DON'T ASK
DON'T TELL

by Claudine Griggs

Published in the United States by
Not a Pipe Publishing, Independence, Oregon.
www.NotAPipePublishing.com
Cover by Gigi Little

Trade Paperback Edition

ISBN-13: 978-1-948120-55-5

To those who suffer and those who resist.
Heroes, all.

PREFACE

The black Lincoln Continental rolled southwest on Interstate 15 across Arizona, not exceeding the speed limit, with visors down against the setting sun. The body in the trunk had been dead less than two hours and would be deposited in a conspicuous place before daylight with a distinctive black and white business card nailed to its forehead.

"God hates bigots," thought the driver. "And if he doesn't, I make up the difference." The man patted a nickel plated Smith & Wesson .357 on the passenger seat hidden beneath a light jacket.

The vehicle was two hours from Vegas. Perhaps he would stop at a bar he knew. "It's not on the official agenda," he thought, "but I might find another queer-hating SOB to join the one already on board."

The man enjoyed his work.

ONE

The English Professor

September 2005

Professor Robert Davenport sat at his kitchen table and skimmed the Friday morning newspaper. Front page, the weekend section, book reviews, a quick look at sports, and finally the society page, which always raised his blood pressure. Despite the call for information on civil unions, the paper never seemed to publish same-sex announcements, only stone chiseled men in tuxedos alongside fantasy women in white lace and heavy lipstick that almost glistened red in the black-and-white newsprint. Proper couples destined for eternal bliss.

There was nothing new about the disparate treatment of gays and lesbians (or even the fat and ugly).

Davenport was an old school gay man who had grown up in the 80's and accepted heterosexism as law of the land. Caring too much or fighting too hard was a waste of energy, so like many professionals of his generation, Davenport had learned to edit his life, almost imperceptibly, to social and career advantage. He used to be good at it, but lately the emotional costs were increasing with no payoff in sight.

Davenport's 36th birthday was next month. No big deal, he thought. Everybody gets older. Yet the approaching anniversary somehow sharpened that soft-blur agitation around the society page—not quite to crystal clarity, but sharper. Davenport might not dream of a castle-in-the-sky wedding, or even respect the concept, but he wanted a piece of the action.

The professor tossed the paper aside. Too bad there wasn't a good afternoon movie to take his mind off things. He had watched *Brokeback Mountain* seven times when it was first released. It reminded him that closets might serve a purpose. And a little over two decades before, at age 15, Davenport had slipped past the R-rating at a multiplex to watch *Desert Hearts*. The graphic affection of two women had both attracted and frightened him, yet he'd walked home after each show with a smoldering emptiness that he could neither understand nor extinguish. In a strange way, that emptiness led Davenport to become an English professor, a dedicated scholar who would study his way through all confusion. But while he had developed an impressive intellectual résumé, his carefully premeditated life remained vaguely uneasy. Now, he cried less and ached more. Davenport wanted a heartfelt relationship someday, and he wanted his hometown newspaper to acknowledge such relationships whether he found one or not.

Davenport sighed, knowing that he should get to work even as he lingered at the table with an extra cup of tea. There were articles to read, assignments to plan, and syllabi to finish—along with the mental adjustment from his summer freedom to the routine of fall semester. That transition used to be easier, he thought. Davenport often bragged that he could "smell education in the air" when September weather began to signal the new academic year. Now, growing concerns about tenure and promotion trespassed on his love of teaching, and his tenure decision was taking longer than usual. But surely his dedication to scholarship and to students would prevail. Surely.

Hoping to distract himself again, he picked up the paper once more and turned to the personal ads. He never responded, of course, but Davenport found comfort in not-so-subtle reminders that gays and straights alike might wrestle with the love demons. Besides, personal columns could be written off as research into popular culture. Davenport grinned.

White single male seeks Bi Black Man for experimentation.

Single white female wants tall sugar daddy with serious intentions.

Single white bi-male into S&M wants fun with male-to-female girlie girl.

Davenport would occasionally laugh out loud, groan about losers and gold diggers, or preach to himself about getting back to work. He was just about to fold the page when he stopped at an item on page thirteen. The language was neither wretched nor desperate, and it did not reek of "middle-aged virgin seeks international supermodel for dinner and first kiss." It called to him like a trumpet. Davenport felt qualified on every point, including his understated yet palpable physical presence.

Wanted: LGBT activists with courage and conviction. Must be intelligent and professional but also inconspicuous. Willing to do what needs doing. Action without recognition. Glory without glitter. A thoughtful *man or woman to fight injustice and become part of a unique organization. Athletic ability a plus but not required. Respond <u>within ten days</u> to <u>xenowrath@justice7.org</u>. If you qualify, we will contact you.*

***

Robert Davenport went about the business of being a university professor. He lectured, graded student papers, held office hours, and reviewed books for next semester's courses, yet Davenport held onto that newspaper ad. He was sure it was some kind of prank, perhaps connected with a reality show. And while Davenport's privileged position with the university offered no room for secret memberships, something would not let him throw the clipping away. Some of this reluctance came in response to rumors about his pending application for tenure with the university, which he'd submitted back in December.

Despite the gossip, he had remained a dedicated teacher, and he knew that more than one student had written in course evaluations that Davenport was "the best professor" they'd ever met. Davenport was, in fact, quite sure that he *was* the best English professor that Yale University had employed in years, and he remained hopeful for a positive outcome in May or June, when decisions were usually announced—and, in fact, *were* announced for all other faculty applications. Strangely, only his decision continued in limbo, and uncertainty had begun to eat away at him.

That week, a sympathetic colleague who served on the English department's tenure advisory committee relayed a few of the dissenting voices regarding Davenport's portfolio, citing insufficient publications— or publications with insufficiently authoritative journals. At first, Davenport disregarded the accounts. His research and writing were solid, his teaching polished and effective, and his growing academic promise seemed on a straight-line path toward full professor. And he wanted to believe, as he has often told his students, that "good work speaks for itself."

But despite Davenport's efforts to suppress any doubts, the words of his friendly informant stirred a dark reminder: homophobia existed in the nation, the community, and the university. Official campus policy denied this, of course, in the same way that Cuba's government denied racism. If only reality could be constructed by legislation. It wouldn't be the first time a gay man or woman suffered institutional prejudice, and the Ivy League did not offer immunity to bias. It was then that Davenport could feel the newspaper clipping from earlier that week all but burning a hole in his wallet.

Despite constant self-assurances about his scholarship and a fair hearing at the university, neither common sense nor professional dignity could prevent Davenport from typing a quick email response to the newspaper advertisement:

September 29, 2005. Found your note interesting and would like more information before involvement at any level. Please send details about the organization to this email address. Thank you. Assistant Professor Robert Davenport.

Davenport reviewed the message, hesitated, and moved the cursor to delete. Then his eyes landed on that title—Assistant Professor—and a sudden anger snapped him to attention. He punched "send" like a boxer fighting a reviled opponent. Then he blushed with regret.

"Oh, well," thought Davenport. "What's done is done."

A few days later, getting cold feet and feeling a bit foolish, the professor sent a second communiqué to the same address: *On reconsideration, I don't really have time for charity work. Thanks, anyway. RD.*

The second email bounced back. The address was no longer valid.

TWO

Death, Accidental

February 2007

Homicide Detective Emmanuel Cerrillo of Pomona, California, scanned the coroner's report. It was too early for this, he thought. Cerrillo moved down the hall toward Captain Ricketts' cluttered office. She had not yet arrived.

Margaret Ricketts was head of the Homicide Division and often worked late into the evening because the eastern outpost of Los Angeles County tended to generate a lot of action. Ricketts was also the Pomona Police Chief but refused to give up her secondary homicide title, though she supervised the city's entire police force. The chief was rarely available before 10:00 a.m. She typically worked past midnight, protesting that with more cooperation around the department she might "have a life" instead of running a school for detective wannabes. It was a hollow complaint. Law enforcement *was* her life.

"Damn it," said Detective Cerrillo to Henry Brown, a middle-aged and over-worked sergeant who had never envisioned himself as an office clerk. "When's the chief coming in?"

"Do I look like a personal assistant?" replied Brown without looking up. "Chief will be here when she gets here. Boss don't answer to me. You need her, call."

An early disabling injury had presented Henry Brown with a career ultimatum—find another place in the department or retire from police work. Brown tried dispatch for a while, supervising the 911 system operators, and finally got an information specialist slot in Homicide. And for Sergeant Brown, being a "secretary" on the force was better than being CEO at IBM. Brown loved his department like a Marine drill instructor loved the Corp.

"Well then," said Cerrillo, "Maybe you can tell me why *Smithfield* is back on my desk. Coroner's report said *accidental overdose*. In case you haven't noticed, the sign in my department says Homicide. Why do I have this garbage before my second cup of coffee?"

"Chief said 'Give it to Cerrillo.' The sign on your desk says *Cerrillo*. That's why it's yours. Talk with the chief if you got a problem."

"Look, Henry," said the detective. "This makes no sense. Some holy roller OD's on smack and I have to read rookie dribble three weeks postmortem. Coroner's satisfied. Boys on the scene are satisfied. Accidental death. Cut and dried. Send a copy to the local news if you want. I got work to do."

"Listen, Manny," said Brown, leaning back in an industrial metal office chair that somehow seemed custom made for the sergeant, "Chief said something stinks about Smithfield. Now maybe that holy roller OD'd, maybe he was an addict, maybe he was crazy, but he was a well-respected crazy. The scene was spotless, and you know the examiner's report shows no indication that Smithfield ever used heroin. He may have been the only guy in California who *never* used drugs. No cigarettes or alcohol neither. Also, boss said there was a similar death in San Francisco a year ago. She wants you to dig around. I got no personal interest, and from what little I gather about Smithfield, the world's no worse off without him. But you know the chief. Once she gets wind of something, she won't let go."

"Ridiculous," said Cerrillo.

"Maybe," said Brown, "but if I was you, I'd make some calls and set a few interviews before our girl gets to the office."

"I don't believe this."

"You can try to beg off the case."

"Would it do any good?"

Brown smiled. "If you value your ass," he said, "I'd start working. Sure, Smithfield's probably a dead end, but read the file—closely—and make an effort. Otherwise, the chief might have you investigating cruelty to hamsters. Oh, and she wants to talk with you this afternoon anyway."

"Damn! You could have just said that in the first place. But I'm telling you my plate's already full. I've got a five-act murder case going to trial next week. The real deal—with guns and bodies. The DA's on me night and day to coordinate testimony and evidence. *And* Judge Hammond is presiding. You'd think the bastard owns stock in mistrials. One loose screw and Hammond will kick our whole case in the toilet. And now Chief wants me to piss away time over a bible thumper who blew his mind in search of Woodstock."

"Cry to the boss. She might care."

"Just tell me when the chief arrives, will you?"

"Okay," said Brown. He was used to detectives throwing off steam while Ricketts wasn't around. But they became procedural models when she was.

Cerrillo softened a little. "Thanks, Henry. It's pointless, but I'll make a few phone calls. Gonna make me a laughing stock... By the way, you don't happen to know anything about that *other* report? In San Francisco?"

"Nope." Brown leaned forward and whispered. "Look, Manny. I know this seems a little weird, but Ricketts is interested in this case. Not sure why. Watch your step. She's smart and doesn't waste time. Don't forget that. And rumor suggests that she's being considered for the number two slot with LAPD. If there's anything to Smithfield, could be it's politically sensitive... Know what I mean?"

"Gotcha."

Detective Cerrillo was sharp enough to abide Brown's caveats. The Sergeant had worked Homicide longer than anybody in Pomona. And he was right about Captain Ricketts. She had more initials after her name than half the professors in California, with degrees in law and political science with street smarts to match. Ricketts grew up in Compton and, through nothing but effort, managed to get a solid education in some of the worst public schools in the country. By seventeen she knew more than the Compton School Board and was accepted at UCLA with a full academic scholarship. She completed her undergraduate program and a dual Juris Doctorate/Political Science Ph.D. in seven years, which was considered impossible.

Cerrillo heard that, as an African American woman with 4.0 credentials, Ricketts had been offered several university teaching appointments without ever having applied. And at least one senator wanted her on his Washington staff. She turned them all down. Despite her "book learning," as Ricketts liked to call it, she maintained a real-world urban clarity. After basic training at the police academy, she fielded multiple departmental offers, including Beverly Hills, but came to Pomona, which rivaled Long Beach and South Central as the toughest beats in Southern California. She passed over a lot of senior personnel, with surprisingly little resentment on their part, to assume the top slot in Pomona's Homicide Division; she was promoted to Chief of Police almost before the ink was dry on her original contract.

There were few people that Cerrillo trusted completely, and Captain Margaret Ricketts was first on the list. He was also a little afraid of her. She arrested two of their own caught selling confiscated drugs as a rather lucrative sideline. Ricketts testified for the prosecution and asked for maximum sentences, which she insisted were not long enough. Growing up "Compton" had done something to her, creating a no-nonsense mindset about as flexible as a bear trap. To be on the chief's wrong side was to be on the dark side of hell.

Remembering this, Cerrillo grudgingly got started on Smithfield.

THREE

Non Sequitur

January 2006

Months passed, and Professor Davenport finished his fall classes, reviewed the final essays, posted grades, attended the Modern Language Association Conference in San Francisco, and then flew to Orange County Airport, California, for winter break. He had two good friends, Daniel Bradford and Mary Anne Shephard, who worked at the Claremont Colleges and the University of California Irvine respectively. Davenport enjoyed escaping from New England in January, but mostly, he enjoyed Daniel and Mary Anne's company.

They would walk the winter sands of Newport Beach in short sleeves or discuss literature in the open-air patio at Walter's Restaurant in the Claremont

Village. For Davenport, this contrasted pleasantly with the breathtaking snows and biting winds of Connecticut, and the three longtime friends might hike the forests of the San Gabriel Mountains or the high deserts of Joshua Tree National Park. But more often than not, they would sit and talk for hours—raving about good books and bad students, drinking too much cabernet sauvignon, eating sourdough bread torn from warm loaves with the sharpest cheddar available, discussing world politics and the imminent rule of philosopher kings who would one day refashion paramilitary industrial economies into intellectual utopias. Such were the dreams of academics on holiday.

And for Davenport, those soul-nourishing moments with Daniel and Mary Anne temporarily supplanted worries about his tenure decision—still pending months beyond university standards—and that foolish fight-for-justice email, now forgotten as a lapse in professorial thinking.

***

June 2006

On a day in early June, Davenport spent the morning at the university library working on a summer research project about the nonfiction of Willa Cather, made a few phone calls, and sent emails to several scholars with whom he wanted to consult, including one at the University of Nebraska and another at Oxford. Davenport then hit the gym for a light aerobic workout, barely acknowledging a bodybuilder with whom he'd had an affair two years ago, an affair that somehow earned him grapevine criticism at work for "promoting the gay lifestyle." Davenport hated that phrase. When did gay love become a marketing platform? Nonetheless Professor Davenport had henceforth proceeded with extreme caution regarding his personal life, which he'd already been quiet about. This further step backward into the closet had translated into completely omitting intimate relationships. "Just until after tenure," he told himself. Then things could change.

On the way home, Davenport stopped at a sports bar for a cheeseburger and Coke. The Red Sox were losing. Baseball wasn't a real interest of his, but some attention to the Sox seemed a prerequisite for New Englander status, especially during a live broadcast. Forty-seven minutes later, he pulled into his driveway and all but leapt from the car. He would quickly check any new emails and then settle into his favorite chair with *The History of the Decline and Fall of the Roman Empire*, which had been on his to-read list for a decade. This would be the summer of Gibbon.

As Davenport entered his living room, a chill ran through his body. He began to tremble. Someone had been in the house. He knew it. Davenport remained motionless for several seconds, still clutching his leather briefcase.

Something was different. But what? Nothing had moved as far as he could tell. The newspaper was on the breakfast table, along with a half cup of tea. The living room drapes were open. Did he leave them that way? Yes. Stacked books rested on the end table and corner desk, just as they had for months. He dropped the briefcase and moved slowly. Front and backdoors locked. All the windows, too. No sign of damage or forced entry. What about the housekeeper? No, she wasn't due for three days and didn't have a key. Davenport always scheduled her visits for when he was home.

He prowled around the house. Kitchen window, locked. The stove, microwave, a dish in the sink, and sponge on the counter—all as he had left them. He checked the guest bedroom; a bit stuffy but pristine. No detectable entry. It occurred to him that perhaps the previous owner had clandestinely decided to revisit the homestead, but he dismissed the idea. Davenport bought the home from a woman after her husband died, and she had moved to Florida with her daughter. Furthermore, Davenport had changed all the locks and added deadbolts. No one else had a key.

Davenport shook his head but kept looking. Absolutely nothing appeared out of place. No physical disturbance of any kind. Yet he was certain someone had come while he was away.

"Hello. Anybody there?" Davenport called out, surprised by his approach and then ashamed of it.

"Okay," he muttered. "Now, I'm talking to myself in my kitchen. Maybe I'd better relax with a comic book instead of Rome." Despite his background and training in exalted literature, Davenport was still a Marvel and DC fan, which he publicly referred to as graphic novels. "Must be working too hard. I'm starting to generate home-invasion theories."

Davenport recomposed himself, opened the refrigerator, and reached for a bottle of Perrier. He would sit with a cool drink, skim the *Chronicle of Higher Education*, and sketch out a few more ideas on the Cather research. Thank god he didn't have to face a batch of semi-literate freshmen papers. He twisted the cap off the sparkling water and moved to the La-Z-Boy recliner with a pen and yellow notepad. But he did not sit down. He did not read the *Chronicle*. He suddenly knew what was different.

Davenport had not had a visitor in two weeks. Yet as he approached the chair, he smelled a soft body fragrance that was not his. Someone had been here. He couldn't determine if it were a man or woman—probably a woman—but someone had sat in this chair, someone who was very skilled at entering and exiting without detection.

Then, even as he thought about it, he wasn't certain. Maybe he was imagining things. Could one's sense of smell be so precise? Something inside his head whispered "presence," but he did not trust the voice. Physical beings leave physical evidence. All Davenport had was non-dimensional fragrance.

Within ten minutes, Davenport wrote off the whole affair as fantasy. He regrouped with pen, paper, and Perrier at the recliner. But before he read the first headline, he froze. His senses had not betrayed him. In the center of the coffee table lay a single white business card with engraved raised black lettering: Don't Ask, Don't Tell. There was nothing else on its face. He hesitated, looked around the living room, and reached for the card. On the back was a handwritten note.

Dear Dr. Davenport: Thank you for responding to our job listing in September. Your preliminary qualifications are impressive. Continue to be patient. We will contact you regarding an interview.

***

After receiving the Don't Ask, Don't Tell business card, Robert Davenport became wary. He no longer felt crazy or uncertain. He was scared. He opened the door to his home more slowly. Sometimes he called "hello" as he entered. He scrutinized people, wondering if they might be watching him. He looked in the back seat of his car before sliding into the driver's seat; and twice, he checked the trunk because of a vague apprehension. He never found anything tangible other than the card, but he remained suspicious.

Davenport sent two additional emails to the mysterious website, and they bounced back. The address was invalid. If not for the copy of the newspaper advertisement and that business card tucked in his wallet, he might have convinced himself that the whole affair was a dream. He considered talking with someone in the

New Haven Police Department or even the FBI, but dismissed the notion. Despite the emerging millennium of diversity, Davenport had cautionary mistrust of authoritative agencies because older gays and lesbians often carried physical and emotional scars from the dark years. And Davenport grimaced as he imagined sitting down to tell the story:

"Well, Officer, I sent an email to a strange personal listing, and the website no longer exists. Then I found a note in my house. No, nothing was stolen or damaged, and I don't know how they gained entry, but I suspect somebody is watching me. Maybe a student or colleague because somebody entered my house without permission. Here is the card. Do I suspect anyone specifically? No. Is there an address? No. I realize that you are working on other cases—murder, armed robbery, and assault—but would you please investigate Don't Ask, Don't Tell? I know this sounds weird, but I have a weird feeling that something weird is going on... No, this has nothing to do with alien abduction!"

Even the most tolerant detective would probably escort the professor out the door, so Robert Davenport did not go to the police. He did not consult with colleagues. He did not call his mother, who probably wouldn't pick up even if he did. Instead, Davenport remained silent and focused on the business of a college professor running against the tenure clock, which was definitely ticking slowly in his case—now a year overdue. His application had been perfect. He'd assembled copies of his publications, statements about current and future research, faculty and administrative letters in support of tenure, and personal testimonials about ongoing support of the English department, undergraduate and graduate students, and the humanities in general. Davenport had expected to receive notice of tenure and promotion by early summer of last year at the latest (almost guaranteeing lifetime job security at the university), but it had not arrived.

New rumors suggested that the president, on advice from the dean, would delay the decision until August. A protracted decision was unusual but not absolutely unheard of among the Ivy Leagues; still, Davenport felt a spasm of not-unreasonable fear. According to well-accepted procedure across academia, if denied tenure, he would have an additional lame-duck year at the university before receiving the boot. He would necessarily enter the job market again. He would lose the power and prestige of an elite, highly selective school. He would search for a new position who knows where and under the stigma of a failed tenure bid.

He researched, wrote, revised, and wrote some more. He called an assistant editor at *College English* to inquire about the status of his previous submission, which had been sent out to an independent referee for review, the obligatory next step. Davenport studied his lecture notes and re-read texts that he had used during the fall semester. His teaching schedule comprised an honors section of freshman comp and a graduate seminar on the 20th Century Novel. He had taught composition many times, yet he prepared as though every new section were a personal audition for the Pulitzer Prize. Davenport didn't particularly enjoy reading freshman essays, but he knew that Introduction to Academic Writing might well be the most important undergraduate experience at any university, and he insisted that *his* students leave the course with improved communications skills.

The first week of August, however, Davenport stopped all work and flew to Wyoming, where he met with his closest friends, Daniel Bradford and Mary Anne Shephard. Shephard was finishing up the second half of a two-year post-doc in Women's Studies. Davenport was sure that she would receive multiple tenure-line offers, but Shephard was holding out for a position near San Francisco, where she wanted to live. Bradford, a 37-year-old full professor in the History Department at Pomona College, occasionally taught in the Claremont Graduate School. He came from a financially endowed background, which made teaching his personal hobby. Bradford could have bought a small private college and had cash left over for a professional sports team, but he, like Davenport, loved the classroom.

In some ways, Bradford, Davenport, and Shephard were unlikely companions (the billionaire, the gay, and the activist), but they had emotional ties stretching to their undergraduate days at UC Berkeley. All three graduated early from high school and, despite assurances from their teachers, had worried about college success. In her first semester, a 16-year-old Mary Anne Shephard admitted to a 17-year-old Robert Davenport while eating lunch, "I don't know how I got into Berkeley."

Robert, who'd still been clinging to a facade of heterosexuality, joked, "Maybe that body of yours outranks your GPA!"

At this, to his surprise, Mary Anne burst out crying, and before Robert could even say he was sorry, Daniel Bradford, who was sitting across the table and heard the remark, threatened Robert with a "royal ass whipping." Shephard looked at Bradford, then at Davenport, and couldn't help but laugh. Bradford appeared to be half Davenport's size and fragile to boot.

"I wish I had your self-confidence and courage," said Mary Anne to Daniel, "but you'd better let me handle the whipping."

Davenport fell all over himself apologizing. Shephard kissed him on the cheek, and soon all three were chuckling. They became unflagging cheerleaders for one another throughout their three years of accelerated undergraduate studies. And, when time permitted, they piled in Bradford's SUV for hiking trips in the

Pacific Northwest, Rocky Mountains, or the Southwestern high deserts, trips which continued to the present. They loved these trips almost as much as they loved each other.

This summer, they met in Jackson Hole, Wyoming, rented a Subaru Outback station wagon, purchased supplemental backpacking supplies, and drove to their first trailhead in Yellowstone National Park. The routine was almost identical every year: stay the first night at a comfortable hotel (this time the Wyoming Inn), hammer out a three-day route, burn in their boots at 20 miles per day, and then check into the best place available to recuperate with one night of clean sheets, hot food, and an indoor Jacuzzi. After that, back on the trails rain or shine until their bodies ached as much from physical exertion as their brains had once ached from the rigor of doctoral research. And on the seventh day, circling back to the rental car and returning to civilization, they began an all-out closing celebration in the best accommodations they could find. Hors d'oeuvres, hearty dinners, a $90 bottle of wine (or two), and breathless late-night conversation of temporarily reunited friends about to disband.

They had been lucky this summer. A few afternoon thundershowers passed through on Tuesday and Wednesday, but the rest of the week had been clear with cooler than average temperatures that peaked near 85 degrees. They hiked and marveled and talked and talked. They discussed men and women, geology and space-time, fauna and flora, religious pogroms, historical madness and popular delusions, the Red Sox and the Angels. But they absolutely did *not* talk about their respective universities or preparations for fall semester. That single prohibition had been settled at the first summer. It was an easy rule to follow.

But now, after a glorious week and heartfelt good-byes, Robert Davenport sat alone in his room at the

Jackson Lake Lodge. He wallowed in self-doubt. He expected a headache.

Mary Anne and Daniel had already boarded Sunday afternoon flights out of Jackson Hole. Davenport's plane would not leave for Connecticut until Monday morning, and he stared out the great lodge window overlooking the Teton Range and wondered whether his declared friendship was a fraud, whether he was a fraud. The Don't Ask, Don't Tell business card remained in his wallet. He had wanted to show it to Shephard and Bradford, tell them about the strangeness, and ask for their advice. He wanted to share his new secret, but fear had stopped him. Even now, Davenport wondered at his silence. He had obeyed the card's instructions without really meaning to.

FOUR

Police Sabbatical

March 2007

Detective Emmanuel Cerrillo walked into Captain Margaret Ricketts' office three days after his conversation with Sergeant Brown. Case files were stacked everywhere. Ricketts sat at her desk in the best swivel chair of the department, which still looked like Army Surplus. There were two small, mismatched, unpadded chairs facing the desk. They were uncomfortable, but she didn't hold long conferences. Her days raced like a 33-rpm record played at 45. At just past 11:00 a.m., her wastebasket was already overflowing with discarded memos.

"Look," said Captain Ricketts, "I'm supposed to meet with the Mayor in half an hour, and then I drive into L.A.

for a sit-down at County: talk about municipal waste. So I don't have a lot of time. Give me the condensed version of Smithfield."

"Nothing new," said Cerrillo. "Preacher's still dead. Loaded with enough smack to kill a horse. Everybody says accidental overdose. His doors were locked from the inside. He was alone."

"We don't know for sure," said the chief. "When you write the report, say something like 'the evidence *suggests* the victim was alone.' Sorry to interrupt." Ricketts liked Cerrillo, but he had not yet learned to properly question evidence and authority, at least not enough to suit Ricketts. An investigator should mistrust everything until facts were checked and confirmed and re-checked. And Cerrillo still believed some people were above suspicion; he worried about hurt feelings, which was natural enough for a young detective just two years into his position. Experience would fix that. Cerrillo was smart, dedicated, and learned fast. Ricketts predicted that he would become one of the county's best detectives.

Cerrillo corrected himself. "Right. He appears to have been alone. Everything, and I mean everything, points to a drug overdose. The initial report and witness follow-up. The guy was not ... uh, did not *appear* to be psychologically depressed, wasn't in financial difficulty. In fact, the church coffers were solid in the black. The guy had money. Seems to have been happily married. No significant family problems. And by all accounts he loved his church. So despite the way the body was found, there is no real evidence to support a motive for a suicide, which I assumed you might be wondering about." Cerrillo realized that he had gone overboard with verbal qualifiers.

"What are you saying?"

"Smithfield was no suicide."

"And?"

"It was not an accidental overdose either."

Margaret Ricketts smiled. "But you just got through telling me all indications point to a simple drug overdose."

"I know. But Smithfield was too straitlaced. He didn't *pretend* to be a holier-than-thou jackass. He really was. I interviewed his personal physician, checked medical records, that kind of stuff. This guy complained about taking aspirin even when his doctor recommended it. Said pain meds violated the will of God or some such. So Smithfield doesn't figure for drugs or alcohol." Cerrillo glanced at a notepad resting on his knee. "He got hard onto anti-drugs seven years ago after a psychiatrist prescribed Thorazine. Smithfield was apparently hearing voices, went to a shrink—I have the details if you need them. But he eventually stopped treatment. Said the voices were from Heaven. Smithfield apparently enjoyed the conversations and quit worrying. The doc said, as far as he knows, this was the only time our preacher took any medication though the guy's mental health continued to deteriorate from a psychiatric perspective. A couple years ago, Smithfield had a dentist fill a small cavity without Novocain. That's how strict the guy was. He stopped going to the doctor altogether last year, placing himself 'completely in God's hands.' Again, that's according to his physician. Then the voices really started to sing."

"Okay," said Ricketts, "But people go crazy all the time, and many folks cruise along for years without a problem. They're clean and sober pillars of the community, and then, wham! Something goes haywire and they take the plunge. Drugs, alcohol, gambling, or everything combined. Smithfield may have started ahead of the pack, but what's different about this case?"

Cerrillo sighed. "I don't know. But it is. If somebody told me Smithfield stepped off the edge of the Grand Canyon because God told him he could fly, I could believe that. But drugs? Not him." Cerrillo leaned forward.

"The pathology report said, except for the heroin, the guy's blood was spotless. Not a trace of nicotine, caffeine, alcohol, or aspirin. He was cleaner than most narcotics agents. And even if Smithfield finally let his hair down to experiment, he wouldn't dive off the Acapulco cliffs first time out. He'd start with a bottle of Manischewitz, something accessible. Plus, our preacher wouldn't have a clue about buying heroin, let alone how to inject. But mostly, he would not have done it, period.

"I interviewed some of the parishioners, fifteen or so, about those heavenly voices Smithfield carried on with. His church groupies said Smithfield was in direct contact with the Lord Almighty, and God told him three things. First, the preacher had been selected—alone—to hear the word. Second, homosexuals were abominations created by Satan to tempt true believers. And third, drugs of any kind would cut off Smithfield's hotline to God. So while I might certify the guy as an overripe fruit basket, I guarantee that he did not die from accidental heroin overdose."

"Then what happened to him?" asked Margaret Ricketts.

"Somebody killed him."

"Why?"

"Don't know."

"Any suspects?"

"None."

"Any conjectures?" asked the chief.

"Nothing that makes sense."

"Sounds pretty thin to be so confident, Detective."

Cerrillo nodded but continued as if this were irrelevant. "Well, you read the file. Too many reasons to live. I mean, Smithfield was wealthy. Skimming off the collection plate, which I assume is typical. Apparently God never told him *that* was a sin. And he indulged in a few non-Biblical luxuries—limousine and driver, a maid, an $80,000 grand piano that he couldn't play, and trips to

Vegas a few times a year for a little gambling. Nothing spectacular. But Smithfield's church, even if they suspected double dipping, strictly worshiped the man. They apparently believe that God *had* chosen Smithfield for a special purpose. And despite his quirks, the preacher fit in pretty well with the broader religious community. He made political donations to the right people, and he never ventured far from his, uh, support base. But Pomona has a lot of fringe churches, a lot of fringe people for that matter. Smithfield didn't stand out much there. But I'm telling you, Chief, our half-baked preacher man didn't shove heroin into his veins. *Someone else* did, and it wasn't God."

Ricketts leaned back in her chair and looked at Detective Cerrillo. "So what do you suggest?"

"Well," said Cerrillo, thinking about his response, "I know this doesn't seem urgent. And, strangely, with passing time, not too many people seem upset that Smithfield is gone. The assistant preacher has taken over Sunday sermons; the parishioners have survived the loss with just a few extra 'amens' during service; the wife still runs the business office and doesn't seem too distraught about inheriting a chunk of money. But I don't think she knew how much cash existed until after Smithfield's death. If she were somehow involved, she would have put on a much better act as the suffering widow. I talked with her three days ago, and you would have thought the guy had been dead for ten years. She says, 'Well, I'm sorry he passed away. But the Lord's work goes on. My husband and I came together for the love and glory of Jesus.' And trust me. The good Mrs. Smithfield doesn't have the brains for beneficiary murder."

"Murder? I don't think you've used that word in this case before," said Ricketts. Then she smiled. "And when you got this assignment, didn't you say something like,

'Who cares? Accidental death!' And, oh, yes, a 'waste of time.'"

Detective Cerrillo made a mental note to kick Sergeant Brown in the ass and said, "Yep. That's what I thought, Chief, at first. And I'll tell you one more thing. If Smithfield had died in a car accident or tripping down stairs or even from an accidental overdose, I would have figured good riddance. One more lunatic off the streets. But I'm a cop, born and raised in Pomona, and I don't appreciate murder in my town. I can't say how it was done, or why, but the preacher was killed and somebody thinks they got away with it. I want to dig around some more."

"People will say you're as crazy as Smithfield."

"Three days ago, I would have said the same thing. Not now."

"What's the next move? You said you got no suspects, no motive, and no leads." Captain Ricketts knew what she'd recommend. Pretty simple. But she wanted Cerrillo to direct the investigation.

"The way I see it? Okay, we got nothing. And I suspect that we're not going to find much around Smithfield's neighborhood. Just a gut feeling. But that letter, the report you gave me from San Francisco. I talked with a detective about that case. SFPD says there's no connection. But maybe I got a hunch. With your permission, Captain, I'd like to take a few days off. See Frisco. Snoop around that other situation, talk with witnesses, relatives—see if I can nail down a missing piece in one or both cases. I mean, they're different, but yet ... they both smell the same kind of weird."

"How?"

"Well, the victim up north served on the local school board. So that's different. But the woman was almost as loudmouth crazy as Smithfield about two things. 'Drugs and faggots.' Her words, not mine. And, of course, in San Francisco, that is not, uh, politically correct. You

know, Harvey Milk and all. There was a growing movement to throw her off the board. And they would have
succeeded, but she died. The official report says suicide,
that she was depressed because she was about to be
ousted."

"And you don't think so."

"Suicide, my ass. Some first-year rookie wants me to
believe that this woman killed herself. She was a creden-
tialed teacher who could have found a dozen other jobs.
Alabama probably would have elected her governor. She
had a burr up her ass about gays, and she might have
been upset about losing her reign on the school board,
but she did not inject herself with cobra venom. That's
beyond bullshit. First of all, do you know how hard it is
to get venom from a King Cobra? This woman had a degree in elementary education, not zoology or
snakeology. And she spent most of her professional life
working with second graders, who may have been
smarter than the teacher from what I hear. It's pretty
clear that Mrs. School Board didn't milk the snake herself, and this whole Queen of the Nile routine is a cover-
up for murder. And if I didn't know better, Chief, I'd say
some of the department boys up there know it. I'm telling you. There might not be a direct connection between
our Preacher and Cleopatra, but these two cases stink
worse than the victims."

Cerrillo had become noticeably animated. "Sorry,
Chief. Didn't mean to get riled. I had a cousin killed in
Mexico City a few years back, when I asked the local detective for an update, he said their chief had been told to
'look the other way.' Not sure who got paid off or why.
Maybe my cuz jumped into some risky business, but he
was a good man. After I became a cop I promised his
mother that I'd never turn away from facts that don't
add up. Pisses me off."

"Sometimes a little agitation promotes justice." Margaret Ricketts leaned forward and put her elbows on the

desk. "I figured when you read the San Francisco report you might do a turnabout. You're learning fast about skilled liars and appeasers—and about evidence that's too tidy for real life. Now, when you inevitably begin to worry about hurt feelings or stepping on toes, think about your cousin and how the cops should've handled the investigation. Then you'll know what to do."

Cerrillo nodded and then asked, "And how about my heading north for a few days?"

"You know we don't have the budget, especially for a police cruiser and expense account. We're short on equipment and manpower, and the Mayor never stops complaining about money." Ricketts looked at her watch. "Damn! I forgot about His Honor. Gonna be late for the meeting." The Pomona Police Chief paused for a few seconds. "Tell me, Detective. Do you mind using your own vehicle in this deal?"

"Why the hell do you think I bought a Corolla? Thirty-eight miles to the gallon. Just give me the go-ahead."

"Okay. Pack a few things and fill the tank. After I finish off the Mayor, I'll stop by First Federal and pull out a few hundred in cash. You might need a hotel, but maybe you can talk to SFPD about bunking with one of the locals for a couple nights. That's typical."

"Chief, I can't take your money. Just give me the time off. I'll handle expenses. The seats lean back. I can sleep in the car."

"No. This is business. We may not have an 'official' budget, but I'm the one sending you on a potential goose chase. I can damn well pay for it."

"But Chief…"

"Don't feel guilty," said Ricketts. "You won't live well. San Francisco is a $250-a-night town, and I'm offering $300 total. If you spend more, I'll have you arrested. Not a penny over three hundred."

"When can I start?"

"As soon as I get back from City Hall and the bank. I'll meet you here."

"But I thought you had to go to L.A., too."

"Oh, Christ! Forgot about that. Somebody must have spiked my coffee." Captain Ricketts reached for her handbag, pulled out an account book, and wrote a personal check payable to "cash." She handed it to Cerrillo. "Look, I can't make this out directly to you. It wouldn't look right. Hell, it probably isn't right. Go to the bank yourself. You're a cop. You won't have any problem."

"Not to worry, Chief." Cerrillo folded the check and slipped it into his jacket. He had no intention of cashing it.

"And tell Sergeant Brown to assign any urgent matters to somebody else. Routine stuff can wait until you get back. I'll alert SFPD you're coming. They won't like it much. Jurisdiction and all. Keep a low profile and report back to me if you find anything juicy. Otherwise, fill me in when you return. Let's call it four days."

"Right."

"One more thing, Cerrillo."

"What's that?"

Margaret Ricketts let out a slow breath. "Watch yourself. If this turns out to be murder, that means somebody can kill with heroin, squeeze venom from a cobra, pump it into a victim, and get in and out of two crime scenes without leaving so much as a fart behind. That kind of somebody has brains and self-control! He's dangerous. I don't know if these two cases are connected, but I want you looking over your shoulder like a virgin schoolgirl until we get a better idea of what's going on. First, talk with, oh, what's his name, the officer who filed the initial report. Walk softly and play nice, but see what you can dig up."

"Don't worry, Chief. I'll give 'em my special Colombo routine."

Ricketts knew that Cerrillo could skillfully feign incompetence. She smiled and said, "Fine. Just remember there's no script to follow. Real killers are generally smarter than Hollywood, so pay attention. We want a conviction not an unsolved mystery."

"Absolutely," said Cerrillo.

"And one more word of advice."

"What's that?"

Chief Margaret Ricketts looked directly at the detective. "When I was young, I once said at a conference that we would have true justice only when police investigate the death of a homeless drug addict with the same rigor as a murdered cop. More than a few people laughed. Others were insulted. From what I hear, the school board victim was not well liked in San Francisco. Sometimes paperwork creates inertia, and sometimes people do. But if she was murdered, then there's a killer on the loose, and I don't give a damn about his motives. I want him stopped."

"I get it, Chief," replied Detective Cerrillo. "But as I said. I don't appreciate murder in my town ... or anywhere else. I'm not likely to be stonewalled."

FIVE

The Case for Tenure

August 2006

Soon after Robert Davenport returned from Wyoming, he received a message on his answering machine. "Dear Dr. Davenport," said a man, "I am from Don't Ask, Don't Tell. We would like to schedule an interview, subsuming tenure. However, because of the delayed decision at the university—and success in this area is at least as important to us as it is to you—we have postponed our face-to-face. We believe, however, that you are a prime candidate for..." The message ended but was followed by another. The caller spoke more rapidly. "Sorry, Robert. Your voicemail has a 30-second cutoff. As I was saying, we are interested in your application and will be in touch soon regarding a personal meeting.

Sorry for the slow response, but we're waiting on your tenure. It's imperative. We've also been working on a couple of interesting new projects, which we think you'll appreciate later on."

Robert Davenport was angry. He didn't like mysteries or anonymous callers or being reminded by strangers about his pending tenure. And he hated presumptuousness. "*Subsuming*," he thought. "What kind of usage is that?" Don't Ask, Don't Tell was beginning to remind him of a pseudo-intellectual freshman who sought time with the professor about issues unrelated to the classroom. He deleted both messages, and then regretted it. Should have saved them for the police, he thought. The business card, newspaper listing, and phone messages were evidence that Davenport was not delusional. He was being stalked.

Davenport decided not to go to the authorities just yet. Who needed them? Davenport was a professor, a trained and skilled researcher. With a little investigation, he could track down a few clandestine lunatics, maybe even gift wrap them for the police.

Davenport went to the computer. He started with a Google search for "Don't Ask, Don't Tell," and received 1,170,000 hits. No good, he thought. Refine the search. Next, looking at that initial newspaper clipping, he tried "xenowrath@justice7.org." Zero. He tried again without the "org." Nothing. "Justice7" brought back 23,800 hits, which seemed to direct him to a rainbow of sites that soap-boxed about "right" and "wrong" and "justice" and "injustice." The World Wide Web gave every incoherent screwball a communications platform.

Looking at the advertisement, Davenport tried "action without glory." To his surprise, there were only two hits. One was about an April 1997 article on Hong Kong's return to China. The other (Davenport didn't open it) seemed to be a gay-porn site that had something to do with "action without glory hole." Davenport didn't want to guess what that meant, but he was pretty sure it had nothing to do with Don't Ask, Don't Tell. He grinned. Suppose it does. Davenport Googled "unique and righteous organization," expecting many hits from groups and people who were bound to believe that they were both unique and righteous, but this bounced a zero unless the quotation marks were dropped.

Almost as earnestly and quickly as Davenport began his investigation, he stopped. He considered using the subscriber search engines at the university library but was somehow sure he would not find a tell-tale beating heart to direct him to the DADT corpus. This probably wasn't even their official name. And Davenport didn't know any person who belonged to the group, which might be operating under an umbrella among thousands of nonprofits or corporate entities. Don't Ask, Don't Tell might even be a government surveillance agency or sting operation. Who could tell? Without more specific information, or at least a ballpark lead, there was little hope of finding whoever had left the phone message or the business card. Davenport did check telephone records through an AT&T friend, and the incoming call had originated from a payphone near Penn Station in New York. That lead would be essentially worthless, unless he wanted homeless alcoholics who fingered payphones for loose change. In fact, thought Davenport, the whole DADT affair now seemed pointless. "Screw 'em," he thought.

Davenport had other things to worry about. Fall semester would start in two weeks. Faculty meetings and other sundries began in six days. Davenport had yet to prepare his advanced literature course, order the textbooks, schedule a library session for freshman comp, and generally get his "mind right" for the return to the classroom. The delayed tenure decision was weighing on him so heavily that he didn't feel his usual excitement for the start of the year. Still, Davenport's intangible personal loneliness and professional angst must be put on hold, and DADT must be tossed aside completely. Being a professor required attention, and once Robert Davenport set about the business of teaching, he was relentless.

***

Professor Davenport began classes and survived the first week's add-drop madness, with its seemingly endless stream of 18-year-olds who searched for lost classrooms and instructor offices, discovered the right room in the wrong building, or purchased textbooks for Professor Joe's course instead of Mary's. A running joke for the most confused was, "Send 'em to Harvard." Once, a baffled young man turned up in Davenport's 8:00 a.m. class and insisted that the professor and all the other students were in the wrong space. Davenport somehow refrained from laughing and said, "Try three doors down the hall to your left." Davenport hoped that when he got there the student might tell the Administrative Vice President she was in the wrong office.

There were the usual freshmen who missed the first week of classes and thereby made room for one or two lucky bodies from the waiting list, holding their breaths to add courses with professors rumored to be easy or sexy or interesting. A semester launch made it difficult to get meaningful work from students until at least the third week. They were often frightened or unsure of their worthiness for a prestigious university. Some were just plain homesick and had to be nurtured into student life. More than one freshman had told Davenport, "I really don't know how I got in," which reminded him warmly of Mary Anne.

It was unusual for a literature specialist to teach freshman composition, which required distinct skills and training, and many senior academics considered first year writing an underling's chore most suited for greenhorn faculty or adjuncts whose function was to weed out the intellectual deadwood. Davenport requested, sometimes pleaded, to be assigned a composition course each fall.

Davenport greeted his freshman writing class as if they were the sons and daughters of the U.S. Congress. Some might have been, but all Davenport needed was a room and a roster. Those were *his* students, and it was Davenport's charge to begin their expansion from adolescent scholarship toward the rigors of the athenaeum. Despite the sometimes overwhelming desire to do his own research, Davenport was a dedicated teacher. He believed in *cura personalis*—caring for the whole person—which were more than mere words to Davenport. He vowed early in his career to always remember that students were people, knowledge could change the world, and a liberal education offered the best collective promise for social justice.

Many faculty considered it cliché to use the word *love* regarding the profession, something that naïve graduate students might utter about their planned academic careers. And while Davenport self-censored the expression among colleagues, he felt it deeply. The university mission underpinned his personal mission to help create better lives for his students and a better society across the board. His friends Daniel and Mary Anne might reside on the far side of the continent, but Davenport's love of the classroom offered an internal companionship that would have been the envy of the most satisfied professionals.

Scholarship and teaching had always been a kind of salvation for Davenport, delivering a temporary reprieve from suppressed longings for a committed relationship and for courage to stand publicly against homophobia and its concordant injustice against gays and lesbians.

He believed that his tenure and promotion would enable such courage.

***

During the third week of the semester, immediately after his 11:00 a.m. Tuesday class, Davenport checked his email and then prepared to read the first batch of formal papers—the personal essay—from his freshmen. His graduate class had likewise submitted brief personal biographies and their preliminary research proposals on Willa Cather, but he would save those for the weekend. The Cather group met only once a week, Mondays, and there was no particular urgency regarding their proposals. In a peculiar sense, despite longer writing assignments, more stringent documentation requirements, and much heavier reading requirements (eight novels, two book-length works of nonfiction, and a dozen or so critical essays for the semester), Davenport's graduate seminars were generally easier to teach than freshman composition.

Davenport checked his email again. The panel proposal that he and two colleagues jointly submitted to the Conference on College Composition and Communication had been selected for review. If accepted, this would support his tenure case, and he enjoyed CCCC. This year's conference would be in New York, which he also savored, so he completed online registrations for the conference and a room at the Hilton. He would still have to write his paper, which would discuss helping first-year writing students conceptualize "audience," but the conference wasn't until late March, and Davenport already had a mental outline entitled, "Beyond the Big Game and My Most Serious Prom Disaster." He had read too many student essays about the spiritual ecstasies of game-winning little league home runs or prom night mishaps that miraculously turned out to be part of the perfect evening. But one of Davenport's teaching objectives was to help students understand that middle-class America was not the way of the world, that for a large portion of the planet's population, food and health care were bigger issues than high school Homecoming. He prodded freshmen to consider cultures, political systems, ignorance, poverty, race, bigotry, violence, benevolence, and maliciousness. There might not be clear answers, but Davenport believed in the questions.

As Davenport was lost in thought, an unfamiliar woman knocked at his open office door.

"Hello," said the professor slowly looking up.

"Hello," said the student. "My name is Tanish Padgett. I'm sorry to come to you after start-of-semester. I know it's troublesome, but I'm sort of a special admission and would like to audit your Monday evening graduate course."

The student offered Professor Davenport an official looking add-drop form with the university logo and apparently signed by the humanities department secretary. Davenport wondered briefly why this didn't come from the English Department, as did typical graduate admissions. He assumed it had something to do with the "audit" designation. Or perhaps the student was third cousin to an Alabama senator and felt entitled to bend rules; although, at 5'7", blonde, and strikingly pretty, she could undoubtedly bend most rules on her own.

"You know," said Professor Davenport, "this is highly unusual. You've already missed two class meetings. That, by itself, is irregular in a graduate seminar."

"I understand, Professor. And I don't want to create extra work for you. I just want to sit in for personal enlightenment. Professionally, I'm trained as a zoologist, and I've spent considerable time in the Southwestern United States and the Australian Outback. I study reptilian habitats."

Davenport glanced sideways. "You're a long way from home."

"Yes. But I've done research in New England, and I have a short-term consulting project in Connecticut. Probably be around for eight months to a year."

Robert Davenport was only half listening, wondering how to get this student up to speed in a course in its third week. And he also was annoyed that the university admitted her at this late date even as an *audit*. "I'm sorry, Miss, but this is highly irregular. We already finished discussing one novel, and the students have turned in their preliminary research proposals. I strongly suggest that you wait until next semester."

"Dr. Davenport, please hear me out. I know this is unusual. But I'm not interested in any kind of credit. I don't need a grade. And I won't create extra work for you. I just want to sit in, read a few good books, and listen. I'll catch up and try to contribute to the dialogue. I promise not to burden you with papers. I'll be an observer only. And please, call me 'Tash,' as my friends do."

Davenport was silent.

Tanish Padgett added, "If you want to be formal, call me Dr. Padgett."

Robert Davenport jerked noticeably.

Padgett smiled. "I already have an earned doctorate."

Professor Davenport dropped his shoulders and grinned. "Okay, who put you up to this? Rothbard? He's been pranckstering since I came here and has tried to push more than one good looking woman my way. He doesn't get it."

Tanish Padgett shook her head. "No, no. Nothing like that. I just want to audit your course. My own interest in Willa Cather and the geographic regions of her fiction. I like books, and you have a solid reputation, Dr. Davenport."

"Perhaps, but my class doesn't relate to zoology or, what did you say, 'reptilian habitats.' Although you might find a few cold-blooded residents around the humanities department. Are you sure Rothy didn't put you up to this? Are you faculty?"

"No. I don't know Rothbard. Let's just say I'm considering a second Ph.D. in literature. Auditing this course is a good way for me to explore that option. And who knows," she smiled a little too warmly, "maybe I can add something to the class. Might surprise you." She paused and asked, "Did you want to see my permission form again?"

Davenport bristled at the implication. "You know, Miss—I mean Doctor—there is no rule that I have to let you in my course, with or without a note from the humanities secretary ... or the governor. I am not overwhelmed by a piece of paper."

"I know, Robert," she said. "That's why I came to your office beforehand. I wouldn't put you on the spot like that in class. And, of course, I will respect your wishes. But I have an interest in you ... your course. I am considering professional options. And I don't want any other instructor, Dr. Davenport. If you say 'no,' I'll retreat quietly." She crumpled the add form and threw it in the trash. "This is now completely unofficial. What do you say?"

Davenport nodded, flattered by her singular interest in *his* course. She plainly understood the value he brought to the institution more than the tenure advisory board did at the moment. And it was clear that Padgett knew academic etiquette.

"So," Padgett continued, "may I audit your seminar?"

The professor reached toward the second drawer of his file cabinet and removed a syllabus for English 720a. "Okay, Doctor Reptilian Zoologist with a special interest in literature," said Davenport. "Here's your ticket to the show. Be sure to read *My Ántonia* along with the assigned critical essays by next class. And if you're late or haven't done the work, I'll send you packing back to Rothbard plenty quick."

"Thank you, Doctor... May I call you, Robert?"

"You already have. And, yes, I typically invite students to use first names."

"Great."

"But there is one thing," said Dr. Robert Davenport.

"What is that?" asked Dr. Tanish Padgett.

"You might help me understand what you're really trying to accomplish this semester. I don't want to offend you, but a herpetologist in a graduate English listing doesn't seem quite legitimate." Davenport played vocabulary trump with "herpetologist."

"Well," said Padgett, smiling. "It seems that you know some terminology not found in the literature handbook. That might strike some as illegitimate, too."

"I read widely."

"Indeed," said Padgett. "But don't worry, Professor. As soon as I have a precise answer about what I'm trying to accomplish, I'll tell you."

SIX

San Francisco

March 2007

Detective Emmanuel Cerrillo arrived in San Francisco at 8:30 p.m., six and a half hours after he'd left Pomona, and checked into the Nob Hill Motel. It was in the Russian Hill/Pacific Heights district, so even the regular rates of $100 to $165 per night were a bargain. And Cerrillo wanted a private room rather than trying to shack up with a local cop for three days. He was partial to maid service, and the manager always gave him a deal. There weren't many perks for police work, but hotel and restaurant discounts could be good.

The Nob was one of those unknown gems of the city that provided a three-diamond room at a double-cut rate. Cerrillo remembered his first vacation visit seven years ago, during his rookie year on the force. As he was leaving the hotel for an early morning walk, he stopped by the front desk to ask about local geography, public transportation, restaurants, etc., and was amused when the clerk, Joe, pulled out a street map, circled several areas, and said, "It's okay to go here during the day, but not at night." Then he pointed south and said, "*Never* go there, day or night." Cerrillo had smiled at the slightly overweight, middle-aged man and thanked him. They had a laugh the next day when that manager discovered Cerrillo was a Pomona cop and that San Francisco had more to fear from him than he from it.

Since then, Cerrillo had returned five times to the same hotel. For the detective, having grown up where even gang members were afraid to go out after dark, the streets of San Francisco compared as London, Paris, Rome, and Beijing all rolled into one, the grand adventure of a mystic land. It was also the farthest Cerrillo had been from his Southern California birth place. And tonight, when he called from the outskirts of town on his cell phone about a room, Joe instantly recognized his voice.

"How long you in town?" asked Joe.

"A few days," said Cerrillo.

"Business?"

"Murder investigation."

"They're sending beat cops for this?"

"I'm a detective, now. Homicide."

"I can hear you grinning," said the manager. "Pretty damn proud of yourself, I'll bet. You're not gonna turn into a crazed Supercop and scare off my *good customers*?"

"That depends on how well you treat me."

"Same as ever," said Joe.

"Maybe I'd better find another hotel."

"What? And miss the local color? Come on. We'll turn down a bed for you."

"That's better."

"But if you're still driving that dented Corolla, park it around the block. Don't want to drag down the neighborhood or embarrass the drug dealers."

"How would you like a ticket on your windshield tomorrow?"

"All right, Detective. Pull in the lot. I can tell people it belongs to the night maid."

"Thought you'd see it my way."

"Hey, listen," said the manager, changing tone. "We're only 80% booked. I'll set you up in a King Suite for the homicide special: $200 total for three nights? How's that?"

"Great," said Cerrillo.

"And I'll send our runner to get a three-day Trans-pass tomorrow morning. Usual deal."

"You reading minds, now?"

"Basic requirement for the hotel union."

Cerrillo hated driving in San Francisco and always got the Trans-pass. No worries about traffic, parking, narrow streets, or steep hills. And the Corolla's brakes had seen better days. But between the buses and cable cars, he could hop off at a doorstep almost anywhere and anytime in the city.

"And one more thing," said Joe.

"What's that?"

"Congratulations on your promotion, Detective."

Cerrillo laughed. "Wow. That's the nicest thing you've ever said to me."

"Don't let it go to your head, Flatfoot. The only reason I bother is because one of your ancestors probably helped settle California, though I expect they was running from the Federales when they got here."

"I love you too, Joe. Be there in twenty minutes. Keep the lights on."

"Starting to sound like a commercial... You hungry?"

"I haven't seen food since early this morning."

"Well, got a few cold cuts in the fridge and some sour-dough. I'll scrape off the mold and pull a sandwich together. Leave it in your room with a couple bottles of beer. Unless you'd rather fend for yourself. The streets are still open for business."

"Nope. On the road seven hours. I'm done. Take pot-luck."

"It's yours."

"Thanks. See you in twenty."

Cerrillo was never quite sure why Joe was so accom-modating. A strange, take-my-hospitality-and-like-it kind of guy. Joe wasn't afraid of cops, either, so that wasn't it. Many people were, but not Joe. Didn't seem infatuated either. Cerrillo knew very little about Joe, who was loose-lipped regarding everything except him-self. He had served two tours in Vietnam; been shot twice and married once. He loved beer, bourbon, and te-quila—especially tequila.   And every two or three months, Joe would try, as he put it, to drink his way through the city. It would take a couple days to recover, but he referred to those ventures as Saloon Therapy. Aside from that, Joe seemed a moderate drinker, and he was secretive about his life. He might have been a serial killer or an eccentric millionaire whose hobby was man-aging hotels, but Cerrillo was sure of one thing: Joe watched over him like a cop watching out for his partner. And beyond that, he could rustle up a great late-night sandwich.

***

Cerrillo slept until 7:00 the next morning and formu-lated a loose investigative strategy. He seemed to do his best thinking in isolation. It could be difficult to concen-trate in the Pomona office—too many clicking keyboards, phone calls, and the very annoying *rat-tat-tat-tat* of an industrial gauge Underwood typewriter, a fifty-pound museum piece that one of the older detectives still used despite his upgraded computer terminal. When Cerrillo needed to focus, he would sneak across the courtyard to the Pomona Public Library, hide out in a corner, and try to grasp the underbelly of murder.

Many cases didn't require real police work, no piecing together of motives and evidence. Murder was often so blood-simple that a myopic librarian could finger the suspect. Pomona didn't attract sophisticated underworld hustlers or international jewel thieves. It was a bastard-disrespected-me-so-I-shot-him kind of town. Charges typically came from drunken brawls, family fights, liquor store robberies gone bad, or jealous boyfriends and girlfriends. Socioeconomic violence was easy to follow.

During the last fifty years, Southern California had become an interlinked asphalt megalopolis of twenty million inhabitants and a hundred municipalities. Riverside, San Bernardino, Los Angeles, San Diego, and Orange counties alone had more people than some Eastern European countries. So legal jurisdictions sometimes blurred because the bad guys didn't respect county lines any more than they respected human life. And the real estate could range from third-world blight to presidential royalty.

Detective Cerrillo feared neither the grit nor the glitter. He would knock on any door—a back alley fire escape in Riverside's Badlands or the front lobby of the glass-enclosed downtown Bonaventure Hotel—and he would go with or without backup. Though he would never openly admit it, Cerrillo didn't particularly disapprove of nonviolent crimes like prostitution or gambling or even drug use, and he had looked the other way on these more than once. But murder was the unforgivable sin, and it had nothing to do with Cecil B. DeMille or the Ten Commandments. It was about snuffing the breath of someone who had no desire to stop breathing. Cerrillo might turn a blind eye toward the personal stash in a teenager's car, but if that teenager pulled a trigger, there would be consequences.

Cerrillo picked up the three-day bus pass at the Nob's front desk at 8:20 a.m. Joe was not around, which was unusual, but Cerrillo didn't ask why. There was a lot to do. Cerrillo wanted to stop by the Richmond and Taraval District Police Stations, both in the Golden Gate Division that patrolled the outer regions of San Francisco. Mrs. School Board's body had been found in her home (Richmond jurisdiction), but many of her acquaintances lived or worked elsewhere, so Cerrillo planned to circulate. And because the death had been ruled a suicide, few of the victim's colleagues had been interviewed, and Cerrillo wanted to correct that oversight. He would also contact family members, which could stir resentment, but he didn't care. A little resentment often produced information, and because Cerrillo believed that Mrs. School Board and the Preacher had been murdered, he would ruffle as many feathers as needed.

Chief Margaret Ricketts had already alerted the Golden Gate Division the day before, so they knew that Detective Emmanuel Cerrillo was coming and the official report would be changed from "suicide" to "under investigation." This meant that a local officer would be reassigned to the case and would blame Cerrillo for the extra work.

Cerrillo made a mental note to visit Golden Gate Park and talk with workers in the zoo's reptile exhibit; also, stop by the University of San Francisco to chat with hospital staff about the victim's medical history, perhaps peek at her records. A police badge would sometimes deliver information despite privacy laws simply because it was easier to help a cop than to explain why they couldn't. But Cerrillo could play hardball with sanctimonious hospital academics who viewed the rest of the world as lab assistants. The how-would-you-like-to-discuss-this-at-the-station or where-were-you-at-such-and-such-time carried a lot of clout.

And the zoo: there was just a chance that someone—biologist, naturalist, keeper, or janitor—might have seen something related to cobras or venom. The odds were low, but some cases were solved by long shots. There could be relatives or coworkers of Mrs. School Board in North-Central, but if possible, he preferred to stay out of SF Metro Division. Chief Ricketts and one of the Metro big wheels didn't get along (apparently some long-ago falling out), and Cerrillo knew that the animosity would leak down to him. Metro might not be necessary, and unless Cerrillo got a few tangible leads, there would be no point.

Preliminary information suggested that many of Mrs. School Board's associates hated the woman almost as much as whoever killed her, so that might be an angle. As an afterthought, Cerrillo scribbled on his yellow pad to check with the emergency room doctor at Loma Linda Medical Center when he returned to Southern California. He'd seen part of a television program about a physician who specialized in snakebites. Cerrillo wondered whether snake venom deteriorated over time. If so, how long did it take? How much would be needed to kill a person? Then, almost as quickly, the detective decided to look for religious connections between the Preacher Smithfield and the woman. That might take him somewhere.

Cerrillo was so preoccupied with jumping ideas that he missed his bus stop. When he finally got off, he had to backtrack six blocks along Geary Boulevard to Sixth and the red-brick Romanesque building that housed Richmond District offices. Cerrillo felt a twinge of jealousy as he climbed the steps. Practically a mansion compared with the cinder blocks and drywall of Pomona, he thought. But when he entered the building and made his way past the civilian reception area, this badge brigade seemed much like any other. There was a general hustle of clicking keyboards, bleeping phones, the metallic resonance of industrial file cabinets, conversational skirmishes of officers and suspects—most of them loud, angry, tearful, or drunk—and the occasional whiff of vomit from a DUI who couldn't make it to the holding cell before throwing up. Cerrillo was sure, for a moment, that he even heard an old Underwood typewriter in the mix. Perhaps they were still standard issue for old guys.

"Hey," said Cerrillo to the nearest uniformed officer. "I'm looking for Detective Lieutenant Mertwile. Drove up yesterday on the School Board murder case."

"Like I give a shit," said the young woman, bent over a stack of papers and taking a careful sip of coffee from a Styrofoam cup filled to the brim. "Lieutenant Kiss-My-Ass could be anywhere. Does he know you're coming?"

"Yes."

"Then you can be almost certain he isn't here." The young woman looked up. This time she smiled with some empathy. "Hi. My name's Josie. Excuse the fine how-do-you-do, but I've only been here an hour, and already my ass has been chewed twice, including by a Neanderthal who said it was my job to make coffee."

"Chewed out *only* twice in an hour. That wouldn't qualify as an honorable mention in Pomona."

Josie laughed. "Well, come to think of it, about the only time supervisors are nice to anyone around here is just before that anyone is suspended. So maybe this isn't such a bad start. What's your name?"

"Detective Emmanuel Cerrillo. From Pomona." He was still too insecure in his promotion to drop the title upon introduction, but he quickly downsized his formality. "Call me Manny or Cerrillo."

"Okay, Detective." Josie was a natural contrarian. Cerrillo liked that.

"So, I take it you haven't seen Mertwile," he said.

"Nope. Haven't seen him. Don't want to. Two doors down the hall." She pointed. "Duty sergeant keeps tabs on everybody. If Mertwile isn't here, and if he didn't sign out on the big board, I won't be the only ass-chewing recipient today. That sergeant of ours, when he swims in the Bay, even the Great Whites run and hide. Toughest SOB I ever met."

"Down the hall?"

"Second door," said Josie.

"I'll check," said Cerrillo. "Thanks."

"And when you do find Mertwile, after you get done hearing how he graduated from Stanford in only three and a half years, ask if I can go with you today. I don't care what case you're working or where. Got to be better than filing reports on community awareness meetings and seventh-grade truancies. Please save me from file-clerk hell and say you need Josie to show you around the District. If I'd known cops had so much paperwork, I would have signed up to be a bus driver."

"I'll see what I can do. Stanford, huh?"

"Yep. Everybody on the force has heard that story a dozen times."

"I suppose the lieutenant won't think much of my Cal State," said Cerrillo.

"Best not to mention it. But don't feel bad. To hear Mertwile tell it, Harvard and Yale were his backup schools."

"Thanks for the tip."

Cerrillo liked Josie already. She starched-ironed her uniform like a rookie searching for brownie points, but she talked and acted like a veteran cop who already had enough points for two careers. Still, Cerrillo didn't really need help, and even when he did, he wouldn't admit it. He just wanted to find Mertwile, read the case file, and talk with people in the field. His only hope for a lead was to stumble onto it, and the only chance of stumbling was to get out and move around. Cerrillo walked down to find the duty officer, and he suddenly reconsidered having Josie tag along. "Local clout," he thought. This would constitute *help*, of course, but a good detective just might convince himself that a beat cop was privileged to ride with him.

At the second doorway, Cerrillo turned toward the desk sergeant inside an open-bay office, a middle-aged, potbellied Billy goat whose uniform appeared one size too small. He looked at Cerrillo's civilian clothes. "Who the hell are you?"

"Detective Emmanuel Cerrillo. Pomona Homicide."

"Oh, right. Mertwile said something about *a jackass stirring up the suicide*. He's out. Left the file on the counter." The sergeant thumbed toward a too-thin manila folder.

"That's the whole file!?" asked Cerrillo in disbelief.

"Yep. Until you and your boss lady got involved, it was a done deal. Dead woman. Simple suicide. Case closed."

"What do you think?"

"I pass out assignments as instructed. Don't decide how they're handled. And it's not my business to second guess the results."

"Where can I look this over?" asked Cerrillo, glancing at the documents.

"Find a vacant desk. Anyplace is okay by me. If you're in somebody's territory, you'll be informed plenty quick." The sergeant took a breath and said, "Sorry, I can't offer you more, Detective. We're pretty informal around here; too busy for anything else. Might be an empty interrogation room."

"Don't worry about it. I won musical chairs in second grade. Just surprised that there isn't more in the file."

"Like I said. The whole deal was cut and dried. That's everything we have, though I doubt it will help you much." The sergeant added, "But don't get us wrong. We got good cops. This is a big town. Everybody's stretched pretty thin. Sometimes we need to go with the obvious. I'll admit that snake-oil jazz seemed a stretch, but I wasn't the detective."

"I understand," said Cerrillo. "And from what I know, suicide *would* be the logical conclusion, except for some additional info we got down in Pomona. Anyway, I have to check it out. My boss is finicky about loose ends." Cerrillo knew that shuffling responsibility to a mystic boss could be a good tactic.

"Yeah. I get that. So there's the file. Have at it. If Mertwile comes in before you leave, I'll tell him you're here." The tone suggested that the conversation was finished.

Cerrillo picked up the manila file. "Oh, one more thing," he said. "I ran into an officer out front. Name of Josie."

"Yeah?" The sergeant looked up again, seemingly annoyed.

"I'm going to visit the Taraval District, talk with a few witnesses, maybe interview school board members. Basically make a nuisance of myself over the next couple days."

"I'm starting to believe you're good at it."

Cerrillo ignored the remark. "Helpful to have a local cop along. Someone familiar with the layout, who's who in crime and punishment, that sort of thing. Don't suppose you could assign Josie to the investigation while I'm here." Detective Cerrillo was surprised by his own change of heart. He generally preferred to work alone, but he liked people with a backbone, and something about Josie suggested "good cop."

"Would that get you out of my hair for awhile?" The sergeant grinned.

Cerrillo nodded. "Almost certainly."

The sergeant walked over to a laminated wallboard that listed the names of about twenty-five officers. He uncapped a felt-tipped marker and wrote "field investigation" next to Josie Waller's name. "Tell her to sign back in when she's done," he said, "and to finish her damned reports. That woman's paperwork is always late ... but fieldwork is important, too."

"I'll tell her. Thanks."

"So long, Detective."

"So long." Cerrillo was almost to the hallway when he turned back. "Oh, one more thing."

The duty sergeant looked up again, visibly annoyed. "I thought you already used up *one more thing*."

"Sorry. Is Josie a good cop?"

"Everybody here is a good cop!" That struck a nerve.

"I mean," said Cerrillo, trying to seem conciliatory, "is she easy to work with? Does she know her business?"

"Seems to me," said the sergeant, "that a *good* detective might ask those questions before having her assigned to the investigation."

"Touché," said Cerrillo. "An afterthought."

"Don't worry. Waller's good. Smart. The right amount of attitude. And she's lived here all her life. You'll do well as long as you don't ask her to get your coffee."

"I already figured she didn't win Miss Congeniality at the ladies home companion charm school."

"More likely kicked out for building hand grenades."

Cerrillo laughed. "My kind of girl. Thanks, sarge."

"You're welcome. And now, young Mister Homicide from Pomona, if there's nothing else, please pick up the case file and get the hell out of my office."

"Just leaving."

"And tell Officer Waller to see me before leaving!"

"Absolutely."

"And now I have one more thing," said the sergeant.

"Yes?"

"If you lose any part of that file, *our* captain will have to call *your* captain..."

Cerrillo clutched the legal-sized folder. "I'll guard it with my life."

SEVEN

The Quiet Woman

November 2006

Dr. Robert Davenport found Dr. Tanish Padgett to be an annoyingly polite student. She sat, she observed, she rarely spoke, and when she did, her commentary often sounded like an excerpt from an online essay that she might have read the night before. Had Padgett been a regular student, she would have been in danger of failing. At the very least, Davenport would have discussed her apparent disconnection from the course material. But Padgett was simply auditing the class, and Davenport was busy with other responsibilities—teaching, reading student papers, and, especially, second guessing his tenure decision, which was now delayed a year and a half beyond expectation. So it was easy for him to ignore

Padgett's lukewarm scholarship. She was pleasant enough, almost invisible. Davenport had no idea whether she was getting what she wanted from the class, but by mid-term, he decided that he didn't care.

Davenport's casual indifference toward a student seemed strange to him, almost frightening. Maybe he was slipping. Logically, he had everything he should want. Davenport had been teaching for eight years, and he loved the concept and reality of the university as a world of ideas. But in the last few months, intermittently, he wondered whether he could stomach another thirty years of the classroom. The doubt scared him. He felt the slow burn of an unreasonable tenure delay, of collegial isolation, of an ethereal hostility hovering overhead. Davenport had always planned his life with scholarly precision, he had succeeded beyond expectation at an Ivy League school, yet somehow he'd been short changed in satisfaction. And for the first time at his job, he had a gnawing suspicion he was getting screwed behind the scenes.

Davenport handled this confusion in typical fashion: he tried to pretend it did not exist. He graded papers, held conferences, prepared and refined lectures. He had trained to teach, and so he would teach. To back away from a prestigious university post would be inconceivable.

Professor Robert Davenport might have held on for thirty additional years of teaching and led a comfortable life, but in the twelfth week of that fall semester, Tanish Padgett stopped coming to class. Davenport found himself peculiarly annoyed. He had gone above and beyond by allowing her to audit, and then she turns up AWOL.

"That's just rude," thought Davenport, and he called the Humanities Department secretary to ask about Padgett's status at the university.

The secretary reported, "There is no Tanish Padgett listed anywhere in the rosters. She's not a student."

Davenport had another thought. "Could she be part-time faculty?"

"Hold on and I'll check," said the secretary. A few minutes later she came back on the line. "Hello? Dr. Davenport?"

"Yes."

"Nothing on Padgett. Although if she is a recent hire, it can take administration a while to log adjuncts into payroll. Do you know what department she might be with?"

"No. And I suspect that she isn't on the faculty. Never mind. If she shows up in class, I'll..." Davenport paused and then asked, "Tell me. Do you remember adding any student to my class during the third week of the semester?"

"Of course not, Dr. Davenport!" The secretary sounded offended. "In a graduate course? Here? If I tried something like that, the professors would have me drawn and quartered! Even when I receive such requests, which happens, I send students directly to the graduate office. I follow the rules, Professor."

"Well, don't worry about it," said Davenport. "When our mystery student shows, I'll find out what's going on. Sorry to trouble you."

"No trouble at all. But, remember, she could be a part-timer. They can come and go pretty quickly. You could check with payroll in a few days. We've got people here three or four years I wouldn't recognize if I sat next to them. In fact, Dr. Davenport, no offense, but I'm not sure that I would recognize you."

Davenport laughed. "Point taken. English faculty do tend to keep to themselves. Sorry."

"Think nothing of it," said the secretary. "I have enough trouble with some of the *personalities* in our department. Professors are ... different."

Davenport felt some empathy. It couldn't be easy for a secretary working with academic egos. Being a colleague was tough enough.

"Oh!" said the secretary, suddenly concerned, "should I alert security about this Padgett? They might track her down."

"No," said Davenport. "Undoubtedly some kind of bureaucratic mix-up. I'll handle it."

"Okay. Bye."

Professor Davenport gritted his teeth as he hung up. He was a professor, a pretty smart guy, and some con artist had apparently put something over on him. But why would a woman with a scientific Ph.D. audit a class in the Yale English department? And why just sit and watch without much effort? What could she possibly want from all this? Davenport flushed with embarrassment as he suddenly made a regrettable connection.

"Don't Ask, Don't Tell," he said out loud. "She's with them."

It was the only thing that made sense. Davenport suddenly knew he would see Tanish Padgett again—but not in class.

***

April 2007

Months later, on April 13, after an unprecedented and probably illegal delay, Professor Robert Davenport finally received official notice from the university that he had been granted tenure without promotion. This rarely happened because tenure and promotion to Associate Professor were generally conjoined, and a professor typically earned both (or neither) in the journey from assistant to associate and then full professor, with each step accompanied by substantial increases in salary and prestige. The university's decision put Davenport in an awkward position. On the one hand, he had received a rather significant professional distinction; on the other, a rather significant slap in the face. Davenport and the Dean of Arts and Sciences met that week to discuss the right and left hands of academia.

"Dr. Davenport," said the dean, "let's be candid and avoid animosity. The university granted tenure based upon your qualitative contributions to scholarship. Yet the review committee withheld promotion based on quantitative considerations, i.e., insufficient publications. They were especially disappointed that you have not produced a book-length monograph. And two advisory members were concerned with your predilection toward teaching freshman composition instead of scholarly research in your primary field."

Davenport listened quietly. The dean continued with a clipped cadence that promoted silence even as he extended an olive branch. "Now, despite the delayed decision, earning tenure at this institution, and especially in your department, is no small accomplishment. Only forty percent make it. We might further assume that, in your case, promotion to Associate Professor will be granted in due course. I personally think it's a foregone conclusion. However, a friendly word of advice from your colleagues: focus on the graduate school and develop a substantial piece of scholarship. Good teaching is fine and dandy, but Yale did not build preeminence with good teaching in freshman composition. It came through a faculty dedicated to research."

Davenport wanted to mention a connection between the school's reputation and its substantial endowments, but he did not. He listened and nodded at appropriate deferential moments.

Finally, Davenport unclenched his teeth and said, "Thank you for the guidance and for your confidence in helping me to secure tenure." As he stood to leave and shook the dean's hand, he added, "And don't worry, Sir. The department's concerns shall not go unanswered."

The dean left the meeting with the distinct impression that he had helped a fine young assistant professor properly refocus his career around the university mission. Davenport left the meeting not sure whether he should give up teaching, scream at the sky, or get drunk. The dean was right about one thing, however. Tenure was an achievement. But why no promotion? Professors almost always went up or out. Why the weird middle ground in his case? Should he be grateful for tenure or furious about non-promotion? Davenport was again disturbed by emotional uncertainty because he was sure he should have one feeling or the other. What was wrong with him?

Because Davenport met with the dean on a Friday afternoon, and because he did not have classes or office hours afterward, Davenport went home, poured himself a glass of wine, took a special muffin from the freezer that he had been holding for such an occasion, started a DVD of *Raiders of the Lost Ark*, and settled into his stuffed recliner. He would relax and allow the baked marijuana and wine to work their calming magic. As he ate the muffin, which tasted distinctly herbal, he wondered why he had given up this pleasure during the last several years. A psychology department colleague who had been through the tenure process the year before—and failed—provided the muffin four months earlier after Davenport mentioned the extreme delay regarding his case. Davenport's friend said, "Hold this in reserve. If your tenure doesn't go well, the home-baked therapy will help you survive the first day, which is the worst part. And it will give you strength to begin a new job search, which is the second worst. I'm speaking as a trained therapist, and California gold is my prescription."

Davenport had accepted the muffin but still felt confident that, while he might enjoy the treat someday, he would not actually need it. Now, faltering from anger and self-doubt generated after his conversation with the dean, Davenport appreciated his friend's advice and gift. Even though he had earned tenure, the sense of rejection was almost unbearable, and he felt great empathy for his fallen colleague, who was now finishing his final year at the university and would begin teaching at a community college in the fall. But as Davenport sunk deeper in the recliner, he soon found himself artificially relaxed and the soundtrack of *Raiders* artificially enhanced.

In a symbiotic relationship of fantasy to reality, Davenport envisioned a character-driven adventure that involved his skilled manipulation of a bullwhip across a host of English Department bodies. He smiled, closed his eyes, and listened to the familiar background of sound effects and thematic film score. And sometime before the Ark of the Covenant had been safely tucked away by top men in a government warehouse, Doctor Davenport fell asleep. He did not care further about tenure. He did not care about promotion. He did not hear the knock at the door or the note that dropped through the mail slot into his living room.

***

Davenport awoke at 8:30 the following morning. Cloudless New England sunshine streamed through the cracks of the blinds. His eyes hurt from the glare, but he felt alert. He lay sideways across the bed with a pillow braced under his head. There was a pain in his ribs, and he rolled over to find one of his Nike running shoes. The other was still on his foot.

Davenport tossed the offending footwear to the floor, stood up, and looked at himself in the mirror. If he had been a twelve-year-old after a seventh grade slumber party, the image might have seemed appropriate. Davenport laughed. "Okay. You had a rough night. Let's regroup. I want you in the shower and into clothes that haven't been slept in. Then, a quick breakfast and the gym. And for god's sake, brush your teeth!" he said, tasting what seemed like soured red-wine glue stuck to his palate. "Later, we'll grade a few papers and go..."

Davenport's determination suddenly collapsed. He was about to say "go celebrate tenure," but he realized that there was nobody in his life to celebrate with, just as yesterday there had been no one to help him bear the pain. His emotional comfort had come from a muffin, a DVD, and a shoe in the ribs. Davenport shook his head, lonely and tired. He decided to take a hot shower to try to wash away these feelings, but as he removed his shirt and drifted toward the kitchen to brew his morning coffee, Davenport noticed the envelope that had been pushed through the door's mail slot.

"Probably from a sympathetic colleague," he thought. "The news must be getting around."

He sat, almost fell into the living room chair, and opened the envelope. There was a handwritten note accompanied by the now-familiar white business card.

Dear Dr. Davenport, Don't Ask, Don't Tell invites you to join our organization, and we have scheduled a meeting for you with two members of our New England chapter a week from Sunday. A car will arrive at your home at 1:00 p.m. to take you to the appointment, at which time you will receive limited disclosure about who we are and what we do.

The note was signed by Dr. Tanish Padgett. A postscript read:

The University withheld promotion because we live in a homophobic world. But DADT can help. Justice is our profession.

EIGHT

Binding Tie

March 2007

Officer Josie Waller and Detective Emmanuel Cerrillo left the Richmond Police Station at 10:00 a.m. Beforehand, Cerrillo pulled Waller into an empty interrogation room, offered a condensed version of the Pomona preacher case, and discussed the San Francisco file with her.

Waller was interested. She had been on the force two and a half years, and it seemed to her that she was too often relegated to community service details—safety presentations at elementary schools using hand-puppet characters who always walk their bikes across intersections and never talk to strangers; scared-straight dramas at city high schools with heavily muscled and tattooed but otherwise tamed prison inmates who testified against the pitfalls of crime; and, what Josie hated the most, speeches to retirees and middle-aged housewives about community neighborhood watch programs who then felt obligated to call 911 whenever a leaf dropped out of place or a trash can fell over.

She did regular patrols, too, often on the graveyard shift, which meant a higher percentage of drunk-driving, disturbing-the-peace, or domestic-violence calls, along with in-your-face alcoholics who were necessarily part of the scene. Josie had already developed a reputation for dependability and guts. She was five-foot nine, ran three miles a day, worked out at Gold's Gym four days a week, and had always been physically robust. And yet, somehow, if one didn't look too carefully, she could seem delicate. Waller was also pretty, which was a double-edged sword in male-dominated professions, and her womanly shape might elicit sexist remarks from cops as well as those she arrested. But Officer Waller carried a hard body and no-nonsense attitude, and she weathered her share of blows from taller and heavier suspects. Waller knew she would be an asset to Cerrillo's investigation, and her first contribution was a shiny new patrol car for their use over three days.

"Okay," said Waller from the driver's seat as Cerrillo slid into the passenger side, "Where first?"

In a moment of inspiration, Cerrillo decided to trust local intuition. "You know the area and the case better than I do," he said, "What do you recommend?"

"First," said Waller, "I know little about the case, only what we discussed at Division, but I'm glad to tag along. My boss has me on an unofficial punishment detail. That's why I was trapped in the paper chase. It's good to get back in a patrol car."

"Unofficial punishment?" asked Cerrillo.

"Yeah. Not much of a story, really. A few weeks back, I roughed up a DUI suspect who roughed me up first. Asshole deserved it, but the chief took some heat."

"I bet. Media problems?"

"Not too much; otherwise, I'd be screwed. Half our job these days is avoiding lawsuits. I got lucky. The automated dash-cam didn't catch the whole *arrest*."

"You *were* lucky. Once 'police brutality' makes the news, there's no stopping it."

"Tell me about it. Still a pisser, though. When it was all over, I had more broken body parts than he did. But I suppose the chief's right. A cop can't afford to lose control. Ironic though."

"Why?"

"Officially, I was praised. 'Injured in the line of duty' is what they said in the report. Unofficially, I'm typing service reports until S.F. elects a Republican mayor."

"That long?"

"Anyway, thanks for bringing me along. Might help me get out of the doghouse."

"Fine by me," said Cerrillo. "Now, do you think anybody might want to kill Madam School Board? Or did she do herself?"

"Herself? That scorpion bitch would eat her own babies before she'd commit suicide. People said she was depressed about losing her job. Horseshit. The holy-rollers who backed her anti-gay crusades had money and jobs. And they loved her."

"Did you know the woman?"

"No, but some just like her. They don't have much hold over the Bay Area these days, but in some parts of the country, homophobes do a lot of damage."

Cerrillo decided to push, to know if they were going to be able to work together. "So you're in favor of faggots teaching children?"

Waller kept her eyes on the road but took her foot off the gas. "That's right, Detective. I support faggots in all kinds of jobs. Perhaps we should stop and discuss it in more detail? Don't mind my cracked knuckles."

"Just talking here. Wanted to know where you stand."

"And?"

"Me? I salute *anybody* who's willing to teach these days. My concern is this. Suppose School Board was murdered. Are you going to help me find the killer or look the other way?"

"First, I already told you the woman was murdered. Had more enemies than Richard Nixon. And second, I'm in a police car with you. If I didn't want to be, that shiny detective's badge of yours couldn't make it happen. So, yes, I want to find the perp, and I'll do my damnedest to find him. We straight now?"

"Yeah."

"Good, cause I'm not," said Waller, feeling better but still gripping the wheel too hard. "Look, Detective. I'm with you on the case, and I'm a lesbian. No more fag remarks, even in jest. Okay?"

"Agreed."

Waller loosened her grip on the wheel. She hadn't noticed, but her fingers were numb.

Cerrillo paused and said, "You know I'm here because Preacher Smithfield wasn't an accidental overdose either. But the only connection I can think of is they both hated gays and died from poison in their veins."

"Not much to go on. And do you know how many homophobes sit in church every week talking about brotherly love? And how many teetotalers do drugs? How many cops, for that matter? Welcome to the Golden Age of Hypocrisy. Your little clues probably narrowed the suspects down to a million."

"I know. But tell me how a preacher who's never touched drugs in his life dies of an overdose. And tell me where some elementary schoolmarm gets cobra venom..."

"I say let's visit the death house. Forget about the woman's political views. And forget about the snake juice. Irrelevant. If she didn't kill herself, then she didn't obtain the venom. And if these two cases *are* related, then that somebody is at least two or three people because multiple skills are involved. Smart as hell, too. We don't need snakes, and we don't need interviews with the School Board. We need a compass to point toward the guilty, and the most likely place for evidence is the crime scene. If we don't find something there, I doubt that other leads will help."

"I'm game," said Cerrillo. "I'm not sure about multiple suspects though? Might be one crazy. Pros kill for money, and how do you turn a profit by offing a couple of fag haters? Sorry, homophobes."

Cerrillo and Waller both smiled. They were starting to click. This almost surprised Cerrillo, who generally disliked having a partner, but Josie struck him right off as *simpatico*, and he believed in her before he had time to think about it.

Waller said, "I have no idea about the profit margins in murder, but the place for answers is the house. The obvious conclusion was suicide, so the investigating officers were probably in and out pretty quick. Who gives a damn about self-abuse, right? They might have missed something, and maybe it's still there. Plus, you have information about the other case, so we might connect a few dots they didn't have."

"Is there anyone at the home to let us in? If not, we'll need a search warrant."

"Don't know if anybody's there now," said Josie. "If the house is on the market, might be sitting empty. San Francisco property values have dropped, which is weird, because it's easier to believe in alien invasions than declining real estate around here. I think the woman was separated from her husband, but let's go see who's there."

Cerrillo said nothing.

After a few seconds, Josie took a breath. "Well? You got a better idea?"

"We still need a judge to sign off on this if nobody's home," said Cerrillo.

"We need evidence, Detective, and nobody's gonna give us a warrant in this case. I'd feel stupid even asking. Besides, I have a very nice Wal-Mart crowbar in the trunk."

***

Waller and Cerrillo parked in front of the victim's Richmond District house. There were no cars out front. The place appeared empty, but the grass had been cut within the last few days.

Officer Waller said, "Listen, Manny. Before we get out, you're the detective on this case, but this is my town, my district. Just follow my lead. If there's anything here, we need to find it. If not, we'll know soon enough. Deal?"

"You're not planning to break in and leave a horse's head in the bed?"

"What do you mean 'break in'? I'm a gentle female police officer. I'm gonna politely knock on the door and ask for permission."

"And if nobody's home?"

"I'm going to investigate a potential burglary in progress and uphold my duty as a law officer sworn to protect private property. I further suspect that a back window might already be broken at this very moment, leading me to reasonably believe an intruder could be inside the home."

"Wow," said Cerrillo, wondering how far she might bend the rules. "I can't even see the back of the house from here. You're some cop."

"I take pride in my duties. You don't know where we could get a horse's head, do you? It would look cool in the report."

"No thanks."

"Too bad." Waller glanced toward Cerrillo and gestured with open palms. "So, follow my lead?"

Cerrillo tried to sound confident. "Let's do it."

They exited the patrol car without reporting their location to headquarters and approached the house. Waller rang the doorbell several times, knocked, and then pounded on the door. She nodded to Cerrillo. "Wait here. I'll grab the crowbar from the trunk and move around back."

A slightly overweight elderly neighbor approached from across the street and called to them. "Hello, Officers. Can I help you?"

Waller spoke first. "I don't think so, ma'am. I'm Officer Josie Waller from the Richmond Police District. And this is Detective Cerrillo. We're on a special investigation regarding, well, you know, the unfortunate incident that occurred here."

"Oh, yes," said the woman. "A terrible tragedy. But nobody's home."

"Did you know the victim, ma'am?" asked Waller.

"Indeed I did," said the woman. "We kind of looked out for each other. California neighbors. Since they lived right across the street, I used to get their mail and feed the cat when they were out of town, that sort of thing. They would do the same for me. After she separated from her husband, she invited me over for tea a couple times. It was pleasant enough. Very shocking about the suicide."

"You said that no one is home, ma'am?" asked Waller.

"That's right. Her older daughter—they had two children—is the executrix of the estate. They plan to sell the property when values recover. I have the daughter's phone number if you need it."

"I don't think that's necessary," said Waller. "What is your name, ma'am?" Waller pulled out a notepad as if she were interested.

"I'm Harriet Quail. A retired social worker. My husband died three years ago."

"Glad to meet you," said Detective Cerrillo, "and sorry for your loss."

"Me too," said Officer Waller.

Harriet Quail suddenly looked embarrassed. "You're probably wondering, since I was a social worker, why I didn't recognize the signs of depression. But I swear, the woman never let on at all. And it was funny, because I used to think with all that was going on in her life, separation from her husband and the, uh, school board problems, that she *should* be depressed. But she never said a thing, just went about her life almost rosy like. I swear there was absolutely no sign of depression."

"Well, to tell you the truth, Mrs. Quail," said Waller, recognizing an opening, "that's why we're here. Detective Cerrillo and I are a little suspicious. We're not entirely sure that this case *was* a suicide"

Mrs. Quail's eyes opened wide.

"But you must understand," said Waller, holding up her hands suggestively, "this is strictly off the record. Please don't let anyone know that we're investigating. Those social worker instincts of yours might be correct. We're not sure the victim was depressed or that she killed herself. But we don't want to tip our hand. If there is a perpetrator, we prefer they believe the case is closed."

Harriett Quail nodded. "Oh, I see. You can count on me, Officer."

"We wanted to look around the crime scene for possible clues, anything that might be out of order. Routine." Waller sighed and shook her head. "But since no one is here, I guess we'll have to check back later."

Mrs. Quail became Citizen of the Year. "Oh, no need for that, Officer. I have a key! I'll let you in right now."

This surprised Waller and Cerrillo even though it was exactly what Waller was hoping for.

"Really!" said Waller. "That's great!" She looked at Cerrillo. "Tell me, Detective. Should we wait for permission from the victim's daughter? Might need a search warrant, and I wouldn't want to violate the rules."

Cerrillo played along, apparently thinking. "It should be okay as long as we have permission." Cerrillo looked at Mrs. Quail, "I'm sorry to sound inquisitive, ma'am, but it's my duty as an officer. How do you happen to have a key to the house?"

"The daughter *asked* me to help. She lives in Arizona, you know. It's very hard for her to come back and forth to San Francisco. I sort of keep an eye on the property."

"Oh," said Cerrillo, "you have explicit permission from the owners?"

"Yes. Very explicit."

"Then it's perfectly all right," said Cerrillo. "Sorry if I sounded doubtful, Mrs. Quail, but we must proceed by the book. It's my job to ask these questions."

"Not at all!" said Harriet Quail, smiling. "If you don't mind my saying, we need more officers like you. I'll get the key. Do you want me to call the daughter and let her know?"

"No!" said the detective, too quickly. "In fact, we would prefer that you didn't."

Mrs. Quail seemed confused, suddenly troubled.

Waller stepped closer to Mrs. Quail and said in a low voice. "ma'am, we wouldn't want to further upset the family without cause. We're not entirely sure of our facts. No need for the children to think that the mother might have been, you know ... at least until we have more information."

Quail nodded.

"And ma'am, until we finish our investigation, we'd just as soon that you not mention this to anyone. Like you, we're suspicious but might be wrong. You understand, don't you?"

Quail let out a sigh. "Of course! It will be our secret. Why bother the children until we're sure? It would be terrible for that poor family to go through more than they have already. Such a senseless tragedy. Please wait while I get the key."

Mrs. Harriett Quail went back into her house, returned, and escorted Waller and Cerrillo to the victim's front door. As a demonstration of her confidence, she handed the key to Waller and said, "Please return this to me when you're finished? I'll be right across the street if you need anything."

"Thank you for your cooperation, Mrs. Quail," said Officer Waller. "You have been a great help."

"Thank you," said Quail.

"And one more thing, ma'am," said Detective Cerrillo.

"Yes?"

"Here is my business card. If you notice anything suspicious the next few months, would you please call me directly? If it's not too much trouble."

That marked the final approval for Harriett Quail. "Absolutely, Officers! I'll be your silent partner. And if you don't mind my saying..."

"Yes?" asked Waller.

"Based on my training and forty years experience as a social worker, it's my opinion that the woman did not commit suicide. I'll testify to that in open court."

"We appreciate that, ma'am," said Waller. "We might need to talk with you further."

"My pleasure," said Quail, satisfied that she had probably cracked the case for the officers. "I'll be home if you need me." Quail marched back across the street.

Cerrillo shook his head. "I'm guessing that this is the most exciting thing that's happened to her in five years."

"Probably twenty," said Waller. "But I'm almost disappointed that I didn't get to demonstrate my special home-access techniques. A key is so passive."

"Works fine for me. I prefer a pass card."

"That by-the-book scene was very convincing, Detective. Something you picked up in high school drama class?"

"Just following your lead, as requested."

Waller inserted the key into the lock, but it would not go in all the way. "Damn!" said Waller. "Our brilliant social worker gave us the wrong key."

"Try again," said Cerrillo. "Salt air. Might have been awhile since the locks were used."

Josie Waller pushed and turned and pushed again, but could not get the key fully inserted. She pulled it out. "Won't go all the way. Must be corrosion."

Cerrillo reached for the Chapstick in his pocket. "Smear a little of this on it."

Waller applied the balm and reinserted the key. She pushed hard and turned. The bolt slid back. She grabbed the knob and opened the door. "I'll make a note," said Waller. "Chapstick in my utility belt."

"I'm surprised you don't already have some," said Cerrillo. "Thought that was a lesbian trademark."

"Watch your step, Detective."

They entered the living room and closed the door behind them. "The air stinks," said Cerrillo. "Every window must be closed."

"That's a bigot you smell," said Waller, gesturing toward the oversized crucifix hanging above the fireplace amid a photographic array of famous evangelical ministers.

"According to the report, the body was found in the master bedroom. Let's see what's upstairs."

Together they looked around the victim's bedroom and adjoining bath, checked the hallway, and passed briefly through two other bedrooms. Nothing stood out.

"If someone broke in, evidence would be downstairs," said Waller.

"Probably."

"Tell me something, Detective."

"What's that?"

"Now that we're actually here, any idea what we should look for?"

"A connection. Something. Anything. Maybe nothing."

Waller hesitated. "After all our talk, I'm suddenly wondering if we're as crazy as the two victims. I mean, maybe they did kill themselves. People turn wacko. It happens. And more than one preacher has OD'd."

"Maybe. But I want to make sure. Look for the missing link."

"What if we don't find it?"

Cerrillo gestured around the living room. "With all the religious paraphernalia, we could hold a hell of a prayer meeting." He shook his head. "Just keep looking."

"Okay. I'll re-tackle the master bedroom. Holler if you need me."

"I'll check down here for forced entry."

Five minutes later, Detective Cerrillo yelled from ground level. "Hey, Josie! Come down here!"

Her reply was muffled and annoyed. "What do you want!? I'm under the bed."

"I found Sasquatch."

Josie hurried downstairs, still irritated. "Where are you?"

"In the kitchen."

Waller joined Cerrillo, expecting a smoking gun or bomb or another body, but saw nothing out of the ordinary.

Cerrillo pointed. "There!" he said.

"What?"

"The refrigerator," said Cerrillo.

"I don't get it. If you're planning to make a baloney sandwich, I suggest you check the expiration date?"

"No. Look. Under the magnet. I saw one exactly like it at the preacher's house in Pomona. Didn't think about it at the time. In fact, I didn't even remember it until just now."

"I still don't...? What? Preacher had the same ice box? Interior decorator? Kitchen curtains? Tell me!"

Cerrillo pointed to a plain white business card with raised black lettering. "What does that say?"

Josie Waller looked. "Don't Ask, Don't Tell."

"Exactly. The bastards left a calling card right under our noses and we didn't notice."

"Are you sure?" asked Josie.

"I'm not only sure," said Cerrillo too slowly, "I am also angry. Yes, indeed, very angry. And before this investigation's finished, I'm going to shove a whole box of those cards up somebody's ass."

Waller smiled. "I wonder what our neighborly social worker would say about that."

NINE

Business as Usual

March 2007

"Listen, Manny," said Captain Margaret Ricketts as she glanced at Detective Cerrillo's report, "this business card deal is pretty slim pickings. Do you expect the DA to file charges with that?"

"No," said Cerrillo.

"Then why are you pushing?" Ricketts did not give Cerrillo time to answer. "There were no fingerprints on the cards. They were printed on different stock. The inks don't match. There is absolutely no indication that..."

"I know, Chief. But it's not just the cards. It's the victims. Not only the way they were killed, but who they were. There is something being worked on us here, and those cards are important. I don't know how, but I'm sure they're connected."

"Probably a coincidence. *Don't Ask, Don't Tell* is used all the time. I ran the phrase through Google and got over a million hits. Thousands of groups have bones to pick about gays in the military or the policy against gays in the military. Those business cards could be a campaign stunt. Like the old *Queer Bills* circulated during Clinton's campaign. Who knows?"

"But Chief, I don't think the DADT folks have a bone to pick about gays in the military or anyplace else. And if I'm right, they're making corpses out of people who do. I mean, have you ever seen a business card with nothing but a name? No address or phone, no sales pitch, no 'vote for Shoeless Joe'? Further, have you seen this particular card anywhere but the refrigerators of these two victims?"

"Nope."

"And it was only an accident that I even noticed the damned things!" Detective Cerrillo sounded like a man who had discovered the smoking gun, but Captain Ricketts didn't smell gunpowder or see a weapon.

"Chief," he continued, "this was murder, and a slick murder at that."

"And what do you propose we do without concrete evidence? I'll support you as far as I'm able, but I've already had my ass chewed about this case. San Francisco PD hates me more than you. And the District Attorney's Office has received complaints because," Ricketts looked at a paper on her desk, "and I'm quoting here, *active court investigations are falling behind schedule*. And would you like to hear what one of your fellow detectives said about the 'preferential treatment' you are receiving from me regarding 'plush' assignments."

"What!" stammered Cerrillo.

"Oh, yes. Apparently the streets of San Francisco are an exotic and envious geographic destination. Wouldn't surprise me if someone thinks you're having an affair with the Police Chief as part of," Ricketts glance at another memo, "uh, *a continuing pattern of deferential and selective management.*"

Detective Cerrillo spoke through clenched teeth. "You'd better arrest me, Chief."

"What for?"

"Well, as soon as we finish our meeting, I'm going to fire several rounds into the testicles of a couple fellow officers."

"If it weren't a violation of department policy, I might help you. But in the meantime, I've got a better idea ... First, close my office door and then sit back down."

Cerrillo complied. Ricketts was sure that she could feel heat radiating from Cerrillo's face. He was angry. Ricketts was harder on him than anybody, and now his comrades accused him of slacking off. She worried that Cerrillo might actually break heads.

"Now hear me, Detective, and try to calm down." Margaret Ricketts picked up several memos from her desk and stuffed them in a manila file folder. "I'll respond to the memoranda. And when I'm done, one particular gentleman might have preferred your methods over mine. Let me worry about inter-office diplomacy. That's my job. Besides, I've wiped my ass with tougher memos than these."

Cerrillo cracked a smile.

Ricketts continued, "But I want you to know the kind of trouble you've stirred up on this preacher case. So you'd better dig up something besides a hunch and a couple of business cards—fast. Otherwise, this first wave of complaints will escalate ... and despite my genial nature, I'm apt to become disagreeable."

"Got it," said Cerrillo, relaxing his jaw.

"All right, then. So far, nobody's found diddlysquat about Don't Ask, Don't Tell. That's okay. Every investigation starts somewhere, and there's nothing wrong with gut instinct. More cases are solved with it than without it. You might be onto something. And, oh, I faxed a copy of that card to the local FBI. Agent Smithers, I think."

"Do we have to bring in the Bureau? There's no federal jurisdiction here. If we uncover Jack the Ripper, I don't want those bastards hijacking the investigation. I've dealt with them before."

Ricketts smiled. "Unfortunately, so have I. But they've got some good people, and they have interstate access that we don't. I've asked Smithers to crosscheck any lines between Preacher Smithfield and, what's her name, Mrs. School Board. We probably won't get much, but it's worth a try."

"Maybe. But if they impose on my case..."

"Your case?"

"Yeah. My case. Okay? It's my case! There's something going on. Josie Waller and me, we're on it. I want those DADT sons of bitches, whoever they are. The only thing worse than murder is dispassionate murder. And whoever is behind this is cold blooded to the max."

"Hmmm," said Ricketts. She generally liked resolute enthusiasm, and she liked seeing Cerrillo eager to work with another cop. He relied on himself too much. "All right. As much as possible, this is *your* case. We probably won't get much from the Bureau anyway. Nobody's been on the lookout for this kind of, uh," she hesitated, looking at a copy of the business card, "artifact. And people have a tendency to see only what they're looking for, and who could expect a crazy calling card to mean anything. Still, there's a chance the Bureau might make a connection."

Cerrillo nodded his head. "I didn't at first. Not until I stumbled on the second one."

"I also sent a copy to one of my criminal law professors at UCLA. He's got a couple billion former students who are now judges and district attorneys. And I think he's a frustrated cop at heart."

"Slim chance, there. Academics are a waste of life." Cerrillo wished that he had not said that. First, the comment suggested the chief was an idiot. And she had more formal education than many professors.

"Perhaps," replied Ricketts, "but remember that even a lowly Police Chief can play a hunch, just like when she sent you to San Francisco to poke around. Or she can also assign you to less exotic duties..."

Cerrillo swallowed hard. "Sorry, boss. I meant no disrespect."

"Detective," she said, "I want this case solved. I'll handle the mayor, the budget, and halfwit memos. I'll even snoop around on my own, with or without your permission." Ricketts leaned forward. "But you were wrong when you said there's nothing worse than dispassionate murder. Worse is an unprosecuted murder. So follow your nose wherever it leads. Go to Istanbul or Red Square. Play golf with O.J. Simpson for all I care. But you had better turn up something quick about Smithfield—for your sake and for Officer Josie Waller. From what I've been told, her ass is hanging pretty thin in Frisco right now."

"She's a good cop. A damn good cop."

"That might not make a difference. So do everybody a favor and put a finger on the bad guys. Or confirm that it's nothing but coincidence. That would be a good investigative result, too."

"It's not a coincidence," said Detective Cerrillo. "Pretty soon we'll find another dead homophobe with a DADT calling card."

TEN

God Hates Bigots

April 2007

A black Lincoln Continental rolled in front of Robert Davenport's home at one o'clock Sunday afternoon. Tanish Padgett emerged from the rear seat, and the professor greeted her before she reached the door.

"Hello," said Davenport. "Nice to see you, again." His tone suggested otherwise.

"Hello, Robert. I'm sorry you're a little annoyed with me, but perhaps you'll understand after our meeting today. Remember, you contacted us first. We're here at your invitation."

"And who is *we*?"

"That's one of the things to discuss." Padgett motioned toward the car. "Are you ready?"

"Not sure. I don't even know you, Doctor Tanish Padgett, or whatever your name is."

"True. You don't really know me. But in a couple hours, I hope you'll know more about me ... and yourself."

Davenport got mad. "I'm sick of the games! Just tell me what you have to say and get the hell off my property."

"Robert, please."

"Who are you?"

"My name is Tanish Padgett of Don't Ask, Don't Tell. We are a righteous organization. I am part of your interview committee."

"Christ! A front-yard infomercial!" said Davenport, glancing skyward and turning his palms up. "I haven't asked to be interviewed. As a matter of fact, after what I've been through the last couple weeks, I don't particularly care what you or anybody else thinks of my qualifications about anything. I do not care to be evaluated or clucked over. So spit out your message, right now, or crawl back in that hearse and heave ho."

"No. We can't talk here. We're meeting at a neutral, a safe location. The supervisor is not part, uh, will not be part of your ... activist group. But he will answer questions about who we are so that you can make an *informed decision*."

"My decision is that you, Tanish Padgett, are a liar. Probably crazy to boot. Tell me I'm wrong."

"You are wrong."

Despite Davenport's determination to be resentful, he somewhat liked Tanish Padgett. She was smart, had a purpose (though Davenport did not know what it was), and somehow seemed more in control of her life than Davenport was of his. And, truth be told, the professor's bruised professional ego was pleased that *someone* thought he might be a hot prospect.

"So you're telling me," said Davenport, "that cock-and-bull fable in my office was legit? Don't make me laugh."

"I told you that I wanted to audit your class for my own enlightenment. That was true. I was enlightened. More than that, I was pleased."

Davenport tried to conceal a faint smile. "Like I should care?"

"I think you will." Padgett moved a little closer. "Robert, listen. We're on a tight schedule. Not me, but ... others. And if you remember, our advertisement called for courage, conviction, and patience. The third part seems to be your sticking point. You've waited this long. And you've achieved tenure, which is important, because we want someone over the long haul. We are now prepared to offer full disclosure about Don't Ask, Don't Tell. And I have risked a lot through my faith in you."

"What!? I'm not particularly fond of you," said Davenport, "but there is nothing to fear from me."

"Not from you, Robert. Not from you."

Davenport glanced toward the waiting automobile, remembering there was another person in the vehicle. "Level with me for a moment ... if possible. Who are you?"

"That can be explained only at the meeting. I'm sorry, Robert. Don't Ask, Don't Tell is bigger and more important than I am. My cards are on the table. What happens next is beyond my control. You'll either come or you won't. But if I leave without you," her voice choked, "you'll never see me again." Padgett wanted Davenport in the organization, but she also wondered what her superiors might do if he declined. She had vouched for him; they could both be at risk.

Davenport tried to appear lighthearted. "You'd get over it." Then he turned bitter, again. "I know I would."

Padgett said nothing and motioned toward the waiting vehicle.

Davenport was just angry enough to agree. "Okay," he said. "It won't hurt to meet the mystery man, but I hope you're buying lunch. I haven't eaten."

"Absolutely."

"Wait a second," said Davenport. Then he ran back into his house to retrieve a small leather attaché. He reemerged, entered the car, and said, "For informal meetings. I'll probably regret this, but let's go!"

"You won't regret it, Robert. I have already bet my life on that."

***

Professor Davenport slid onto the rear seat, which seemed too luxurious for a passenger car yet deficient for a limousine. Tanish Padgett sat beside him and spoke to the driver regarding climate control because the interior, even with smoked-glass windows, had become too warm. From Davenport's Connecticut home near the university, they drove north on Interstate 95 for an hour. Davenport remained silent during the trip through annoyance; Padgett, through concern; the driver, according to orders.

Finally, the Lincoln pulled off at the Rhode Island Welcome Center just past the state line and parked beside a modest looking motorhome.

Padgett got out of the vehicle. "This is it," she said.

"What?" asked Davenport. "A rest-stop parking lot?"

"The motorhome. It's *our* version of Air Force One. A mobile office and conference center."

"Not exactly the Oval Office," said Davenport, his regard for Don't Ask, Don't Tell falling faster than a first-round elimination from *American Idol*.

"We may impress you yet," said Padgett.

Davenport chuckled. "Nothing too dramatic, I'm sure. But this *is* my first trailer-trash conference, and my initial observation suggests that your righteous organization is under-funded."

Padgett said nothing and knocked on the motor home. A lean, tall, middle-aged man wearing wraparound sunglasses, a beard, and what appeared to be a short-haired wig opened the door. Davenport struggled to keep from laughing. "Hello, Mr. President," he said, playing on Padgett's Air Force One comment.

"Doctor Robert Davenport," said the man with welcoming deference and extending his hand. "Very pleased to meet you. Won't you come in?"

Davenport nodded and shook hands at the door. The professor gave a quick glance inside before entering. No one else was there, and surprisingly, Davenport trusted Padgett enough that he felt more humored than suspicious. He assumed that the president was crazy but harmless and stepped into the trailer.

"Pleased to meet you," said Davenport.

The vehicle interior was contrastingly plush. From the outside, one might think rented-blue-collar vacation. From inside, bullion and bearer bonds. Leather covered furniture, gleaming chrome, expensive liquor.

"Please come in," said the man. "We generally use codenames or aliases, so you may call me Gulf Stream." The man smiled, anticipating Davenport's thoughts. "Not to be confused with Prometheus, Blood Queen, Solomon, Tiger Lily, Ramrod, or some of our other covert operatives, or even Tanish Padgett, one of our few members who kept her real name, although most of our people assume it's code so it serves just as well. Besides, she's just naturally inconspicuous... Of course, I don't know everybody in the organization. Come to think of it, I'm not sure anyone does."

"That's fine, Mr. President," said Davenport, no longer able to suppress a laugh. "But have you checked the RV's exhaust system? Some of the fumes may have leaked into your brain."

Gulf Stream laughed and nodded at Padgett. "A sense of humor under pressure. I like that."

"And further," said Davenport, "I'd say you are a long way from the Caribbean, Mr. Gulf Stream."

"That's true. But I have operated in the gulf—a lot of work in the southern states. Let's just say I got promoted. However, I adopted my stage name because of my private aircraft. If one must fly, a Gulfstream executive liner is really quite accommodating. You see, Dr. Davenport, we are not as under-funded as you might think, though I can't speak for everyone." Gulf Stream paused for effect. "Some of our cells get their jobs done with almost nothing except courage and conviction. But come, Professor. Sit down. And, Tash, please close the door and join us."

Gulf Stream motioned toward the rear of the vehicle. "How about a glass of wine to enhance introductions and promote organizational bonding. We have an excellent cabernet sauvignon, K-J's 1997 California Vintner's Reserve. You can pay more, but it's difficult to find superior decadence in a bottle."

"Why not?" said Davenport. "Uncork the bottle. We'll toast to your upcoming therapy. I might even get new material for a short story."

"Tanish, old girl," said Gulf Stream, "I think you've found a winner. Can't thrive in our business without the ability to relax in all situations." He opened the bottle of deep colored wine and poured it into three glasses on the conference table at the back of the motor home, which was surrounded by four plush beige leather captain's chairs. "Please, sit. But allow the wine to breathe a few minutes."

"Isn't breathing done before pouring?" Davenport knew something about wine, and he wondered whether Gulf Stream was posing wealth and sophistication that did not exist.

"True, but I'm an impatient man," said Gulf Stream lightheartedly. "And though it would be shamefully uncivilized, this particular vintage is so delicate that one could enjoy it straight from the bottle. Make yourself comfortable."

Gulf Stream gestured again toward the chairs. He then turned to the small refrigerator and removed a platter of assorted cheeses, fruits, shrimp, and other hors d'oeuvres, along with a bottle of sparkling water, which he set on the table. "You'll be surprised how well this selection complements the wine, especially the Vermont cheddar. That alone will be worth your trip, Dr. Davenport. Absolutely to die for."

"Call me, Robert."

"Fine, Robert. And I should tell you that we are thinking *Shakespeare* or *Chaucer* as an appropriate codename should you decide to join our little band. Isn't that delirious! You can pick your own moniker, of course. Perhaps something less British."

"Whatever you say, Mr. President." The professor couldn't resist a bit of ridicule. It helped suppress his fear that the man might be dead serious.

Robert Davenport, Tanish Padgett, and Gulf Stream positioned themselves around the table beautifully constructed of solid rosewood, which even the professor knew was difficult to obtain. Davenport lifted a glass of wine. "If you don't mind," he said, "I'll drink without further breathing."

"Absolutely," said Gulf Stream, likewise reaching for a goblet, then standing, and motioning to Padgett to do the same. "And I'd like to offer a toast! To justice, and to the organization that makes it happen!"

Gulf Stream held his glass forward. Davenport and Padgett chimed the crystal rims together. They drank and sat.

Davenport suddenly changed the subject. "Look, it's clear that you at least have some resources to work with here, but if we're going to talk awhile, don't you think we should invite the driver in to share the bounty? I hate excluding folks."

"No, Robert," said Gulf Stream. "The driver is on duty. And should you decide to link up with DADT, you will meet him later as part of the New England Chapter. He's quite capable, but for the moment, our driver will remain on guard. Purely precautionary. Later, he'll take you home. In the meantime," said Gulf Stream, sounding more like an executive, "you will not be allowed to communicate with anyone but me or Tanish inside DADT until you commit to the organization."

"All right," said Davenport. "If that's the way it is—the wine is very good, by the way—but if you don't mind, I've had a rough year. I'm tired of grubbing for tenure, tired of clueless colleagues and a phantom student from an organization I probably should never have contacted in the first place. So tell me, plainly and quickly what you do and why I'm of any interest to you. Or, let's call it a day." Davenport gulped the last bit of wine in his glass.

"Right," said Gulf Stream. He reached for an unlabeled file folder on the counter behind him and extracted a news clipping and several glossy photographs that showed protesters holding up memorably distasteful signs like, "God hates faggots," "Burn in Hell," and "Homosexuality is Abomination." Gulf Stream refilled Davenport's wine glass and pointed to one particularly egregious glossy. "Do you know where this photograph was taken?"

"I do," said Davenport, suddenly angered.

"Tell us," said Padgett.

"This whole god-hates-faggots thing has been done before, too often. But those particular snapshots look like the self-righteous gangsters who showed up at Matthew Shepard's funeral."

"Correct," said Gulf Stream. "In very bad taste. And this is the same kind of venom, you might say, that inspired Don't Ask, Don't Tell. Cops beating gays and lesbians, people losing jobs, professors not being promoted, violence, harassment, religious terrorism, and out-and-out murder. The hetero-agenda did more than turn our stomachs. It converted soft-core political activism into guerrilla warfare." Gulf Stream spoke like a commander. "And as a logical corollary, we drew upon the military policy towards gays and lesbians in our move toward justice."

"I don't need a lecture," said Davenport. "I'm an English professor. I can read newspapers, but most reasonable people oppose the nonsense in those photos."

"Do they, Robert?" asked Padgett, breaking her silence.

Gulf Stream said, "I don't think so, Professor. Some of your *reasonable people* hide behind turned collars, as-usual politics, diversity euphemisms, and campaign slogans. Some of your *reasonable people* would stand silent while fanatics build a gay Auschwitz with a crucifix over the entrance. They will look the other way. They will preach tolerance. They will supply the matches. That's what I learned from Wyoming."

Davenport shook his head. "It's not all gloom and doom," he said, pushing the offending photographs back toward Gulf Stream. "Madmen preach the rules of their own asylum. We don't have to take them seriously."

Padgett said, "Tell that to Matthew Shepard or Brandon Teena."

Gulf Stream added, "I remember a 1927 news article that claimed the Nazis were an inconsequential fringe group soon to be extinct. The writer was ultimately killed by the SS, and I don't plan to wait for some foamed-mouth preacher to tie *me* to a fence post, Professor. And Don't Ask, Don't Tell isn't sitting around waiting for the gay equivalent of Nuremburg Laws to come out of Washington. We have a new message: God hates bigots. And we're taking the battle directly to the homophobe asylum." Gulf Stream held up his wine glass and nodded toward the stack of photographs. "I don't know if we can send those bastards to hell, but we can remove a few from the earth."

The three were silent for several seconds. Gulf Stream retrieved a photo from a second file labeled *Good Deeds* and said, "Here's a sample of DADT activism. Our agents traveled to San Francisco for this case. And thanks to the special zoological talents of our own Tanish Padgett, Ph.D., one school board fascist is now feeding fungi."

Davenport recognized the victim's name. Mary Anne had mentioned the Bay Area campaign to remove this woman from office. Davenport glanced at Gulf Stream and said, "I read that she committed suicide."

"That was the official report," said Padgett, pride underlying her tone.

"She screamed like a pig," said Gulf Stream. "But that isn't what really bothers me. No one seems to have figured out there's a new anti-terrorist organization at work, and we left enough clues that a newbie rookie should have known something was up. I mean, credit where credit's due, especially now that DADT is expanding."

"Well, if you really killed her and wanted somebody to know, why didn't you leave a note for the police? Or stop off at the station on the way to the morgue? Seems to me the investigators would have appreciated the gesture." Davenport remained sarcastic, too naïve to be frightened.

"That's just the problem, Robert! We did! But, *paaah-leeez*," said Gulf Stream with stereotyped inflection. "We're new wave artists here. DADT has left business cards at over 200 hundred events, and not once have we received proper recognition. The heterosexists have a collective foot on our closet door. They won't let us out."

"Perhaps a more direct approach," suggested Davenport. "The Unabomber communicated his brand of insanity directly."

"Oh, God!" said Gulf Stream. "Kaczynski was a random act of violence, a bomb-and-hand-grenade guy who hated everybody and killed indiscriminately. That's just plain wrong. We never took down anyone who didn't deserve it several times over. And Teddy's little catch-me-if-you-can police tauntings: using a number code to authenticate messages and publishing a gibberish manifesto that led to capture! One must have a little style, Robert. Surely you tire of leading your freshmen hand-in-hand through every detail of the simplest story. And what has college education come to in this country when a trained homicide detective can't follow DADT clues that stand out like Ru Paul in green stilettos?" Gulf Stream took a breath. "But Phase Two will take care of that. We'll leave a trail of blood crumbs."

Robert Davenport finished his second glass of wine, not quite sure what to think about these folks. "You know," he said. "It's Sunday, and I might be talking with two Bellevue residents on a weekend pass, but I'm willing to hear a little more as long as the wine and cheese hold out."

"You shall, Dr. Davenport," said Gulf Stream. "And after you do, try not to over-identify with our early murder-by-stealth-in-the-shadows phase. DADT hopes to one day reshape the psychology of a nation, and for that, our methods and madness must go public."

"We are at a crossroads," said Padgett.

"I, and others like me," said Gulf Stream, "are going to break out of the covert closet and take payback into the open air."

Padgett added, "Altering a methodology that has carried us very far, very successfully. And we have lost only a few operatives and eliminated a lot of human debris. Silent and deadly."

This sounded personal to Davenport; he would soon learn why.

"I wouldn't worry about that," said Davenport, pouring himself another glass of wine. "Sooner or later, if you're doing what you say you're doing, people will figure out that it's murder, which you don't seem to understand is immoral, nefarious, unethical, illegal, and not nice, et cetera, et cetera, et cetera." Davenport, now on his fear-suppressing third glass of wine, punctuated these phrases like an imperious Yul Brynner.

"It's not murder," said Padgett with dry emotion. "It's retribution."

"We can debate semantics another time," said Davenport. "First, tell me something. If you go around killing *homophobes*, what makes you any better than folks who go around killing *faggots*."

"Self-defense," said Padgett, "which is not only a God-given right, it's a somber responsibility. Otherwise, the bad guys win by default."

"Quite frankly, I do not believe any of this," said Davenport while trying to pour wine from an empty bottle. "But I've heard that Thorazine can work wonders for your kind of delusions."

"Robert," said Padgett, "I think that it's more likely that you do believe us. And, furthermore, that you *want* to believe."

Gulf Stream smiled as if he had been waiting for this moment and said, "Delusions!" He stood, reached for a box of surgical gloves on a shelf behind the conference table, removed a pair, and passed the box to Padgett. "The real question is, Doctor Davenport of the English Department, what will you do when you are convinced? Slink back to your non-promoted university pedestal? Write a few more scholarly essays about injustice that nobody will read? Or will you risk something? It's 1933, Professor, and the brown shirts are gaining votes in America. But let me show you what Matthew Shepard and my murdered Jewish grandmother taught me about political activism."

Gulf Stream pulled the surgical gloves tight around his hands and moved toward a coffin-sized cupboard that Davenport assumed was a utility closet. He opened it, and Davenport's willing suspension of disbelief tumbled down the rabbit hole.

Gulf Stream held a skull, cleaned and whitened with hydrogen peroxide, a small entry wound between the eyes and a much larger exit wound behind what would have been the left ear, a death smile resembling one of the photos Davenport had just seen, and a two-inch golden crucifix jammed between the incisors like the dog tags of a fallen soldier.

"This was my first Mission Statement for DADT. The bitch survived Matthew Shepard's funeral by two weeks."

***

Three hours later, the black Lincoln Continental returned Robert Davenport to his New Haven home. It was not quite dusk, yet his vision seemed obscured with shadows. Davenport said nothing to Padgett as he exited the vehicle and moved toward the house. His hands were shaking so violently that he could not fit the key into his front door lock. Davenport paused, wrapped both hands around the key, and steadied himself enough to engage the bolt. He entered and slammed the door, jumping at the sound.

Almost immediately, he wondered if, perhaps, he had imagined the entire afternoon. Things like this just didn't happen in civil society. Then Davenport dropped his briefcase and ran to the bathroom. A disturbing mixture of cheese and wine emerged from his stomach. His body continued to tremble. His acidic throat burned. But what was most disturbing to Professor Davenport at this moment was that he could not accurately interpret his physiological responses to recent events.

Was he trembling out of revulsion or exhilaration? Davenport looked into the mirror. The image hinted at an answer.

ELEVEN

An Early Recruit

April 2007

Tanish Padgett stewed over her second bourbon at Mary's Bar near Boston College. In her mind, Gulf Stream's trailer demonstration was too blunt for a potential new recruit, especially Robert Davenport. Padgett had protested beforehand, but Gulf Stream proceeded. Now, a day later, she remained angry. First, she did not want to risk losing Davenport. Second, she did not like men telling her what to do.

There were other concerns. Padgett was the only DADT member that Davenport could identify, and Gulf Stream was humorless about organizational security. If necessary, he would sacrifice Padgett to protect DADT's integrity.

On the other hand, Tanish Padgett could take care of herself.

Gulf Stream had given Davenport six more days to make his decision. If he wanted to join, he was to post the number 6923 in the rear windshield of his vehicle using 210-point font; then at 11:00 o'clock Saturday morning, he should drive to the university, park in the faculty lot, eat lunch at the main dining facility, and return home. Somewhere along this route, a DADT agent would receive the message. If Davenport's answer were "no," he need do nothing. He would not hear from the organization again.

Neither Gulf Stream nor Padgett believed that Davenport would go to the police, but if he did, there should be no leads to DADT. The professor had no real evidence of what he'd seen in the motorhome; and for some reason, Padgett had a gut feeling that Davenport wanted to sign on. If he did not, it could be bad for her and possibly Davenport, but that wasn't what was bothering her. Padgett stopped caring about mundane particulars of life when her mother died, and she stopped caring about life itself after she killed the man responsible. Death, she thought, might even be a blessing. But in this instance, she wanted Davenport to join her fight for justice, and she was afraid Gulf Stream might have spoiled the chance.

***

Tanish Padgett's mother, Elizabeth, had been a single woman living near Greenwich Village during the 1960's. She worked as a legal secretary in Manhattan, made a decent living, and loved and cared for her only daughter, Tanish. Elizabeth was a lesbian who had gotten married at age 20 to a man she didn't love. And like many girls of her generation, she adopted the notion that women *should* be married. Despite a confused attraction to women, Elizabeth would do the "right thing"—get married, raise children, and adjust. But for Elizabeth Padgett, the wedding night was almost unbearable, and after two years, she could no longer tolerate marriage. Her husband had been a decent and loving man, but he was still a man.

Elizabeth filed for and obtained a divorce, gaining sole custody of her daughter since the husband did not protest. After several years of unquestioning solitude, and to her own surprise, Elizabeth began to explore the possibility of a relationship with a woman.

Even Tanish, who was five years old at the time, noticed a pleasant change in her mother. Despite long hours at her job and the burden of raising a daughter as a single mother, Elizabeth Padgett seemed younger, happier, as if she were invigorated by even the thought of companionship. Four years later, the former Mrs. Padgett met a young and ambitious New York attorney and fell deeply in love for the first time. Elizabeth and her partner were cautious, but after the two women had known each other for a year, they decided to buy a home together. That decision, however, was never implemented.

As a couple, they made an offer on a property in an exclusive area of Long Island, realizing they would both have to work hard to afford it. But someday, when the attorney made partner in a law firm, Elizabeth could quit her secretarial job, go to college, manage the home, and enhance the quality of life for themselves and for Tanish. Their love generated unlimited optimism.

After signing the purchase contract, the two women stopped at a gay and lesbian bar to celebrate the dawn of happiness. As misfortune would have it, the NYPD chose that same evening to raid the bar. These systematic uniformed attacks predated the Stonewall riots and were brutal and consequential. The patrons were rounded up, some were physically or sexually assaulted by police, and all were taken to the station for booking. Names appeared in newspapers the following day.

Elizabeth Padgett was immediately fired from her secretarial job and escorted from the building for the unnatural crime of being *accused* of being a lesbian. Two days later, Elizabeth's girlfriend was likewise terminated from her position as an associate attorney, but the most devastating blow was yet to come.

The local bar association filed charges against the young lawyer on the indefensible grounds of "moral turpitude" and asked that the New York State Bar revoke her license to practice law. Both women knew that a lesbian attorney would be allowed no defense. Gay liberation was not yet even a fantasy in this era, and often, the most destructive part of heterosexist propaganda was that the victim herself might believe it, might surrender without a fight. Thus, after the State Bar Association moved against her, Elizabeth Padgett's first and only love—a young, promising, and idealistic attorney—hung herself from a drapery cord in the house they had just bought.

Elizabeth Padgett would be less fortunate. She was not only unemployed and accused of lesbianism, but she suffered the greater sin of beauty. Prescriptive heterosexuality might allow an ugly woman to die gracefully, but not a feminine elegance that had turned against natural order. The evening after Elizabeth's fiancée committed suicide, one of the original arresting officers came to Padgett's apartment. The man had no warrant, no legal authority, no legitimacy, and no humanity. But he was a police officer with a public and judicial license that sanctioned all attacks on homosexuality. Humanity was not required.

When Officer X (Tanish would never refer to him by name) showed up at Elizabeth Padgett's door, she was a jobless single mother whose lesbian lover had just committed suicide. The officer gave Elizabeth few options.

Unless she wished to lose her daughter to child protective services and be implicated in the "jealous murder" of her girlfriend, then she was to do whatever Officer X commanded whenever he commanded. Officer X would teach Elizabeth to respect the proper roles of men and women, as had been ordained by God, church, and society. He would ensure that little Tanish Padgett did not repeat the moral crimes of the mother. Any resistance would send Elizabeth to prison and her daughter to a foster home.

That evening, Elizabeth said nothing. She nodded and complied with every instruction, every debasement, every detail. The first night turned into weeks, then months. And finally, by the time Officer X brought other men to her apartment to share in the moral instruction, Elizabeth could smile on demand.

Elizabeth Padgett learned the lessons of heterosexuality, month after month, as every orifice of her body was assaulted by multiple teachers. Her soul leaked into the carpet, never to be recovered. And because Elizabeth had no power to resist, she began to prostitute herself in the employ of the officer who defined her feminine virtue. Unlike her fiancée, Elizabeth died gradually over many years, her loving spirit systematically crushed before, finally, a random drunken trick beat her into a coma, leaving Elizabeth unconscious in her own bed with nine-year-old Tanish crying in the next room.

Tanish Padgett had seen much of her mother's anguish and degradation at the hands of others; she remembered all of what she saw; and she sautéed her hatred of policemen and, especially, Officer X for two decades. It was a burning, self-nurturing hatred that propelled Tanish through high school, college, and doctoral studies in zoology. And it was the same glorious hatred that led Tanish Padgett on a deliberate and circuitous route back to Officer X, long after he had retired with distinction from the police force. She became his housemaid.

But Padgett was not a victim; she was an avenger. She courted Officer X's trust, which did not take long, because Tanish, as her mother before her, was beautiful, and Officer X was old, caustic, and lonely. He easily convinced himself that he deserved a loving young woman to serve him. Finally, after several long years, with exquisite timing and precision, Tanish Padgett moved against the oppressor. And she watched with great satisfaction as the prolonged effects of *amanita phalloides*, a particularly deadly mushroom she had added to his pasta sauce, attacked the demon's central nervous system, leading to abdominal pain, vomiting, and eventually, following a brief remission, paralysis and respiratory arrest. But Padgett's finest moment came in telling Officer X, after his voluntary muscle control had abandoned him, exactly why she had come, why she had befriended him, and why he was dying. With the unflinching exactitude of a trained scientist, Padgett explained what the officer might expect during his final hours of consciousness as the paralytic toxins penetrated every cellular structure in his body.

Tanish Padgett had not planned a life beyond the execution of Officer X because she assumed that she would be arrested, convicted of murder, and sent to prison. But mushroom poisoning was so rare that most doctors did not recognize it, and because the victim was almost 70, the coroner attributed death to acute liver and kidney failure, which were certainly among the effects of amatoxin consumption. And ironically, because Tanish Padgett had been the victim's beloved caretaker, and he had no other kin, Officer X left her considerable financial resources under the terms of his Will. The man had used his badge to gather a sizeable estate, larger than Padgett realized. He had once bragged, "I did well. A passable salary plus whatever I could steal. The 60's and

70's were heydays for smart cops with guts." Tanish Padgett wondered what part of her inherited wealth had come from her mother's stolen, tax-free body.

With vengeance satisfied and a secure financial horizon, Padgett worked as a part-time lecturer at several colleges in the Boston area. She was twice invited to apply for full-time teaching jobs, but never did. Padgett discovered that revenge, once achieved, left little ambition in its wake, which did not concern her. Padgett had succeeded in killing Officer X, and that was enough. She'd earned the right of sloth.

Padgett might have drifted indefinitely, but on a lark, she responded to a peculiar personal ad for LGBT activists in a Boston newspaper that led her to Don't Ask, Don't Tell. The organization became Padgett's opus in settling scores, an all-purpose fellowship of vengeance, righteousness, and amends, not only for her mother, but for the world history of injustice against gay men and women. It was a task for many lifetimes. Padgett would never be directionless again.

When Padgett first met an anonymous representative, he explained their mission and asked, "Are you interested?"

Padgett laughed and said, "I became a member before either of us knew the group could exist. And now you want to know whether I will join the fight? I think DADT should join *me*. I am pretty good at this work."

The recruiter nodded. "Together we can send a unified demand for life, liberty, and the pursuit of happiness, which is a post-dated check that gays and lesbians have never been allowed to cash."

"Fine," said Padgett. "But I mean to pursue every cent of the balance due, and I expect DADT to hold up its end of the bargain."

The representative wondered who was recruiting whom?

After bonding with Don't Ask, Don't Tell, Tanish Padgett defined the cause. She scanned all horizons for injustice and bigotry. She looked at businesses and schools, in governments and churches, on television, in books, magazines, shopping centers, parks, alleys, bars, and scientific conferences. And when she saw something that turned her stomach, she proposed DADT counter-measures. Padgett initially gained a reputation for recklessness but soon tempered her enthusiasm with the coolness of stealth, which, she said, was the logic of dys-topian resistance. The mission was everything. Danger was nothing. And she would have been content with ex-istence in just this role—until she sat in Professor Davenport's classroom.

Now, something less certain stirred within her. Padgett wanted a friend, a real friend, perhaps more than a friend. And if she succeeded, it would mark the first time that she had genuinely cared for another per-son since her mother died.

***

Tanish Padgett decided to meet with Robert Daven-port before his decision deadline. This presented some risk and would never have been authorized, but Padgett believed the danger was minimal. If Davenport went to the police, Padgett could be arrested, yet authorities would not be able to trace DADT farther than her own involvement. If a smart cop got lucky, he might track down Gulf Stream or the driver, but he wouldn't get be-yond than that.

Emulating the French Underground, Don't Ask, Don't Tell had arranged their operational cells by threes, and one member of each cell knew only one member in another. Those individuals communicated at predeter-mined times and locations, often indirectly, leaving signals or notes that would be incomprehensible to anyone outside the cell, including others in DADT. Things like, "Red Bull, Crescent Green, Chair Against the Bay," which would presumably make sense only to the intended recipient. There were no home phones and addresses in the business.

Three operating cells comprised a squad, and each squad was directed by one member of a command section. It was possible for individual members to encounter colleagues without recognizing their shared affiliation. So if law enforcement apprehended one, which was bound to happen, they would have great difficulty penetrating beyond the local cell, even with cooperation from the suspect, which was unlikely. The first generation recruits were selected primarily for their single-minded resolve, and each was provided a cyanide capsule (if desired) in case of emergency. Further, as far as Tanish Padgett could tell, DADT was relatively new, probably not more than 10 years old. It grew cautiously, and in her estimate, the entire U.S. membership was around fifty. She was aware, however, that some assignments had crossed national borders, and cells might soon be established in Central America, possibly Europe.

From what Padgett knew of the selection criteria, early recruits were kamikaze spirits. They had suffered a direct loss and were on a mission of personal vengeance, which they might have pursued without DADT, and few expected to survive beyond their hetero-war. But as the organization began to prosper, so did its vision. Don't Ask, Don't Tell was becoming corporate. It might well survive its founders.

Padgett belonged to the first-wave recruits. She stumbled into the organization and expanded the work in her mother's memory. But Robert Davenport belonged to a new breed. He was managerial stock. Whoever ran DADT (Tanish did not think it was Gulf Stream) was looking toward a sustained guerilla war on homophobic soil. They wanted to bring the battle to the doorsteps of self-exalted fascists as well as polite, mild-mannered bigots; and the fight would not be rhetorical. Not this time. It would be bloody and political. DADT would not be dragged to a burning stake or to a frozen Wyoming fence post.

Someone had learned the lessons of Vietnam, so the Founder might be a veteran, a gay man who had dodged bullets in Southeast Asia and at home, a man that knew enough not to challenge the U.S. in head-on military conflict. That was suicide. But jungle fighting in Southeast Asia proved that the little guy could win through sustained, long-term, and invisible combat. Heterosexist tradition preferred a fifteen-round boxing match with Goliath wearing the stars and stripes and his opponent wearing handcuffs and a blindfold. Not this time. DADT moved secretly among homeland institutions, and like the Viet Cong, they would visit in darkness and withdraw to invisible lairs while extracted night-blood seeped into the ground. Psychological insecurity would be one of their most powerful weapons.

Robert Davenport would belong to the evolving breed, and Tanish Padgett approved. He was an established professional with a life beyond DADT, a "respectable" who could operate above suspicion and reproach in the second-phase declaration of war. Tactics would soon become explicit, but the missioners themselves would remain implicit. And when DADT operatives were ultimately exposed, even that would further the objectives. It would proclaim that five percent of the suburban population might harbor invisible killers. There, just down the street, any street, in Mister Rogers' Neighborhood, lurked a different drummer on a silent death march. Another lesson of Vietnam. Bloodshed is the penalty for ignorance and arrogance, and a prime motivation for enlightenment.

The body count was about to escalate. One house or the other would fall.

***

On Friday afternoon, Padgett telephoned Professor Davenport. "Hello, Robert," she said. "It's Tanish. I want ... need to talk with you before tomorrow's deadline."

Robert sounded as though he somehow expected her call. His voice was firm. "Hi, Tash. Look, I have to stop at school for an hour or so. But afterwards, suppose we meet for dinner?"

"Great." Padgett was surprised at how happy she felt. "Where?"

"Come to my house at six. We'll go somewhere. I know an Italian place."

"Fine. I'll drive down from Boston. Should make it by six." Padgett hesitated a second, remembering why she called, trying to find words. "Robert, mmmm, I was wondering, uh—How are you?"

"Good." His voice was different. Subdued but not downtrodden. "Better."

"Glad to hear it," said Padgett.

"Look, Tash. Don't worry. Can't explain at the moment. I've got to run. We'll talk tonight. Okay?"

"I'll be there. Six o'clock."

"See you then."

TWELVE

A Professor of Law

March 2007

Detective Cerrillo checked his voicemail messages from off-site. There were five, which was higher than usual. Josie Waller came first.

"Hey, Manny. It's Josie. Striking out up here. No real leads. People seem pretty closed mouth about this school board case, which strikes me as odd because folks typically love to blab. Everyone seems afraid to defend or condemn Ms. School Board lest they upset one side or the other at election time, but I'll keep looking. Let me know if you've come up with anything on your end and—" The voicemail cut her off. Josie's report was disappointing, but Cerrillo made a note to call as soon as he returned to the office.

The second message came from a recent assault victim who preached, "Why haven't you arrested my mugger, who is probably a terrorist and should be on the FBI's most wanted list, and I want you to refer me to a good lawyer who will sue the police department and City of Pomona for five million dollars and take the case all the way to the Supreme Court for failure to protect my civil rights and keep vicious criminals off the streets, and call me immediately with a full report about everything being done on my case if you actually care about innocent victims in this town. I'm a taxpaying citizen, so just remember—" Cerrillo hit the delete button. The Department limited messages to 30 seconds; otherwise, crime victims might, literally, preach for hours about their theories of justice or injustice.

The third call was from Alfred McDaniels, the UCLA law professor that Margaret Ricketts had contacted about the DADT business cards. "Hello, Detective," said Professor McDaniels. "Maggie suggested that I contact you if I discovered anything related to the evidence you turned up in San Francisco and Pomona. She also tells me that you don't think much of law professors or professors in general. For that matter, I'm not sure I can disagree with you. Strangely enough, however, I have a friend who used to be a Municipal Court judge—I hope you have no predisposition against judges—but he now teaches part-time at—" The recorder cut off at this point.

"Damn it," said Cerrillo, curious about any new information but thinking that his impression of rambling long-winded academics might be on target. Fortunately, the next message was also from McDaniels.

"Ah," said the Professor, speaking slightly more rapidly, "It seems the answering machine has a time limit. Very sensible. You wouldn't believe the whining, self-ingratiating messages I get from students—future lawyers mind you—pleading for higher grades despite general incompetence and sloth. Please call me, Detective. My friend, the former judge, received one of those little business cards in the mail almost six years ago. He never really understood why, but it was sent to his home, which is very unusual because personal information about the judiciary is highly restricted. Anyway, he received just the card in an envelope with no return address and no other enclosures. I'm sure you can appreciate the—" The recording cut out again.

"Jesus, Joseph, and Mary!" said Cerrillo. "I should have quit this job long ago." He advanced to the fifth message. It, too, was Professor McDaniels.

"Sorry, Detective. Time limits can be a good thing but I don't really like them. Do you? Anyway, give me a call. By the way, on the back of that strange little business card was a hand-written inscription, 'Good job on People vs. Alexander!' That was probably the only reason he kept it. Judges get so few compliments. Like professors and probably detectives. Talk with you later. Bye."

This time Professor McDaniels ended on his own accord. Cerrillo was furious that McDaniels did not leave a telephone number. He started to call Chief Ricketts, but then decided against it. Ricketts worked 70 to 80 hours per week, and she did not like to "play secretary to lazy detectives." Nor would she be amused by an investigator who could not track down a full professor at one of the largest universities in the country. Cerrillo decided to wait until he could get on a computer terminal and pull up the UCLA faculty directory.

It occurred to Cerrillo that he could just drive to the school and talk directly with the absent minded professor, and it might be inconvenient and possibly embarrassing to Professor McDaniels should a police detective on a murder investigation drop by his classroom or office unannounced. Cerrillo smiled. "That might be entertaining," he thought, "but a phone call should suffice." Besides, McDaniels and the Chief were colleagues.

***

Detective Emmanuel Cerrillo returned to Pomona PD, fired up his computer, and visited the UCLA campus website. As he looked through some of the university photos, he felt a twinge of envy. He had gone to college, sure. One could not become a detective without at least a bachelor's degree, but Cerrillo had gone to Mt. San Antonio, the local two-year school, and then transferred to Cal State for his junior and senior years. They were accessible schools where Cerrillo managed to get a solid education, but even the pictures of UCLA smelled like learning and Nobel laureates. And they had a real football team! That was one thing Cerrillo had missed. UCLA had over 35,000 students, and he was suddenly jealous of every one. Cerrillo wished he could be a young man starting his educational journey right there in the center of the universe. Then, just as quickly, he imagined sitting again through torturous introductory classes in chemistry or world literature and was pleased to be out of school and carrying a badge. But the campus seemed impressive, and Cerrillo felt he understood a little more about Chief Margaret Ricketts.

Detective Cerrillo found the faculty directory, located Professor McDaniels, and dialed the number. After the third ring, he wondered what sort of rambling message he should leave as payback when a soft, midrange voice answered. He recognized it as McDaniels.

"Professor Alfred McDaniels," the man greeted.

"Hello, Sir, this is—"

"Might you be Emmanuel Cerrillo from Pomona?"

"Yes, Professor. I'm Detective Cerrillo. How did you know?"

"Oh, a fairly easy deduction. We professors might not be as incapable as some people seem to think."

"I'm a stranger," said Cerrillo, still curious. "You've never heard my voice and we've never met. Plus, you didn't know I was calling. Doesn't seem like an easy deduction to me."

"First, my dear detective. Do you have any idea how officious you sounded in just those first words? A deaf man could have detected your police manner. Put that together with a Pomona area code, and Maggie's recent request, and I've got an easy deduction on my hands."

"Impressive."

"I am pleased to finally meet you, even if it is over the phone. Maggie has bragged about you on several occasions. You are a favorite son, don't you know."

Cerrillo was surprised. "She could fool me. Ricketts is tougher on me than any cop in the pueblo. I'll try to remember that 'favorite son' business the next time she chews my ass out."

Professor McDaniels laughed. "If she ever stops the ass-chewing, that's when you should worry. We reprimand only those who can be instructed. Otherwise, it would be wasted effort. And if it's any consolation, ask Maggie about some of the indelicate scoldings she received around this hallowed institution when she was a young woman. I once overheard her complain to another student that we were all against her from the start." McDaniels chuckled. "But for the record, Maggie finished in the top five of her graduating class. And as far as I'm concerned, she was the best of the five. Smartest and toughest student on campus. A little rough around the edges at first. Undisciplined. But the faculty weren't about to let her kind of talent go unchallenged. I'd say that we succeeded beautifully."

Cerrillo didn't want to like Professor McDaniels, believing that most academics were skilled at avoiding real-world issues, but he did like him. "Damn," thought Cerrillo. "First, I connected with Josie Waller, now,

McDaniels. If I ain't careful, I'll end up on Facebook trying to collect a thousand BFFs."

It was also nice to hear that even the infallible Margaret Ricketts had suffered a few ass-kickings at the hands of the Law School. Made her seem more human, less invulnerable, less super cop. "Well, to hear Ricketts talk about you these days, Professor, you might easily pass for Kris Kringle in *Miracle on 34th Street*."

"I can afford to be amiable with everyone *but* students. And I'm happy to say that many of my former apprentices—those who survive—go on to become friends and colleagues." McDaniels paused slightly. "Tell me, young man. Have you ever considered law school?"

Cerrillo laughed from surprise. "Not a chance. Had my fill of higher education after four years. I'm done... Perhaps we can discuss those telephone messages you left."

"Oh, yes," said McDaniels, "I almost forgot why you called. But never say never regarding law school, young man. It's much more than job training and licensure. The law is a way of looking at the world. Very interesting field."

"I'll keep it in mind, Professor, but right now, I'd settle for locking up a murderer. And I'm pretty sure there's one running loose in the Golden State."

"Yes, yes. Looks like you may have stumbled on some nasty business. I don't have a class until 2:00 o'clock today, so we can chat a bit. I'll tell you what I know. Oh, and by the way, I took the liberty of ordering a copy of the *People vs. Alexander* case file for you. It should be delivered to your office within two days."

Cerrillo was again surprised. He briefly resented uninvited help on an investigation, but McDaniels knew Cerrillo would want the file and acted accordingly. Not bad.

"Thank you, Professor. I appreciate it. Although, I'm sorry to see you spend your time and money. The department would have requested and paid for any copies in the investigation. I'm sure that, uh, I mean, on a teacher's salary..."

"Think nothing of it, Detective. I am a full professor at a major law school. My salary and benefits might surprise you."

Cerrillo gave a responsive whistle. "Well, I'd better get on with the investigation before Chief Ricketts writes me up for loitering and dereliction of duty."

"I shouldn't worry about that," said McDaniels. "You are on duty. And if there is an official question about that, let me know and I'll have a state Supreme Court Justice or perhaps the U.S. Attorney General call your office to put in a word for you. In any case, Maggie knows you're talking with me, and I rarely waste time.

"Now," continued Professor McDaniels, "I don't know a lot about *People vs. Alexander*, but the bits and pieces of a court file, when properly dissected and reassembled, often create recognizable images. Your job is to see the greater picture."

"I'll do my best," said Cerrillo.

McDaniels smiled to himself. "Undoubtedly. If not, your boss would be disappointed, and that's not going to happen. I sense that you love the law as much as she does, Detective."

"Thank you, Sir."

McDaniels paused briefly and said, "So, if it's all right, I'd like get back to my primary function, which is to find the next Margaret Ricketts in our school and make sure she knows that brilliance is never enough. Entering the world of movers and shakers is a distinct privilege, and I want my students to consider their contributions to humanity along the way."

"Absolutely, Sir."

After he hung up, Detective Cerrillo wondered about Professor Alfred McDaniels. Did this aging law professor really have connections to the Attorney General or

Supreme Court? Cerrillo's gut reaction said yes. He had learned long ago that the smartest and most powerful folks often downplayed their credentials, and he suspected that Maggie's 'Kris Kringle' was more than met the eye.

***

Two days later, after Detective Cerrillo had reviewed the *People vs. Alexander* case file, he called Waller.

"Hello? Josie?"

"Yes."

"Glad I got you. It's Manny. Can you hear me okay? Our phone system's been acting up."

"I hear you." Waller was pleased Cerrillo called but skipped the pleasantries. "What've you got!?"

Cerrillo laughed. "Hey, you're supposed to ask how I'm doing, what's the weather, did I see the last episode of NCIS."

"Knock it off, Detective. The fact is I don't care how you're doing. Just give me the lowdown on DADT."

"Talk about a dyke on a mission!"

"Remind me later to slap you..."

"Sure," said Cerrillo. "You probably hit like a girl anyway."

"And just ask the last guy I arrested how that felt."

"Never mind," said Cerrillo, remembering what Josie told him about the drunk that roughed her up and her double-fisted response. She was a real cop, all right, though Cerrillo would never grow tired of ribbing her now and then. "Any doings in Frisco?" he asked.

"Frisco? Really?" Waller asked, sounding disgusted.

"What?"

"Such a tourist," she remarked. "I interviewed some of Mrs. School Board's coworkers and church fellows. I think she belonged to Looney Tunes Anonymous. Real Termite Terrace. The woman's professional contacts seemed to be distancing themselves, and a few admitted that our special lady was having a mental meltdown. But her church groupies swore she was receiving *holy visions*."

"Sounds like our Pomona preacher. I dislike fruitcakes but would choke down two of them for a lead on that business card."

"Basically," said Waller, "I confirmed that Mrs. School Board's church is on the cutting edge of crazy. Not much else."

"No surprise there. Look, Josie. Professor McDaniels, that UCLA guy I told you about, sent me a copy of the *People vs. Alexander* file. The only tie-in is that note to the judge on the back of the business card. The case itself—about a high school teacher accused of molesting a teenage boy—is pretty limited. But by local newspaper accounts, some parents and religious leaders called for gay blood like something out of the Middle Ages. The judge dismissed the charges for lack of evidence."

"And?"

"A month later, the *child* in question, the sweet little innocent, was busted for stealing a car with his boyfriend. He then *admitted* to lying about the molestation because he was mad at the teacher for failing him. Some joyride, huh. Anyhow, I'll send you a copy of the file."

"Why?" asked Waller. "I'll take your word it's nothing."

"There are a lot of names of witnesses, teachers, even a few students. And the judge offered some sharp criticism of the prosecutors."

"Names of students? I thought juvenile records were sealed."

"Not a juvenile case. Filed in the Criminal Court Division against the teacher, remember. And a few *witnesses* were seventeen-going-on-Folsom-Prison, so the judge did not seal the record. I'd like you to glance through the file to see if any names wrap around Mrs.

School Board." Cerrillo paused and then said, "Hope I don't sound like I'm giving orders."

Waller noticed his tone and liked it. Felt like partners on a mission. "Maybe just talk with the judge who got the note. See what he knows."

"Died three days ago," said Cerrillo.

"You're kidding."

"Nope."

"You don't think...?"

"No, no. Not a murder. The judge fell dead from a heart attack while surrounded by five friends in a very public restaurant. Natural causes. Confirmed and reconfirmed. Besides, our DADT playmates weren't mad at the judge, remember? They complimented him."

"Right. Right."

"Look, Josie. Not sure what we're up against so just keep your eyes open. I got a feeling this involves more than one nut howling at the moon. Plus, the *Alexander* case dates back 10 years, and if DADT has operated a decade without getting tagged, they have serious method in their madness."

Officer Waller became defensive. "I can take care of myself."

"Sure, but even good cops get killed, and I'll feel better when we size up the opposition... You know, there are still moments when I wonder if our imagination is chasing ghosts ... but don't lower your guard until we know whether we've got a deal or a misshuffle."

"It's no fantasy that we've got two very dead victims and three very weird business cards. And *somebody* wrote that note to the judge. They're tied together somehow."

"That's my guess. Read the file, Josie, though parts might be missing. When some of the Muni and Superior Courts merged, files got tossed around or transferred or copied onto microfiche. We might dig around the clerk's office for more. Anyway, read what's there and let me know if you make any Nobel Prize discoveries."

Waller laughed. "I'd settle for enough to file charges."

"Me too."

"Okay," said Waller. "We both keep looking. Sooner or later, luck will stumble something our way."

THIRTEEN

The Fourth Card

April 2007

Almost seven weeks later, Officer Josie Waller of San Francisco's Richmond District called Detective Emmanuel Cerrillo at his Pomona office. "Hi, Josie," said Cerrillo. "Glad you called. Did you ever score with that case file?"

"I never even opened the box. Been working on something else." Waller paused for effect. "We've got a lead, partner."

Cerrillo felt a twinge of hope. "What?" he asked.

"A fourth card turned up."

"You're kidding? Another murder?"

"No," said Waller. "Just a really weird coincidence."

"Come on, Josie. Spill it."

"There's a copy of that business card on my desk, see. And I walk down the hall for a cup of coffee, minding my own business, and a beat cop says to me, 'Hey, what's the deal with Don't Ask, Don't Tell? Some kind of new gay club?'"

"Who asked this?" asked Cerrillo.

"A cop on patrol."

"Did he make an arrest?"

"No. He knows less than we do. But this rookie saw one of those cards taped to a driver's dashboard during a traffic stop. Can you believe it? Pulled the driver over for a burned out taillight. Didn't even give him a ticket. Just told the guy to fix it and sent him on his way."

"Josie, get to the verbs!"

"Well, our guy ran a routine license plate check. Standard Operating Procedure. The plates were clean, but dear sweet officer remembered the card. Thought it was peculiar, and the engraved gothic lettering is pretty distinctive, so when he saw the copy on my desk, he wondered if he was out of the loop about something. He said our card looked the same as the one in the vehicle. That was enough for me. I ran a check on the registered owner. Squeaky clean. That burned out taillight is probably his worst offense since birth. But I *unofficially* drove to the address, found the car, and looked through the window. The damned card is still on the dashboard. The guy's not even trying to hide it."

"Does he know you're snooping around?"

"Don't think so. I haven't approached him."

"Good," said Cerrillo.

"I tried to get a search warrant for the vehicle and house, but the judge laughed. I mean belly laughed. After he caught his breath, he said, 'Issue a warrant for a man with no criminal history because you discovered a business card on a dashboard with a phrase that a million people use every day? You must be a comedian,

Officer Waller.' Then he laughed some more for good measure."

"Well," said Cerrillo, "you can't blame the judge for common sense."

"I suppose not. We're the only people who know there's a criminal connection. The judge is probably backslapping my joke all around the courthouse." Waller hesitated and said, "But I still want to talk with the driver. He might volunteer something. Maybe even let me in the house."

"Wait a day, Josie! I want to be there... You sure it's the same business card?"

"Yeah. I mean, the car was locked, but it's posted in plain sight. Same white stock. Same raised lettering. This guy's involved somehow."

"He could also be the next victim. We don't know. Listen, as soon as we finish talking, I'll head north. Be there in six hours. Wait for me. Tomorrow morning, we'll have a word with the guy."

"Suppose he clams up?" asked Josie.

"Then we'll *know* he's involved. That, by itself, would be valuable. What kind of work does he do?"

"No idea, but it must be lucrative. Lives near El Camino del Mar and drives an L.L.Bean edition Subaru Outback. Plush. I'd say he makes more dough than you and me combined. But not a blotch on his record. He could be Mother Teresa's little brother."

"Don't care about his family. I want to find out if he sidelines in milking cobras. Wait for me, Josie. I got to be there."

"Okay. I'll read the *Alexander* case file to pass the time, but step on it. I'm anxious to see if our new friend has a spare business card."

"I'll clear with the chief and hit the road. See you at the station."

"Let's just meet at my apartment. You can sleep on the couch and save a little money."

Cerrillo hesitated and said, "Don't worry. I get a special deal at a local hotel. No need to burden you."

"Cut the crap," said Josie. "I'm not gonna chase down my partner at a hotel when something turns up. This is business, Manny, and we're sticking together. And I got a feeling this case is about to spill its guts."

***

Detective Cerrillo arrived at Waller's apartment at 6:30 p.m. after a seven-hour drive. San Francisco rush hour is worse than Los Angeles, and Waller lived off California Street a mile from the Richmond District station. Waller wasn't home when Cerrillo parked his car, but he knew she was on her way because he had called her from his cell phone as he dropped onto the surface streets. There was still plenty of daylight, and Cerrillo wanted to interview the witness that evening. Josie had stumbled onto something, and Cerrillo feared that another victim was in the making if they did not take action.

Five minutes later, Waller pulled alongside Cerrillo's Corolla. She was still in uniform. "Hop in," she said through her vehicle window, "before anybody discovers that I know the owner of that wreck you're driving."

Cerrillo grinned. "Then perhaps you shouldn't shout about it to everyone in the pueblo."

"Oh, don't worry. I'll say I arrested a suspicious derelict."

"Thanks."

"Here," said Waller, tossing Cerrillo a yellow-green ticket stub, "Slip this under your driver's side windshield wiper."

"What is it?"

"A dummy citation. Can't park here between 2:00 a.m. and 4:00 a.m. This will stop one of my coworkers from writing you up in case we work into the night."

Cerrillo shook his head, tucked the paper under the wiper, and slid into Waller's patrol car.

"Have you eaten yet?" asked Waller.

"No, and I was wondering if you'd be willing to visit our suspect *now*?"

Waller shifted the vehicle into drive and pulled into traffic. "Don't mind at all. But he isn't home. I just drove by the place. That's why I'm late. Car's not there."

"Damn," said Cerrillo. "I'm anxious to meet this guy."

"Look," said Waller. "The sun won't set until about 8 o'clock. Let's get a bite. I know a good hole-in-the-wall Mexican joint. Then we catch Mister Business Card at an inconvenient moment."

"Inconvenient for whom?" asked Cerrillo. "I just spent seven hours on the road. I'm tired, hungry, dirty, and would rather be sipping tequila at the poolside."

"Want to hold off 'til tomorrow?" asked Waller.

"No!"

"Me neither. And I was thinking it's better if we show up in the prowler rather than civi-wheels. Bells and whistles can make an impression."

"Sometimes," said Cerrillo. "But if our guy's as plush as you say, he probably won't be intimidated by a black-and-white. We might stiff-arm a high school dropout on a probation tightrope, but not somebody with money. Our badges should serve just as well. At least you're still in uniform. Might even be a turn-on for him."

"Not funny, Detective. Although if it helps to break the case, I could play hetero for up to fifteen seconds. After that, repulsion-seizures would take me out."

"Let's just do dinner and then see if our guy is home. What's his name?"

"Uh, wait a second, oh, Craspen. Alex Peace Craspen or Peace Alex Craspen. Something like that. The info's in the manila folder on the floorboard."

Cerrillo picked up the file. "Strange name."

"Not for San Francisco. The 60's flower children had babies and gave those babies inspired call letters. We have more Moonbeams, Chastities, Sweet Seraphs, Lucy Sky Diamonds, Glory Roads, Rainbows, and NoNarcs than any city on the planet."

"NoNarcs? You made that up."

"Believe it or don't."

Cerrillo laughed. "Well, I can remember a time 'Cerrillo' was considered outlandish, even in Southern California. So maybe I shouldn't talk."

"No worries now," said Waller. "In twenty years, everybody south of Seattle will be es-speaking es-Spanish... Here we are." Waller nodded toward a glass and steel door in a rundown red-brick building.

"Sure it's safe to eat here? They don't grind cockroaches with the beef?"

"That's an insult, Detective? No self-respecting Mexican cook would ever use ground beef. Shredded only! Don't know about the cockroaches, but whatever they do, it's sex on a platter. They've got a smothered burrito that will warm your belly today and ass tomorrow. The absolute best in the City."

"Maybe I'll get a burger."

"Don't act so gringo. It's embarrassing."

"Hey," said Cerrillo, "I *am* Hispanic."

"Yeah, but once you go mainstream, civilization can bleed the color right out of you. I've seen it happen too many times."

"That's pretty rich coming from the whitest girl on the planet."

"Then order a double-jalapeño burrito, Manny. We'll see who's descended from Zapata."

Cerrillo preferred burgers but felt culturally challenged. "Fine!" he said. "I'll eat the shredded beef cockroaches. But no jalapeños."

Detective Cerrillo and Officer Waller went inside and ordered two smothered burritos, chips and guacamole, and two bottles of sparkling water. Beer would have tasted better, but they were on duty and neither of them wanted to show up at the Peace Palace with alcohol in their system.

Halfway through dinner, Cerrillo said, "You're right, Josie. Zapata would appreciate this place. Good."

"Told you." Waller bit into a side-ordered fresh jalapeño.

Cerrillo grimaced. "Those will kill you."

"My veggies for the day," said Waller.

Cerrillo chewed slowly, took a drink of water, and leaned back. He had never been so at ease with a fellow cop. Shop talk mingled with personal ribbing as naturally as inhaling and exhaling. She was right, too. Partners should be at hand when tightening the noose on an investigation. He refocused and said, "Okay. When we talk with this guy, let's start out nice. Just a couple of officers looking for possible leads on an ancient murder case." Cerrillo never used the term "cold case." No matter how long an investigation might have languished, a murder investigation was open and unsolved and never *cold*. "We'll ask this Peace man to be upfront, matter of fact, help the police like a good citizen. See what he knows and what he's willing to tell."

"Okay. And if the guy's uncooperative?"

"I'll turn *L.A. Confidential*. Bad cop gone wild and you counter with by-the-book."

"Sounds good," said Waller. "But if Craspen is DADT, and if the group is tight, it'll be a wasted interview, especially since we don't have a search warrant."

"Just do the best we can. Scope the house and car. The suspect might finger himself."

"Worth a try."

"Besides, you haven't seen my bad cop routine. It's a prize winner."

"Okay, Señor Auuw-nuuld. I'll play along. But keep the game below a felony. You're out of jurisdiction. Our judge has a sense of humor only up to a point. So when I pull back on the reins, take heed!"

"Got it. I'll respect your turf."

"Now, partner," said Waller, squeezing a wedge of lemon on her hands and wiping them on several damp paper napkins, "Let's find out who's printing business cards."

FOURTEEN

The Interview

April 2007

Detective Cerrillo and Officer Waller arrived at Alex Peace Craspen's home at a quarter to eight. There were about 30 minutes of daylight remaining, and the Subaru Outback was parked in the cramped driveway. Cerrillo glanced inside the vehicle. The DADT business card was still on the dashboard and looked yellow around the edges, as though it had been there for months.

"Unbelievable," said Cerrillo. "Our unsuspecting suspect has balls."

"So do I," said Waller, "but remember what we talked about, and be prepared to ease back your bad-cop frenzy if we go there. Don't want to screw up potential evidence with illegal search and seizure."

"That wasn't how you phrased it earlier, but I get the message. And who knows, maybe the guy's a Republican who can't keep his opinions to himself. He might spill his own beans."

"A Republican in San Francisco? Not likely. Let's try granulated sweetness until we find where he stands. Now, get nice like you mean it."

As they turned toward the front door of the house, a young man, perhaps twenty-five to thirty years old, emerged to greet them. "Hello, officers," he said. "I saw you examining my vehicle but suspect you're not looking to buy a used Subaru."

Waller smiled. "No, sir. But if you have a few minutes, we'd like to talk."

"Of course," said the man, who was actually thirty-six. "However, if you *are* interested in an Outback, I can highly recommend them. Fun to drive. All wheel traction. Heated seats, which are delightful on damp City mornings. Wasn't it Mark Twain who said his coldest winter was a summer in San Francisco?"

"Yes, sir," said Waller. "I think so. But I'm Officer Josie Waller from your local Richmond Division. This is Detective Cerrillo from Pomona Homicide. We'd like..."

"Pomona!" The man looked at Cerrillo. "I'd say you're a long way from home, Detective. Must be an important case."

"Yes, it is," said Cerrillo. "Do you mind if we come in?" Cerrillo wanted to get in the house.

"Not at all. Please and welcome. It's not everyday Homicide visits my humble home." The man gestured toward his front door. "I make divinely decadent cappuccino with fresh vanilla and dark chocolate."

"That won't be necessary," said Waller.

"Nonsense," said the man. "If I invited two visitors and didn't offer refreshments, my poor dead Alabama grandmother would roll over three times in her grave. And to demonstrate the relative importance, she only rolled over twice when I came out fifteen years ago as a gay man. The only thing more unforgivable than homosexuality, I'm afraid, is to compromise the rules of Southern Hospitality. If you want to talk, you simply must have a cappuccino, and then perhaps you'll even share a brandy chaser."

Cerrillo wondered why this man seemed unsurprised and very much at ease with two unannounced police officers at his home. As Waller and Cerrillo approached the doorway, Craspen extended his hand to Cerrillo. "Alex Peace Craspen at your service, sir. And ma'am. Please come in."

"Thank you," said Waller.

"Please make yourselves comfortable in the living room while I crank up the espresso machine."

"Really, it's not necessary," said Cerrillo.

"It *is* necessary if you want me to discuss Don't Ask, Don't Tell."

Cerrillo glanced at Waller. Could Craspen read minds?

"All right, Mr. Craspen," said Waller. "You have our attention. We'll have coffee." Waller paused and, worried that their host might suddenly clam up, added, "This is an informal visit. You're not a suspect. We're just interested in that business card."

"Of course, of course," said Craspen. "Police always go out of their way for *informal* visits. And call me Alex. I'm an attorney—though I hope you won't hold that against me—and all day long it's Mr. Craspen this and Mr. Craspen that. In my own home, please use Alex. Some of my friends call me AP, for Advance Placement, but they do it to annoy me I'm afraid. So, please, call me Alex. Don't make me insist."

"All right, sir," said Cerrillo. "Do you mind if we sit in the kitchen? We can chat while you're working. Take less of your time that way."

"Oh, dear me!" said Craspen. "You're not going to talk-and-run, are you? After all the trouble you took to find me." Craspen busied himself about the counter, measuring coffee and water and wiping porcelain cups with a paper towel. He sighed. "But of course. Please, pull up a chair."

"I'm investigating a possible murder in Pomona. Probably no real connection up here, but I am looking for information." Cerrillo had a thought and asked, "By the way, were you getting ready to leave when we arrived? You came outside just as we were about to..."

"Impeccable timing, but not accidental," said Craspen, pointing toward two small black and white video monitors mounted on the kitchen wall. "I have cameras fore and aft, I mean front and back. Saw you coming. Like to keep an eye on things. Figured you weren't just looking to buy a used car. So now we're in my kitchen, and you keep insisting that you're not really looking for a special connection in a murder, that you just randomly dropped by at random. Detective, I'm not much of a believer in coincidence. Except for desperate missionaries, people generally have better things to do than chat with strangers. And I don't think you're selling Bibles."

"All right," said Cerrillo. "For starters, that business card on your dashboard. Where did you get it?"

"Ahhh! That doesn't sound casual at all. Much better. I like a man with purpose."

"So?"

"I'll tell you what, Detective. First, you tell me why you think that card has any special significance, and then I'll *spill my own beans*, as you say. Deal?" The cappuccino steam began to hiss. "Don't mind the froth-maker. I'm listening."

Waller said, "I can tell you something about that card, Mr. Craspen."

"If you call me mister once more in my own home, I'll pour our refreshments down the drain, take the 5th, and go straight to my room. It's Alex, *please*."

"All right, Alex. Years of police training can hinder familiarity."

"Isn't that the truth," said Craspen. "Life becomes a bad habit if we're not careful. So tell me ... by the way, 'officer' sounds so ... so Georgia plantation, so prison lockdown... May I have your names again?"

"I'm Officer Josie Waller. 'Josie' will be fine."

At this point, Waller would have performed a fan dance to keep Craspen talking. So would Cerrillo for that matter.

"Call me Emmanuel," said the detective. "Or Manny."

That's better," said Craspen. "Now, Miss Josie, you were about to tell me why my little dashboard insignia is of interest."

"There have been two reported suicides that we suspect were murders. We might be wrong. We found business cards at each of the crime scenes." Waller purposely didn't mention the Municipal Court Judge and the third business card. "And now, quite by accident, we stumble upon an apparently identical card in your automobile. You can understand our curiosity."

"Absolutely," said Craspen. "The cappuccino is ready. Smells heavenly, doesn't it?" He poured three servings, added whipped cream and a sprinkle of chocolate on top, set the cups on a serving tray, and motioned toward the living room as he walked. "Let's get out of these harsh lights and relax in the parlor. Please follow me."

Waller and Cerrillo complied. When they all were seated around an antique coffee table and had taken a few polite sips of cappuccino, which really was delicious, Waller set down her cup and asked. "Where did you get that card, Alex?"

"Right here." Craspen opened a drawer in the lamp stand next to his stuffed chair, removed a small box, and offered several cards to the officers. "Take them," he said. "Spread them around. They were printed to call attention to that widely accepted and despicable social policy." He took a sip from his cup. "Mmmm, I think a little more vanilla next time. Wouldn't you agree? Though I'm very pleased that you have taken an interest in my personal DADT ad campaign."

Cerrillo firmed his voice. "Mr. Craspen, I'm not interested in your political agenda. I'm interested in who killed a Pomona resident and whether it's the same person who killed a woman in San Francisco. And with this box of cards, I also think I have justification to bring you to the precinct for questioning."

"Oh, nonsense, my dear Emmanuel. Better talk to him, Josie girl. I'm merely an intellectual property rights attorney, but even I know my Bill of Rights and habeas corpus fairy dust enough to believe that you have nothing. Besides, let me assure you, I will happily give you, right here in my humble abode, as much as I would in even the most brutally manly police station. And isn't it the information you really want? Not little old me?" Craspen did a fair imitation of a wilting Southern Belle.

"Unless you're the killer," said Cerrillo.

"Oh, paaah-leeze," said Craspen, rolling his eyes. "The last thing I killed was a jar of fire ants when I was nine years old. And I still have nightmares. If you are half as smart as you must be to find your way from Pomona to my doorstep, then you should know that I'm not in, oh, what's the Godfather argot, um, I'm not in the muscle end of the organization. I handle legal affairs, contracts, financing, and all around stylistic flare. And there are so many buffers between me and what you want, I couldn't help you get there even if I wanted, which I don't."

"Before you say any more," said Cerrillo, "perhaps I should advise you of the Miranda Rights."

"If you do," said Craspen, using a straight voice, "I'll clam up immediately until I talk with a dozen attorneys." Craspen then reverted to Southern Belle. "But since I am my attorney, my advice to my client is that you and I should remain friends, and we can have our brandy and keep chatting so pleasantly. Wouldn't that be better? After all, I've practically bragged about the cards, and I'm happy to keep talking. What do you say, Emmanuel?"

Waller tried to soothe Craspen. "Like I said, Alex, we're looking for leads. You are not a suspect. And in matters of detention or arrest, the Detective has no jurisdiction. That would be my department. And I prefer to talk here."

Craspen looked closely at Waller. "You know," he said, "now that I look at you for a moment, I get the feeling we've met."

Waller did not recognize Craspen. "It's a big city. I'm a cop and get around a lot. Could be we ran into each other."

"No matter. I'll think of it in a minute. But you look familiar." Craspen stood and retrieved a bottle of brandy and three crystal snifters. "We shall drink to your investigation, Detective Cerrillo. Regrettably, I can't, um, *savor* alcohol like I used to, but this XO cognac has been waiting for a special occasion."

"If you insist," said Cerrillo, watching Craspen's movements. They had stumbled onto something, and if Craspen were directly involved with DADT, he might turn violent or try to escape. The brandy could even be poisoned.

"The cost is unimportant, but this one bottle of brandy might exceed the better part of your week's salary." Craspen caressed the container. "One of my quirks is that I don't like warm brandy, so we'll drink it at room temperature. I hope you like it. The quality reflects the occasion." Craspen sighed as he poured into the snifters. "I'm so glad you're here, Josie and Emmanuel. I know you won't believe it. But I'm tired. Sick and tired. It often seems that my poor grandmother, with her simple wisdom, had a better grasp on what's important than I do, with all my years of education and training. Honesty, decency, and hospitality."

Craspen handed a glass to Waller and one to Cerrillo. He lifted the third and said, "Officer Josie Waller. Detective Emmanuel Cerrillo. I'd like to make a toast to Don't Ask, Don't Tell. Without them, I should have died five years ago from boredom." Craspen was not talking to his guests when he added, "Thank you."

Cerrillo and Waller barely sipped their drinks. They were focused on Craspen, who, on the other hand, swirled the brandy snifter, took a deep breath of its fragrance, tasted a few drops of the liqueur, and then abruptly emptied the glass. He sat down and poured again. "So," he said, "What would you like to know?"

Cerrillo decided that something had changed in Craspen. He still seemed relaxed but also more serious. He might provide answers. "The brandy is very good," said Cerrillo.

Craspen laughed. "You barely tasted it. Tell me. Do you believe I poisoned your drink?"

Cerrillo thought and said, "No."

"You hesitated too long, Emmanuel. Let me assure you. There are no toxins in your glass."

"I believe you," said Cerrillo, taking another drink. "But do you know anything about the murder of a Pomona preacher by the name of Smithfield? Or the San Francisco school board case?"

"Only that the two creatures are dead and that I approve. Strange, isn't it? I have nightmares about those poor ants and hardly a thought about the good preacher. I wasn't there. Perhaps you'd like me to inquire about the details?"

"What do you mean?" asked Waller. "Maybe it *is* time that we read your rights."

"Don't spoil my big moment," said Craspen. "I was about to suggest ... in the other room is a shortwave radio. Phone lines are so easy to trace. Let's go to my office. With your permission, I'll try to reach a *friend* who can provide helpful information."

"That's fine," said Cerrillo, shifting his hand to the shoulder harness under his jacket. "Just be sure to move slowly."

"Well, that's interesting!" said Craspen. "Here I am, an unarmed citizen escorted by two armed police officers, and it seems that the gun-wielding detective is the one who's afraid. You might soon find this amusing."

"You have the right to remain silent..."

"Skip it, Josie girl," said Craspen pleasantly. "Everybody in America can dance with Miranda. Besides, I have nothing to hide. And as I indicated, there is someone else you might want to talk to." Craspen turned courtroom serious. "And the only connection to him is through me...! Now," said Craspen, friendly again and slapping his thighs, "shall we try to raise him on the radio?"

"Let's go," said Cerrillo. "Call your playmate. But just remember..." Cerrillo flashed his jacket to reveal the holstered Smith and Wesson. "And don't forget that Officer Waller is a very capable backup."

"Not to worry. I'm kitten harmless and a little tipsy besides. Please follow me."

Craspen moved toward a side room with a large oak desk and, sure enough, a compact electronic system that confirmed itself as a shortwave radio. Craspen turned it on. "Want to check my FCC license?"

"That won't be necessary," said Waller.

"Too bad, cause I don't have one..." Craspen laughed. "Oh, really, Miss Josie! That was funny. You must never forget how to laugh. Perhaps you've been watching reality police shows. Very distasteful. The bad guys and the cops are so *mean* to each other."

"Are you telling us the murder of a preacher wasn't *mean*," said Cerrillo, ready to arrest Craspen on the spot though he wasn't completely sure of the charge. But he decided to wait a few more minutes. Craspen might be crazy or know something. Cerrillo wanted to find out which.

Craspen reached for a small box of breath mints, carefully selected one, and offered the box to his guests.

"No thanks," said Waller.

"Not for me," said Cerrillo.

"Okay," said Craspen, placing the mint in his pocket and taking another drink from the snifter.

He turned toward the radio microphone, which was made of stainless steel and seemed hopelessly outdated. "This is an early 70's system," said Craspen, now more than tipsy. "Solid state circuitry. One generation above vacuum tubes, but you'd be surprised what it will do. I've talked with Australia."

Cerrillo and Waller were quiet.

"Hello. This is Peace Pipe calling Gulf Stream. Peace Pipe to Gulf Stream. Over."

Nothing.

"Peace Pipe to Gulf Stream. Over."

Nothing.

Craspen turned a dial and again activated a switch on the microphone. "Peace Pipe to Gulf Stream. Over."

Nothing.

"Perhaps your friend is confined to a lock-ward," suggested Cerrillo.

"Why, Detective! You made a joke. Even while on duty. I'm very impressed. Give me another minute or two. This isn't my regular check-in, so I might not reach him, but the chances are good. The man is a serious workaholic."

"Just keep trying, Peach Pie," said Cerrillo.

"That's Peace Pipe to Gulf Stream. Come in, please. Over." Craspen released the microphone switch. "By the way, Josie, I just remembered where I saw you. And I want you to know that DADT is working on your behalf. Actually, we're working on everyone's behalf."

"Whoever they are, I want no part of them," said Waller. "Murder isn't my bag."

"Don't be so Dragnet," said Craspen. "And don't condemn us until you know us. Self-defense is justifiable... Anyway, I'm glad you came tonight, Josie. It's nice that a sister will put an end to this."

A static-muted voice responded. "Gulf Stream to ... Come back..."

Craspen straightened himself, turned another knob, and keyed the microphone again. "Hello, Gulf Stream. This is Peace Pipe. Do you read? Over?"

"Got you, buddy." The voice was now crisp and clear. "Confirm cell code. Over."

"Sorry, sir. Can't do it this time. Triple seven, triple niner. Over."

There was a long pause. "Damn," said Gulf Stream. "Sorry to hear it, friend. Who's with you? Over."

"I'm having drinks with one of San Francisco's finest and a comely homicide detective all the way up from Pomona. They are asking about our nice business cards, and I'm afraid I let my pride get the better of me. Had one posted on the dashboard in my car, and it *finally* led these good folks to my doorstep. Not that I really mind. Over."

"I understand," said Gulf Stream. "And this could turn in our favor. I've been campaigning for Phase Two—out of the closet and in to the streets. I hope you're not overreacting," said Gulf Stream. "There's no way they could prosecute you. Over."

"I know. But our new friends, Detective Emmanuel Cerrillo and Officer Josie Waller..." Craspen pronounced the names slowly and clearly and the officers frowned. "They seem determined, and I'm, tired. Spending too much time at the clinic. T-Cells very low. Don't want to fight anymore. Over."

"What do you want from me?" asked Gulf Stream. "Name it. Over."

"They asked about a dead preacher in Pomona and that tarantula excrement who once served on the school board here. Thought you might have information for them. Oh, by the way, I like these officers. They're not the enemy. Just cops doing a job. And I stuck my foot out to get their attention." Craspen pulled the mint from his pocket, slipped it in his mouth, and downed it with a little more brandy. "Uh, Gulf Stream, I don't have much longer. Over."

"I understand, and maybe your sacrifice will push some of our more timid patriots all the way to boldness. Over."

"I hope so. Just wanted to say it's been an honor to serve under you..."

Cerrillo and Waller glanced at each other in confusion.

"The pleasure has been mine," said Gulf Stream. "And I must congratulate you. Though we've never met face to face, the San Francisco cell has done fine work. A big help. Your group will continue, I promise. I'll contact the necessary affiliates tonight and get things moving. Over."

"Thank you. I'm starting to feel the effects ... not pleasant..." Craspen appeared to be struggling to remain conscious.

"Something's wrong with him!" said Waller

"Are you in pain?" asked Gulf Stream. "It's not supposed to hurt. Over."

"Not exactly pain," said Craspen. "Hard to breathe. Butterflies slamming against my chest. I think... Over and out."

Craspen collapsed, and Waller grabbed him before he hit the floor. Cerrillo immediately called for an ambulance.

"He's foaming at the mouth!" said Waller. "That was no breath mint. Damn it!"

"Try to keep him awake," said Cerrillo, holding his cell to his chest. "Medics are on the way. We need him alive!"

"He's convulsing!"

"Hello, Detective Cerrillo, and hello, Officer Waller," said Gulf Stream. "You've cost me a good soldier, though he seems to think well of you. I was there when the scorpion queen died. I missed out on the preacher but received a detailed report. And I'm disappointed that those are the only two cases you seem to have connected. We've done everything but post messages in the *New York Times*. Perhaps only a few cops can read. Over."

"Let me talk to that son of a bitch," said Cerrillo, tossing Waller his cell and grabbing the microphone. "Listen up, whoever you are. If you're so high and mighty, why don't you drop over to your friend's house and we'll hash things out right now."

Cerrillo glanced at Craspen, whose unconscious body was twitching all over. Waller braced him in a sitting position as she spoke with the dispatcher.

"Don't worry Detective! You and Waller will hear from me soon enough, or I should say that you'll hear from Don't Ask, Don't Tell. In honor of Alex Peace Craspen, I am about to bring our mission to your doorstep. The next business card will be personal. Over."

Josie told Cerrillo, "Ambulance is almost here, and I called for backup along with a full investigative unit. Craspen must have hidden cyanide in the breath mints. I suppose we can look around this place now as a crime scene."

"We can," said Cerrillo, "but I bet we don't find much except the cards the guy already showed us. And

Craspen's gonna be dead before the medics arrive—if he isn't already."

The convulsions had stopped. Cerrillo released the microphone intercom switch, which he'd accidentally gripped in frustration.

Gulf Stream sounded back. "I'd say you're right, Detective. Craspen was a smart fellow, so you won't find much beyond what he wanted you to find. But don't worry. You'll hear from me very soon. I give you my word."

Cerrillo screamed into the receiver, "Where are you, you son of a bitch?"

"Where?" Gulf Stream laughed. "I'm right next door. We're beside everyone in the darkness. Good night, Detective. DADT will be in touch. Over and out."

The radio hissed with serpentine static.

FIFTEEN

Out of the Closet

April 2007

Gulf Stream was a big man—six feet two, athletic, and strong—with an elite engineering education that had been financed through a sizable Trust established when he was five years old. At twenty-five, the Trust remainder was conferred to him, and now, at forty-five, he had invested and reinvested those funds, profiting obscenely, as he said, in the tech-stock expansions of the 90's; and with almost supernatural foresight, he sold eighty percent of those holdings before the dot-com bubble burst and purchased blue chip stocks that would reemerge as trendy following 9/11. Despite his wealth, Gulf Stream kept up professional appearances as a consultant for two aircraft parts manufacturers in Brazil and Texas, but, under the radar, he worked as a squad supervisor with Don't Ask, Don't Tell. He was a briefcase rebel with a cause.

Gulf Stream had grown up in Southern California, New York, and Boston. He felt at home anywhere, and at twenty-two, unfortunate circumstances drove him to claim fierce ownership of his right to life as a gay man. Gulf Stream suffered a brutal bashing along with two friends in New York during the spring break of their college senior year. But what offended him most was not the physical assault, but the discernable amusement of the police investigators. Unknown to anyone at that moment, including Gulf Stream himself, the incident lit a slow fuse that would ultimately burn down to an explosive mixture of keen intelligence, substantial financial resources, and simmering rage.

During the assault, Gulf Stream had suffered minor physical injuries compared to his companions. He returned to MIT, said nothing about his bruises, cracked ribs, or anger, and calmly finished his senior engineering project, which was a computer-controlled automobile system designed to prevent drunk driving by not allowing engagement of the ignition unless the driver could enter a numerical sequence in a preprogrammed "sober time." But he also completed an unofficial project—a molded and polished alloy baseball bat about half the size of a Louisville Slugger. After receiving his undergraduate degree in robotic manufacturing technology, Gulf Stream returned to New York, walked gaily one evening through the neighborhood where he and his friends had been assaulted, and was approached by a suitably aggressive homophobe. The young engineer christened his low-tech Slugger against the skull of a potbellied, drunken, unshaven dimwit who never suspected that a faggot might fight back or even claim the right to do so. Surprise was this man's last emotion.

For Gulf Stream, that act of vengeance proved to be adrenaline enhanced ecstasy, and the psychic rush became addictive after a single experience. But Gulf Stream soon learned that this addiction, like many others, required progressive escalation of the dose. Each subsequent act demanded a more deserving victim than the last, and the search carried Gulf Stream to seedier and seedier redneck bars, cult religions, underground white supremacist meetings, or even the neighborhood supermarket. The man could play any part, fit any role, speak in tongues, slap backs, and buy beers. He hunted prejudice with skill and patience. Sometimes he got lucky and found easy prey on business trips. But wherever he found it, Gulf Stream plotted against it. New York would pay a heavy price for the bashing of three college men, and the penalty was doubled for the city's willful failure to investigate and prosecute that attack.

Had the idea occurred to him, Gulf Stream might have become a founding spirit of Don't Ask, Don't Tell, but that brilliance came from another. Gulf Stream had simply expected to dish out vengeance until he was arrested or killed. Systematic, organized opposition never occurred to him. And while the police never seemed to notice that there was a peculiar wave of attacks against heterosexuals or connect Gulf Stream with them, someone from DADT did notice, and Gulf Stream became an early and eager associate. The organizational Founder was a man that even Gulf Stream could admire for his precision, forethought, morality, and long-range planning. The Founder was a visionary philosopher. By comparison, Gulf Stream, despite his MIT technical training, considered himself no more than a talented plumber. Within months, Gulf Stream would have willingly died for the Founder. But that was not demanded of him. Instead, the Founder's first and more difficult request was that Gulf Stream surrender his addiction to street justice.

"Don't Ask, Don't Tell," said the Founder, "is not an instrument of random violence and retribution. We are the sword of Damocles. And as a member, you shall guide this sword toward a greater social good. Either that, or you will not hold authority under our mission." The Founder demanded loyalty, a sense of duty, and exquisite self-control. Gulf Stream delivered. He carried out assignments with cool efficiency on some of the most deserving souls in the country, and DADT agents uncovered the best of the worst for special treatment. Their sword of Damocles could fall almost anywhere; and soon, Gulf Stream loved the Founder and his undertaking.

But after ten years of devoted service, Gulf Stream was about to break ranks to bring Don't Ask, Don't Tell out of the closet ahead of schedule and without explicit authorization. He would play General Patton instead of Bradley. Certainly, as part of the Board of Directors, they had discussed long-range strategies, and it was agreed the guerrilla war should one day be carried into the open. Visible carnage was an important rhetoric, and they believed that the progress of Martin Luther King, Jr., and the civil rights movement would not have fared so well without the likes of Malcolm X and a few burned cities along the way. Reasonable people might be persuaded by reasonable arguments, but bigots must be moved by half-sized Louisville Sluggers and those willing to use them. Gulf Stream would leave great thinking to the Founder. It was time for his personal Phase Two.

Gulf Stream had held back one exceptionally deserving victim, waiting for the moment he could take sweet revenge *and* make a public declaration. After he lost Alex Craspen to the cyanide capsule and taunted Detective Cerrillo and Officer Waller, Gulf Stream planned a solitary march on Washington. The focus would be a former FBI agent, a department supervisor who had once investigated other agents for the "crime" of homosexuality and sacrificed the careers of his fellow gay men and women.

Once, during the more enlightened 90s, as the LGBT movement began to pick up energy, Gulf Stream had asked the man if he felt any particular remorse for those sacrifices. The supervisor responded, "Not really. Most individuals moved into other fields, and only one that I know of committed suicide. Besides, discharge was department policy, which I carried out efficiently and which earned me two promotions. They should have followed my example and stayed in the closet."

Gulf Stream nodded with fierce self-control, but he remembered, smouldered, and waited. It would be very easy to get at this now retired FBI supervisor because Gulf Stream and he were enduring lovers, and Gulf Stream kept him very close. He made sure that the man remained addicted to Gulf Stream just as Gulf Stream remained addicted to the idea of killing him. There was nothing that Gulf Stream hated more than a closeted homosexual who victimized other gays and lesbians—a hatred that sanctioned retribution. And for Gulf Stream, contrary to popular wisdom, revenge was a dish best served warm, personal, and bloody.

The man loved his work.

***

May 2007

Three days after Cerrillo and Waller had talked with Gulf Stream on Alex Craspen's radio, each of them received a call from the Los Angeles divisional office of the FBI. A representative came to Pomona to see Cerrillo, and he immediately ushered the detective and Captain Margaret Ricketts into a private conference room in the Superior Court Building next to the police station.

"Detective Cerrillo," said the FBI agent, "I don't have time to beat around the bush. What do you know about a group called Don't Ask, Don't Tell?"

"Not much," said Cerrillo. "What's going on?"

"How about you?" asked the agent, gesturing at Chief Ricketts.

"Detective Cerrillo is your man in this case," said Ricketts. "He has more information than anybody. We made inquiries with your office several weeks ago. Sent a copy of the DADT calling card. Have you come up with something?"

"Yes," said the agent, "and I almost wish we hadn't." He opened his briefcase and took out several color glossy photographs. "We're gonna visit Officer Waller, too. I'll fly to San Francisco this afternoon. The Bureau wants everything, and I mean everything, you have about this group." The agent paused before handing over the photos. "I hope neither of you is squeamish. These aren't pretty."

Cerrillo looked at the first. A naked middle-aged white man was strapped hand and foot to a four-poster bed. His throat was cut. There were multiple stab wounds. Nailed to the middle of his forehead was a plain white business card with raised black lettering.

The FBI agent handed Cerrillo another photograph. "When that card was removed during autopsy, we found a note on the back. There was not much blood, so the coroner says it was attached postmortem."

Chief Ricketts and Detective Cerrillo looked at the enlargement of the handwriting: *A personal gift for Emmanuel Cerrillo of Pomona Homicide and Josie Waller of SFPD. Forgive me for not wrapping it. More to follow. G.S.*

"That bastard," said Cerrillo under his breath.

"There's more to the story, I'm afraid," said the agent. "A small brown package was mailed to the Director in Washington. It contained another business card along with this man's testicles and a tube of red lipstick. The inscription read, 'In remembrance of J. Edgar Hoover.'" The agent turned toward Cerrillo. "So tell me, Detective.

Why does a lunatic hack up a retired G-man and bequeath what's left of the body to you and Waller?"

Emmanuel Cerrillo shook his head looking at the photo. "I don't know, but I hate to break the news. Gulf Stream is no lunatic. Neither are the people who work with him. Have you alerted Waller that she might be in danger?"

"Yes. But frankly, I want to find out how you and Waller came to be on a first-name basis with the devil himself."

Cerrillo stood up. He didn't like the insinuation that he and Waller and Gulf Stream were somehow pals. "Let's find out, instead, how fast I can kick your ass down the stairs!"

"That's enough! Both of you!" said Ricketts, stretching her arm in front of Cerrillo and turning toward the agent. "And I suggest that the FBI get on the ball—fast! We sent a heads up months ago, and you seem to have done nothing until now. Cerrillo and Waller will give you their reports. Every detail. Let's focus on finding the man with the knife."

The agent and Cerrillo sat down, temporarily regrouping. "Sorry, Detective. Sorry, Chief. I've never been on a case where one of our own got ... butchered like an animal ... and the killer sent souvenirs."

"I understand," said Cerrillo with surly rebuke. "But if anything happens to Waller while you're second guessing who done it, you're gonna look worse than the photo."

"Settle down, Detective," said Ricketts. "I'm telling both of you for the last time. Quit the bullshit!"

The FBI agent didn't like that tone from a local police chief, especially a woman, but then again, Ricketts sounded like she might be able to get away with it. Cerrillo already knew she could. Both stewed quietly.

"That's better," said Ricketts. "Now take a breath and try to act like cops. We've got work to do."

SIXTEEN

Drs. Padgett and Davenport

April 2007

"Tell me, Tash," said Robert Davenport at their dinner meeting, "Why does DADT want me? How did they know I might be interested? Come to think of it. There's no way *I* could have known I would be interested... With everything going on, I just liked the idea of social justice, and the ad struck me as *different*."

"Weren't rumors starting to circulate about your tenure progress?"

"Yes," said Davenport, "I was paranoid, of course, but it seemed a little farfetched, then, that prejudice might be a factor. I thought academia was above that. Hell, I didn't even know I could be so angry. Thought *I* was above that."

"I'm not privy to everything about DADT," said Tanish Padgett. "You're acquainted with my story, pretty much. I did what I did. I have no regrets. But whoever's behind our organization is way beyond me. That newspaper ad? They have psychologists who develop a recruitment pitch by region, personality, even unconscious qualities they're looking for. Then responses are screened when they come in."

Davenport served himself another helping of fried rice and motioned to Padgett. "Would you like more? And be sure to try the sweet and sour. Good stuff." They had decided to meet at a Chinese restaurant in New Haven.

"No more for now," said Padgett, sipping on the warm tea and focusing on Davenport. "Basically, DADT picks a region where they want to expand." She hesitated. "Or sometimes they must replace someone who's been lost. The business is not without hazards. So they run a carefully worded ad for LGBT justice fighters and collect email responses for ten days, sometimes longer, and on the posted deadline, they print the contacts and close down the site.

"You'd be surprised how many hits we get from a typical listing. Mostly from superhero wannabes, do-gooders who think we're some kind of big charity outfit with cushy, high-paying jobs that don't require calloused hands or hard work. People are amazing. They write, knowing nothing about us, and demand six figure salaries, a private secretary, no travel or lots of travel, corner office space above the 20th floor or below the 5th, or whatever. People ask if we're connected with Area 51 or Roswell, New Mexico. One guy wanted to know if he'd be working in the Batcave. Quirks are eliminated immediately. Others get tossed after a soft background check. But if we find a professional with some skills and who is not off his rocker, he'll get a hard screen. And candidates must be gay, LGBT supportive, or anti-otherism."

"I'm kind of surprised I made the initial cut—and then made it through the full screen. I mean, if my tenure were important to them, there must have been other professionals in secure positions who responded to that newspaper ad." Davenport paused a few seconds and said, mostly to himself, "It's apparent I haven't dazzled my university or my department." He was still smarting from his sketchy tenure process and the lack of promotion.

"You were short-listed right away. I don't know how our psychologists rank the candidates—the science of psychology always smells a bit like witchcraft to me—but I know you started at the top. Our people have developed pretty sophisticated recruit profiles and might be better at it than the FBI. They typically want multiple recruits for multiple operating cells, but I think you were the only New England candidate to make it through the full background screening."

"How do you know?"

"I was assigned to your investigation. That's why I audited your class."

"Lucky me," said Davenport, almost sorry that he hadn't met Padgett under different circumstances. He was secretly enjoying the second-hand account of his number one applicant ranking with DADT. It was nice to feel like a hot prospect with somebody, especially since that morning he and his colleagues had received an email rejecting their academic panel proposal for an upcoming conference.

"As a reminder," said Padgett, "you can still back out at this point. You haven't met any identifiables but me. Gulf Stream wore enough of a disguise that even I wouldn't have recognized him. And DADT could eliminate your connection to me."

"How would they do that?"

"Oh, send me very far away, where there would be zero chance you could track me down or that we might accidentally run into each other." Padgett paused and took another sip of tea. She wasn't eating much. "If they really believed I might present a danger to the organization, they would kill me."

"I don't believe it!" said Davenport. "That's unreasonable. Downright uncivilized!"

"It's very reasonable, I'm afraid, given our line of work. Like I said, I don't know everything about DADT, but discipline runs cold and deep. They're dedicated and growing. They mean business, Robert, and will declare open warfare pretty soon. They can kill me if they want, not that I would roll over for anyone, even DADT. But the organization comes first. I support that. My life is expendable."

"Not if I have anything to say about it. Still, why their interest in an English teacher. I might be good with words—like to think so anyway—but why recruit a broken down scholar for this type of game. After seeing that skull at the trailer with you and Gulf Stream..." Davenport shuddered. "I'm not sure I fit in."

"Not everyone does the ... uh, hands-on work. Although, if you were battle scarred like some of our members, you might be a better fit than you think."

"So Gulfy was wounded?" asked Davenport.

"Yes. He and a couple friends were bashed. Not that uncommon during the 80's. Gulf Stream got out with cracked bones and bruises, but one of his close friends went from MIT doctoral student to a group home for the disabled in a moment. His brain was so addled that he never recognized his best friend again. The poor boy had weekly seizures, even when he was in the coma. Died three years later from a brain hemorrhage.

"Gulf Stream's ribs healed, but his rage grew year by year. He quit being human long ago. Can't say that I blame him ... or some of the others. One thing you must understand, Robert. Gulf Stream and folks like him are singularly devoted to the organization. They've been hurt beyond repair, and DADT gives them pain relief. A kind of battlefield morphine."

"But I'm not like that. Why do they want me?"

"I can't say for sure. Perhaps you're a bit more like Gulf Stream than you believe, that once you get a taste of ... self-defense, you'll volunteer for the front lines. A variation on the corruptive value of absolute power."

Davenport laughed. "You're not going to tell me that DADT thinks it has absolute power. If so, those psychologists haven't been screening for self-delusion."

"Of course not," said Padgett, too calmly. "They have a good handle on their relative position in the world. Gays and lesbians are rabbits. The rest of society are wolves. But people like Gulf Stream are passing out Uzis to the cottontails. And as long as they don't stumble onto a similarly armed hetero-pack, the bunnies are likely to come out on top." She paused. "And in a real sense, they do have power over their victims ... so far. Near as I can tell, there's nothing more absolute than murder. And rabbits suddenly endowed with muscle can foster a pretty fierce Thumper Rebellion."

Davenport smiled. "That still doesn't explain *me*. I don't plan to carry a weapon."

Padgett nodded. "I believe you, Robert. I suspect the real reason DADT wants you involves the new phase that's about to begin. You're for strategic planning, information, propaganda. I remember a friend, well, a kind of associate, who was a Vietnam Veteran. He was in the Air Force, served in the Strategic Air Command as a journalist. He worked from eight to five, five days a week, in the news office. Managed the flow of information in and out of the base, edited to military specification. He said he never shot anybody, killed anybody, or supported the war. His hands were clean."

"So?"

"Well, while he never directly engaged in the Vietnam War, he supported the machinery of war. I think that's why DADT wants you. There are rumors of some kind of Manifesto. Very hush, hush. They're planning a big offensive that will make people stand up and take notice, and they want a document to follow immediately after. My guess is you'll be approached to collaborate in the writing of that document and to get it to the newspapers. So even if you don't fight on the front lines, you'll be part of the machinery, part of the mission. But I don't really know. I'm not in management, just a file clerk who can sideline by milking cobras. If DADT tells me to punch somebody's number, I do it. I'm a yes-ma'am."

Davenport laughed. "Somehow, Tash, you don't strike me as the file-clerk type."

"Since we met, a little bit of the old me has resurfaced. I mean," she added, "most of Tanish Padgett got lost somewhere along the way. But she liked you right off. Like a kid brother. Made her feel alive again"

"Not sure I want to be anybody's kid brother. Having family almost always means getting hurt sooner or later. An emotional kick in the teeth."

"That's the truth," said Padgett, sipping again on her warm tea. "But after awhile, Robert, I'll tell you, I'd rather take it on the chin than be ... empty. I don't know. Maybe I'm getting soft in the head. I just want to care about someone. And you wouldn't exactly have to be my kid brother. I'm one of the few straight recruits."

Davenport was surprised. His head jerked visibly.

"Sorry," said Padgett. "I wasn't insinuating ... or trying to put you on the spot, oh, or make you uncomfortable. I wouldn't do that."

"No," said Davenport. "It's just..." He laughed, regaining his composure. "You know, I caution my students over and over about making assumptions, and here I am, the wise professor who assumed that everyone in DADT would be gay. That's like saying everyone in the women's movement is female. Stereotypes and preconceptions."

"Sorry if I caught you off guard. We're just talking, right?"

"Yeah," said Davenport.

"And, you know, Robert, even though I've been hetero all my life, I probably wouldn't turn down a relationship with a woman if I met the right one. Not sure. Sounds weird, doesn't it, even to me. But after my mother died, and especially after my hooking up with DADT, I really didn't think about love. I just focused on revenge. Figured that when it was all over, if there were any pieces of me left, I'd somehow put them together. I never really expected to get out alive. But one thing is certain. Without DADT, I would have evaporated long ago."

"So who created the organization? How did it start?"

"I don't know," said Padgett. "I don't even know anybody who does, though Gulf Stream might, and he's not talking. But whoever runs DADT understands people, and how to manipulate and motivate them. Some of the demands are beyond belief, and recruits never seem to squawk."

Davenport pushed his plate aside. He'd eaten all the sweet and sour pork he could handle. The restaurant was practically vacant, so he felt easy about their conversation. "I don't generally stuff myself like a Christmas turkey, but I was a little depressed, a little angry. Food sometimes calms me. I'm really glad you called, Tash. Glad you drove down to New Haven tonight."

"Me, too. I wanted to see you before the final decision, Robert. It's hard to back out once you're in—possible, but difficult. And I admit that I want you in the club because I don't want to lose touch with you. Selfish, maybe, but I don't care. Wanting something is better than wanting nothing." Padgett shuddered. "That's like living in a black hole, and I've been there."

"To tell you the truth, when I finally got the news about my tenure decision, I was so angry at my beloved colleagues that I would have signed a DADT contract in blood with Faust looking over my shoulder. I was mad at the school, people, fate, society, religion, you name it. But I've calmed down. Even without the immediate promotion to associate professor, I can still carve out a pretty good life for myself," Davenport almost sounded like he was trying to convince himself rather than Padgett. "Might be lonely at times, and, sure, there's injustice in the world, but I doubt that Don't Ask, Don't Tell is really going to make a difference. And they don't need me either way."

Padgett leaned forward. "They do, Robert. It's true they can get another body, but they need *you*." Tanish Padgett chanted like a soft-core infomercial. "DADT will be hard pressed to find anyone better. You will contribute to DADT much like you contribute in the classroom. Does teaching make a difference? Yes, and so does the pursuit of justice. You matter to the organization, and we are already making a difference in the world.

"We're about to make a big move. I don't know what it is, exactly, but in two or three years, DADT will be a front-page, high-stakes reality show. Individuals and institutions that preach hatred against gays and lesbians will learn to walk softly and leave their sticks at home. We play for keeps."

"You can't win that way."

"Perhaps, but I know we can't win by doing nothing. And if we go down in flames, I'll die happy for having tried. Because I tell you, Robert, my mother was killed by ignorance passing itself off as morality, murdered by a social presumption that homosexuality is bad. She was defenseless. We are not."

"You're starting to argue like an academic, Doctor Padgett," said Davenport.

Padgett smiled. "Bottom line, Robert. I'm not sure of the absolute right or wrong of DADT methods, but I'm absolutely sure about the rightness of their goals. I'll go down with the ship if necessary, and in the long run, we *are* going to change the status quo."

"Maybe," said Davenport as if he were amused, "but I'd feel more comfortable working for a company if I knew who sat at the top of the organizational pyramid. I mean, I wouldn't necessarily have to like the guy. Hell, I can't stand the university president for that matter, yet I can work for the son of a bitch. I just like full disclosure. Secrecy is an itch I can't scratch."

"That's where I come in," said Padgett. "It's the best disclosure DADT can offer at the moment. I believe in what we do, Robert. Justice is not easy. It can be dangerous. But that's what we will continue to do. With or without you. On the bright side, our Northeast cell averages one assignment per year. We plan it carefully. We do the job and get out. A perfect record for ten years. The rest of the time, when we're not on active duty, life goes on routinely. We work, do research, make widgets, go to church, pay taxes ... whatever. Your having tenure is one of the reasons you passed the background check. DADT is in this for the long haul. And they need people who can remain inconspicuous even as we begin to go public. Stealth is our great strength. We learned it from the Viet Cong, and from our government. Oratory is another kind of weapon. And that's why they want you. We think you will be good at it."

"I see," said Davenport.

"But remember, whatever you decide, casualties on both sides are about to go up. If it makes you feel any better, I believe that the sooner we persuade people against hatred and bigotry, the sooner our killing will stop, the sooner DADT can retire. There might be fewer casualties overall if you join."

Davenport seemed to be thinking. He appeared relaxed, more than Padgett would have imagined.

"You seemed concerned," said Padgett. "There is still time to bow out, though I hope you won't because it

could mean trouble for me. Gulf Stream is a harsh over-
seer, and he's blood-serious about internal security. But
that's not why I'm here. I think we'll get the job done
better with you than without, and I care about you, little
brother. I'll carry on either way." She paused briefly and
added, "You can still extricate yourself, Robert. Go back
to the safe world of teaching, writing, and kissing the
asses of those who blocked your promotion."

Robert Davenport smiled. "Nice try, Tash, but a
wasted effort. I've already decided to join DADT. Here,
tonight. I have doubts, sure. But when you called this afternoon, I knew I wanted in. Still, I'd like to find out
who's running this show. It's all research to me."

Padgett nodded, noticeably relieved.

"So you won't have to worry about Gulf Stream killing
you for breach of security. I wouldn't have allowed it anyway. He's not the only one who has suffered in this
world. Could be that cumulative rejection hurts more
than broken bones, and enough pain over enough time
might drive anyone to the 'hands-on' work you mentioned."

"I don't think that would suit you, Robert. You're not
like him ... or me."

"Even a tenured professor can learn. And I won't be a
part of an organization that I can't support from the
ground up. It's true that my talents lie in white-collar
work, which I'm good it, but more than a few homophobes have earned blue-collar treatment. Gulf Stream
showed me one of their skulls in the trailer."

Tanish Padgett smiled, pushed her cup of tea aside,
and nodded. "It seems that our psychologists know their
business better than I guessed. Now I'll have a shot of
bourbon to celebrate."

"Me, too," said Davenport.

SEVENTEEN

Temporary Duty

May 2007

Police Chief Margaret Ricketts called Detective Emmanuel Cerrillo into her office. "Close the door and sit down."

Cerrillo obeyed. "What's up, boss? I already reported everything I know." He smiled. "I haven't learned anything else since yesterday."

"But I have," said Ricketts. "A Fed-X package will arrive this afternoon from Virginia. It contains a temporary federal gun permit in your name, Detective. You're being assigned to the FBI, which will allow you to carry firearms across state borders, on airliners, etc. Waller is getting the same treatment. You two are now part of the national DADT investigation."

"Waller and I are already on the case. Our case! Every lead is being—"

"*Cállate*, Manny! There's more. Even our grandest suspicions about Preacher Smithfield were short of the target. We guessed murder. We didn't figure serial-murder and conspiracy-to-commit-who-knows-what. In twenty-four hours, the FBI has turned up at least four additional incidents. They suspect more. Agents are suddenly remembering those business cards and pulling things together. This is no longer a local matter, and because you and Waller were the first to become, ah, enlightened, and because you somehow tracked down Alex Craspen—that was good work, by the way—you're on the case."

"Like I said. Waller and I are making progress. There's no need to bring in—"

"Forget it. You're with the FBI, and nobody's asking what you want. You need federal jurisdiction anyway. DADT is bigger than we thought, and you'll be crossing state boundaries. Listen, Cerrillo. You have stumbled into a hornets' nest. Maybe it was pure luck, or maybe good police work. Doesn't matter. You got results. Also, these Don't Tellers have a personal interest in you. It's a link that we might be able to use." Ricketts leaned back in her chair, seeming satisfied. "Now that the FBI's interested, I suspect DADT will be short lived. They can't be too big or too sophisticated, because not many people go in for hacking off body parts. With extra federal resources, we'll track 'em down."

Cerrillo shook his head. "I'm not sure, Chief. Like Bush's ventures into Iraq, the crap might be deeper than we know. That Craspen guy. Peach Pie or Peace Pipe or whatever he called himself. An intellectual property attorney, and yet I watched him roll over and die for the cause without so much as a whimper of regret. Waller talked with the members of his law firm. Nobody knows nothing about Don't Ask, Don't Tell. Craspen never mentioned it. In fact, they knew very little about Craspen himself, except that he was good at his job, very smart, and had been with that firm for nine years.

"Now, Craspen told us he worked in DADT finances and, oh, *stylistic flare*, or some such. But he seemed to also have talent for international money laundering because all his personal assets 'disappeared' the day after he died. Money in offshore accounts—gone. Tangible assets like the car and house were leased. Craspen's entire estate, all but pennies on the dollar, vanished like spit in a hurricane. Waller is chasing the paper trail but her computer geeks keep hitting firewalls. Numbered accounts in Europe, Asia, the Cayman Islands—all with multiple barriers that were cleared by wire transfers to other numbered and tiered accounts. Craspen's money has turned to smoke. Even the IRS doesn't know how much, where it came from, or where it went. That's control, Chief. DADT is banker smart and lawyer crooked."

Cerrillo took a breath. "Waller's still searching," he said, "but fly-by-night gang bangers don't recruit attorneys. Nope. DADT is the Pro Bowl and won't go down easy. We might round up a couple linemen, but if Craspen's willpower is any indication, the organization plays hard and will die to protect the quarterback."

Margaret Ricketts nodded and smiled. "That's why you're now heading up the FBI investigation." Ricketts leaned forward. "But don't think you're gonna run off forever to some lap of luxury. When the Feds are done with you, I expect you back at a desk in this office. You belong to Pomona PD. Remember that."

Cerrillo smiled. "Why, Chief. That is the nicest thing you've ever said to me."

"A temporary mental lapse... And one more thing, this matter is confidential, even within our department."

"You're joking," said Cerrillo.

"I'm not. Sergeant Brown is the only person aside from me who knows the whole story. Relay any messages through him if I'm not available. I trust our people, but until we learn more about DADT, the fewer involved with the investigation the better."

Cerrillo shook his head. "I hate secret-agent crap. But I'm glad Henry is in the know. A solid chunk of cop."

"Even so, talk directly with me when possible. If DADT recruited a high-ball like Craspen, there's an even chance they have a few cops on their team... Now, there's an Agent Scott Randall coming by the office tomorrow morning. He'll fly with you to San Francisco from Ontario to debrief Waller. She will be provided an FBI vehicle and driver."

"Hold on, Chief. Waller and I would prefer to work alone!"

"Shut up and listen," snapped Ricketts. "This is for your protection. Gulf Stream mentioned you by name in that note. Waller, too. And we all saw what he did to the other guy. So until we find this psycho, you'll have a driver who doubles as a bodyguard ... and to give you additional time to focus on the case." Ricketts stood and leaned on her desk. "But FBI credentials or not, Detective, I want you back in Pomona when this is finished. And if Gulf Stream hacks you into little pieces, I'm going to be very unhappy."

"Can't say I would appreciate it either."

"Stay on your toes," said Ricketts, "and stick with Waller. She's a street cop who knows the City and the gay scene, which appears linked to DADT. Watch each other's backs at all times. And when you fly to other jurisdictions—you *will* be traveling on this case—a federal agent will accompany you for added safety. Keep your eyes open. Grow them in the back of your head. Be on guard 24/7. You can relax when that Gulf psycho is behind bars ... or dead."

Cerrillo sighed. "I doubt that Waller will like having a babysitter, but I understand."

"And there's another thing."

"Don't worry, boss. We'll be careful."

"This is different. When you and Waller get your temporary federal walking papers, they will be at a supervisory level. Both of you."

"Oh, shit!" said Cerrillo, realizing the problem.

"Exactly. Some long-term FBI folks will be working under you. There could be more than a little ... professional resentment."

Cerrillo let out a sigh. "You're saying that some of our partners might be more dangerous than Gulf Stream."

Ricketts laughed. "Maybe not that bad, but let's say they might be *unenthusiastic* about your investigation. But remember, when necessary, you're the boss. Follow the DADT trail anywhere it leads. *Anywhere.* Send subordinates where and when you need them whether they like it or not. They can fetch coffee for all I care. You and Waller are lead investigators. I would rather you had a few more years under your belt before taking this on, but you and Waller have authority to throw your weight around if there are any problems with the hired help."

"I understand," said Cerrillo. "And don't worry. The feds will love us after me and Waller throw Gulfy into a padded holding cell."

"I'd appreciate that myself," said Ricketts.

EIGHTEEN

A Point of No Return

May 2007

"Recruit One to Gulf Stream, over," said Tanish Padgett during her usual check-in. She paused a few seconds. "This is Recruit One, over."

"Gulf Stream to R-One. How are things on the East Side? Over."

"The stars are aligned. Shakespeare is on board. Over."

"Glad to hear it. How *sure* are you? Over."

"Absolutely. By the way, I heard rumors about a premature Phase Two ejaculation. What's the scoop? Over."

"Afraid so," said Gulf Stream. "I probably over-reacted. Legal eagles are on the lookout but haven't gone to the media yet. Cowards. Soon our public announce-ment will be ... insuppressible. Stand out like a drag queen in Congress. We're on the move. Over."

"Might have been better to wait for the rest of us, Gulfy. Hope you didn't tip our hand too early. But at least we've hooked the Professor." Padgett intentionally used language that Gulf Stream would want to hear. "A great recruit. Over."

"No doubt, but we must be *sure* he's with us. After my 'gift package' to the FBI, our internal security is even more important. And radio transmissions might not be as secure as a public phone anymore." Gulf Stream switched to commandant. "Listen, I want Shakespeare to commit himself past the point of no return. Under-stand? Over."

"What's the job? Over." Padgett knew something was on tap for Davenport, but she worried that it might be too soon.

"I talked with Little Boy. He assigned an extra mis-sion for your New England cell. Sweet and easy. Take Shakespeare. If he's in for murder, he's with us. Over."

"I don't like the M-word," said Padgett too quickly. "That's *not* who we are. Self-defense is justifiable homi-cide. Over."

"Fine by me, but I doubt the FBI will abide by your distinction. If any of us get caught and don't use the cy-anide escape clause, they will stand trial. And you can imagine the kind of homophobic zealots who'll be in the DA's cheerleading section. We will be convicted and sent to prison or death row. Shakespeare is smart enough to know that. Over."

"I know. But to tell you the truth, I'd be happy to stand trial. In fact, I hope to someday. That would give me a chance to tell a few of the world's assholes what I think of them." There was a prolonged radio silence. Fi-nally Padgett said, "Over."

"Down, down, girl. You're in this deal on principle. I admire that. But some of us enjoy uncontaminated revenge. We expect to crash and burn, which is still easier than swallowing bullshit year after year. Never mind, I'll hash out the details with LB. Sorry about the extra work. You've done more than your share for the year. But since we're getting ready for the big one, we must know where the Professor stands. Pearl Harbor is in eleven months." Gulf Stream paused for effect. "But our version will be ... different. Anyway, that's The Founder's call. LB will want to meet Shakespeare and a few other eggheads to start the Manifesto. Without a declaration of purpose, the violence could be wasted. Over."

"I agree. Over."

"We lost a good man in San Francisco. One of our core associates. I think he was moonlighting on the Manifesto Committee. Over."

"I'm sorry to hear about the loss." Padgett took a slow breath. "Would you do me one favor, Gulf Stream? Over."

"What? Over."

"I like Daven ... I mean, the Professor. Oh, I'm getting sloppy about names. He's a good guy. He could have backed out and lived a good life without DADT. I'd like you to watch out for him when you meet with Little Boy. And afterwards, if possible. Okay? Over."

"Listen, girlfriend. You've been with the organization a long time. One of the earliest and best. You understand our program. We are at war. It might be a defensive war, but people die when bombs fall. It's the mark of the beast. If you like the Professor, fine. But handle this mission as ordered, whatever comes down. I'll do what I can to keep everybody safe, including Shakespeare. So will the Founder. But war is nasty business, and we didn't start the fight. They did. We're going to give the enemy their fill of it very soon. If this means sacrifice of the

Professor, or even you or me, so be it. But we must do our assigned jobs. Are you hearing me, Recruit One? Over."

"Loud and clear," said Padgett, "and don't worry about me. But, if possible, take care of our new member. The man loves his work and ... still has something to live for, even if he can't see it right now. He reminded me what that felt like. Over."

"I'll do what I can. Remember, most Phase Two recruits have lives beyond DADT. They're middle managers. But the old-timers? We're a slow-burning fuse that's about to explode all over the sanctimonious bastards who preached against us." Gulf Stream spoke as if he were dictating a memo. "And Pearl Harbor will make *me* very happy. If I die in the process, fine. If not, I will enjoy the looks on their rosary faces, all those white-laced mobsters who slept peacefully while their heavenly Hetero Hell crushed our minds and bodies. Our Pearl Harbor will dish out justice to Elm Street, it will be worth every pint of blood on either side, and it will be *my pleasure*." Gulf Stream took an angry breath. "Over."

"You sound like a committed man," said Padgett. "Over."

"Just remember our purpose and plan. We might die on D-Day, but the organization will keep on trucking, bigger and better, and it will march toward full citizenship. If I didn't believe that, I wouldn't have been able to squash that FBI cockroach last week. Over."

"You *sure* the Big One is going down in eleven months? Over."

"That's what I'm told. By the way, we have Dirty Mary."

"Jesus Christ," said Padgett. "Do they know how to handle it? Over."

"Let the techno-geeks worry about that. There will be lots more goodies in the schedule, but Mary will set them down hard. The clock is ticking, and we need Shakespeare on the Manifesto. I'll contact you later with mission specifics—should be fairly routine—but the real objective is Shakespeare's initiation. We no longer have the luxury of long-term observation, and with or without him, we storm the beaches in eleven months. Over."

"And if Shakespeare should falter?" asked Padgett. "Over."

"Standard operating procedure," said Gulf Stream without hesitation. "He's already in too deep to back down. Over."

"We know that, but he doesn't. Over."

"He will soon. One way or another. Over and out."

NINETEEN

Rising Temperatures

May 2007

Las Vegas can be hot even during mid-May, and at 2:00 p.m., it was 95 degrees. The humidity hovered around 12 percent, so the day seemed comparatively cool. Detective Emmanuel Cerrillo enjoyed the desert climate. Officer Josie Waller found it disagreeable. But neither had time to contemplate the weather. They'd just received a radio message to proceed immediately to the airport. A special agent would meet them with further instructions, and they would leave for Boston on the next available flight.

"There goes dinner," said Josie Waller.

"Don't worry," said Cerrillo, "You'll get an on-board snack pack."

"Prison food."

"You know, Josie," said Cerrillo as they departed their off-the-strip hotel room, "We've been running for about two weeks, and as far as anybody can tell, not a peep from Don't Ask, Don't Tell since Gulf Stream sliced up the last victim. And now we're being sent to Boston?"

"I wonder who's dead?" asked Waller, wishing it were a joke.

Waller and Cerrillo parked the navy blue Ford Crown Victoria in front of the Las Vegas Airport. A gruff security officer told them they could not leave the car there unattended, but Cerrillo flashed his FBI credentials and said, "Make sure nothing happens to this vehicle. Our driver-bodyguard will pick it up within fifteen minutes."

The officer wasn't sure if this was exactly legal, but he had respect for the federal agents in unmarked vehicles. "Okay," he said.

En route, Waller had called their assigned driver (they had given him the day off) and told him about their trip to the airport. Waller used her personal cell phone because Cerrillo's boss would be furious to discover they had ditched the bodyguard. Margaret Ricketts suspected that DADT might be watching them. Neither Waller nor Cerrillo worried about it because they were imperiously confident in their tag-team defensive capabilities.

"Hey," said Cerrillo to the airport officer, "Where is the main security office? We're supposed to report in."

The man pointed inside the terminal. "Go to the end of the ticket counters until you see a TSA uniform. Talk with whoever's wearing it. They'll take you inside."

Cerrillo nodded. "Thanks." He looked at Waller. "Let's go."

They entered the terminal, which was air conditioned about five degrees below comfortable, and proceeded as directed. At an exit near the end of the building stood an Asian TSA officer who looked more like a high school student than airport security. Waller approached and flashed her badge. Before she could ask for directions, the young man said, "Oh, yes. Officer Waller and Detective Cerrillo. I received a message to be on the lookout. They're waiting for you. Please follow me." The young man took them behind a counter and, using an electronic card key, opened an unmarked steel door. "Down this hallway, please."

They found a security control room that made Cerrillo's and Waller's home departments look impoverished. Closed-circuit monitors focused on hundreds of locations around the airport with armed personnel scanning screens from luxurious chairs that bulked out like first-class recliners on Air Force One.

"Plush," said Cerrillo. "Caesars Palace could take lessons."

A voice called down the hallway. "Detective! Officer! This way please." The new agent, who looked too young and too pudgy to be in the FBI, glanced at the TSA officer. "That will be all. Thank you."

"Yes, sir," said the man as he turned to go back to his station.

"Cerrillo and Waller, I presume."

"Yes," said Cerrillo. "Mind telling us what's going on?"

"Not at all," said the agent. "But may I see your IDs. Sorry. I haven't met you before, and we operate on personal recognition around here."

Waller and Cerrillo pulled their identification. The agent looked displeased. "*Special* credentials," he said, obviously less impressed than a moment before. "They seem in order, but I hate it when we get temporary help. What's so important that real FBI can't handle it? We don't need amateurs with federal authority."

Tired, hungry, and irritable, Waller was in no mood for departmental arrogance, especially from a man. "Look," she snapped, "now that you know who we are, run off and grab us a cup of coffee and a bagel. And don't get one for yourself because it looks like you've put on a few pounds beyond regulation. But I suppose sitting all day in this grand ballroom doesn't allow for much real police work."

The agent turned, ready to square off with Waller, when Margaret Ricketts emerged from a washroom, saw Cerrillo, and waved to them both. "This way," she said. "Meeting's in the back. "

"Chief!" said Cerrillo. "What are you doing here? You *never* leave Los Angeles."

"Arrived this afternoon. Flying home tonight. Let's go!"

Waller gestured to the impertinent agent. "You'll have to excuse us, Mr. Real FBI. We temporary flunkies have an investigation. Forget the bagels for now."

The young agent turned purple with anger, and Margaret Ricketts, seeing this, called again to Cerrillo and Waller. "Come on! We need to get you up to speed. And I have a department to run in Pomona while you are chatting so pleasantly. Move it!"

Waller and Cerrillo started toward Ricketts. The chief shouted at the agent behind them, "You, too, Ellington. You're on the clock like the rest of us. So, if it's not too inconvenient, let's go!"

Ricketts led the trio to a small back office. A middle-aged man was shuffling a stack of papers. "Come in," he said to everyone.

Ricketts, Waller, Cerrillo, and Ellington sat down. Cerrillo and Waller dropped their bags on the floor. The man closed the office door and returned to the head of the table. "Gentlemen ... and ladies," he began.

"Call me Captain or Maggie," said Margaret Ricketts.

"Ditto," said Waller.

"Agreed," said the man. "My name is Samuel Judd. Sam. First, from this moment on, our discussion is classified. Understand?"

All four nodded.

"Fine." Judd nodded at Cerrillo and then Waller. "We're not quite sure what you two have stumbled onto, but it's beyond a couple murders and neutered FBI agent." Judd passed a packet of papers to everyone. "This is a transcript of a radio message that was intercepted ten days ago."

Cerrillo interrupted, "If this is important, why did it take ten days to get to us?"

"Quiet!" said Chief Ricketts. She was firm but not harsh. "Listen to the man, Emmanuel."

"A fair question," said Judd. "I'll answer it in a minute. And you will have time to go over the transcript in detail when you're on the flight. The government has reserved an entire first-class cabin for you." He nodded toward Cerrillo, Waller, and Ellington. "That will also give you three a chance to get to know each other."

Ellington and Waller glared at each other across the table.

"I'll provide the short version of what we know, which isn't much," said Judd. "I work with ... a number of agencies, sort of a civilian intelligence advisor to Homeland Security, the CIA, FBI, anybody that needs me. Exactly what I do? Well, that's classified too. Anyway, the Don't Ask, Don't Tell dance is rather messy. And the Bureau Director was less than amused by that special gift he received a couple weeks ago."

Waller shifted her body as if she were about to speak, but Ricketts motioned to her. "Please, hear the man."

"Now," continued Judd, "after that package, the CIA and Homeland Security got involved."

Waller quickly interrupted. "I thought the CIA worked only on international ... issues. Doesn't law prohibit them from...?"

Judd held up his palm. "Let's overlook the legal technicalities for now." He smiled. "They're probably classified anyway. But nonetheless, since the 9/11 terrorist attacks, radio and cell phone transmissions are constantly monitored along with just about any kind of communications traffic. We're getting good at electronic surveillance. So," he said, looking at Cerrillo, "to return to your question, ten days isn't much of a delay. You see, all varieties of transmissions are recorded and digitally stored, but it's not possible to individually evaluate every one. The compounded volume would be staggering, even for computers. We plug key words and phrases into a search program, telling the system what to look for. When designated patterns surface, a computer alerts human operators for further screening. That's what happened in this instance, and the DADT folks made it easy. One of the phrases from your report was 'Gulf Stream.' Plus, we knew they were using short-wave radio. Tactically, it was a mistake for them to give you that kind of information. We thought we might be dealing with rank amateurs."

"Hmmm," said Cerrillo. "I'm not so sure they made a mistake."

"What do you mean?" asked Judd.

"They want us to find them. Or find out about them. Or something. But I don't want to be led by the nose down a wrong alley. Anything from Gulf Stream is suspect. My impression was that he is calculating and damned smart. We'll follow the numbers, sure, but let's keep a 360-degree scan while we do it. I prefer to find him on our terms, not his."

Judd glanced at Ricketts and nodded, obviously approving of Cerrillo.

"I concur," said Judd. "Now, back to the transcript. The term 'Gulf Stream' by itself might not have been helpful. It refers to an airplane as well as our deranged suspect. However, when combined with a few other items like 'FBI' and 'DADT,' which we also cross-referenced, the computer flagged this particular conversation as soon as it stored it. The human element bears the primary responsibility for any delay in producing a transcript. Nonetheless, ten days is acceptable considering how little we had to go on. And so far, this one item is all that we have."

Waller flipped through the five-page transcript, not yet grasping its importance. "So why are we here? This looks flimsy enough. Why didn't you email us a copy?"

"Because," said Judd, "there are a few disturbing references in the memo that hint at a coordinated ... event." Judd was going to say "coordinated attack," but his trained habit of political doublespeak dissuaded him, even among peers.

"What do you mean?" asked Cerrillo.

"We don't know yet," said Judd. "But every agency we can think of is trying to find out. And because you two have had some success, we want you involved. Maybe something will stimulate your memory or connect a bit of information from that Craspen fellow. Anyway, you're the closest thing we have to experts, so you're going to Boston tonight."

"Think of it as a working vacation," said Margaret Ricketts, "without the vacation."

"And who's the kid?" asked Waller, thumbing at Ellington.

"We'll get to that," said Ricketts.

"Oh, by the way," said Judd, "Chief Ricketts is in the know and has proper clearance. So you are all authorized to communicate with her. She's digging around L.A. with some of our people, but report only to her or to me." Judd handed everybody in the room his business card. "I wrote my direct line at the bottom. Only about thirty people in the country have it. Try to keep it that way."

"Let me guess," said Cerrillo. "Classified."

Judd laughed.

"And why Boston?" asked Waller.

"Near as we can tell, the transmission from 'Recruit One' originated in the Boston-Providence area."

"You mean with all that high-tech hullabaloo, you can't pinpoint a radio source," asked Cerrillo.

"Another operator problem, I'm afraid," said Judd. "They weren't looking specifically for geography in the initial screenings, just content. But with a little back tracking of satellite relays, signal triangulation, and a smattering of calculus, our boys are fairly sure the transmission originated within 50 miles of Boston. If DADT used cell phones, we'd probably have them in custody by now." Judd took a breath. "Now listen up. I want the three of you to read that transcript twenty times on the plane." Judd pointed toward Cerrillo and Waller. "Bring Ellington up to date as best you can. His doctoral thesis was in criminal psychological profiles. Tell him everything you can think of about your conversations with Craspen and that other chap. The government is paying for the entire first-class cabin, so you'll have privacy. Get to know one another and work together."

Waller and Ellington glared again across the table, but perhaps less harshly than before. "Does the kid have a first name?" asked Waller, thumbing at her nemesis. "Don't tell me it's Duke."

"Jim," said Ellington without the hint of a smile.

Judd continued, "You two can make friends on your own time. For now, try to think like the *National Enquirer*. No matter how wild the story, look for any link with DADT." He paused and let out a sigh. "The transcript makes reference to a Dirty Mary. So it is *very important* that we find these guys."

"Who the hell is Dirty Mary?" asked Ellington, and, unable to resist, added, "unless you're talking about Waller here."

"You'll think Hail Mary when I throw your ass across the room," said Waller.

"Hold on, guys," said Cerrillo. He looked at Judd. "So who or what is Dirty Mary?"

"We're not absolutely certain, and *this* is why the matter is classified." Judd leaned forward. "We suspect a bomb. Maybe nuclear, maybe chemical, maybe biological, but *dirty*. Our interrogators would very much like to sit down with Mr. Gulf Stream and discuss the whole affair. And there's something happening in eleven months they're calling Pearl Harbor. Dirty Mary is part of it, and we can assume she's not an island rum cocktail." Judd glanced around the table. "Are you starting to understand? Their Pearl Harbor might make the Oklahoma City bombing or even 9/11 look like a street fair. Now, I want you to locate this Gulf Stream, Recruit One, Shakespeare, and the Professor, or anybody else on Gilligan's Island. And this time," said Judd, looking at Cerrillo, "I want a live body to question! There are to be no cyanide capsules unless *we* supply them. Further, the Agency isn't too particular about how you manage the job. Just find Gulf Stream."

"I understand," said Cerrillo.

"Holy shit," said Waller.

"I don't know how holy it is," said Judd, "but you're right about the second part."

TWENTY

The Devotion of Solomon

May 2007

Professor Robert Davenport became part of Tanish Padgett's New England Operating Unit, which she sometimes referred to as "New-U." Their first mission would be in a week on the following Saturday, and even Davenport understood that, once completed, he would never really return to business as usual. This was a good thing. It was why he had joined the organization.

The assignment was a straightforward elimination. Routine. Easily executed. In fact, Davenport wondered why the job was so uncomplicated in light of the planned program expansion in eleven months. He deduced that this was a training mission designed specifically to see how he reacted under pressure, a kind of one-day boot camp. And he resolved to get an "A" on the test, if that's indeed what it was.

The target was a simple-minded religious zealot and sidewalk preacher who incessantly protested the "homosexual agenda" in Massachusetts and who had descended into an almost nonstop verbal exhortation after the state recognized same-sex marriage three years earlier. Further, his venom contained political ambitions, which concerned DADT. A German news reporter claimed in 1925 that Hitler and the National Socialist Party were an inconsequential gang of thugs; DADT would not wait until the Massachusetts' Mad Hatter became "consequential." Theirs was a preemptive strike. But the real mission concerned Davenport. The organization needed to confirm that Shakespeare was "in," and they needed to do it quickly.

Davenport, Padgett, and Solomon-X (the third member of the New England cell and the chauffeur for Davenport's first meeting with Gulf Stream) drove to Northwestern Massachusetts in a utility van provided by Padgett. In mid-morning, they cut the residential hard line to the victim's phone; fifteen minutes later, they magically and conveniently arrived to restore service. Padgett wore a "Preserve the Sanctity of Marriage" button on her simulated phone company uniform, and the victim welcomed all three service agents into his home. Once inside, Solomon-X said evenly, "Don't Ask, Don't Tell says hello," and offered two quick shots to the man's head, splattering blood on Davenport.

Davenport wanted to scream but remained silent. He had never seen a gunshot victim, let alone someone who'd been shot at close range with a .45. The violent noise, smell of gunpowder, and bodily carnage caught him completely off guard. Further, Solomon used soft-point cartridges, so Davenport didn't need close examination to see human brains scattered across the floor like crimson oatmeal. He dropped to his knees and vomited on the carpet.

Solomon patted him on the shoulder. "Be easier after the first time," he said. "Remember we're at war." Pointing to the dead preacher he added, "He is enemy."

"Take a minute to catch your breath, Robert," said Padgett. "Think about all who have suffered because of men like this one. Think of *our* victims sent to prison or fired from jobs or killed because of malicious ignorance."

Soon there was nothing left in Davenport's stomach, but his dry convulsions continued for a full minute.

The professor's prolonged anguish stunned and then disgusted Solomon-X. He said, "DADT don't teach English. You knew that! Maybe you coward after all!"

The words stung Davenport almost as bad as the words from some of his tenure-committee colleagues disdaining his "inadequate" scholarship. He would not be thought of as a failure by Solomon. "Don't worry about me," stammered Davenport, wiping the back of his hand across his mouth, struggling to his feet, and accepting a hand from Padgett. "I just ate too much breakfast. That's all..." He took another deep breath and looked directly at Solomon. "Let's finish the job and get the hell out of this place."

Solomon said suspiciously, "Maybe you be okay. Maybe not."

Padgett glared at him. "He's going to be fine, Solomon! The first mission can be hard. You know that. And Robert hasn't had the same kind of ... life motivations we've had."

"Professor not look like right man," said Solomon, holding his gun with a purpose. "Maybe kill coward for our protection."

Padgett understood exactly how to control Solomon. "The Professor is the right man! He was personally selected by the Founder for our cell and to work on a special project, and nobody goes against the Founder. Nobody! But we must help Shakespeare learn our ways. That's a big part of your job now, Solomon, and the Founder is counting on you more than anyone!"

Solomon nodded reverently, holstered his weapon, and said, "You right. Founder is never wrong. I apologize to you, sir, for doubt. May God and Founder forgive me."

Davenport steadied his body enough to speak. "Just a temporary weakness. It won't happen again." Picking up on Padgett's lead, he added, "I would never dishonor the Founder."

Solomon went back to work as if the whole incident were now forgotten. He eyed the body on the floor.

Padgett placed a DADT business card on the refrigerator, came back to the living room, and tried to further assure Solomon with levity about Davenport's nausea. "Let's clear out and stop for pizza and beer on the way home. I suspect the Professor will be hungry soon because his breakfast is spread across the carpet."

Davenport grimaced.

Solomon-X laughed and said, "We go eat. But first, you watch."

"We really should leave," said Padgett.

"You and professor man watch," he replied.

The preacher had an eight-foot wooden crucifix mounted on the living room wall, and Solomon decided it would be a bonus message to nail the victim to his own cross. He retrieved a claw hammer and pack of four-inch galvanized nails from the garage; and then Solomon, who stood six feet with heavy muscles, grabbed the frail corpse by its neck, lifted it high upon the cross, braced it against the vertical beam with his left elbow, and drove two nails through the deepest flesh under its chin.

"Christ," said Davenport under his breath, awed by the sight. He mentally pictured a helpless young gay man, beaten, tortured, and tied to a fence in freezing temperatures. Could a dead preacher represent justice?

Certainly the man on this cross had suffered less than Matthew.

Padgett offered minor assistance as Solomon pounded nails through the wrists and each foot. After completing his windfall project, Solomon buried the claw end of the hammer in the skull of the victim, kneeled, and offered a silent prayer.

Davenport, his adrenaline-infused pulse throbbing in his ears, struggled not to become nauseated again.

Padgett noticed and said, "Are you still okay?"

Davenport inhaled and exhaled. "Not sure," he said, letting out a breath. "I knew the mission, what we planned, but damn..." He tilted his head back and exhaled again. "Oh, brother. Solomon's right. It's not like teaching English... Wow."

Padgett waited a moment and said, "Listen, Robert. We don't care much about one man's personal prejudice, but when he starts campaigning to move that prejudice toward government policy, even local policy, we move to stop it. And we do it hard and fast."

"I know," said Davenport. "I know. But on-the-spot violence ... caught me by surprise. Gulf Stream's cleaned and sanitized skull in a trailer is one thing. Fresh brains leaking on a blood-stained carpet is another. I was ... part of ... murder."

"We do God's work," said Solomon-X. "Pray. He will help you. I help, too, like Founder wants."

"Don't worry," said Davenport, strengthening his rhetoric once more. "I'm in the show now like it or not. It's just that nailing someone to a cross..." He straightened his body, looked at Padgett, and said slowly, "I am Shakespeare. I am DADT!" And somewhere inside himself, Davenport knew he was certifiably part of the organization. He remembered the photographs of the hateful protesters at Matthew Shepard's funeral, the dean's subtle condescension when consoling him about the English department's lack of support for tenure and promotion, and, especially, one of his students who'd recently committed suicide after the boy's family had rejected him for being transgender. And there still existed the Don't Ask Don't Tell military policy supported by people whose enthusiasm seemed better suited for the burning stakes of the Dark Ages.

Then, looking at the man nailed to the wooden beams, Davenport approached and dipped his finger in the oozing blood and traced the letters DADT on the wall next to the cross. "I'm with you now," he said to Solomon-X. "I'm with you."

Still wearing their blood-smeared surgical gloves, they shook hands.

A minute later, as the group was preparing to leave the victim's home, they noticed a handsome wooden cashbox sitting on a table near the crucifix. It contained roughly $7,000 in crisp hundred dollar bills, five gold Krugerrands, and several rolls of silver dollars. They left the money in place, but Davenport later questioned Padgett when they were back in the van.

"I'm curious as to why you didn't take the money?" he asked. "It might have been used to finance some of your, uh, our campaigns."

Not waiting for Padgett, Solomon-X responded. "Our mission is justice! We came to kill, not steal. We are servants of God, not common thieves."

Solomon projected the crystal conscience of singled-minded devotion. He had not even been tempted to steal, and, unlike Davenport or Padgett, he could have really used the money.

Solomon-X worked as a bartender in a rough section of East Providence, Rhode Island. The patrons were hardcore down-and-out alcoholics, addicts, prostitutes, ex-convicts, or future convicts. And Solomon lived in a small, under-funded apartment complex six blocks from his job. He could not afford a car and walked to work even at night in the dead of winter. Emotional and physical scars ran deep from his childhood, some disguised by tattoos, and DADT was Solomon's new religion. With the fanaticism of a true convert, he believed that the mystic "Founder" of Don't Ask, Don't Tell, whom he had never met, could walk on water.

After the assignment, Tanish Padgett drove to Providence and dropped Solomon at his residence. As Davenport and Padgett merged onto southbound Interstate 95 toward New Haven, Padgett relaxed and spoke more casually.

"I know what you're thinking," said Padgett.

"What's that?" asked Davenport, contemplating the day's activities while simultaneously numb and exhilarated.

"You're wondering how Solomon made it into the organization. He's nothing like you or Gulf Stream."

"Well, he doesn't seem typical, not that I really know what typical is. But that place where he lives. Depressing. I wouldn't leave a stray cat there."

"I know," said Padgett. "But in some ways, Solomon is one of the happiest people around. He never seems confused by ... what we do. I mean, I handle violence by trying not to care. He seems to love it. Told me once that DADT was his personal ticket to heaven. Solomon-X has faith."

"Is Solomon...?" Davenport decided not to ask.

"What? Go ahead, Robert. You can ask anything now. You're in."

"Oh, I don't know. Just talking with the guy. I wondered if he were developmentally disabled. Hard to tell. If he were one of my students, I'd probably refer him for testing."

"I don't think he has a diagnosis. He's too self-sufficient. And he's broke. People don't care that you're sick unless you have money to pay for treatment. I think of Solomon as a 25-watt light bulb in a 100-watt world. But for him, 25 is the Goldilocks Zone."

"How old is he?" asked Davenport.

"What do you think?" asked Padgett, curious.

"I'd say thirty-five, maybe thirty-seven. He's very strong."

"He's twenty-six with a body aged by street life. Told me that he worked blue-collar jobs since a teenager ... long, hard days. Mostly construction after he dropped out of high school, including winters when he could find work. And, because of his, uh, let's say temperament, he seemed to get the worst jobs on any site. People took advantage of him. And when Solomon discovered he was gay, which he hated as much as anyone, you can imagine how he was treated in the construction field. Worse than a woman..."

"Damn. Didn't he have family to help him?"

"Solomon didn't come from the kind of family that would support anything, let alone a dimwitted gay son. They treated him worse than his coworkers did. Kicked him out of the house when he was sixteen or seventeen. Solomon was homeless for two years and lost several toes to frostbite. One of our DADT members found him in a hospital after he attempted suicide. Talk about your proverbial clay ready for the Maker's hand. Solomon would have followed a warm bowl of soup and a little kindness straight to hell. We set him up with on-the-job training as a bartender, arranged for an apartment, and paid a few months rent while he got on his feet. He's been with us ever since, about five years now. At first, Solomon was kind of a DADT rover. Worked with different cells as needed, but he's been with me for the last couple years when I asked for him permanently. His devotion is boundless. If we asked him to swim across the Atlantic and attack Portugal barehanded, he would probably try."

"Did you send him for counseling or something? He seems stable, if not very bright."

"No. After his confinement on a mental ward, he wanted nothing more to do with doctors. But his initial DADT recruiter—it wasn't me if you were wondering—helped Solomon semi-accept his homosexuality."

"Semi?" asked Davenport, wondering how that would work.

"Well, it's strange. Solomon is a young man. Hormones and all. And yet as far as we know, he's completely celibate. Doesn't even talk about sex. Societal homophobia and rejection by his parents did a real job with him. He acknowledges that he's gay but dislikes it. Sad."

Davenport understood what she meant. He witnessed similar struggles in some of his gay and lesbian students, pride versus self-loathing. It was hard for some to escape family teachings, even when they wanted to. His own family had inquired about "conversion therapy" on the recommendation of a family pastor, but Davenport was smart enough to avoid that and soon assured his parents that he had met a girl in high school who was helping to cure him of homosexuality. Then he walked resolutely into the closet until he could provide for himself. Davenport sometimes wondered if the self-inflicted skullduggery had hurt him more than the potential social costs of being out. But how does one measure such an effect?

"Solomon might be a sad case," said Davenport, "but self-contempt can also be dangerous, unpredictable."

"Not with Solomon-X," said Padgett. "He's a rock of ages. And sometimes a 25-watt bulb offers the perfect light."

Davenport felt somehow disturbed but said nothing. He did not know why this should make him uncomfortable.

After a few moments of silence, Tanish Padgett said. "Robert?"

"Yes."

"After we go back to New Haven, after I drop you off at home, it's likely you will be contacted by Gulf Stream in a few days, perhaps even Little Boy."

"That reminds me, I was going to ask about LB. Still don't know a lot about the organization. I wasn't sure if he was real or a referential piece of Pearl Harbor."

"Little Boy is both. He's a Coordinate Supervisor. Works directly under the Founder. Gulf Stream receives assignments from Little Boy and then dishes them out to one of his three cells. I'm not sure whether Gulf Stream knows the Founder. My guess is that he does. Anyway, someone will probably talk with you soon."

"About the Manifesto?"

Padgett hesitated, which Davenport noticed. He felt a twinge of apprehension but suppressed it. Then Padgett said, "Yes. About the Manifesto."

TWENTY-ONE

Closing the Gap

May 2007

Emmanuel Cerrillo, Josie Waller, and Jim Ellington had been at their Boston hotel for less than twenty minutes when Cerrillo was called to the lobby.

Returning to the hotel suite, he said, "Forget about the radio transcript for now. We're heading to western Massachusetts."

"What's happening?" asked Waller.

"Yeah," said Ellington. "We're up all night on the red-eye, hit the ground staggering, and now we're supposed to saddle up. How about a hot shower and something to eat? And if it's not too much to ask, a couple hours sleep."

"Later," said Cerrillo, holding a fax that he had re-trieved at the lobby. "A business card on a refrigerator along with some joker nailed to a cross in his living room."

Ellington shook his head. "Looks like we're gonna miss lunch, too."

Waller reached in her overnight bag, pulled out a Snickers bar, and tossed it to Ellington. "Eat this. It will tide you over. Drink a Pepsi along with it and you won't need sleep for ten hours. Real cops know that." She nod-ded to Cerrillo. "How far's the drive?"

"Hundred miles or so. But the vehicle hasn't arrived yet. They were supposed to have it at the hotel when we got here. Damned government can't do anything right. Better call..."

The hotel phone rang. Cerrillo answered. "Detective Cerrillo here."

"Hello," said a young, nervous voice. "This is the front desk. There's somebody from the FBI who says you're under investigation for conspiracy and conduct unbe-coming and that you should please handcuff yourself immediately and report downstairs."

Cerrillo did not laugh. "Tell whoever's there that I'm in no mood for fun and games. We're on our way to the lobby, and if this character doesn't have our transporta-tion, there might just be a little conduct unbecoming." Cerrillo hung up the phone. "Grab your hats, gang! We got a visitor."

"The car better be comfortable," said Waller. "If the FBI has gone cheap on us and delivered a Metro, I'll call Avis and request a Hummer on the government expense account."

"Don't you worry," snapped Ellington, chomping on the Snickers. "We're supposed to have a full-sized four-door. I just hope there's room in the trunk to stuff your ass. You been getting on my nerves since Vegas."

Waller smiled. "You'd better hit the gym for a few years before you get around to stuffing me anywhere, Darling. I eat tougher cops than you for breakfast. And I got my training on the Streets of San Francisco while you were reading the Hardy Boys and trying to figure out which end of the gun was dangerous."

Waller and Ellington were getting along better after their flight together, but it was hard to tell from their dialogue.

Cerrillo had not liked partners until Josie, and now he had two of them. He knew Waller could take care of herself but worried how Ellington would hold up if things got rough, although it seemed a good sign that the newbie dished back nearly as well as he received. And Detective Cerrillo would accept any kind of help— whether it be psychological profiles or blind luck—to track down Gulf Stream.

"Knock it off, both of you," said Cerrillo. "I want to get to the crime scene before some local yokel rips the victim off the cross with a crowbar and destroys any forensic evidence. You two can kill each other on the way."

"Just try to keep super dyke off me while I do my job," said Ellington to Cerrillo. "I didn't spend nine years in college to have some beat cop shove me around."

"Super Dyke! Thanks for the compliment, kid," said Waller. "But nine years to get through college! I'm surprised you didn't stretch it out to ten. Probably kicked back on mommy and daddy's trust fund while the rest of us worked for a living. Keep your mouth shut and eyes open, and you just might learn something from Super Dyke."

Cerrillo struggled not to laugh. "Come on, Josie. We're gonna need Ellington before we're through. There's no telling what kind of psycho-profile we're up against, and Ellington must know his stuff or Judd wouldn't have sent him along."

"Thanks," said Ellington, relieved. He was sensitive to the 'kid' label among first-line agents and officers. "Just control the dragon lady and I'll do my best."

"The first lesson of police work," said Waller, "is you've got to handle a little ribbing. Comes with the territory. I'm surprised you didn't learn that on the Honor Roll. And another thing, College Boy, try being a woman in an urban police force. You wouldn't last a week."

"If I were a woman in an urban police force, I would kill myself," said Ellington.

Waller pulled her weapon and held it butt-first toward Ellington. She said nothing but raised a Vulcan eyebrow.

"Fuck you," said Ellington.

"Dream on, little man! Have you even seen a woman with her clothes off?"

"Look," said Cerrillo through clenched teeth. "I'm going downstairs, pick up the keys to the vehicle, and then drive to the crime scene. If you're in the car when I leave, great. If not, you can hitchhike." Cerrillo walked out.

Josie Waller grimaced and then motioned toward the door, indicating that Ellington should go first. They made it to the elevator without further comment. In the lobby, a gruff-looking, middle-aged FBI man greeted them.

"Hello," he said. "They told me I would be meeting two men and a woman. Which one of you is the woman?"

Agent Jim Ellington laughed out loud.

Officer Waller pointed to Ellington and said, "That one. You can tell by the giggle."

The agent tossed a set of keys to Cerrillo. He resented serving as a delivery boy for out-of-towners, whether they were in the Bureau or not. "There you go," he said. "The Crown Victoria is parked out front. But if you don't know your way around Boston, you'll be lost in two blocks. Fortunately, there's an on-board navigation system, so you might make it three blocks."

"Let's go," said Cerrillo to Waller and Ellington, otherwise ignoring the new agent.

"Care to tell me what's going on?" said the delivery boy.

"Nope," said Cerrillo.

"Thanks a lot," said the agent. "Not that I really give a damn. But you just be sure to return that vehicle in one piece. If there's so much as a scratch, I'll have you filling out paperwork for three days in a windowless basement that's smaller than the car." Then, quite suddenly, the agent became more sincere. "By the way, they told me you had been up most of the night on the Vegas red eye. That's a bad way to discover Bean Town. I picked up three breakfast wraps and coffees at a little joint I know. A box on the floorboard."

Josie Waller's eyes opened wide. "If I were a woman, I'd kiss you."

"Appreciate it," said the agent. "But 'pretty boy' here might be more my type," he said, gesturing mockingly at Ellington, who blushed. "Good luck with the investigation. What little I've heard suggests it's nasty business."

"Very," said Cerrillo. "What's the damage for the food?"

"You can owe me."

"What's your name?" asked Cerrillo.

"Everybody calls me Serge."

Cerrillo noticed that the agent limped slightly when he walked. "Thanks for the breakfast treats, Serge. And I hope you dropped valium in the coffee. My two partners here have been at each other's throats since we left Vegas."

"Who's winning?" asked Serge.

"Don't know yet," said Cerrillo. "But I've had my fill."

Serge nodded and grinned.

"That limp of yours?" asked Ellington.

"Not that it's any of your business," said Serge, collegially, "but I took a bullet about a year ago. Made a stupid mistake. That's how people get shot, so be careful out there." Serge didn't mention that it was his partner who made the mistake, not him. "Anyway, I was pretty close to retirement, so they decided to keep me around for comic relief ... delivering squad cars to newcomers. On the other hand, if you need to know anything about anybody in Boston—from the Mayor to the streetwalkers who work the lobby of your hotel—you give me a call. That's for real, too. I'm old-school FBI, and I can still earn my keep. My card's on the front seat of the vehicle. Office and home numbers. Whatever I can do for a field agent..." Serge paused noticeably. Everyone felt his pain. There was more to that limp than just torn ligaments and stiff joints. They knew that part of his life had been taken from him.

"Thanks, Serge," said Cerrillo, now a full comrade. "We could probably use inside information when we understand more about what's going on. Need a ride back to the station?"

"Don't worry about me," said Serge. "I'll get where I need to go all right. Hail a cab at gunpoint if necessary."

"Definitely old school," said Detective Cerrillo.

***

"Jesus H. Christ," said Cerrillo. "Haven't you people ever heard of preserving the crime scene!?"

"They've heard of it," said the County Sheriff, spitting at the ground. "And maybe that's how you do things in the big city. But here in Greenfield, we don't leave one of our own hanging on a cross for two days while waiting for the almighty experts to show up and tell us how to run the department. The body's at the morgue. Go take a look if you want, but be sure you're respectful. I don't want you upsetting the family any more than they've already been. This was a good man we're talking about. A devout Christian man. You be mindful of that or, FBI or not, you'll get a hard time from the locals and from me."

"Look, Sheriff," said Cerrillo. "We've got several murders that follow a pattern. I'm sorry about what happened to your man, but people are dying, and I'm sure we both want the SOB who's behind it. I need everything you got, and I hope somebody took photos before you removed the body. And keep everybody else away from the scene. Not that I expect there's much evidence left if your boys haven't preserved it."

"You think we're morons out here in Podunk Massachusetts!? We have real procedures just like Boston cops. There will be more photos than you need. Inside and out. But you can't expect us to leave a man hanging on a wall. He had family. He had neighbors."

"You're right, Sheriff," said Cerrillo, trying to appear sympathetic because they still needed the Sheriff's help. "We'll look at everything, and I'd like to talk with the first officer on the scene. He might have noticed something. By the way, how was the body discovered?"

"That would be Bradford. Lives three doors down. Tried to call the victim several times and got no answer—the outside phone lines were cut. Walked over to check and saw the body through the front window. Called us. What a sight that was."

"Any suspects or ideas?" asked Cerrillo.

"Nothing that makes sense. Bradford said he saw a white repair van parked on the street that morning. Doesn't remember anything more. We're still asking around the neighborhood. Most people had already gone to work at the estimated time of death."

"Did Bradford make the vehicle?"

"No," answered the Sheriff. "He said, and I quote, 'It was either a Ford or Chevy or maybe a Dodge.' Might have been a pushcart for all we know, but it was white. There was no reason for him to really pay attention."

Cerrillo nodded. "We'll look things over and then talk with Neighbor Bradford and the first officer on scene. If you could take Waller to see the photographs, that would be a big help." He turned toward Waller. "Josie, you know what to do. Ellington and I will stay here and get started." Cerrillo turned back toward the Sheriff. "Who found the business card?"

"What card?" asked the Sheriff.

"The Don't Ask, Don't Tell business card. On the refrigerator."

"Don't know nothing about it. Nobody said nothing about no business card."

Cerrillo said, "But I've got a fax here from my home office. Says there was a card on the refrigerator."

The Sheriff waved to a young officer standing next to a patrol car. "Hey, Sam. Did you guys find some kind of business card when you got here? You're supposed to keep me informed, damn it."

"What are you talking about?" asked Sam. "Should we have been looking for something special? Nobody told me."

"Oh, hell," said Ellington, interrupting. "Somebody found the card, or it wouldn't have been mentioned in the fax."

"What fax?" asked the Sheriff.

Cerrillo pulled out a copy of the paper he had retrieved at the hotel. "There!" he said. "Don't Ask, Don't Tell. Business card on refrigerator. This came from the Pomona Police Division. They wouldn't know about it unless somebody reported it."

"Let me see that, again," said Ellington.

"I'd like to see it myself," said the Sheriff. "Sounds screwy. Hey, wait a minute. The letters DADT are traced on the wall in blood."

"Those bastards," said Cerrillo as he handed Ellington the paper. The Sheriff looked over his shoulder.

"Detective?" asked Ellington. "Where is the fax cover sheet? This is page two. And who has the initials G.S.? That's not your chief."

"Gulf Stream!" said Cerrillo grabbing back the paper. "That son of a bitch. They must have misplaced the fax's first page at the hotel. Gulf Stream is one of the psychos we're looking for, Sheriff. He's *the one* we're looking for. The cover sheet probably explained what's going on. Let's check the house refrigerator, Sheriff, and then I'll call my boss. Maybe they can track down the source."

"I doubt it," said Ellington. "DADT is too smart. Bet it came from a copy service, or they tapped into a public phone system."

"All right," said the Sheriff. "Let's go inside the house and take a gander. I'm starting to think the whole lot of you are tetched. But follow me." He gestured toward the victim's front door.

Cerrillo, Waller, Ellington, and the Sheriff entered the living room. The wooden cross had been pulled off the wall and was resting on the floor. Cerrillo expected more blood.

"Around the corner," said the Sheriff.

Cerrillo walked into the kitchen, looked at the refrigerator and then at Waller. "Did they get photos of this room?" asked Cerrillo.

"If they didn't, I'll fire somebody," said the Sheriff.

Cerrillo bent down in front of the refrigerator and examined the DADT business card without touching it. Waller offered him a pair of surgical gloves, which she always carried. "Use these," she suggested. "There could be prints."

"I doubt it," said Cerrillo, taking the gloves nonetheless. "Gulfy has been pretty slick so far." Cerrillo pulled a glove on each hand, gently lifted the refrigerator magnet, and retrieved the familiar looking card as if it were the Star of India. He turned it over. As expected, there was a note in small but delicate handwriting.

Dearest Officer Waller and Detective Cerrillo: Sorry I couldn't be there to greet you personally, but I trust you received my message. Do you like our team's handiwork? DADT will be dormant for a while. I think we shall meet soon after Pearl Harbor. Best, G.S.

TWENTY-TWO

Dinner at Eight

May 2007

Professor Davenport was in his faculty office the week after spring-semester finals. He did not give a final exam for his writing courses and had opted for end-of-term papers instead, which he was now reading. And he hung around the campus to help a few handpicked students add his assigned fall courses, which were typically filled soon after registration began, or to talk with overly anxious souls who "couldn't sleep" until they knew that the professor had read their last paper and calculated the final grade. Davenport looked at the stack of freshman papers on his desk. He simply could not face them, and he likewise dreaded the upcoming commencement ceremonies.

Davenport was bored, which struck him as odd. Academia was still academia. He'd been doing this job for years. But it wasn't academia that had changed; and now, compared with Davenport's recent adventure in Northwestern Massachusetts or the anticipation of the Manifesto writing project, slogging through twenty student essays seemed unbearably tedious. Besides, he had read all of the stories in one form or another. Papers about the cultural significance of television violence (with the strongest support material derived from Wikipedia or the student's roommate) or the ultimate homecoming dance that led to everlasting love for an 18-year-old or the untimely death of a casual friend that helped a student realize that one must live every moment to the fullest. In Davenport's opinion, many freshmen already seemed so devoted to living life to the fullest that they found it difficult to spend one hour of serious work on an academic paper. It was easier to stack back-to-back clichés and believe in effortless brilliance.

Davenport decided to wait on the papers. Grades weren't due for six more days, and he recalled the wisdom of his high school psychology teacher: Never put off until tomorrow what you can put off until the day after tomorrow. So by the time Davenport had packed his briefcase and driven home, he had further decided to flash-skim the papers, give each a generous holistic score, and submit final grades. That's what students cared about anyway. Who would know how much time or effort he spent? And if he padded their evaluations just perceptibly, general relief should forestall any complaints.

As he walked in the door of his home, Davenport's pulse skipped at the flashing light on his answering machine. He hoped it was a call from Don't Ask, Don't Tell, and they would save him from the stack of papers by sending him on a mission.

The message came from Gulf Stream: "On Saturday, I will fly to Connecticut in my private jet. Please pack a small suitcase and expect to be away for two days. You will be taken to meet Little Boy and discuss the Manifesto." The last part revealed: "You might also be needed a couple weeks in July or August, so be sure to consider your academic schedule accordingly. We expect you to maintain the pretense of a scholarly life—it's your cover and ours. Welcome aboard, Professor. My driver will pick you up Saturday at 7:30 a.m. and take you to an airport near New Haven. See you then."

Davenport smiled with anticipation as he erased the message. He would travel by executive jet to an unknown destination and meet a mysterious someone who used a pseudonym and was an officer in a deadly underground organization. Perhaps they would even blindfold him for the flight. This cloak-and-dagger excitement was better than teaching any day of the week. It was decided: Professor Davenport would streamline the grading process of his freshman and graduate courses. He had more important things to do.

**

"Nice to meet you," said Little Boy, a smallish and delicate looking man.

"Same to you," said Robert Davenport.

"You're probably wondering exactly why you're here. And we'll get to that in due course, but tell me, Professor, how did your teaching go this semester?"

Davenport thought this was a strange approach to a first interview regarding a blood-letting group, especially considering the time and expense to bring him here. "Fine," he said.

Little Boy looked at Davenport and waited. He understood the value of silence.

"Well," continued the professor, "it was okay, but after my ... first job with—Padgett's an interesting character by the way—I must admit that the whole college experience has begun to seem kind of lame. Don't know how to phrase it exactly. I'm still analyzing. The university has become, oh, anticlimactic."

Little Boy nodded. "You mean dull and pointless."

"Something like that, but not precisely. In fact, I feel strangely *imprecise*."

Little Boy leaned forward in the stiff leather chair and poured two servings of brandy, offering one to Davenport. "Listen, Professor. You'll be here until tomorrow morning. Gulf Stream is off on other matters, and the main purpose of your visit is for us to get to know one another..."

A servant entered the room. "I'm sorry to interrupt you, sir, but the cook is wondering if our guest would prefer sea bass or salmon for the dinner entrée. There are red meat options as well. Perhaps filet mignon or a more traditional grilled porterhouse. May I suggest the filet mignon? We have some especially beautiful and delicately aged cuts."

"How about it, Professor?" asked Little Boy. "Our chef trained in Europe and worked in several Parisian restaurants before I stole her. She is cooking for *you* tonight. Anything goes. What shall it be?"

Davenport was a little startled. "Oh, I hadn't gotten around to thinking about food. The whole trip—private car and jet and royal treatment—has been a bit overwhelming."

"Well," said Little Boy, "I might offer a bologna sandwich with a deli-pickle, but that would defeat the purpose of a vintage-class wine cellar." He visibly shuddered.

Davenport smiled.

"And besides," said Little Boy, "our purpose is to become acquainted, and I would never trust anyone who does not appreciate the high art of dining. Man should not live by bread alone even if he can."

Davenport nodded. "I'd like filet mignon. Don't get it often on a professor's salary." He looked at Little Boy. "Believe it or not, I still have college loan payments."

Little Boy motioned to the servant. "Make a note to inquire about the professor's outstanding student loans. We will arrange to have them paid off immediately. And tell Sylvia that we'll both have the filet mignon."

"Yes, sir," said the servant. "And with the main course, I'd like to suggest the vintage cabernet that we've been saving. A superb, lingering essence. Your father purchased a case over thirty years ago, and this is the only bottle remaining."

"Perfect!" said Little Boy. "Dad would be pleased, I think, that the last gasp should be shared with our Professor. And after dinner, we will have the California port." Little Boy glanced at Davenport. "This might seem a tad provincial, Professor, topping off Sylvia's cooking with a California wine, but the texture and depth of this particular vintage is as good as the best out of Portugal. I know several vintners ... actually, I own the winery, and let's just say that these particular winemakers are gods of cottage industry."

Davenport smiled. "Fine! What's for dessert?" He meant this as a joke.

The servant replied, "Sylvia is preparing a light cream fudge cake, braced with fresh strawberries and topped with her own special lemon sauce. It won the Paris Expo, and I might add that first place was not good enough."

"I agree," said Little Boy.

"Wow," said Davenport, warmed by the brandy, "maybe we should stick with bologna. I'm starting to feel guilty about what dinner is costing you."

Little Boy laughed. "No need to fret, dear boy. Money is a blessing, but spending it is even better. And besides, I'm afraid that Gulf Stream and I are both victims of lavish inheritance. Though I dare say I am by far the greater victim."

"If that will be all, sir," said the servant, "I'll assist Sylvia in the kitchen."

"By all means," said Little Boy.

"Thank you, sir. Dinner service will begin at eight." He left Davenport and Little Boy in the study, which appeared to be a combination office, research library, and upscale recreational lounge.

Davenport set his brandy on the side table and shook his head. "You'll have to excuse me if I seem out of place," he said, "but I really am. The lavishness is daunting. I'm used to begging the English Department for file folders or whiteboard markers. And my family raised me to believe that opulence was sinful."

"Opulence without purpose *is* sinful," said Little Boy, holding up his aperitif glass and turning it back and forth. The afternoon light reflected against the crystal like spectral fireflies. "But our gathering is a necessity. And treating myself and those around me well makes life worthwhile." He set his glass next to Davenport's and smiled. "Sure. We have business to conduct, but there's no need for business to be miserly and crass. For example, my servants make more than an assistant professor. So I like to think that I treat all my associates well."

Davenport nodded in appreciation. "Do they, your workers, know about DADT?"

"No," said Little Boy, "and I'm afraid we must take care to keep it that way. I assume that most would not mind what kind of work I do. After all, a vote against me would be a vote against their livelihood. But a single mistake about the organization could be disastrous, so there is no need for them to know."

"But how do you keep it from them? Especially if you bring people like me here?"

"Professor Davenport," said Little Boy, "I am a legitimate businessman. The extent of my enterprise and investments would no doubt startle you. There's so much work that filters though this office, sometimes even I don't know what I'm up to from day to day. That little winery I mentioned. It's merely a sideline, and yet the way California land values have increased over the last decade, I could sell it at ten times the initial investment. But I like the winery and don't need the cash. Professor, even my corporations own corporations, and let's just say that DADT is a hobby. A deadly serious hobby. But to paraphrase the underworld, I have a lot of buffers between me and the front line. I'm too old anyway, not that I would ever have been good at the, oh, hands-on tasks. For that, we have people like Gulf Stream, who is one of the best. I am a manager and financier and strategizer. Strictly limp-wristed."

"But despite your apparent modesty and reclusiveness, a lot of people apparently admire you and follow your orders."

Little Boy smiled. "Because I sign the checks ... and I provide a very narrow path to the Founder. People must go through me for that."

Davenport somehow felt sure that Little Boy was less limp-wristed than he claimed. "The Founder?" he asked.

"Yes. An incredible man. Philosopher. Thinker. Visionary." Little Boy seemed reverent. "A manager of people and ideals. If I were religious, I would wonder about the divinity of our Founder. One thing I can tell you: if he asked, I would give him everything. My money and possessions—even that bottle of port. My life, too, and as you might already suspect, there is nothing I value quite as much as living."

Robert Davenport became slightly guarded but wasn't sure why. He had been treated like royalty since he'd met Gulf Stream at the airport. And, of course, they hadn't blindfolded him. Gulf Stream had simply lowered the cabin window shades during the two-hour flight, and Davenport, except for general observations of the hilly terrain when he emerged, had little idea where he was. The cool dry air and old-growth forests suggested the north central United States, perhaps southern Canada. They had driven through a small town to arrive at Little Boy's mountain retreat, which was well accented but not lavish enough to be featured on *Lives of the Rich and Famous.*

Still, there was something disquieting in Little Boy's conversation that felt like gentle double-speak—the grammar too good, the manner too diplomatic, the niceness too nice. Gulf Stream, on the other hand, seemed straightforward, uncensored, in-your-face DADT. Between the two, Davenport assumed that Little Boy was the more dangerous.

Considering Little Boy's last statement, Davenport said, "Yes, living is important." He hesitated, trying to dispel his uneasiness, and added, "Tell me, please. Exactly why am I here?"

"You already know," said Little Boy as if he had expected the question and considered it too obvious to answer. "DADT wants a Manifesto. You're the language specialist."

"I realize that. Recruit One and Gulf Stream told me as much. But let's level with one another. English professors are a dime a dozen, and writing for a semiliterate America doesn't require an Ivy League teacher. A community college sophomore could handle it."

"That might be true," said Little Boy, leaning back and folding his hands across his chest, "so tell me why you think you're here." He waited quietly for Davenport's ego to answer.

"Okay. I'll bite," said Davenport, reaching for the brandy and pouring himself another serving in the ornate aperitif glass. "I don't want to get too light-headed before dinner, but this is exceptional brandy. Imported?"

"Absolutely," said Little Boy. "You just poured thirty-five dollars into your glass." He understood that money, itself, could be an effective flattery.

"Good stuff," said Davenport, also leaning back and now beginning to relax despite his initial apprehensions. "All right, if I were in your position, considering what little I know about DADT, I would probably want a professor with some particularly desirable qualities."

Little Boy nodded without interrupting.

"First," said Davenport, "the organization is about to enter a so-called second phase. My knowledge is limited, but you basically want to transition from an underground, closeted organization, to an overt, aboveground force. You also plan to be...durable, not a bunch of flash-in-the-pan fanatics who burn down their own house to protest real estate prices and then have no place to sleep."

"Nicely put, Professor."

"That's why you waited until I had tenure before offering me a position."

Little Boy laughed. "Go on."

"Second, this new phase requires that you simultaneously communicate with Wheat-Plains Joe, who probably dropped out of school in the sixth grade, as well as the nation's pinstriped power brokers, including politicians and academicians. Not an easy task. Yet it would be pointless to draft a statement that's over the head of Middle America or beneath the people who make decisions. And further, you do not want DADT to come off looking like soft-shell eggheads instead of new-wave Black Panthers. You need *stylistic heat*."

Little Boy was beginning to understand why Padgett recommended Davenport so highly. The professor was exceptionally smart.

"Third, it doesn't hurt that I am a gay man, that I've been recently injured—or at least annoyed—by the system, that I am a preeminent member of a preeminent faculty, or that I can be *physical* when needed. And this professor works out pretty regularly and can hold his own in a barroom brawl even if he does his best to avoid one, which is also important to you. In fact, I would say that my wholesome inconspicuousness is a conspicuous virtue for DADT."

Little Boy nodded and murmured at suitable moments, which gave support for Davenport's continuing self-indulgence.

"Fourth, I did not flinch at the Massachusetts' testing grounds... Well, maybe I flinched a little, but we got the job done. My guess is that Padgett watched me pretty closely and confirmed I have a stomach for and have accepted the realities of DADT. But mostly, you know that I philosophically support the organizational mission, and while ethically opposed to violence, I understand that sometimes the end justifies the means. Short-range force to pursue long-range justice. Without that goal, DADT would be just another gang of common cutthroats."

"Perceptive," said Little Boy. "Very perceptive, indeed, but let's see if you can answer the final question."

"And what might that be?" asked the professor as though nothing could ever be beyond his analytical prowess.

"You pointed out that English professors are dimes to the dozen. What makes you so special? Why did Padgett recommend you as the academic gold standard?"

"That's easy," said Davenport, now holding his crystal glass against the light to inflict its rainbow sparkles around the room. "Because I'm very, very good at my job. I am an established writer with a distinct flare for language. I will turn your Manifesto into literature. People will notice and listen. We will broadcast our message with style and grace."

"Astonishing," said Little Boy.

"Thank you," said Professor Davenport, thinking that Little Boy seemed far too appreciative to be double-speak ominous.

Soon, a soft melodic and operatic chime penetrated the study.

"Aaahh," said Little Boy, "I think we may adjourn for dinner."

TWENTY-THREE

Ivory Towers

June 2007

The middle of June, Robert Davenport received a call from his hiking partner, Mary Anne Shephard.

"Hey, Rob," said Shephard. "Danny and I are looking at Rocky Mountain National Park this year. August 6th through the 12th. We figure to meet in Estes Park, hike for a week, then return to the real world. What do you think?"

Uncharacteristically, Davenport had completely forgotten about his annual affair with Daniel Bradford and Shephard. "Oh, Mary. Hey. Wow. You caught me off guard here. I've been so busy."

"Hell," she said. "You're busy. I'm busy. Danny's busy. Ditto, ellipsis, ditto. But our August debriefings are sacred. A little dirt and sweat puts everybody back together better than all the King's horses. I would disintegrate without these trips"

Davenport felt a little annoyed by the intrusion of his old friend. He was supposed to visit Little Boy at the end of July to discuss draft sections of the Manifesto. These week-long wilderness escapes suddenly seemed foolish to Davenport, like asking a Fortune 500 executive to stop and gather rosebuds. Then, almost simultaneously, he longed to see his old friends. Perhaps he could even hint about DADT... But no. His loyalty was steadfast.

"Look," said Davenport, "I'm really sorry, but I'll have to get back to you. I'm working on a, uhm, special project this summer."

"Well, what's the scoop? You got a book contract? Another university on the line? Come on. Share the wealth."

"No, nothing like that. It's kind of ... confidential."

"Robbie, old boy, have you gone Republican? Not working for the CIA or other white-male subversives?"

Davenport laughed, remembering their undergraduate socialist harangues and glory days of unabashed idealism. "Nothing so bad as that... What were those dates again?"

"Meet August 6. Depart 12th. If those dates are good, I'll book a hotel in Estes Park. And then someplace nice in Denver—five stars—for the-night-before-we-leave bash. Standard operating procedure."

"If you can find a real five-star in Denver, you're a miracle worker." Davenport was buoyed by the thought, but then regained his focus and his mood became grave. "I have to get back to you, Mare. Really might not be able to pull it off this summer. Sorry."

Shephard became concerned. "Rob? You're not ... you're not sick, are you? I mean, in ten years, my little hospital episode was our only summer-trip glitch. And come to think of it, you didn't respond to my last email. Are you okay? What's going on?"

"It's nothing like that. I'm fine. But really, something important came up. I just need to cross-check a few details..." Davenport glanced at his calendar and decided to take the easy way out. "Let's assume the dates are good. Go ahead. Make the reservations. I'll try to mesh things on my end. Don't worry."

"That's better. For a minute I thought the earth was off center. Daniel and I need these summers. So do you, dear friend."

Davenport let out a breath. "You're probably right. Yes, let's make it work." He suddenly felt better. Much better.

"Oh, by the way," said Shephard. "I'm moving to Berkeley. I had three job offers. But I wanted to be near San Francisco, and Berkeley is a lot closer than Irvine or Cambridge. Though Cambridge offered the best money and Irvine the best weather."

Davenport felt a twinge of unfamiliar jealousy. He had predicted that Mary Anne would have multiple offers from top schools, yet Davenport himself had received only one, where he had struggled with tenure besides. "That's great," he said. "Although it would be nice to have you in the Northeast." Davenport meant this, which almost surprised him.

"Well, that's why we must have *August!* Every August. It's the only real possibility to be together again, Robert. We were once closer than the three musketeers, and on those trips we still are. Professionally, we have to go where the work is, and if we're lucky, it's a place we like. And I feel lucky. It's hard to believe this awkward and freckled-faced little girl somehow ended on top of the world at Berkeley. I want you to help me celebrate this August!"

"Okay, okay. I need the trip. And perhaps I've been feeling lonelier than usual." Davenport paused. "Which is surprising because I'm busier than ever."

"Say no more," said Shephard. "I'll book the hotels and email the confirmation so you can arrange your flights. Daniel is already sketching the trail routes. That's his diversion. Plan to hike in and around the park, and expect a hundred miles for the week. So if you've gone soft over the school year, better start getting in shape. Danny Boy is fierce on the dirt, and he ran two off-road marathons last year. We'll have trouble keeping up."

"Based on past experience," said Davenport, "I'd say we'll have more trouble keeping up with you."

Shephard laughed. "I do appreciate hiking you boys into the ground."

"Do your best," said Davenport, imagining the wind and sun and open sky and remembering the deep human connections with his friends. "Do your best."

"You can count on it," said Mary Anne.

Davenport smiled as he hung up the phone. He loved these trips with Daniel and Mary Anne. He loved his friends, too. Sure, he had business with DADT, but maybe Little Boy was right. Maybe it was possible to combine an elite academic life and a little bloodletting without compromising one for the other. And as a tenured professor, Davenport could maintain his university cover while writing a Manifesto worthy of the Ivy League. He would simply meld his professional identities from two distinct worlds—both of which were lucky to have him.

***

November 2007

Gulf Stream met Little Boy at a Manhattan Starbucks. They both happened to be in New York and decided to use the opportunity for a face-to-face. It would not be a long conference.

"What's the latest with Shakespeare?" asked Gulf Stream.

"He's ours," said Little Boy, who had checked in on Davenport's Manifesto progress earlier that week. "Working earnestly on our Manifesto."

Gulf Stream grinned. Little Boy saluted Gulf Stream with a high-held café latte, and they laughed together. Gulf Stream shook his head. "Tash won't be happy. Can't say that I blame her."

"I suppose not," said Little Boy. "A sacrifice for the good of the outfit. Anyway, makes no difference what we or Padgett think. That's how the Founder wants it, and that's the way it's gonna be."

"I know. I even agree, but part of me hates to see anybody played for a fool."

"Maybe. Though don't forget, others have suffered worse. And without some of *their* sacrifices, gay middle-class professors wouldn't be teaching so securely in their ivory towers. The spirit of Stonewall holds those towers together. Ours, too, I suppose," said Little Boy. He took a sip of coffee and then gestured toward the limousine outside. "After we finish, can my chauffeur drop you somewhere?"

"Naw. I know Manhattan like the back of my hand. Find my way blindfolded, and I kind of like grubbing around the neighborhood again. Makes me feel young and sexy. Besides, Pearl Harbor's likely to be my finish. I'd better enjoy my town as much as possible beforehand."

"You'll come out intact if I have anything to say about it. Some of the, uh, events are still being hammered out, but the Founder doesn't go in for kamikazes. You should still be standing when it's over."

"Either way is fine by me, but I'm going all the way. My blood, their blood, whatever it takes. My life's irrelevant as long as we make it hurt. Cut 'em deep."

"Don't worry," said Little Boy. "I can't reveal all the details—you know why." Little Boy clenched his fist in admiration. "But it's beyond imagination. We're slicing to the bone. I tell you, man. The Founder is a military genius! A tiny, inconspicuous giant who will rock the world. They will think the plagues of Egypt have returned."

"When?"

Little Boy smiled. "April 15. Five months."

Gulf Stream nodded. "Hmmmm. Will everything be ready?"

"Yes."

"Why April 15th?" asked Gulf Stream.

"Who knows what's in his mind. He doesn't think like we do. But for my money, it's a good day. We paid our taxes like obedient citizens, yet public services and support were held back or even turned against us. Police power crushed our bodies. Psychiatrists and social workers and tainted research corrupted our spirits. We were expected to finance the war against us, year after year, and then apologize for existing." Little Boy looked across the table and sighed. "Sorry. Don't mean to preach. Anyway, the country will be focused on another tax day. But this one won't be remembered for the color of money."

"And Dirty Mary?"

"She's beautiful," said Little Boy, leaning back. "And there are several cousins to go along with her, and ... like I said, the Founder is a genius. A guerilla in the mist. The bastards won't even see the hand that kills them, by the thousands, great and small. In five months, the Founder is going to shove *don't ask don't tell* down the gullet of the beast. I hope they choke on every syllable."

Gulf Stream sighed. "It won't be enough. Bigotry takes a lot of convincing to change. So if I don't make it, keep the pressure on. Don't let 'em rest, and don't stop at 'tolerance.' God, I hate that word. We go all the way to full integration."

"Pearl should be enough. In the past ten years, we've pulled down a billion dollars of purchasing power. And that's chump change compared to the devotion of some of our converts. That's our real strength."

"One thing," said Gulf Stream.

"What?"

"Until now, innocents have been spared. We've gone after the deserving, which never bothered me. In fact, I enjoyed it. But Phase Two is likely to be... philosophically sloppy. I worry it might make some of our number turn tail."

"Our true believers will understand it as necessary. Sacrificial lambs in the name of justice ... just like our professor." Little Boy glanced at his watch and swigged the last coffee. "Sure I can't drop you somewhere?"

"Yeah. Don't worry," said Gulf Stream. "I'll get reacquainted with the city I love before our new Gorgons are unleashed. Even Perseus' shield won't help them."

"Amen to that," said Little Boy. "Science trumps mythology every time."

"Good financing doesn't hurt either."

TWENTY-FOUR

This and That

November 2007

"They're up to something," said Chief Margaret Ricketts.

"I know," said Detective Emmanuel Cerrillo.

"And our infamous Gulf Stream has dropped off the face of the earth."

"Immediately after he had that guy nailed to the cross and pissed in my face with that damned refrigerator note."

Even after six months, Cerrillo was still burning over the Massachusetts incident. Ricketts wondered if he were getting too emotional. "Listen," she said, "I want you to take a few days of R&R. You need it. That radio transcript has led nowhere. Intelligence has scanned for signs of a suspicious professor, but there are hundreds of thousands of college teachers in this country, as well as intellectuals and pseudo-intellectuals who call themselves 'professor' just for the fun of it. And it's some kind of DADT code anyway. Recruit One, whoever she is, started to say the guy's name, something like D-a-v-e-n. Then she caught herself and stopped. So they've tried search combinations of 'Daven' and 'professor,' but the smallest number of hits was over 40K. Both of these characters are children of the void. I mean, who could have thought 'daven' could turn out to be a real word and a fairly common name. But never mind. You and Waller have busted ass all around the country. Take a few days off. Let research do its job. Then we'll put you back to work."

"That's probably best," said Cerrillo, who had become discouraged. "Me and Waller have found nothing since Massachusetts." But then Cerrillo shook his head. "No! We can't afford to stop. Their 'Pearl Harbor' will be big, whatever it is. I won't sit on my thumbs and wait for Gulf Stream to make his move. The transmission said eleven months, and that was six months ago. It's gonna happen around March or April. What I don't understand is how a bunch of fruit flies can outsmart the FBI, Secret Service, and whoever else Judd has working on this case. Why can't our boys punch the numbers on this?"

"DADT is not smarter than us," said Ricketts. "We just haven't made the right connection. Don't forget. They know who we are. We don't know them. And it's only recently that we even discovered DADT existed. And I tell you, Manny. Every crook screws up eventually. Gets cocky or careless. Looks left when he should have looked right. Takes a piss when he should have held back. Becomes visible. Either that or he digs a hole and hides forever, which is almost as good." Ricketts did not seem convinced by her own words. "We'll find them, and then we'll send Gulf Stream to the dungeons of Alcatraz and throw away the key."

Cerrillo took a deep breath, gaining strength. "Listen, boss. Forget R&R. I don't want to find our gang like they found Timothy McVeigh—after the deed. That won't bring back the dead. Gulfy's had enough laughs. So I'm gonna link up with Waller in San Francisco. That's where we found Craspen, and that's where we'll pick up the trail again."

Rickets waited a moment and said, "I can't really think of anything better. Hey? What happened to that other agent, Jim Ellington, in all this?"

"Oh, he's still on the case, and we talked two days ago. Judd has him double reversing Vegas to Boston. Every time he sketches a new psychological profile, Judd sends him off to investigate. If you ask me, that angle is a waste of time. Nobody has a profile for Gulf Stream. He's too psycho for any chart." Cerrillo grunted. "That bastard may be smart, but we'll get him with old-fashioned police tactics. Knocking on doors, or kicking them down if necessary, and asking blunt questions. Ellington can write his psychological profile when I drag Gulfy's ass to the interrogation room wrapped in a straightjacket."

"I still think a few days' R&R might help you sort through this stuff, come up with new ideas."

"Oh, don't worry, Chief," said Cerrillo. "I'll sit down for meals, and Josie knows the City backwards and forwards and sideways. Too bad she's gay. I could get to like her... Oh, hell, I do like her, and now I'm talking crazy..."

"Not crazy," said Ricketts. "A cop's life can get lonely at times, and their closest friends are often other cops."

Cerrillo nodded and then shook his head again. "There's one thing that's really got me worried about DADT."

"What's that?"

"Well, how many murders are they responsible for? Ball park?"

Ricketts appeared to be thinking. "Confirmed? Maybe fifteen. My guess is that it's more, of course. A lot of their handiwork probably wasn't reported as such. And they were in business long before you and Waller began to smell the stench." Ricketts leaned forward. "And I hate to say this, but I suspect the FBI is holding back information. I doubt that we've received all they have."

"I'm sure of it," said Cerrillo. "Some of those SOB's are almost as neurotic as Gulf Stream. They'd allow a few more murders rather than lose the glory of catching this guy ahead of us." Cerrillo looked across the desk. "That's why we can't stop. That's why me and Waller need to pick up the Frisco trail, ground zero. Gulf Stream's not going to walk to a police station and surrender. We'll have to drag him out of the sewer."

"You got my vote."

"But the point I was getting at, the weird part," said Cerrillo, "with all DADT's previous handiwork, how did they manage to turn the spigot off so quickly? As far as we can tell, nobody has so much as stepped on a cockroach since Gulfy said they were going dormant."

"That's impressive, all right," said Ricketts. "Even after the Japanese surrendered in World War II, it took time to get the word out. And some soldiers were still hiding and fighting years later, even after they knew the war was over. You'd think that DADT would have at least one patriot who would fail to get the memo or refuse to obey it."

"And if they have that kind of organizational control, that kind of obedience, it's not just impressive. It's dangerous and probably means that DADT cells are so busy working on the next project that nobody has time to go rogue."

Margaret Ricketts nodded but said nothing.

"Pearl Harbor could be worse than we think," said Cerrillo, "especially if Judd is right about a radioactive or biological Dirty Mary. The clock is ticking, boss. Nobody should rest."

Ricketts stared into space for a few seconds and said, "If you're worried, I'm worried. Perhaps you and Waller should backtrack. I'll send word to the Bureau that you're headed back to San Francisco."

Cerrillo smiled. "I thought we worked for them."

"So do they."

"Thanks, Chief. It's great when I agree with your recommendations."

"Oh, hell," said Ricketts. "You and Waller been running this case for months."

"Naw," said Cerrillo. "We make suggestions and you take them seriously. That's all."

Ricketts smiled. "Just remember your promise. Lace up Mr. Gulf Stream in a nice warm straightjacket."

"So tight he won't be able to breathe."

***

March 2008

Officer Josie Waller and Detective Emmanuel Cerrillo were back in San Francisco for the fourth time in as many months. Cerrillo received a cheap monthly room rate from Joe at the Nob Hill Motel each time, though he sometimes slept at Waller's apartment, especially when they worked late, piecing together leads that led nowhere. And because Cerrillo might be in the City for days or weeks, depending on what they or Judd or anybody else dug up, he'd opted for a private suite at Nob Hill. Why not? The FBI was paying.

Cerrillo had already wasted the morning on another dead end and was trying to take a catnap in his hotel room when the phone rang. It was Waller, and she said, "I'll be there in five minutes!"

"Huh?" asked Cerrillo. He had been almost asleep

"We're going to the zoo!" said Waller.

"To hell with that," said Cerrillo. "We've already been there. A big zero! Go by yourself, Josie. If someone taught the baboons to deal cards, let me know. Otherwise, I need some sleep."

"They found a body."

Cerrillo bolted upright. "I'm listening."

"Early this morning. Inside the cobra exhibit."

"An employee?"

"No. The staff doesn't recognize him. Don't know how he got in. Speculation about suicide, but if you ask me, this seems a little too cozy with Mrs. School Board."

"Could be suicide," said Cerrillo, fighting drowsiness. "People go crazy. Play with snakes and guns and other toys."

"Well..." said Waller, stretching the punch line.

"Come on, Josie. Spit it out."

"Oh, it's probably not important ... but they found several DADT business cards in the guy's wallet."

Cerrillo stood up. "Get over here!"

"I'm on the way. Eight blocks."

"Where's the body?"

"On ice, pal. At the zoo. The crew pulled the guy out and tried CPR before calling police. They thought he was one of their own and hoped he might be alive."

"Anything else?"

"Nothing unusual," said Waller. "I mean, he wasn't wearing black lace panties under his street clothes."

Cerrillo laughed. "Like I give a shit."

"Never know. Men sometimes get off on that stuff. Anyway, they looked through the guy's wallet. Typical identification, except for the infamous cards, so the District office called us."

"It's about time," said Cerrillo.

"Another thing. Employees found a plastic container with a stretched rubber lid. The kind for milking snakes. The guy must have been a professional handler, and he had already juiced a cobra."

"Yeah? If he was a pro, how come he's dead?"

"Near as they can figure, the victim didn't know there were two snakes in the pit. The victim had the business end of one, and the other got him. Bitten at least three times, so it looks like the snake he was milking also jumped in on the action."

"Jesus."

"The curator said he died within minutes. Can't live long with venom from two healthy adults. The surveillance video isn't very good; but get this, he didn't harm the cobras after the attack and didn't even try to get out of the pit. Just sat down and died. Probably one of those extreme animal lovers. Knew he was dead, got comfortable, and waited..." Waller took a breath. "I tell you one thing. If a cobra ever sinks its fangs into me, I'm gonna bite him back before I sign off."

Cerrillo laughed. "Well, it's bad news for the victim, but good news for us. This is the first real meat we've had in months."

"Manny?" asked Waller, turning cold.

"Yeah?"

"Who do you think the venom was for? I mean, if the guy had got out with it?"

"Probably some homophobe Bible thumper whose life was spared by this accident."

"A sympathetic preacher might call it divine intervention."

"That's okay with me, but I'm recommending those snakes for a medal."

Waller laughed nervously, hesitated, and then turned serious. "Hey, partner. Is it ... possible this guy was planning to come after us?"

The thought had not occurred to Cerrillo, but he dismissed the prospect. "I'm pretty sure Gulf Stream has some kind of sicko attachment to you and me—and he seems to want us around for their D-Day. Don't know why, but I plan to ask him about it someday. Besides,

DADT wouldn't hit us with a reptile sideshow. More likely a direct attack. They know we're onto them, and we can shoot back. But mostly, as bizarre as it sounds, I think Gulfy likes us ... and he's looking for something."

"Studying psychological profiles, are we?"

"No. Just a gut feeling."

"Same thing," said Waller, "and I hope you're right since I don't care to be on DADT's most-wanted list. But that cobra juice was being squeezed for somebody. And, as you pointed out, Gulf Stream knows we're after him... Wonder if he's running scared."

"Not the Ice Man. He doesn't care whether he lives or dies, and you got to care to be afraid. That's why everybody's an atheist in fox holes. They want to live."

"If true, that makes Gulfy even more dangerous."

"Not as dangerous as I am," said Cerrillo, "especially if he hurts my partner."

"Ditto," said Waller.

"Okay. Let's hit the zoo. If we're lucky, one dead fruitcake will lead us to the nuts and chews that built him. Could be our snake charmer didn't get the memo about DADT's hiatus." Cerrillo was silent for a couple seconds. "I just thought of something else, Josie."

"What?"

"They might not be aware that one of their troops is missing. If we play this right, Gulf Stream might be looking the other way when we knock on his door."

"Should we inform the FBI about our dead guy?" asked Waller.

"Hell, no! They'll find out soon enough, and we'll give them what they've been giving us: zip, nada, zilch, and an overall hard time. Let 'em find bodies on their own dime. Plus, there's a reason the precinct called you and not them."

"Right," said Waller. "But if we hook something big with teeth, we contact Ellington. He's a pain in the ass but legitimately smart. And besides, when properly motivated, our young protégé can pinch information and travel vouchers out of Judd."

"You going soft on Ellington?"

"Naw, he's like a kid brother. They're more responsive when you kick them around a little. Makes 'em feel special."

"You *have* gone soft. Next thing you'll be wanting to adopt him." Cerrillo simultaneously heard a car horn outside the hotel and through the phone. He looked through the window. Waller was waiting for him in the parking lot. She reached through her driver's side window and gestured with her unpolished longest finger.

"You should have been downstairs waiting for me," said Waller.

"Let me get my pants on first."

TWENTY-FIVE

Conference Call

March 2008

Soon after the zoo, Cerrillo and Waller set up a four-way telephone conference with Special Agent Samuel Judd in Las Vegas and Pomona Police Chief Margaret Ricketts. Cerrillo and Waller had hoped to keep the new information to themselves, but they needed Judd's assistance for a down-and-dirty search warrant to investigate where the victim worked, lived, bought groceries, went for takeout; to exert pressure on his friends, relatives, neighbors, lovers, or drinking buddies; to rummage through his house, car, office, and trash; and they wanted to do it before Gulf Stream took a breath. Cerrillo and Waller needed an all-purpose federal flashcard that granted broad discretionary power. So they called Judd.

After Cerrillo explained about the cobra victim and DADT cards, Judd said, "I'll have a warrant signed, scanned, and emailed to the Richmond District within the hour. An investigational skeleton key."

"Want the email address or a fax number?" asked Waller.

"Don't make me laugh," said Judd. "We have an obscene database, and I'll send this directly to your divisional chief. Ellington will catch the next plane to SF."

Cerrillo was cautious. "This warrant? We'll be able to, uh, investigate on the fly? We don't know exactly what we're looking for."

"Believe me," said Judd, "when I finish the parameters, you could interrogate a preschooler and log the milk and cookies into evidence."

"Nice and legal?" asked Cerrillo.

"Legal?" said Judd. "Of course it's legal! Probably not Constitutional, but by the time an appellate judge notices, you'll have the information. That's important, Detective, so don't bother me with cautionary details. I'll get the warrant. Use it before some Ninth Circuit do-gooder remembers the Bill of Rights. And if a half-baked public defender shakes his head, hit 'em with choice phrases about *Homeland Security*. That's more effective than most search warrants these days because nobody cares about breaking down doors if terrorists might be on the other side. So get the job done."

"I understand," said Cerrillo. "Oh, one more thing."

"I'll get the warrant! Don't worry!"

"No, this is different," said Cerrillo. "I'm thinking we should keep this quiet, not spread information around the FBI, or even our departments. If we're going to catch Gulf Stream with his pants down, the fewer people involved, the better."

"Agreed," said Ricketts, who had been quiet but attentive during the conversation.

"Me too," said Judd. "You forget that I don't work for the Bureau, and I'm more interested in results than bruised egos."

"We didn't forget," said Waller, "but, sir, we really don't know who you work for."

Judd laughed. "Nobody does, including me! You'll have a blanket warrant. Expect Ellington by day's end. Put him to work as you think best—psychological profiling, burger run, or studying up on snake charmers—just find DADT."

Everyone was silent for several seconds.

"Anything else?" asked Judd.

"No," said Waller

"Not me," said Cerrillo.

"One item," said Chief Ricketts. "If you guys locate Gulf Stream, don't get stupid. Call for backup. We have Special Forces for that kind of work. They shoot straight and don't ask questions. And while we may not be sure who Judd works for, keep in mind, Emmanuel, *you* work for Pomona PD. I didn't spend all these years turning you into a cop for nothing. I want you back in one piece."

"I'm hoping for that myself," said Cerrillo.

"You track 'em down, and we'll wipe 'em off the planet," said Judd. "When it comes to DADT, you won't be invoking *Homeland Security* in vain."

Immediately after the conference, they all sprang into action. Cerrillo and Waller drove to the Richmond Divisional office to pick up the warrant. Judd called Agent Ellington and ordered him to San Francisco. Margaret Ricketts sent an email to Professor Alfred McDaniels.

***

Detective Cerrillo and Officer Waller searched the dead man's Sausalito home. "Get a load of this place," said Waller. "DADT must pay pretty good."

"Maybe they only recruit rich folks," said Cerrillo. "I've never seen so much gold leaf and marble."

"Earns more than cops, that's for sure. What did this guy do aside from loitering in cobra pits?"

"No idea," said Cerrillo. "Judd's running a background check but nothing so far. No record."

"Most people don't have criminal records."

"Not criminal record, *no* record. As far as Judd can tell, Adam Smith doesn't exist. Could be a patron saint out of Rome or head of a drug cartel in Mexico. I've never seen anyone with a blank slate before. Even my grandmother got a parking ticket or occasionally put too many chocolate chips in the Toll House cookies. It's like this guy hasn't left the house since he was born, except that he was never born."

"Another pseudonym," said Waller, fumbling through a stack of papers on an entryway desk. "Maybe he liked *The Wealth of Nations.*"

"Aren't we literary, today," said Cerrillo. "Sounds like you paid too much attention in freshman English."

"It was sophomore economics, but I think Adam Smith—the author—should be studied by everyone. Might give some people a reality check, especially politicians who think taxpayers grow on trees."

"You're talking weird, Josie. I like it better when you're a cop and not a professor wannabe."

"Oh, I'm a cop, but my life ain't over. Could be I'll turn in the badge someday and go back to college. Write articles about incompetent Pomona detectives."

"Give up your badge? That's just stupid. I've worked with you for a while now. If you ain't about busting bad guys, you ain't about nothing. And besides, Professor Waller, what kind of pervert writes about 'incontinent' detectives," said Cerrillo with a grin.

"Less talking and more looking," said Waller. "You found anything?"

"No. Smith has a California driver's license that California doesn't know about, and a Social Security number that was issued to a Nebraskan auto mechanic who died twenty years ago. He has a house that's paid for, but apparently he doesn't work for a living, file tax returns, or have any bank accounts. I'd say he gets an A+ in creative financing."

"The more I learn about DADT, the more confusing it is. Who are these damned people?"

"Bless me if I know, *Mija*." Cerrillo shook his head. "Now I'm starting to talk like my grandmother. Of course, with her intuitive sense, she could probably figure out DADT better than me. Maybe our Mr. Smith comes from Area 51?"

"Makes as much sense as anything," said Waller, still rummaging through papers in the living room desk. "But even if DADT is a band of little green men from Planet Xenophobia, they are killing folks in the City. And I aim to drag their scaly, slime-green asses down to the station in handcuffs. In addition to murder, I'll charge them with illegal immigration."

Cerrillo laughed. "Like I said, busting bad guys... You'll be in uniform after they commit you to an old ladies home. Probably wear your badge to bed. Hey! Look at this. An autographed copy of *Atlas Shrugged*. I was supposed to read this in college but didn't."

"Typical student," said Waller. "You must do well in Pomona. The illiteracy capitol of the world. Rand was a certified economic genius but too wordy when it came to her fiction..."

Cerrillo's cell phone rang. It was Agent Jim Ellington. "Manny?" he asked. "That you?"

"Yeah," said Cerrillo. "What's up?"

"Judd tracked down a little about Smith, alias the Invisible Man."

"And?"

Ellington laughed over the phone. "Well, you'll be very pleased to know that Mister Adam Smith is a retired Russian expatriate now living on a seventy-acre ranch in Australia just outside Sydney. Aside from raising horses, he's an independent computer consultant and does volunteer work at the local youth club helping underprivileged kids."

"Is that right," said Cerrillo. "And why is he on a slab in San Francisco?"

"Hey!" interrupted Waller. "What's going on?"

Cerrillo flashed his palm at Waller. He asked Ellington, "Anything else?"

"Nothing in the U.S. databases. Judd emailed the guy's finger prints to a Russian friend. Used to be KGB. This guy and Judd have some kind of history."

"Some boss you got there," said Cerrillo. "I wouldn't turn my back on him."

"Don't worry," said Ellington. "Judd's definitely on our team, but he'll look anywhere for information. Smith doesn't exist in our domestic files, and even the Russians have very little. Some records were lost in the, uh, transitional government. You know, when the USSR gave up on itself. Files purged to protect the guilty. Anyway, Smith's real name is Brache Luchinko. Czechoslovakian. We don't know why he's here or how he got into the country. Hell, the CIA didn't know that he was in the country. Judd has requested the Soviet files—I mean Russian—and will relay any information, but Luchinko probably isn't the guy's real name either. They think he was in the Czech or Soviet secret service, so there's no telling how many identity flips are involved. If Smith were alive, even he might not know who he really is."

Cerrillo motioned again for Waller to be patient because she wasn't. He told Ellington, "I don't care if the guy used to be Elvis. Smith died here in a cobra pit and is linked with DADT. I want to know how he ended up in California. By the way, where are you?"

"At the Richmond Station," said Ellington. "Be sure to thank Josie for the Snickers bar and potato chips in her desk. I was hungry. Anyway, I just came from the morgue, and you might thank me. I am the genius who sent Smith's prints to Judd to begin with."

"Good move. But don't break an arm patting yourself on the back."

"Should I meet you at the victim's house?"

"No, no," said Cerrillo. "Stay put and wait for Judd's report. Eat whatever you want in Josie's desk. We're checking the house, though if half of what you say is true, we won't find anything beyond lessons in forgery. Smith ever actually in Australia?"

"I'm betting yes," said Ellington. "Likely he came to the US through Sydney. Probably before border security tightened after 9/11. We don't think he could have come in undetected from Eastern Europe. By the time Judd is finished, there are going to be some red faces at the CIA. Somebody screwed up."

"They were probably too busy spying on Americans to worry about ex-Soviets sneaking into the country. Any ideas how Smith fell in with DADT?"

"None."

"I thought you were a genius," said Cerrillo.

"An honest genius. I don't pretend to know what I don't know."

"Anyway, hold tight and wait for Judd's report. When we finish here, let's meet back at the station. I assume Judd has contacted the Aussies."

"Are you kidding? He'll have four continents working double shifts even if he has to bribe three of them. Some of Judd's contacts are very, uh, *un*official."

"Of course. Keep us posted," said Cerrillo.

"Will do," said Ellington. "Later."

When it was clear that Cerrillo was off the phone, Waller, exasperated, asked, "Ellington?"

"Yes."

She rolled her hands over and over each other as though she were expecting to learn the meaning of life. "Tell me everything!"

"What will you give me?"

"A bullet in each knee if you don't." Waller fingered the butt of her gun.

"Don't smile when you threaten someone, Josie. Gives you away."

"Just tell me why Ellington called before my brain explodes."

"Well, our homeboy at the morgue isn't from Sausalito."

"Duh," said Waller.

"And Smith isn't his real name. It's ... shit!" said Cerrillo, shaking his head. "I forgot the name."

"I should really shoot you."

"Smith's some kind of Russian Czechoslovakian spy who lived in Australia and got through border security, according to Judd's underworld cronies. More is on the way, but for now, we keep searching the house. You can get an update at the station, but Smith's important only if he can lead us to Gulf Stream... By the way, Ellington said thanks for the Snickers and chips."

"Fine," said Waller, casually. "I've got enough ammo for him, too. I'm gonna check Smith's bedroom; you hit the kitchen. And for the record, your summary of Ellington's telephone report is wholly inadequate! Stinks!"

"Okay, so I'm a rotten secretary." Cerrillo held up both hands and shrugged. "I can live with that. But before we jostle the crime scene, did the photographers get enough shots?"

"Yes, according to them."

"Good, but try to keep things intact just in case. We still don't know what we're looking for."

"You think I'm a rookie?" said Waller.

"No," said Cerrillo. "But just be careful. I want Gulf Stream, Josie. Pay attention to details ... and try to think like a Bates-motel-psycho-lunatic."

Waller laughed. "A couple margaritas might help. Loosen the neurons." She turned down the hallway.

Both Cerrillo and Waller worked in silence for several minutes. Cerrillo in the kitchen; Waller in the master bedroom. Soon, Cerrillo thought he heard a soft crash and rolling jellybeans.

"Aaaahhh!" shouted Waller.

Cerrillo pulled his gun, his heart in his throat, and peered cautiously down the hallway. He called out. "Josie, are you okay?"

Silence.

"Josie! Talk to me, partner!"

"Yeah, yeah. I'm fine. Just very stupid. I oughta shoot my own knees!"

Cerrillo slid his gun back into the leather and moved down the hallway.

"Damn!" said Waller.

Cerrillo peeked around the corner into the bedroom. Waller was repositioning a small card table. Then she began to pick up the letters from a Scrabble game that had been spilled across the ceramic floor.

"Sorry, Manny," said Waller. "I backed into the table. What a mess."

"It's just a Scrabble set," said Cerrillo.

"I know. Probably not important, but it's the principle. I trashed a crime scene."

"Is there any indication that someone else lived with Smith?" asked Cerrillo.

Waller rattled off what she'd gathered from the precinct. "Lived alone. One car. Neighbors never saw anyone but Smith, and rarely saw him. Shades were always down. The guy seemed nice enough but didn't have visitors."

"Do you suppose he was playing Scrabble with himself?"

Waller hesitated. "You said we're looking for a lunatic."

"Yeah, but do you play Scrabble alone?"

"No. I don't even like playing with others. I'm no good at it. My eleven-year-old cousin can beat me and do her homework at the same time."

Cerrillo shook his head. "Do you know anybody who Scrabbles solo?"

"Nope. Chess, maybe, or Scrabble on the computer. But the board game? Suppose it's possible. Sounds boring to me."

"Me, too," said Cerrillo. "I'm guessing crosswords would be better. Besides, our Russian-Czech-Aussie-DADT secret agent doesn't strike me as the spelling bee type... Listen, Josie. We've been here three hours and haven't found a thing. Let's go to the station. By the time we arrive, Ellington might have the Russian files, and I want to see the photos. If we're lucky, someone got a shot of the Scrabble board."

"You mean before I knocked it over."

"Yes."

"And if not?"

"Another set of knees for you," said Cerrillo. "But police photographers are fairly reliable, and I'd like to know what a foreign intelligence snake charmer Scrabbles when no one is watching."

Waller scooped up the remaining letter tiles and put them on the table. "I can tell you one thing already," said Waller.

"What's that?"

Waller held up two Zs and two Qs. "Smith cheats," she said.

TWENTY-SIX

Manifesto Blues

November 2007

Robert Davenport had been back in the classroom for almost three months, teaching freshman composition and an upper-division literature course. He went to campus three days a week, held office hours, met with students as needed, and from all outward appearances, functioned as an engaged tenured Assistant Professor. The Humanities Dean assured Davenport that he would almost certainly receive promotion to Associate Professor the following year—that the previous decision was simply a gentle reminder to focus on research and writing over teaching—so he should not feel slighted by the board's first ruling.

The dean said directly, "Write it off to the ups and downs of academic politics and don't take it personally. Anyone can be the victim of a team error, but it's the final score that matters. Tenure is the academic standard at this institution, and you won. And while there are no guarantees regarding promotion, we have great confidence in your scholarly potential..."

Outwardly, Davenport appeared comforted. He smiled and nodded and thanked the dean for good advice. Inwardly, Davenport was inconsolable. Gentle reminder! Don't take it personally! I'll show them potential! Still, he smiled on command with colleagues.

Secretly, Davenport wished half of the English Department were on a DADT hit list without regard to race, gender, or sexual orientation. And he focused on his twin meetings with Little Boy about the Manifesto, which Davenport resolved should be more than a statement of purpose. He worked feverishly on the manuscript at home. He envisioned literary comparisons with the Ten Commandments, the Magna Carta, the Declaration of Independence—the undercarriage of which, for Davenport, was identical to that of his Manifesto. Freedom. Truth. Equality. This would be his masterpiece, his best scholarly work. He hoped the dean would someday choke on every word and tremble at every resolution.

Davenport had also traveled to Rocky Mountain National Park during the first week of August to hike with his friends, which had been a good experience. Nonetheless, halfway into the trip, Davenport suspected that something significant had changed in his relationship with Mary Anne Shephard and Daniel Bradford. He felt it. So did Shephard and Bradford, though for different reasons. If someone had asked Davenport about the change, he might have answered, "Oh, I've probably outgrown them and moved on to other things. It happens."

But Shephard and Bradford wondered, "What's wrong with Robert? Maybe he's sick or on drugs? The tenure year can be hard on people, especially with his situation, but something is off." They prodded Davenport with gentle and concerned questions on the hikes, around the evening campfire, or during their last night's wine-infused extravaganza. But Davenport delivered evasive placebos. "Never felt better. Very busy with new projects, but I'm great."

Shephard and Bradford wondered what "new projects" could occupy their friend so completely, and they believed he had suffered a mild emotional breakdown due to stress. After the hiking trip, Mary Anne sent Davenport a delicately worded email urging him to consider counseling or to contact her if he wanted to talk. Davenport deleted the message without response.

He could easily have ignored all opposition to his alter ego except for a strange package from Tanish Padgett. It shook him temporarily from the fictional world of self-exultation. Unfortunately, it did not shake him hard enough to accept Mary Anne's counsel. And, more unfortunately, if Shakespeare had gone to the police at this stage, he almost certainly would have been contacted by Detective Cerrillo and Officer Waller, who might have gotten him off with a few years in prison.

But instead, when Davenport came home from the university on Thursday afternoon toward the end of November with a ridiculous mound of student papers, there on his doorstep was a nine-by-twelve envelope from Padgett. "Thank god," he thought. "Something more interesting than school work."

Davenport poured a glass of wine, relaxed in his living room recliner, and opened the package. His excitement turned to vinegar. The envelope contained a finished copy of the Manifesto of Purpose, ninety-six pages, dated almost one year before Davenport's initial meeting with Little Boy. A note from Padgett was attached:

Robert: I stumbled onto this by accident. There is a lot I don't understand, but didn't you meet with LB during the summer about writing the Manifesto? Aren't you working on it? Gulf Stream seemed upset when I asked him about this document. Let's talk. And please don't speak with anybody until we meet. For the first time in my life, I no longer trust DADT.

***

December 2007

Two weeks later, during the university's reading period, Robert Davenport and Tanish Padget met at a tavern in East Greenwich, Rhode Island. They were cautious.

"What are you going to do?" asked Padgett.

"Find out what this means," said Davenport, pointing toward the Manifesto on the table between them.

"It might be a draft. Maybe they want something better."

Davenport said nothing.

"Maybe," she added, "but it doesn't read like a draft."

"No, it doesn't," said Davenport. "The thing even has a table of contents with page references. It's a final copy ... and besides, you said that Gulf Stream acted strange when you questioned him."

Padgett nodded. "Yeah. He was evasive, and that's not his style with me." She paused, sipped the iced bourbon, and shook her head. "But why ask you to work on a Manifesto that's already finished?"

"I don't know, but I'm gonna find out. I've busted my ass over this project. Little Boy waxed poetically about purpose, long term goals, how the piece should be arranged, and basic content. Said I was the expert writer, and now it appears to be some kind of joke." Davenport looked at the table. "But I am not laughing, and neither will Gulf Stream and Little Boy if they're screwing with me."

"There's got to be an explanation. We're missing something. Whatever one might say about DADT, they don't waste time. Little Boy and Gulf Stream are businessmen, damned good ones, too. From what I hear, they could probably account for half the New England GDP by themselves, and they don't play games or beat around the bush."

"Possibly," said Davenport, switching gears in his head, pointing at the table, and glancing at Padgett. "What do you think of that Manifesto?"

"I don't understand."

"Is it any good? Does it need re-writing?"

Padgett sighed. "No. Says what needs to be said. It's … near perfect."

"That's what I thought, too," said Davenport. "Clear. Straightforward. Sophisticated yet unpretentious. A high school freshman could follow along. And, frankly, it's better than the one I'm working on … so far. Mine was just taking shape." Davenport couldn't bring himself to say it was better than he could write even though that was how he felt. "By the way, how did you find the copy?"

"At the bar in Providence where Solomon works."

"That dump? You're kidding."

"Solomon told me that it had been left for him at home several months ago. Someone came later to find out what he thought about it, ask a few questions."

"What did he say?"

Padgett laughed. "Solomon read it twenty times. Carries it around with him. That's why it was at the bar. He doesn't read well, you know, but he has whole passages memorized. The Manifesto is Solomon's Bible. He worships it."

"Audience response…" mumbled Davenport.

"Huh?"

"Oh, nothing. I was just thinking they sent it to Solomon as a test. If he could understand it, anybody could. And his emotional response was," Davenport stared into space for a moment, "flawless."

Davenport suddenly became suspicious. "And what were *you* doing there, Tash? At that hole in the wall?"

Padgett looked down. "I know we're not supposed to take a personal interest in our cell mates outside of missions. But Solomon ... he's had a rough life. He's nice, just not the brightest fellow around."

"Understatement," said Davenport, coldly.

"Don't let on to Gulf Stream. I occasionally swing by Providence to check on Solomon, sometimes slip a little money under his front door, have a drink at the bar and chat. He's completely dedicated to Don't Ask, Don't Tell, and I want to be sure they aren't taking advantage of him. Solomon would offer his last drop of blood, and even though he supposedly works with me, I sometimes wonder whether Gulf Stream uses him on extra assignments. You know that Solomon is intellectually ... defenseless. Maybe I've got Big Sister Syndrome."

Davenport relaxed, suddenly ashamed of his suspicion that she might be playing him. It had been Padgett, after all, who alerted him to the Manifesto. Now she was apologizing for dropping quarters in a donation box for the underprivileged.

"You don't have any syndromes," said Davenport. "You're a decent woman who grew up too hard and too fast, thrown to society's carnivores. There are probably lots of folks in that situation, but few with your compassion."

"I don't know..." began Padgett.

"I do." Davenport cut her off. "It's a shame that the world has inspired an organization like DADT. But if it must exist, I'm glad that people like you are at its core. Otherwise, I might have regrets."

"Don't you?" asked Padgett. "I do ... sometimes."

"I'm starting to wonder." Davenport hesitated and then said, "No. I don't have regrets about our little episode in Massachusetts. I did a background check on that small town hero—a homophobe fascist in the making. Gulf Stream knows his business, all right. Few people were more deserving of a DADT intervention. I could have survived without nailing the guy to a cross, but let's face it, the method is the message, and with that act, Solomon gave them a boldface memo." Davenport laughed just perceptibly. "I always *believed* I hated violence, but in the end I almost loved Massachusetts. Revenge, power, not feeling helpless. Maybe it's the kid in me. You know, truth, justice, the American way."

Padgett smiled.

Davenport continued. "I'm sick that what we did seems necessary ... *is* necessary. But I don't feel bad about doing it. Does that make the English professor a monster?"

"You're no monster. Neither am I. Neither is Gulf Stream. DADT is self-defense." Tanish Padgett became firmer. "In 1992, the Pope informally pardoned Galileo. Think of it, Robert. The Catholic Church needed almost four hundred years to apologize for mistreating one of the greatest scientific minds in history, a man who offered nothing but truth. Well, *no one* has apologized to my mother, and I don't intend to wait four hundred years. We'll bring hostile homophobes to their knees. We are right."

"Do you really think illiterate Wyoming Bible thumpers will apologize to Matthew Shepard, or their own gay sons and daughters for that matter?"

"No, and I don't need their apologies. They can meet their maker with self-righteous bile streaming from their lips. That's good enough for me, and Pearl Harbor will serve them in kind." Padgett turned to steel. "My mother will receive her apology when they die."

Both were quiet for a moment.

"I am sorry you have so much pain," said Davenport.

"Forget about it. I'm glad for people like Gulf Stream and Little Boy and the Founder. DADT is fighting back. I hurt less by being part of it"

"Tash?"

"What?" asked Padgett, a little softer.

"How much do you know about Pearl Harbor? What they're planning?"

"Don't have many details, just that it's sometime in April. I'm waiting for my assignment. It's big though. Something the enemy can't ignore. And the Manifesto will be released simultaneously. The shot heard round the world..."

"I'd like to ask a favor," said Davenport.

"Yeah?"

"Step back awhile."

"What do you mean?"

"Don't question Gulf Stream further about the Manifesto. Don't let anyone else know that you've given me a copy."

"I wasn't planning to."

"Try to avoid new assignments if possible. Wait quietly in the shadows."

"What for? I won't surrender."

"I understand. Just retreat for a month. I don't want you to get hurt."

"Irrelevant. There's not much left of me to injure."

Davenport leaned back and smiled at Padgett. "Yes, there is," he said. "I didn't know that for sure until tonight."

Padgett didn't believe him. "Get real."

"Stand down. Be patient. Give me a few weeks to crack this Manifesto thing."

Davenport sensed that Padgett was resistant. "Tash?" he asked.

Padgett appeared to have drifted away in thought.

"Tash?" he said again.

"I'm sorry," she said. "What?"

"Hear me out, please. Something is wrong with my role in the Manifesto. I need a little time..." Davenport decided to change direction. "What do you think of me, Tash?"

"I'm not sure what you're getting at."

"You recruited me for DADT. You sat in my class. We've known each other for a year now. If we forget the organization for a moment, how would you rate my intellectual capacity?" Davenport grinned. "I mean, when my head's not stuck up my ass due to general arrogance."

Padgett giggled like a school girl and said, "I've read many of your essays, Robert. I've listened to you speak. You *are* brilliant. Undisciplined at times—you are still a young man after all—and you might have benefited from additional science training. But..."

"Go on," said Davenport.

"You haven't learned the most important thing you told your students. Brilliance is not enough ... though I suppose a little arrogance is justified."

"It's never justified. My work should speak for itself. Somehow I forgot that. But listen, Tash. If you really believe in me, hold back and let me snoop around. I might step on some toes, and I don't want repercussions to fall your way. Understand?"

Padgett seemed concerned. "What are you going to do?"

"I'm going to use my education and training. Engage my research skills." Davenport held up the Manifesto. "I'm going to find out why I'm wasting time on a project that was apparently finished a year and a half ago. I am going to meet and speak with the untouchable Founder, whoever he is, and ask a few questions."

"Robert!" Padgett almost gasped. "Nobody just *talks* with the Founder. Protecting his identity is essential."

"That's one of the problems with DADT. Another oversight of mine. Little Boy has met with the Founder, and so will I. Closets are for losers. They are immoral. And no one is above a dialogue. I'll use humanities bullying, English professors are very good at it, and suggest that I'm *entitled* to meet the Founder. It might work. But keep a safe distance. Go back to Boston and stay there in case anything goes wrong. Please."

Padgett was frightened. "I don't like this."

"Me either."

"I suppose I can retreat awhile. But, Robert, you'll be careful? And, umm, respectful? Many people, even those who haven't met him, worship the Founder. They wouldn't stand for disrespect."

"Absolutely. I'll be diplomatic."

Padgett nodded. "I'm not kidding, Rob. We both know that DADT can defend itself when threatened."

"Don't worry, Tash. You and I got involved in this thing for the right reasons. And we have one great advantage."

"Advantage?"

"We trust each other, and I thank you. Most of my life, I've been afraid of almost everything. No more. I plan to ask the Founder about this Manifesto and my relationship to it. I will listen. I will be nice. But if I don't like the answer, I will *respectfully* suggest that he go to hell."

TWENTY-SEVEN

Practice Makes Deadly

January 2008

Gulf Stream drove to a high desert plateau in Southwestern Colorado to test the radio controls of his model airplane. There were other enthusiasts at the site, people who loved their hobby and the expansive red-stone geography. A few modelers had been World War II pilots, perhaps eighteen or nineteen years old when they entered the Army Air Corps. One man had flown with the Royal Air Force because he had been too impatient to wait for America's entry into the war. He joined the British and, due to his training and skill as a pilot, was immediately put to work in the Battle of Britain. Gulf Stream liked this man within minutes of their meeting, though he seemed almost too old to exist in the Twenty-first Century. The man had constructed an authentically detailed miniature P-51 Mustang that he could bend and roll and barrel across the sky better than a fourteen-year-old Trek fan born of the digital age. Several radio pilots were Vietnam veterans who, having suffered social and professional isolation upon return from their unpopular war, decided that sailing model airplanes and helicopters was more therapeutic than drug rehabilitation programs, and it might ease the pain of failing marriages, struggling on the job, enduring memories of Southeast Asia, or fighting with the Veteran's administration for medical benefits. They found relative comfort in the camaraderie with other veterans in the innocuous world of radio controlled aircraft.

The sport was fun and did not require operators to drop napalm on faceless targets, strafe men and women in remote villages, intercept supplies along the Ho Chi Minh Trail, or secretly invade Cambodia on the orders of Richard Nixon. Nor did it require them to listen to unbathed hippies call them "baby killers" when they returned to American soil. They could briefly forget about Daniel, Stephen, Marty, Angela, or José, their former friends and classmates who had been left in pieces on the battlefield among the seemingly endless rain of lies and deceit. They did not have to think about student protests and political maneuvering while cluster bombs blanketed North Vietnam, killing civilians and children indiscriminately along with the enemy. And they did not have to consider that the South Vietnamese government, which Americans were reportedly defending from communism, might have been worse than the enemy itself. Instead, the displaced veterans could fly miniature airplanes and not contemplate the difference between a good war and a bad one—though the World War II soldier and Gulf Stream believed they knew the difference.

Gulf Stream also believed in guerilla action, and he practiced with the radio controls whenever possible. The new Pearl Harbor was coming, and during that action, Gulf Stream would manipulate a remote-controlled twin-engine executive aircraft with video assistance to carry a deadly weapon. The primary target, a large religion-based university, had been particularly venomous in its right-wing homophobic and anti-feminist political affiliations. Gulf Stream, himself, preferred more personal exploits—hands around a knife or a throat—but DADT's second wave had been designed for a paparazzi splash, carrying the battle to Everyman.

The aircraft would deliver one of their ABC weapons—atomic, biological, or chemical. Gulf Stream didn't particularly care which, but he wanted to be sure he delivered it precisely. So he practiced with models in the field. At home, he used a "Predator Simulator," which provided real-time cockpit views to the remote piloting system that would ultimately guide his converted war bird. It was complex, costly, and sophisticated. It would be lethal.

Gulf Stream smiled and maneuvered the scale model plane through a double loop followed by a perfect four-point roll. He was skilled and nearly ready for Pearl Harbor. As he practiced, Gulf Stream pictured the face of his friend who had been killed all those years ago in New York; almost simultaneously, the bloodied death mask morphed in his imagination with the face of Anita Bryant and her Florida campaign for the "moral majority." A Miss America runner-up merged with Gulf Stream's friend in a grotesque psychic transmutation. Gulf Stream sickened with rage. He worked at the controls, thinking, "Let's see the bastards preach when a 'moral minority' rams an executive jet down their throats."

"Nice move," said the American RAF World War II veteran after Gulf Stream executed a mid-air stall and recovery and followed it with a high-speed mock strafe a few feet from the ground. "You would have been handy in a Spitfire."

"Thanks," said Gulf Stream.

"Where did you learn to fly like that?"

"I have a private jet. Use it a lot for business, but I play with my models."

"It shows. Lord, we could have used you against the Germans."

"By the way," said Gulf Stream, "if you don't mind my asking?"

"What?" asked the veteran.

"How many Nazi sons-of-bitches did you shoot down?"

"Enough," said the old man.

Gulf Stream nodded and replied, "Glad to hear it."

The RAF veteran was surprised later, as were others, when Gulf Stream's model fighter slammed straightaway and at full speed into the side of a sandstone rockface two hundred yards across the open field where they had gathered. They were even more surprised by Gulf Stream's smile.

Several bystanders moaned "Oooooh!" or "Ouch!" or "That's gotta hurt." One man sought to console him and said, "Better luck next time, friend."

Most observers assumed that the radio control system had malfunctioned and Gulf Stream lost throttle and maneuverability. But the RAF man was confused. Only beginners made that kind of mistake, and his new acquaintance was no beginner.

"Don't worry," said Gulf Stream to the group as he closed the antenna and turned off the remote power. "I have an even better back-up machine, and I think I'm ready to use it." Gulf Stream waved, climbed into his rented vehicle, and drove to a distant airport.

TWENTY-EIGHT

The Un-Scrabble

March 2008

Josie Waller and Emmanuel Cerrillo raced across the Golden Gate Bridge toward the Richmond District office. Waller was driving.

"Slow down!" said Cerrillo. "You're gonna kill us before DADT gets the chance."

"Quit whining. I want to see those photos, and speeding is a police perk. We don't get many."

"Cops die in accidents just like regular folks," said Cerrillo. He had never quite gotten over watching *Red Asphalt* during high school driver's education. "Besides, we're in an unmarked car. No lights. No siren. Not safe."

Waller eased off the accelerator. "Well, it's not every day I hit the Golden Gate without traffic. Got to seize the opportunity when it comes."

"I ought to ticket you for speeding."

"Right, like you carry a ticket book. Besides, we're at the exit and just a couple miles from the station. You want to see the photos as much as I do. Admit it."

This was true, but Cerrillo decided not to respond.

"By the way," said Waller, smiling, "I talked with your boss a couple days ago."

"You spoke with Ricketts?" asked Cerrillo.

"Yep. We're becoming pretty good friends. Better be nice to me."

"I think I *will* write you up for speeding."

Waller was quiet, waiting for the inevitable question.

Cerrillo finally broke the silence. "So, uh, what did you two talk about?"

"This and that. Girl talk."

Cerrillo laughed. "Ricketts never wasted a breath in her life. Whatever she spoke about, Josie, it was more than chitchat."

Waller smiled too big. "Oh, basically, she said to watch out and make sure you don't come home in a body bag. Very sweet, Manny. You never told me she had adopted you."

Cerrillo was becoming angry at Waller's meddling but checked it. "The Chief of Police did *not* adopt me. She simply has a community responsibility to ensure that the city's best detective isn't injured or disabled. Purely a professional concern."

They finally approached the station. Waller parked the vehicle. It was 5:15 p.m.

"I hate when it gets dark so early," said Cerrillo. "Feels like second shift."

"With Don't Ask, Don't Tell, there is no shift. They work overtime, and so do we."

As they entered the building, Cerrillo said, "Let's get at those photos."

"That's a great thing about the digital age. Instant gratification. Four years ago, we had to wait for the lab to finish processing. But now? Hundreds of high-definition photos at the push of a button."

Richmond Division office was surprisingly quiet. Most of the eight-to-fivers had left the building, but Cerrillo recognized the desk sergeant, who always seemed to be on duty.

"Hey, Jeffries," said Cerrillo, waving as they were about to pass.

"That's Sergeant Jeffries to you. Every time you're here, we end up with extra work. Now we're busting ass on Adam Smith since he turned up dead at the zoo. You and Waller sure find some weird ones."

"No weirder than Mrs. School Board."

"I'll grant you that..." said Jeffries. "Oh, that kid Ellington is looking for you. At first glance, I figured him for an FBI snob, but he ain't quite the most disgusting Fed I ever run into."

"Not by a long shot," said Waller.

Cerrillo grinned and gestured toward Jeffries. "She's gone soft on the kid."

"He's camped at Waller's desk," said the sergeant. "So if you'll excuse me, I've got reports to read. Mostly because of you."

"Complaining about work?" asked Waller. "You probably came in at four this morning, that is, if you bothered to go home last night. And it's now after five o'clock. Why don't you knock off for the day, Sarge? You've earned it."

"And why don't you mind your own business. I got more important things to do than abide your notions of police work."

"Fine by me, Pops," said Waller. She smiled. "I just thought you might be tired of pushing that pencil around. Pretty strenuous."

"Are you still here...?" said Jeffries.

Cerrillo and Waller walked down the hallway toward her desk. Cerrillo asked Waller, "You two got some kind of game on?"

Waller said, "Jeffries practically lives here. Has about a hundred years of back-logged vacation. Lieutenant Mertwile, our self-exaltus rex, once tried to *insist* that Jeffries take time off, back when the Lieutenant first came on as second shift supervisor. Guess how well that worked out."

Cerrillo laughed. "I've still never met Mertwile."

"Oh, that's right." Waller laughed in return. "You were assigned to him when you started this whole 'wild goose chase.' Glad he shuffled you aside. Got me out of the doghouse and back on the streets."

"Why's Jeffries so attached to his desk?" asked Cerrillo.

"He loves police work, and this place is his life... Want to ask him about it?"

"No thanks," said Cerrillo.

"You're smarter than you look," said Waller.

Cerrillo grinned. "Has advantages."

They went to Waller's desk; no one was there. Ellington called from across the way. "Hey, guys! Over here. I'm spread out in an interrogation room."

As they approached, Waller asked, "You got the photos?"

Ellington held up a compact disk. "Supposed to be on this."

Waller and Cerrillo entered the room with Ellington and closed the door.

"I hate working off site," said Ellington. "It's so disorganized. And I prefer my own equipment and people."

"Welcome to police duty," said Waller. "The good stuff happens out of the chaos. But this place is home to me, so don't knock it."

"Oh, I didn't mean anything," said Ellington. "But whenever I get my way, I prefer familiar turf. I don't get my way very often."

"I hear that," said Cerrillo, surprised by the de-escalation of rhetoric between Ellington and Waller. "Any news?"

"Waiting to hear further from Judd, but don't worry. Whatever can be bought or stolen, he'll get it."

"Bring up photos from the victim's house," said Waller.

"What about the crime scene?" asked Ellington. "I figured you'd start there."

"Cut and dried," said Cerrillo. "One dead guy. Two live snakes. End of story. Let's see the house. Specifically, the bedroom."

Ellington set the CD on the counter. "I think all images are stored on this but nobody's had time to catalog the shots. Nothing's printed either. We'll need a decent computer terminal." Ellington looked around. "Shall we move to an office PC? Better yet, I can bring my laptop in here. Just take a minute."

"Get your laptop, and let's stay here," suggested Waller. "We'll commandeer this room for privacy."

"What if Mertwile objects?" asked Cerrillo, joking.

"Judd can handle the elite Mister Stanford," said Ellington.

"You already heard his college history?" asked Waller. "I didn't think you'd been here long enough."

"I heard it," said Ellington. "Mertwile came around to check my credentials and find out why I'm here. Throwing weight around for show. Spent twenty minutes telling me about his education and all the post-graduation offers he turned down, including the FBI, to work with SFPD, and blah-ditty-blah-blah. Good thing I've been watching you guys in action. I'm learning how to ditch egos run amok."

"That's Mertwile, all right," said Waller. "*Persona summa cum laude.*"

Cerrillo nodded toward Ellington. "If you're not careful, Josie's gonna turn you from a perfectionist nerd into genuine FBI."

"I can live with that," said Ellington. "Let me get my laptop—custom built at MIT. Back in a jiffy."

"Okay," said Cerrillo, "But do you think Dirty Harry would say 'jiffy'?"

Ellington turned pink.

"Forget it," said Cerrillo. "Listen, Waller and I haven't had anything to eat since early breakfast. We'll walk down the street and grab some sandwiches. Get your equipment and start inspecting the photos."

"Right. I'll be ready in five minutes."

"Can we bring you anything?" asked Waller. She was anxious to see the photos, but now that Ellington had them in hand and needed time for set up, Waller noticed she was hungry. And they might be at this for a while.

"A ham and Swiss on rye. Meatball sub would be better if they have 'em."

"They got everything. If you can think it, they can make it. And I'll grab Cokes for everybody. Could be a caffeine-and-sugar night."

"Sounds good," said Ellington. "Um, when I start the slide show ... what am I looking for?"

"Scrabble board," said Cerrillo.

"You're joking."

"I hope not. Just see what you find," said Cerrillo.

"We'll be back in a jiffy," said Waller

***

In fifteen minutes, Waller and Cerrillo returned with sandwiches, potato chips, pickles, and extra-large Cokes in old-style paper cups that were already dripping with condensation. Ellington was busy at his computer.

"I suddenly understand why you might be interested in Scrabble," said Ellington.

"What do you mean?" asked Waller.

"Take a look."

Cerrillo set down the oil spotted food bags, which smelled of hot pastrami and French fries. On his computer screen, Ellington had a clear shot of the Scrabble board. The word groupings seemed insignificant at first glance, except that they were obviously not part of a legitimate game. The writer was doing something else:

```
            C O B R A
            E
            R A G N A R O K
   W A L L E R
            I
   P E A R L   H A R B O R
         P   L            E
   N O I R   O D I N      V
         I            C E R R I L L O
      K I L L E R S      N
      I                  G
      N            W C E R R I L L O
      G U L F S T R E A M
               R
```

"Gibberish?" asked Waller hopefully.

"Not quite," said Ellington soberly. "DADT has you on a watch list."

"Hope it's not a hit list," said Cerrillo.

They were quiet, their food growing cold, reading silently. Then Cerrillo took charge.

"First, send copies of this one to Judd and Ricketts. If there is a decipherable meaning, aside from obvious insanity, they might see it. Second, print a bunch of hard copies for us. We can play around, try to figure out whether it's some kind of cryptic message or random mental flutters of a nutcase. Wish we could ask him about it."

"Looks like you rated two honorable mentions, Detective," said Ellington.

"Three," said Cerrillo. "Two horizontals and a vertical."

"Don't suppose that's good."

"What makes you so special?" asked Waller. "I only got one." She was afraid for both of them but didn't let on.

"Probably nothing," said Cerrillo. "Besides, Smith ran the letters off the board. I hate crazies who violate the rules of their own dementia."

"DADT understands we're after them," said Waller.

"We already know that," said Ellington.

Waller shook her head. "That rag-nark thing... drug talk?"

"Rag-na-rok," said Ellington

"You mean it's a real word?"

"Remember your Norse mythology?" asked Ellington.

Cerrillo and Waller shrugged.

"Didn't you even read Marvel comics? Thor?"

"Couldn't afford books when I was a kid," said Cerrillo. "Too busy finding enough food."

"Comics? Really?" asked Waller.

Ellington shook his head. "Never too late to complete your education. I bet neither of you been to a ComiCon or Trekker convention. I strongly recommend them. Geek-love cleans the soul. Anyway ... Ragnarok and Odin. One of Odin's jobs is to postpone Ragnarok for as long as possible."

"And what's Ragnarok?" asked Cerrillo.

"The day when heaven and earth will be destroyed."

Waller laughed. "DADT has visited one ComiCon too many. Even drunk, Gulf Stream can't possibly believe they will destroy heaven and earth."

"Not for everybody," said Cerrillo. "Just for the unlucky few caught in their Pearl Harbor..."

"They're going to give gays and lesbians a bad name," said Waller.

Ellington punched the send button. "I just emailed the photo to Judd and Ricketts. These DADT people make it hard to form a psychological profile beyond *unpredictable*, which is quite possibly the most dangerous profile there is."

***

"I'm exhausted," said Josie Waller. It was almost dawn, and they were still in the interrogation room looking at photos. "Been Scrabbling so long I can't tell vertical from horizontal..."

"I'm done in, too," said Cerrillo. "At this point, if Odin or Ragnarok or Gulf Stream bit me on the ass, I'd surrender. We've cross-talked all night. Nothing from Judd or Ricketts. They're probably sensible enough to be sleeping."

Ellington smiled and interjected. "You old folks wear down more easily than us young bloods. Don't worry, I'll cover for you."

Waller yawned. Cerrillo was silent.

"Wow," said Ellington. "You must be tired! That was one of my best put-downs ... And by the way, Ragnarok is an event, not a person."

Waller glanced at Cerrillo. "I'm too tired to kill him. Let's get some sleep. Smith probably set up the chess board to torment us."

"Scrabble board," said Cerrillo.

Waller nodded. "Either way. Adam Smith was crazy."

"Don't care. Let's call it a night." Cerrillo reached for his jacket. "I'm heading to the motel and crash until Tuesday."

"No you're not!" said Ellington, barring the doorway. "Neither of you!"

Waller and Cerrillo snapped awake, startled by Ellington's boldness.

"Sorry," said Ellington, more gently, "but one thing we know for sure about Smith's message is that you're in it, which means DADT likely has you under surveillance. We can't be sure about details, but you can't be alone, especially in your present condition. You're both punchy. Everybody stays at my place tonight."

"I want my own bed..." said Waller.

Ellington ignored her. "I have a suite, and until we learn more about Gulf Stream's whereabouts, consider yourself under my protection."

Waller laughed. Cerrillo followed suit. A sleep-drunk exhale.

"Yes, sir, Captain Young Blood." Waller snapped to mock attention.

"Fine by me," said Cerrillo. "As long as there's a bed and a pillow, I'll play. You wouldn't have a shot of tequila at this super-suite?"

"There are two queen-size beds," said Ellington. "I'll confiscate a bottle of anything you want from the hotel bar. You and Waller can take the beds. I'll spread out on the sofa. But neither of you is to be alone until we find Gulf Stream."

Waller laughed again. "We're cops. I think we can handle a killer with a hypodermic syringe and snake oil. My .380 magnum strikes faster and has greater range. And Cerrillo can outdraw the Waco Kid."

"Even Waco can't shoot half asleep. Right now, I doubt either of you could hit the wall with a shotgun."

"Hit it!" said Cerrillo, flexing his eyes, "I can barely see it."

Waller relaxed. "You'll get no argument from me, General Young Blood. Just point to the bedroom. I sleep. You protect. We go now." She tossed Ellington the keys of the Crown Victoria. "Designated driver."

Ellington slid them in his pocket. "Thanks," he said, "but we'll take my car. It's a cinch DADT knows your vehicle. Better odds they don't know mine. Stay in the building until I pull around back to the fire exit. Don't come out until I knock on the door. By tomorrow, we might have an update from Judd, and maybe then I'll let you out of my sight."

"Hmmm," said Cerrillo. "I might be fuzzy around the edges, but he's starting to make sense."

"Told you we'd turn him into a cop," said Waller. "We are good."

"Wait two minutes," said Ellington. "And if there is so much as a crippled bag lady within five blocks, remain inside until I give the all clear."

***

"This federal protection racket is sweet," said Waller. "We lounge around, take our meals indoors, watch cable TV as much as we can stand—and a personal gofer fetches booze, burgers, and USA Today at all hours." She glared at Ellington. "But three days is enough. It's time to work, and I'd rather DADT kill me than watch one more episode of *The Munsters*. And I love *The Munsters*."

"I feel like a prisoner in the White House," said Cerrillo, gesturing around the hotel room and then at Ellington. "How did you rate this setup, Ellington? Are you sleeping with Judd?"

After three days and two nights confined with Waller and Cerrillo, Ellington was learning to dish it back. "I don't rate the room," he said. "DADT does. After Smith's body turned up, headquarters figured we might be here awhile. They gave me extra space in case we need more agents or have to set up specialized equipment. Technical FBI stuff that wouldn't interest you."

"He's sleeping with Judd," said Waller to Cerrillo.

Ellington was exasperated. "If you juvenile delinquents could hold your breath for five minutes..."

Then four things happened simultaneously. The fax machine signaled a transmission and began to print airline tickets. Chief Margaret Rickets called Cerrillo; Special Agent Judd called Ellington; and someone knocked on the door.

"Oh, shit!" said Waller.

***

Four hours later Cerrillo, Waller, and Ellington were on a flight from San Francisco to Providence, Rhode Island. Adam Smith was no longer a primary concern, nor was his Scrabble board. The Providence Police Department was holding a live suspect, a half-witted local bartender who had beaten a patron to death for disparaging remarks about gays in the military. The perpetrator called himself Solomon-X. That was the only name he would give police, who took fingerprints and began a standard background check. Solomon's rough-used body—scars, muscles, and tattoos—suggested a criminal record, and authorities wanted his real name. But there were several things that caught their attention, aside from the murder itself. First, Solomon hadn't tried to run; claimed he was proud and would do it again. Second, when asked about it, Solomon said he was a freedom fighter and expected to die like a soldier. Third, he carried a DADT business card.

Police departments across the country had been instructed by the FBI to look for the DADT calling cards but received no information as to why they were important. Authorities were simply to detain suspects for questioning, protect the crime scene, and inform Special Agent Samuel Judd and/or Police Chief Margaret Ricketts immediately. Thanks to two attentive Providence cops on the night shift, the system worked, so Waller, Cerrillo, and Ellington boarded another redeye en route to T.F. Green Airport. They were scheduled to touch down at 6:30 a.m. None would sleep on the way. Too much adrenaline. Too many racing thoughts.

Unlike Adam Smith, Solomon-X was alive. He could be questioned and seemed willing to talk. And the three investigators did not want to blow this opportunity. It was clear from the preliminary reports that Solomon's IQ was low-average. It was also clear that Solomon had a hot temper and fierce pride. The ideal suspect for interrogation. And if they could topple one DADT domino, the resulting progression might crush Gulf Stream and his Ragnarok dreams.

The stakes were rising, and the tables might be turning.

TWENTY-NINE

The *Other* Professor

March 2008

Professor Alfred McDaniels called Chief Margaret Ricketts several days after she informed him about Adam Smith's body in the cobra pit. "Listen, Maggie," said McDaniels. "I've got information about Smith. It's classified, however, so I can't reveal anything. Sorry."

Ricketts laughed. "Well, Professor, I might wonder why you're calling."

"I think we should have an early lunch tomorrow. Say eleven at the usual place. For old time's sake. I would like that."

"Sure," said Ricketts. She knew McDaniels well enough to infer that he couldn't talk by phone. "I have to shift a few appointments, but it's always a pleasure to see you." She also understood that the usual place was the Good Earth Restaurant near Westwood, which McDaniels purposefully did not mention by name and was a short walk from the UCLA campus.

Ricketts arrived early the next day and ordered a cup of hot tea with honey and lemon. She loved the Good Earth's special English blend and, especially, her afternoon teas with Professor McDaniels when she had been a young, tough, and overly ambitious student. In those days, she never allowed anyone the impertinence of distracting her from study, but an hour with McDaniels was more educational than ten in the library—and a lot more fun.

The professor arrived five minutes after Ricketts. Both had a habit of showing up twenty minutes early whenever they got together. Such opportunities were rare.

McDaniels greeted Ricketts as the waitress showed him to the booth. "Hello, Madam Police Chief. Shoot anybody today?"

"No," said Ricketts. "I've been trying to cut back." They shook each other's hands with the grip of a Sousa march and held it longer than business required. "Hello, Professor."

McDaniels turned to the waitress. "I'll also have tea. And then we'll order lunch in perhaps thirty minutes. Thank you, Maria." The waitress hurried away. "So, how have you been, Maggie?"

"Busy, I'm afraid. The last few weeks, not much on my mind besides Don't Ask, Don't Tell. And now that we've seen the Scrabble board, I'm even more worried about Cerrillo and Waller."

"Quite right," said McDaniels.

Ricketts hesitated. "I understand that you might have some information."

"Yes, but as I said..." McDaniels stopped. Maria set his tea on the table, along with an extra carafe of hot water. The professor would take afternoon tea once or twice per week, sip the warm liquid as he reviewed textbooks or read student exams, or sometimes stare blankly into the tablecloth, thinking thoughts that he never discussed. Maria often waited on him and was used to making things the way he wanted.

"Thank you," said McDaniels.

"You're welcome," said Maria, glancing at her watch. "I'll check back in thirty minutes." McDaniels was always precise in his time requests.

"Fine," he said.

Ricketts smiled. "I remember Maria from when I was a student. How long has she worked here?"

"Long time," said the professor. "She predates César Chávez. An incredible woman. Somehow managed to send three children to college on a waitress's salary. Not many of my privileged law students have her resilience or depth of character."

It had always seemed to Ricketts that Professor McDaniels loved and understood working people. She remembered when McDaniels invited several janitorial and cafeteria staff to talk about their lives in his second-year law course, "Topics in Legal Philosophy." When one of his students later asked what those discussions had to do with becoming an attorney, Professor McDaniels had replied, "Ladies and gentlemen, the law is not a factory for widgets or beer. It's a governing philosophy of life *with* your fellow man. It's about people, the men and women all around you. And, with that in mind, I expect each of you to know the names and brief histories of the individuals who clean your dormitories and prepare your meals at the dining facilities. And let me assure you. There will be related questions on your final examination in this course. I suggest that you have something to say."

More than a few UCLA campus workers were pleasantly surprised (some were suspicious) in the coming weeks when a small flurry of law students suddenly seemed interested in getting to know them. Some of the students were in turn surprised when, later, a few janitors and cafeteria workers began to take avuncular interests in them in return, dropping off baked goods or notes of encouragement at their dorm rooms.

From this experience, Margaret Ricketts had become acquainted with a Mrs. Socorro Cerrillo, who took the bus each day from Pomona to work at the campus dining center, and who had a son in high school who dreamed of going to college. Ricketts eventually met that son (Emmanuel), advised him during his college years, and ultimately supported his application for the Los Angeles Police Academy. And now, the Pomona Police Chief was concerned about that same young man who had become a detective and was traveling across the country in search of Don't Ask, Don't Tell. Ricketts didn't know if other students understood that McDaniels was a defining spirit in the humanities, but she did. She loved him for helping to dismantle her youthful resentments about hardship and race, helping her to focus on future goals, and for caring about students and others beyond any requirement in a standard faculty contract.

"I hope Maria is happy," said Ricketts, sipping her tea.

"I think she invented the concept. Stoic on the outside; radiant on the inside."

"Tell me, Professor. Why don't we get together more often? How long has it been?"

"Many months," said McDaniels, "which is how it should be. I didn't spend three years turning you into a Philosopher Cop so that you could live in the nostalgic past. We had good times at the university, and occasionally we'll have more. But there's work to do in the world. Our pathetic little contribution to humanity."

"Is it really pathetic?"

"In the grand scheme, almost certainly," said McDaniels. "But put together a million contributions from a million concerned citizens, and who knows? Civilization might make it to the end of the 21st Century without Ragnarok."

Ricketts grimaced. "Oh, yes. I almost forgot why we're here."

"I talked with my Washington contacts. There are some things about Adam Smith."

Ricketts sipped her tea and set down the cup. When McDaniels offered no further information, she said, "Well, we're fairly sure he came out of Russia and somehow made it to the U.S. via Australia. He certainly didn't cross the Mexican border in a coyote's beat-up '68 Dodge. Smith had financial resources, a phony passport that looks better than one from the U.S. State Department, and some potent historical baggage. Probably old school U.S.S.R., Cold War KGB, and almost certainly dropped out of Sunday school." Ricketts looked at the professor. "What else can you tell me?"

"Legally, nothing." McDaniels smiled. "And here I am, an esteemed law professor about to break the law. You really should arrest me."

"I won't pressure, but rest assured that, as far as I'm concerned, this meeting never took place. I won't be able to remember any information ... or where I got it." Ricketts smiled. "In fact, who are you?"

McDaniels laughed. "I'd put my reputation in your hands any day, Maggie. And sometimes, bending rules can enhance those pathetic contributions, turn them more substantial. My informants—I can't remember their names either—violated several orders of security in talking with me, but there is no better security than absolute trust in the person who receives sensitive information."

"Thank you, Professor."

"You already know most of what there is about Smith. But there's one more item. He got out of Russia with fissionable plutonium, perhaps as much as ten pounds. I'm no physicist, thank god, but sources tell me the stuff is particularly nasty. No one believes that DADT has the capacity to construct a nuclear bomb, and "Dirty Mary" probably refers to a conventional device that will kick up a cloud of toxic and radioactive debris. Dirty is an understatement, especially if it's an airburst. Anyway, Smith had access and opportunity. My sources are worried."

"Christ," said Ricketts, shaking her head and thinking that suddenly the tea tasted strangely metallic.

"Those sources also suggest that this Pearl Harbor will likely take place in April. It will involve multiple incidents, perhaps biological and chemical." The professor seemed both subdued and troubled, which was rare.

"What's wrong, sir?"

McDaniels hesitated, as if he had just become aware of his emotions. "Oh, I don't know, really. This sort of thing makes me tired."

"Thing?"

"Violence. Maybe I'm getting old. Students have been coming and going in my classes for thirty years. I've lectured all over the world. I've had protégées go on to outstanding careers. And a few, like yourself, have become wonderful people besides. But this Pearl Harbor. Retaliation. Killing people. Cold bloodedness. Even if they have a legitimate gripe, I have no stomach for it. My whole being—the law school, the court system, the Constitution—is about finding another way. Now and again it seems that the arm that bears the sword is the arm that controls the world, and I wonder if the rule of law stands a chance."

Ricketts empathized with McDaniels as she would a loving grandfather. "Sir," she said, patting the .45 caliber pistol under her jacket, "civil authority rules this weapon. You taught me that. And it is the law, backed up with lead, that will subdue Don't Ask, Don't Tell. The law might someday eliminate their gripe as well. In the meantime, we will stand against the likes of Gulf Stream. That's my promise."

Maria returned to their table. "Are you ready to order, Professor?"

"Yes," said McDaniels. "I shall eat whether queasy or not. My usual chicken salad sandwich on toasted whole wheat."

Ricketts asked for a tuna wrap and fruit cocktail.

"I'll also bring a fresh pot of hot water and extra tea bags," said Maria as she walked away.

"There isn't much else regarding Smith and DADT," said McDaniels after Maria had gone. "The next best hope is that suspect in Providence, Rhode Island. Your detective is there?"

"They arrived this morning. Cerrillo, Waller, and the kid, Ellington."

The professor nodded. "A fine crew for the job." McDaniels looked up. "They *will* be careful?"

"You bet," said Ricketts. "Interview the suspect at the police station and have an armed escort to and from each session. Don't worry, Professor. Cops are good at protecting their home turf ... even if the rest of the city is burning. We learned that during the Rodney King affair." Ricketts wished she hadn't said that.

"Organizations are comprised of people, and people have self-interest," said McDaniels. "In fact, if I were in charge of DADT and its forthcoming attack, I would, at this point..." The professor stopped.

"Yeah. I know. Gulf Stream must be thinking that right now. Kill the messenger. Kill Solomon."

"Along with anybody who might be with him."

"Professor?" asked Ricketts, sounding a little like a student again.

"What?"

"Any chance we might be overestimating DADT? I mean, all we really have are a few murders and some grandiose proclamations."

"Along with a platter of missing plutonium and a dead Russian-Czech intelligence officer. Remember the crystal morning of September 11? Beautiful and routine … until that moment it wasn't. My greater fear is that we're *under*estimating them."

Ricketts nodded. "I'll call Providence. Request extra precautions…" Then she smiled. "I'm very glad we didn't have this talk, whoever you are."

"What talk?" asked McDaniels.

THIRTY

Between the Ides

April 2008

"Listen to me, you refugee from a failed rehab," growled Cerrillo, "I don't care what the guy said. You killed him. And you're going to prison for the rest of your natural life, which, if I had my way, wouldn't be long."

"Ease off, Detective," said Waller, placing her hand on Solomon's shoulder. "We can't blame him for getting riled. You don't know what it's like for someone to spit 'faggot' in your face. Me and Solomon do." Waller turned toward the suspect. "Still, you can't go around killing people. I know you got mad. Lost control. Acted in the heat of the moment. Special circumstances can make the difference between the death penalty or life in prison.

Talk to me." There was no death penalty in Rhode Island, but neither Waller nor Cerrillo knew that.

Solomon did not take the bait. In fact, he had said nothing during the first two days of questioning, which had prompted Cerrillo and Waller's move toward more aggressive tactics. "When in doubt," said Waller, "revert to the classics." And since Waller was a lesbian and might form a connection with Solomon, as she had with Craspen, they agreed that she would be the good cop. On the other hand, Cerrillo would do his best to imitate the kind of person DADT sought to eliminate.

"You're wasting time," said Cerrillo. "I say we ship this homo-fuck to prison where he belongs. Maybe a good Samaritan will stick a dull shiv in his liver."

Waller, standing behind Solomon, nodded at Cerrillo. "Knock off the homo-crap, Detective. You know I'm gay. I don't have to take that."

"I'm talking to the scumbag, so don't take it personal, Super Dyke. Doesn't matter to me who you sleep with."

"Let's just keep the interrogation professional," said Waller. "Could be the defendant gets off with a lesser charge. He was provoked." She patted Solomon on the shoulder, walked in front of the table, and said gently, "Tell us what happened. If I'm going to help you, we need facts."

"My name is Solomon-X. I am a prisoner of war. My orders are clear. You get nothing."

"Bull shit," said Cerrillo.

"Are you a military veteran?" asked Waller, trying to appear sympathetic. "Post-traumatic stress could be another mitigating factor."

"The Army wouldn't let a degenerate pervert like him in," said Cerrillo, stepping away. "That's a slur against all veterans as far as I'm concerned."

"Detective," said Waller. "If you don't quit insulting the defendant, I'll have to ask you to leave. We're trying to find out what happened on the night in question. Perhaps the man acted in self-defense."

"We know what happened," said Cerrillo. "Mr. Homo Erectus sliced up some poor drunk at the bar. And for what? Cause the guy called him a bad name. Like I give a shit. The victim was a family man. Salt of the earth Christian. And Solomon here is going down. Maybe we can get him a cell at the zoo if the gorillas don't object." Cerrillo turned to Solomon. "One thing is for sure, the big house knows how to handle dimwitted pansies. You listening, sweet thing?"

Solomon looked at Waller as if Cerrillo were not present. "I would like a pizza."

Waller nodded sympathetically. "Sure. I could go for something myself." She motioned to the officer standing by the door, who was really Agent Jim Ellington dressed in a Providence PD uniform. His task was to watch and evaluate Solomon. "Pepperoni okay?" asked Waller.

"With black olives, please," said Solomon. "I like black olives."

"You got it."

"Beer?" asked Solomon.

"No beer allowed in the station," said Waller. "How about a Coke?"

"Okay," said Solomon.

"Wasting time," said Cerrillo. "Maybe the prisoner would like a massage and conjugal visit, too? Pizza, my ass. He can eat slop like every other convict."

"He's only a suspect at this point. You've heard of the Constitution. Innocent until proven guilty. So while we're interrogating the man, we can spot him a large pepperoni and black olive. One human being to another."

"Pretty liberal definition of human if you ask me," said Cerrillo, thumbing toward Solomon. Cerrillo leaned in close. "You might get empathy from Officer Waller here. She's not much smarter than you about some things. But I didn't fly cross-country to play footsy with the likes of you, and I don't give a damn about your underprivileged childhood or how many times your uncle molested you. I don't even care about the asshole you wasted in that worthless dive you call a job. I want to know about Don't Ask, Don't Tell."

Solomon-X smiled. This was the first time anyone had named the organization. "I'm a soldier. I've mangled tougher mans than you. And I follow orders." Solomon seemed amused.

"Better be careful, General Patton. Tough guys are sometimes found hanging in their cells. I want info about DADT. Not tomorrow or next week, but now! Or you might not walk out of here."

"Loosen these handcuffs," said Solomon. "We see who walks or be hanged."

"Genius," said Cerrillo, shaking his head. "I'm talking to the smartest moron on the planet. Probably opens bottles with his teeth. DADT wouldn't work with this guy. Too stupid."

Cerrillo had struck a nerve.

"That not true!" yelled Solomon. "You don't know nothing. I'm a soldier. Plenty soon, you see."

"See what!?" said Cerrillo. "I doubt that you could wet your pants without supervision. No way you're DADT."

Solomon suddenly hated Detective Cerrillo, and he was sensitive to people calling him stupid. That was worse than faggot. He sat straight and said, "You are a pig. I work with professor. A real professor, like Harvard. And a science lady, too. I help *them*. Ha! Even the Founder knows me. I am friend of Gulf Stream. You are nothing."

At the mention of Gulf Stream, Waller and Cerrillo reflexively turned their heads.

Solomon noticed. "Maybe you show respect now. Gulf Stream makes you afraid, I think. He laughs at pig cops."

Ellington listened and watched, standing motionless. He suddenly wondered if the Founder and Gulf Stream might be the same person.

"Who is this Gulf Stream?" said Waller, innocently. "Is he your ... boss?"

Cerrillo interrupted and stuck his finger in Solomon's face. "Gulf Stream wouldn't have anything to do with this kind of lowlife. The headman of DADT doesn't waste time with simple-minded fools."

"I am not afraid of you," said Solomon, bursting with pride. "Gulf Stream would die for me, and I would die for him."

Cerrillo laughed. "Go ahead. We ain't stopping you."

Solomon turned red. "You're not worth talking to. I know things, and..." Solomon hesitated as if trying to remember. "Between the Ides of March and the Ides of May, justice in America will find its way."

Waller pulled up a chair across from Solomon. She placed her palms on the table, tense but struggling to remain calm. "A poem? A riddle? What does it mean?"

Solomon-X seemed embarrassed, waited, and then repeated, "Between the Ides of March and the Ides of May, justice in America will find its way." This was apparently explanation enough.

Waller realized that Solomon was reciting memorized lines that he probably didn't understand.

"That's great!" said Cerrillo. "My Cocker Spaniel can sit and roll over, and our soldier boy can squawk like a parrot, but he's not as smart as an African Grey." Cerrillo flapped his elbows. "Solomon want a cracker?"

"Leave him alone," said Waller. She looked at Solomon. "Did Gulf Stream teach you that?" she asked and then tried to sound reverent. "Do you *really know* him?"

"I know him," said Solomon, proud and too angry to hold back.

"Liar!" said Cerrillo. "He wouldn't waste time with you. And from what I hear, DADT is running like scared faggots. Not a peep in over ten months. Gulf Stream has turned yellowbelly. The Founder, too." Cerrillo wasn't sure if the Founder was a myth, but he threw the pitch anyway.

Solomon forgot that his legs were shackled to the metal chair and tried to leap across the table at Cerrillo. Everyone except Solomon heard his ankle snap as he twisted against the chair, which caught on the table. Solomon screamed with pain. Then, he clenched his teeth and hushed himself. "I am ... a ... soldier," he said. "We will win!"

Waller tried to help Solomon back into the chair. He yelped.

"I'm sorry," said Waller. "Lie still." She shouted to Ellington. "Send for an ambulance!" Then she looked Solomon in the eye. "Listen to me. Your leg is broken. Near the ankle. I'm going to unlock the cuff that's holding you to the chair. Don't move." Waller could see a bone fragment protruding just underneath the skin.

Solomon nodded. The pain was severe, but detaching the shackle should help.

Waller was no longer playing good cop; she became a real cop again. "Solomon! Remain still when I release the shackles. You're still handcuffed. If you go after Detective Cerrillo, we'll hurt you. Understand?"

Solomon nodded.

"All right." Waller motioned to Cerrillo. "Hand me the key."

"I don't have it..." said Cerrillo, earnestly. "Really!"

"Yes, you do!" said Waller.

"No, I don't." Cerrillo reached into several pockets to confirm. "Oh, damn!" He pulled the key from his jacket and handed it to Waller.

Waller braced the prisoner's ankle with her knee to immobilize it. "Solomon, this might hurt. I'm sorry. Once I get the cuff loose, you should feel better. Okay?"

"Yes," said Solomon, through clenched teeth. "I won't hurt you, sister lady."

"Glad to hear it," said Waller.

Agent Ellington returned to the interrogation room. "The paramedics are en route! Five minutes."

Waller struggled but couldn't open the shackle. "Ankle's swollen! This thing is really tight. Give me a hand!"

Before Cerrillo had a chance to move, Solomon shouted. "Not him! *No one* insults the Founder."

"Let me help!" said Cerrillo.

"Stay back!" commanded Solomon. "Or I'll kill you."

Ellington stepped forward. "What can I do?" He looked at Solomon's leg. "Geez, Louise. You weren't kidding. That swelled up fast. Better wait for the medical team. They might have to cut it off."

Solomon began to thrash wildly. He was a strong man, even with a broken leg.

"No, no!" said Waller. "Solomon! Listen! He didn't mean your foot! He was talking about the shackle. I won't let them hurt you!" She realized that Solomon was part wild beast—angry, wounded, and afraid.

Solomon seemed to relax a bit.

"That's better. It will be all right." Waller spoke to Ellington. "If you can hold his leg, I think I can pry open the cuff."

"Okay," said Ellington, clutching the ankle with both hands.

Waller looked at Solomon. "Here we go. I'll try to be quick. Ready?"

Solomon nodded. Waller inserted the key and pressed as hard as she could. Solomon screamed. The shackle popped open. Solomon groaned as blood rushed into his foot. Then he was silent, and it seemed to Solomon that, for the first time in his life, he had an intellectual moment, a flash of brilliance. The police officer who was assisting Waller had not removed his revolver.

Despite the confusion and pain, Solomon understood that he had already said too much about Don't Ask, Don't Tell. Cerrillo had deliberately provoked him. Waller had deliberately befriended him. But by the grace of the Founder, Solomon was a blood-baptized soldier in a holy war, and he would protect his unit and commander at all costs. After this interrogation, the FBI would surely question him further, perhaps using drugs or torture, until they got what they wanted. He might not be able to resist. An immaculate voice told him what to do, and Solomon-X moved with lightning speed. Cerrillo saw everything in slow motion.

With both hands cuffed together, Solomon twisted hard and somehow reached Ellington's revolver, pulled it from the holster, and maneuvered the barrel under his own chin. He squeezed the trigger. A single shot echoed from the interrogation room. The bullet tore through the side of Solomon's skull and into Josie Waller.

THIRTY-ONE

Seeking Counsel

February 2008

Robert Davenport called Tanish Padgett. He didn't want to leave a recorded message, so he tried several times. Finally, they connected.

"Hello, Tash," said Davenport.

"Oh, hi, Robert," said Padgett. "Nice to hear..."

Davenport cut her off. "I talked with Little Boy. I'm scheduled to meet the Founder."

"Jesus! They agreed to that?"

"Yeah. Reluctantly, I think. Little Boy—god I hate that name—waited over a month to confirm the meeting. Said they had to make special security arrangements. Apparently, nobody meets the Founder but through L.B."

"That's what I've heard."

"And that's what bothers me. Even a CEO at IBM will sit down and chat with the managers now and then. Business schools preach open-door policies, but DADT seems to think they're too good for dialogue."

"We're not a typical business..."

"Still, in the last few months, I've gone sick about skulking around. Secrecy might be necessary, but we don't have to sneak like purveyors of the Black Plague. Less Berchtesgaden and more Fire Side Chat if you ask me." Davenport hesitated. "After all, I'm a member of the organization. My hands are stained. I expect to be kept in the loop."

"Did you ask Little Boy about the Manifesto?"

"I tossed the copy in his lap, demanded to know who wrote it and why I wasn't clued beforehand." Davenport softened his tone. "I didn't mention how I got it."

"They'll probably find out," said Padgett. "Solomon won't hold back anything if they trace the copy to him. He would slash his wrists for the Founder."

"Doesn't matter. I set the meeting. I'll ask the Holy Father what's going on."

"Robert, be careful. Little Boy ranks high in the organization and can't be trusted. And despite the finished Manifesto, they want you for something." Padgett sounded sad. "DADT started out as an LGBT avenger. Whole and clear. But since moving into Phase Two, they seem to be changing ... for the worse. Justice should be as clean as a laser. I'm worried, and we should both be on guard."

"Like I said, I'll ask the Founder about this."

"When's the meeting?"

"April 14. Gulf Stream will pick me up early afternoon and we go from there. Usual protocol."

"That's about two months," said Padgett. "Why are they waiting so long?"

"Don't know."

"Robert, how did Little Boy sound when you first asked about the Manifesto and Founder?"

"What do you mean?"

"Was he worried? Surprised? Did you get any kind of sixth sense?"

Davenport paused. "Now that you ask, I'd say he was expecting this. In a way, he was, because I made arrangements through Gulf Stream for the preliminary talk. You can't just pick up a phone and call LB. I can't, anyway. But still, he didn't know exactly what I was going to say because I didn't tell anybody. I told Gulfy it was urgent, and he agreed to fly me up there. But again, Little Boy didn't seem caught off guard."

"And what, uh, how did you phrase it, exactly?"

"I asked pointblank why they had me wasting time on another Manifesto!"

"And?"

"The son-of-a-bitch sipped his brandy—never seems to be without it—and nodded as though I'd told him the sun rises in the east."

"And then?"

"Little Boy said that I was working on the Manifesto because the Founder requested it. That was good enough for him, and it should be good enough for me. I think he expected me to apologize and go home."

"But you didn't."

"I asked to speak with the Founder."

"And."

"He calmly set down his brandy and said it would take a month or two to make the arrangements. It seemed strange, Tash. I felt almost certain that he had already scheduled the meeting ... like he was just waiting for me to ask."

Padgett began trembling. "How will you actually meet the Founder? Where?"

"No idea. Gulf Stream and Little Boy are figuring out the logistics. It's apparent they trust me less now because I'm asking questions. I don't think they're used to that."

"Robert, you must not go!"

"I have to find out what's going on! Who knows? Maybe he's a nice guy and will offer a legitimate explanation for double dealing."

"They're going to kill you," said Padgett.

"If that's all they wanted, there'd be no need to wait. I would already be dead. So I'll meet the Founder to ask a couple questions before I die. And listen, Tash. I might be a lowly English professor, but I used to be a man, a physical man who could throw his weight around. Besides, I'm learning fast in this organization, and I might not be so easy to kill."

"Don't Ask, Don't Tell invented that game, Robert, and they have a big advantage. You'll be outnumbered and outgunned. Your intellect and motives won't protect you. They aren't an Army who throws out members via dishonorable discharge. Your body will be stuffed in a trunk and dumped on a scrap heap." Padgett drew a deep breath. "Let's run, Robert. Right now! Before it's too late."

"We can't run from homophobia." Davenport suddenly felt that this was the wrong thing to say. "I mean, no more running for me, Tash. Don't worry. Maybe things aren't as bad as we think. I'll talk with the Founder and find out."

"Please, please, don't go!"

"The meeting's on April 14. Just remember to keep a low profile. Hopefully they won't connect my copy of the Manifesto with you." Neither believed this. "And if you don't hear from me by April 15, pack up and run. Don't let the bastards find you."

Padgett was silent for several seconds. She said, "If they kill you, Rob, I won't run, just like I couldn't run after my mother ... died. I fought, instead. That's why I'm asking you not to go. If we leave together now we might have a chance. Robert ... I ... care..."

"Don't say it, Tash. Please. Everything will be okay. Have faith."

"I'll try... If you should change your mind..." Padgett's voice choked, but she continued, "Can I ask a question on a completely different subject?"

"Sure. Anything."

"How are your classes going?"

"What?"

"You know. The university?"

Davenport chuckled with surprise. "Everything's great. Breeze through my course prep. Cancel office hours on a whim. I tell students what they want to hear instead of what they need—the administration probably loves me now. I read student papers in one-fifth the time it used to take. It's amazing how easy teaching can be when a professor doesn't care."

"I'm so sorry, Rob."

Davenport paused for a moment and then chuckled with sadness. "I guess I've become an all too average teacher ... and I so wanted to be special." Suddenly his voice strengthened. "Don't worry, Tash! On April 14, Doctor Faustus intends to reclaim his soul."

THIRTY-TWO

Sorry

April 2008

"When can I see her?" asked Detective Cerrillo

"Officer Waller is still in surgery," said the Rhode Island Hospital emergency room nurse. "Another hour or two. The doctors won't know exactly until they get in and see the damage. X-rays tell only part of the story. But we've worked with gunshot wounds before. Your friend is in good hands."

"She's more than a friend," said Cerrillo. "She's my partner... Her hand looked like ground beef when they brought her in."

"Don't worry," said the nurse. "By the way, does she have family to notify?"

Cerrillo hesitated. Josie had once described her rather *unpleasant* family rejection when she when she came out as a lesbian. "No," he said. "No family to notify."

"I'm sorry. I'm so sorry," said Jim Ellington to Cerrillo in front of the nurse. "It's all my fault. I forgot my training. I forgot everything ... and I'm supposed to understand the criminal mind. God, I'm sorry!"

"Skip it," muttered Cerrillo through clenched teeth. He wanted to beat the hell out of Ellington but remained civil on the expectation that Waller, herself, would sling more than a few choice phrases at Ellington when she came out of the anesthesia.

"I'm so sorry," said Ellington once more. "She might have been killed."

"I said skip it. The worst will be when you tell Judd our star witness is dead. Solomon was our only direct DADT connection, and now he's in the cold room." Cerrillo paused long enough to reveal his agony. "And the best cop I know is in surgery."

Ellington nodded. "We'll check Solomon's apartment and workplace again. Maybe find something. Judd's gonna be pissed, all right. Probably transfer me to the Aleutian Islands unless he can find someplace colder."

Cerrillo was silent but approved the idea. The nurse listened quietly, knowing that the officers needed emotional release.

"I'd better call Judd," said Ellington. Both Cerrillo and Ellington had their cell phones turned off because of hospital policy. "I'll have to step outside."

"Okay, but I'm not leaving this spot until Waller comes out of surgery." Cerrillo could not hide his bitterness. He pointed toward the exit across from the nurses' station. "Go."

"Listen," said the nurse, interrupting gently. "Both of you please try to relax. Your friend has one of the best orthopedic surgeons in New England. Two years ago, he stitched a seven-year-old boy who accidentally shot himself through the hand with his dad's pistol. That kid now pitches little league. Pretty good from what I hear." The nurse was a tall middle-aged woman who had walked hospital tiles for thirty years in almost every department. She didn't know whether the surgeon had really worked on a bullet-through-the-hand kid, but she knew how to calm emergency room families. She also knew that police partners were about as close as *family* could get. "Settle down, boys, and don't worry. In six months, Waller's hand won't know the difference."

"I hope so," said Cerrillo.

"Okay," said Ellington.

Cerrillo hesitated, wanting further reassurance. "So the doc's pretty good?"

"He could graft wings on a hummingbird, and the entire operating team is top rank. You can relax, Detective. Take a walk around the parking lot. Get some coffee. Visit the Dunkin Donuts down the street. The surgeon will talk with you soon. Probably send the patient home in a day or two."

Cerrillo began to feel better. "That kid's really pitching baseball?"

"Yep," said the nurse. "Got a mean curve ball."

"All right," said Cerrillo. "I'll prop myself up in the waiting room. Holler the second the doc comes out."

"Absolutely," said the nurse. "And if you want," she whispered, "I'll bring a cup of coffee from the nurses' lounge. It's New England sacrilege, but I'm not that crazy about Dunkin Donuts myself."

"Thanks," said Cerrillo. "Coffee won't be necessary."

The nurse smiled and went about her business. Ellington and Cerrillo moved from the emergency room to the regular waiting area, where a few other people were sitting.

After several minutes of silence, Cerrillo asked, "Before you call Judd, tell me what the hell happened, Jim? How did Waller catch a bullet?"

"Not sure," said Ellington. "It was all pretty quick. The video playback could help, but the table might be in the way. Somehow Solomon reached my gun, and before I knew which end was up, he had it under his chin. Waller tried to stop him ... I think she reacted on instinct. Bullet went through Solomon's head into Waller. Maybe the video will tell." Ellington took a breath and shook his head. "Doesn't matter though. I screwed up. Almost got her killed."

"That's pretty much the way I saw it."

"If he'd wanted," said Ellington, "Solomon could have probably wasted both me and Waller."

Cerrillo spoke more gently. "How could the guy fire a weapon so fast with his hands cuffed together? Houdini couldn't do that... But if anyone's dead, I'm glad it was Solomon. Not you or Waller."

Ellington understood the tenuous reconciliation. "Stay here and keep an eye out for the doc. I'm going to call Judd. Might as well face the music. You want me to check in with your boss, too?"

"Don't bother. Judd will spread the news. Besides, Ricketts is a first-line cop. She'll know that I'm waiting on Waller's surgeon."

"Right," said Ellington. "Back in a few minutes. God, he's gonna be pissed."

Now that Cerrillo was starting to worry less about his partner, he was becoming increasingly frustrated that Solomon was dead. They had no other legitimate lead. And Cerrillo didn't want Gulf Stream to quarterback Pearl Harbor Day without someone running interference. Solomon's "between the Ides" recital might offer a clue, but they already knew Pearl was scheduled sometime in April. They'd look at the interview tapes, send them to Judd and Ricketts, and pray there was something worthwhile. Maybe DADT *was* running scared. No, Solomon had bragged they were on the move, and dim as he was, he seemed like he would be one to know.

Cerrillo glanced at his watch, wondering when Waller would come out of surgery. He suddenly imagined her parading around Rhode Island with a bandaged arm and bitching at anyone who offered sympathy. She could shoot straight with either hand, and one thing was certain, if the doctors tried to keep her off the job, *they* would need a visit to the emergency room. DADT had drawn her blood, so Waller now had "first rights" in the investigation. Nobody wearing blue would argue that.

Ellington had been gone twenty minutes, and Cerrillo suspected that the conversation with Judd was heated. This was a rookie error in the World Series of interrogations, and Ellington was the chief rookie. Of course, Cerrillo admitted to himself that he should have been looking out for his teammate, so some of the blame was his.

"Detective Cerrillo?" called a man's voice.

The nurse pointed toward Cerrillo. "Over there, Doctor."

"Detective?" asked the doctor again.

"Yes, sir."

"They're taking your friend to recovery. You may see her now."

"How is she?" asked Cerrillo.

"Came through without a hitch. The bullet did less damage than I expected. Passed cleanly. The nerves and tendons to her ring finger got the worst of it. Time will tell how they heal."

"She will still, uh, be able to handle a ... be a cop?"

"No problem. She's a healthy young specimen, all right. Rock hard. Should be running with the bulls in no time."

Cerrillo laughed, obviously relieved. "Thanks, Doc, but if you knew Josie, you'd worry more about the bulls."

"This way, Detective," said the doctor. "Nurse, would you please show him to Recovery B-Q." This was code for the private recovery room reserved for VIPs.

"Yes, Doctor."

"I'm sorry, Detective," said the surgeon, "but I can't accompany you. Got another stitch-er-upper. A kid, a bike, and a car. Too common on the streets of Providence, I'm afraid. Teenagers think they're immortal. Cars don't care."

Cerrillo nodded. "I hope the kid's throwing curve balls soon."

The doctor smiled and walked away but had no idea what Cerrillo was talking about. "Good luck to you and the other officer," he said, looking back.

"This way, Detective," said the nurse. "I told you our team would put her back together."

"That you did."

"Follow me."

Josie Waller was asleep. An IV was taped to her left arm. A heart monitor signaled its gentle beat. And the white gauze bandage on Waller's right hand seemed hardly more than an oversized Band-Aid about three inches square.

"I was expecting a bigger bandage," said Cerrillo, almost to himself.

"Oh, Doc stitched her with real small sutures. Heals faster with a light dressing and strong antiseptic. Less scar tissue. Giving her antibiotics, too, which she'll probably take for a few days." The nurse glanced at the patient chart. "Nothing remarkable. She's in good shape. Released in a day or two." The nurse sighed. "I sure hate to see a uniformed officer in the emergency room. One of my brothers is a Massachusetts State Trooper. I know what they go through. We're gonna take good care of this girl."

"Thanks," said Cerrillo. "Mind if I just sit here until she wakes up? I got to know she's all right. From her."

The nurse smiled and pointed to a chair. "Have a seat. The recovery room chairs aren't too comfortable. On purpose. But you won't be here long. They'll take her to a regular private room in about an hour or two. Should be awake by then. If you need anything, you ask for Jennifer. I'll get it plenty quick."

"I appreciate that," said Cerrillo. "And thanks for the private room."

"Standard policy for an injured officer." She chuckled. "Some years back a cop was shot in the line of duty and the state's insurance company beefed about the cost of a single. Said the policy covered a twin. Just coincidence that a couple of blue boys pulled over the company's chief executive next day for a routine traffic stop and had a little heart-to-heart. Said that next time they might find a pound of cocaine in his trunk. And guess what? Shot cops get private rooms from start to finish along with round-the-clock nursing care. Period. Of course, we were giving it to them even before we had official authorization... Look," said Nurse Jennifer, "I'm gonna check in on other patients. Just hit the call switch if needed, and we'll all come running."

"Thanks," said Cerrillo, sitting down. He suddenly felt very sad, realizing how helpless Waller was at this moment—and how mortal. For a moment, Cerrillo wondered if caring so much about a fellow officer might hamper his *professional detachment*. "To hell with that," he thought. "I'm not gonna pretend to hold back feelings based on some professor's theoretical proclamations about objectivity, and my partner taking a bullet's got nothing to do with theory." Cerrillo then considered the members of his team—Ricketts, Waller, Ellington, even Judd. Maybe he was a better cop with the lot of them than without.

Waller moaned and twitched her neck. She mumbled something incomprehensible and then lay still, asleep again.

Cerrillo had no idea how they were going to pick up the DADT trail from this point. They would return to Solomon's apartment, of course, or maybe Adam Smith and his Scrabble board could lead them. Unlikely on both counts. Still, the intelligence agencies were looking into Smith's Russian connections. Something might turn up. But DADT was not predictable. Cerrillo personally knew of two instances where operatives chose suicide rather than be questioned—Craspen and Solomon. Yet sooner or later, a link in their murderous chain would break. Nothing remained secret forever.

"Hey, partner." Waller blinked her eyes in quick succession, trying to focus. "Why aren't you out looking for Gulfy...? And you look like a train wreck."

"*You* look marvelous," said Cerrillo. "How you feeling?"

Waller had already fallen asleep again. Cerrillo didn't care. She was alive, able to recognize him, and to crack wise. She would be okay, which was more than could be said for Gulf Stream if Cerrillo had anything to do with it. The matter had gone way beyond 'professional detachment.' It was certifiably personal.

***

The nursing staff soon moved Waller to a private room, where, with residual anesthesia, she slept through the night. Cerrillo refused to leave and dozed intermittently in a padded armchair next to Waller's bed. Several nurses checked on Waller throughout the evening, and a freshly starched white uniform entered the room at 6:00 a.m., took the patient's pulse and temperature, and removed the IV still dripping into Waller's arm.

"Good morning," said the nurse to Cerrillo, who roused before Waller. "After sleeping in that chair all night, you may need an appointment with a chiropractor. I can recommend a good one. But don't tell the doctors I said so. They seem to think chiropractors all graduate from Voodoo Tech."

"Don't worry about me," said Cerrillo. "I've slept on worse stakeouts than this. How's our girl doing?"

"Why don't you ask her," suggested the nurse.

"Oh, she's awake!" Cerrillo stood painfully. "Hey, super cop! You were out the whole night. How you feeling?"

"Like shit!" Waller tried to push herself up in bed but flinched from a sharp pain. "Ugh!"

"Don't put weight on your hand!" said the nurse.

Waller lay back. "Forgot I took a bullet. Not that I didn't deserve one, losing a witness like that." She hesitated and then, with faint hope, asked, "Solomon?"

"Dead," said Cerrillo.

"Thought so," said Waller. "The splatter sure looked like it."

"I'll be back in an hour to help you bathe," said the nurse. "They serve breakfast at eight. In the meantime, I'll leave you alone for police talk, although it sounds pretty tame compared to the emergency room. We've seen it all." She smiled. "Use the call button if you need assistance. I'll be back."

After the nurse left, Cerrillo said, "Solomon was not your fault, Josie. Might blame Ellington and me, but mostly it was Solomon himself. He pulled the trigger."

"Thanks for the sugar coating, but we screwed up. I screwed up. A witness is not supposed to die during interrogation. By the way, where is Ellington? Was he hit?"

"No. He went back to the hotel last night after we figured you'd be okay. The poor sap talked with Judd yesterday. I'm surprised his cell phone didn't melt. Judd would have sacrificed any of us over Solomon."

"Judd could be right. If this Pearl Harbor deal is bad as he thinks, our mistake will cost lives." Waller paused and appeared to regroup. She was still fogged with anesthesia. "Help me up. I gotta pee."

"Let's call the nurse."

"Never mind," said Waller. "By the way, what are you doing here so early? It is morning, right?"

"Very. Only been light for an hour, but I had to protect my partner."

Waller pointed at the stuffed chair. "Slept there?" She grinned when it was apparent that he had. "Gee, I didn't know you cared."

"Don't let it go to your head," said Cerrillo. "Cops look after cops. I'd do the same thing for a K-9."

"Sure, sure," said Waller, still smiling. "I won't let on about your growing sentimentality." Waller moved again to sit up. "Damn. This hand of mine hurts!"

"Bullets will do that."

"Isn't there some kind of electronic bed control? Help me raise this. I want to get up."

"We should check with the doctor. You just had surgery."

"To hell with that!" said Waller. "When I was fifteen, a doctor tried to tell me that I was working out too hard at the gym! If I'd listened to him or the school counselors, I'd be teaching kindergarten or punching the clock as a secretary. Makes my skin crawl to think about it." Waller looked at her bandaged hand. "Well, maybe kindergarten has some advantages."

"Are you kidding? Los Angeles first graders pack hand grenades in their lunch boxes, right next to the peanut butter sandwich and Uzi. You're safer on the force or working a coal mine." Cerrillo found the controls and elevated the head of the bed. "I still think we should call a nurse."

Waller ignored him. "Give me the switch, and lower the guardrail. I've got to use the bathroom. My hand might be out of commission, but the bladder's working fine."

With a little assist from Cerrillo, Waller stood, maintained a shaky balance, and walked eight feet to the bathroom. As she returned to the bed, Waller said, "Don't go barefoot around here. The floor is like ice."

"I'll make a note of it."

"And speaking of flagrant sentimentality, thank you for the flowers." Waller gestured toward the windowsill. "Just what the doctor ordered. When did you have time to get them?"

Cerrillo noticed the bouquet for the first time. "I didn't know they were there. Must be the boys at the station." Cerrillo cleared his head. "Wait a minute. Those weren't there when I went to sleep last night. And who delivers flowers before 6:00 a.m.?"

"You got me," said Waller, untroubled. "I'd say we've got a dedicated florist on our hands. Alert the media! Somebody probably dropped them off at the nurses' station and they brought them in during their shift. Why don't you look at the card? It will tell us."

Cerrillo suddenly became concerned and drew his weapon.

Waller laughed. "Are you going to shoot the carnations or the roses? Nobody's in the room but us."

"I'm telling you that those things were not there when I went to sleep last night around two in the morning." Cerrillo walked slowly to the bouquet. Looked at it from every angle. He pulled latex gloves from his pocket and delicately and slowly removed the attached envelope.

"The bomb squad moves faster than you do. Read the card!"

Cerrillo opened the tiny envelope. "He's probably too smart to leave fingerprints, but we can't be too careful."

"Don't worry. If we need to track down a sweet-sixteen FTD delivery girl, we can call and ask. You just don't remember the flowers. The department must've had them delivered."

"I was here the moment they brought you in. I haven't left the room." Cerrillo looked at the note and shook his head. "Besides ... Gulf Stream doesn't work for the department."

"Quit screwing around," said Waller, now serious.

"I'm not screwing around. That bastard was here last night." Cerrillo handed her a glove and the note, stepped outside Waller's room, gun drawn, and glanced up and down the hallway. Nobody but hospital staff. He holstered his weapon and returned to Waller.

Josie had difficulty focusing, but she was able to read the printed message.

Dear Officer Waller: Sorry about your misfortune. I am also sorry about _our_ misfortune. Solomon-X was a reliable DADT citizen. Not the brightest light in the box, perhaps, but his faith in our mission was stellar. We shall miss him at Pearl Harbor.

I hope the flowers will cheer you up. By the way, if you were not a sister, you'd be dead right now. Love, Gulf Stream. There was a PS handwritten below the text. *You are beautiful when you sleep. So is Detective Cerrillo.*

"This guy is beginning to get on my lesbian nerves," said Josie Waller.

"Mine, too," said Cerrillo, in empathy.

Waller laughed. "I won't tell anyone you're a lesbian if you don't tell about the flowers. A girl's got to protect her tough-guy reputation." The delayed effects of anesthesia suddenly pulled at Waller. "I need a little nap. Then I'm gonna get out of bed, track down Mister Gulf Stream, and make him seriously regret his error."

"What error?" asked Cerrillo, anticipating the answer.

Waller replied, "The fool should have killed us while we were sleeping."

THIRTY-THREE

Waiting Game

April 2008

Gulf Stream fidgeted with a ten-stack of Krugerrands. He loved the sound and feel of gold; and with hardly a thought, he manipulated the coins in a one-hand shuffle that rivaled high stakes gamblers holding thousand-dollar chips. Gulf Stream also kept rare silver dollars and early American double eagles, but most of those coins were for investment and aesthetic appreciation. Krugerrands were for tactile enjoyment. King Midas without the curse.

Gulf Stream took great pleasure in his wealth—the freedom of throttling and rolling a private jet at 30,000 feet, the most expensive wines and foods, an abundance of trained servants and managers, and the distinctive caress of bearer bonds, offshore bank accounts, and electronically held gold bullion—but the satisfaction of mere money paled in comparison with the blood ecstasy of Don't Ask, Don't Tell. Every assignment reverberated as a personal victory, and the bridled wait for Pearl Harbor grew more and more difficult. Gulf Stream felt like a sniper who, after days of stealth, focused the crosshairs on his target, yet military strategy dictated, "Hold your fire." It was torture. He burned with the nervous impatience of a younger man. He wanted to fight and win, of course, but primarily he wanted to fight. Action was everything. And like the poet Marvell, Gulf Stream heard time's wingèd chariot breathing fire at his back, mocking his youth and vitality as if they might waste away before the appointed hour.

Pearl Harbor would be in two weeks. Dirty Mary was ready. The controls of the aircraft were ready. Gulf Stream was more than ready. And the anticipatory flush of adrenaline had become almost too much to bear. Perhaps a little side action would settle his nerves. What could it hurt? The Pearl would still be there.

Gulf Stream shuffled the Krugerrands for over an hour, attempting to sedate a psyche that craved vengeance and a body that trembled from the physical denial of aggression. He didn't know if he could wait until April 15. He could almost feel the pulse of a victim's throat between his steel fingers. Death was so intimate.

His thoughts circled like vultures. The Krugerrands continued their dance. Gulf Stream added bourbon to the mix and soon left to find pleasure in the darkness.

***

April 2008

Professor Robert Davenport had a week off from the university. His classes were of minimal importance, and he worked as little as possible to meet university requirements; but now, idle time provided disturbing moments of reflection. Davenport questioned whether Don't Ask, Don't Tell had warped the fabric of his life the way a black hole warps the fabric of space. Certainly, an academic career had once been important to him, as were his friends Daniel Bradford and Mary Anne Shephard. He had allowed DADT to deform those connections, but the error was not his alone. Social prejudice and isolation made their contributions as well, kindling a slow-burn resentment during his lifetime.

Davenport was scheduled to meet the Founder on April 14, two weeks away. Tanish Padgett said that he would likely be killed; however, if DADT expected a complacent victim, they'd receive a lesson in the American tradition of resistance. The once mild-mannered professor had purchased a nickel-plated Smith & Wesson .380 revolver, ironically dubbed "Lady Smith" by the manufacturer and marketed to women for self-defense. All his life, Davenport considered himself too Gandhi to bear arms, but DADT had rearranged that perception. The English professor would not go gently into the night, nor would he passively allow the organization to murder innocent people. He would talk with the Founder, reason with him, and discuss the escalating violence of Gulf Stream and Little Boy. Justice had taken a wrong turn, and the Founder should know.

Davenport did not precisely understand how DADT had faltered, but he understood enough to buy Lady Smith and a box of hollow-point cartridges. He was a language specialist, he studied the rhetoric of lies and deceit, and he had been asked to write a Manifesto that was already written. There were reasons for this. Davenport would discover them and evaluate his options. Lady Smith was one of them.

THIRTY-FOUR

Back to Basics

April 2008

The next day, Margaret Ricketts was on a conference call with Josie Waller and Emmanuel Cerrillo, who were in the Rhode Island Hospital security office. "We think Pearl is going down April 15 or 16," said Ricketts. "I talked with Professor McDaniels at UCLA. Judd, too. Even re-read Shakespeare's *Julius Caesar* for good measure. Not that I got much more out of it this time than the first."

Waller and Cerrillo laughed. "*Julius* couldn't hurt," said Waller. "A wandering soothsayer might do better than we have at tracking down DADT." She waved her bandaged hand in the air. "Probably wouldn't get herself shot in the process either."

Cerrillo felt out of his league with literary references, but it didn't bother him. "I'm just a working man," he said. "Avoid Shakespeare whenever possible and take Hemingway with a shot of tequila." Cerrillo tried to imitate Huck Finn. "Too much book learning tangles the brain sompin' powerful."

Waller re-directed the conversation. "So who figured the date?"

"Mostly Solomon," said Ricketts. "Between the Ides. Mid-April."

"And how do we know Gulf Stream isn't jerking us around with Solomon's nonsense?" added Cerrillo. "I'd like to shove a billy club between both their Ides."

"The Scrabble board also mentioned April," said Ricketts. "Solomon's poem—hurts me to call it that—referred to the Ides of March and May. Ides fall on the fifteenth."

Cerrillo interrupted. "These Ide things? What about *April* 15th"

"There are no April Ides," said Waller. "In some calendars, like the Romans, the ides came on the thirteenth. So they might be off a day or two, but Solomon called March and May. And if I'm any judge, he didn't lay down the strategic plan. Just repeating what he heard."

"I agree," said Ricketts. "Still, DADT might throw a curve. They like to mix violence with moral platitudes."

"Similar to the people who pissed them off in the first place," said Waller.

"Anyway," said Ricketts, "we expect an attack around April 15."

Cerrillo said. "Less than ten days."

"It's nine," said Waller, almost to herself. Then she spoke clearly into the speaker phone. "How bad do you think it will be?"

Ricketts had not told Waller and Cerrillo about the missing plutonium. She wouldn't put that extra weight on them. "Might be nasty," said Ricketts. She paused. "We have agents scattered across the country, but DADT isn't flashing their business cards these days, and disgruntled LGBT folks look like everybody else. That makes them hard to spot in a country that harbors cartoon stereotypes of bearded terrorists with automatic weapons and foreign name tags. Gulf Stream hides behind American mannerisms and business suits."

"The briefcase drill team," said Waller, thinking of the Los Angeles Doo Dah Parade.

"Say, what happens to Caesar in that story?" asked Cerrillo.

"Treachery and assassination," said Ricketts.

"Waller, listen up!" said Ricketts. "What's the status of your wound? You fit for this kind of work?"

"As long as I don't have to go hand-to-hand with anyone over the age of two. Aspirin eases the pain. The doc gave me something stronger if I need it."

"Level with me, Cerrillo. Should we put Waller on the disabled list?"

"She'll do fine."

"You can't pull me off this case, Chief!" said Waller. "I got a score to settle with Gulfy. Don't appreciate a man walking into my sleeping quarters without permission even if he brings flowers."

"She's all right," said Cerrillo again.

"Against my better judgment but..." began Ricketts.

"Thanks!" said Waller

"What do you need to make it work?"

Waller chuckled. "I'd settle for finishing this job and heading back to California. Rhode Island in April is *cold*. A frozen wonderland without the wonder. The sooner we throw Gulf Stream in jail, the better I'll like it."

"Oh, I don't know," said Cerrillo. "A homeboy could get used to this place. Snow's kind of pretty. Beats grey skies and choked freeways."

"In case you haven't noticed," said Waller, "the white stuff is frozen water. I've busted my ass twice slipping on ice and been shot besides. I'm beginning to think Rhode Island doesn't like me."

"See what I mean, Chief. That bullet ain't mellowed her attitude."

"Attitude won't stop DADT," said Ricketts. "We ought to pull her off the case until she's better, but I know how she feels."

"Thanks," said Waller again.

"Don't thank me," said Ricketts, "I might get you killed."

"Worth the risk," said Waller. "I want Gulf Stream."

"What happens after you leave the hospital this week?"

Cerrillo nodded to Waller. "We'll comb through the recording of Solomon's interview. See if we missed anything. Then go back to his apartment."

"The stink's hard to take," said Cerrillo, "but we'll manage."

"Then we'll re-interview people at the bar, which smells worse than the apartment."

Cerrillo interjected, "Ellington's headed back to San Francisco. Snoop around the Smith house, which is furnished like a damned museum. There's some Chinese flowerpot worth half a million. One of the paintings is a Pollock. Looks like something from a yard sale. I still don't know how these jokers got so much money. Terrorists are supposed to be young, broke, and stupid. Anyway, Ellington will crosscheck Smith's connections."

"Solomon's apartment is probably the best bet," said Ricketts. "Try to find something fast." Ricketts trailed off briefly and then came back strong. "Another thing, I want security to review all the video surveillance tapes, inside or outside the hospital. Maybe a camera caught Gulf Stream entering or exiting—a guy with flowers at three in the morning should be easy to spot. We're checking whether someone at the hospital or police department tipped him off about Waller's room, which seems likely."

"Waste of time," said Cerrillo, regretting his insubordination immediately.

"Perhaps," said Ricketts sternly, "but you don't mind if the Pomona Chief of Police does a little police work?"

"Nope. Sorry, boss."

"The lab hopes to track down where that florist's note card was made or purchased. Maybe somebody at a store will remember something. Or they might have a surveillance tape. But nine days is short order for this kind of work. Billions of greeting cards are produced and sold every year."

"From Wal-Mart to Hallmark," said Cerrillo

"Don't forget the Internet," suggested Waller. "And self-printed cards."

"For a thousand reasons the odds are against us," said Ricketts

"On top of that," added Cerrillo, "Gulf Stream is a slick son of a bitch."

"Do you say sick or slick?" asked Ricketts.

"A two-for-one special."

THIRTY-FIVE

Davenport's Plan

April 2008

Robert Davenport finished his preparations to meet with the Founder of Don't Ask, Don't Tell. The itinerary was simple. A driver would pick up Davenport on Monday, April 14, at 2:00 o'clock, and he would be escorted to the airport. Similar to the travel arrangements for his conferences with Little Boy, the professor would be transported to a clandestine location.

Padgett repeatedly warned Davenport not to go to the meeting, suggesting instead that they gather as much cash as possible, drive to Mexico, open several discrete bank accounts in U.S. dollars, and bribe their way into the invisible heart of a rural culture. From there, they might eventually travel to South America or Europe.

After Pearl Harbor, she said, anyone connected with DADT would be pursued by every law enforcement agency in the country, and the two of them would additionally be hunted by Gulf Stream—double jeopardy. The best they could hope for then would be that the FBI caught them first. Their best chance for survival was to evaporate, now, and begin new lives.

Davenport believed that Padgett was probably right, but inner pride pushed back at him. Davenport wanted to know whether or not DADT had played him for a sap, a chump, a liberal arts geek with postmodern gibberish for brains. He wanted to talk with the Founder and learn the truth about the Manifesto. And afterward, it still might be possible to slip into the bowels of Central America with Padgett. Maybe he could be a real professor again, rejoining the profession with a much greater potential to foster social change than the murderous dreams of Little Boy and Gulf Stream. Somehow he had forgotten that education could lift the humblest person to the greatest heights, forgotten that he was a teacher and not an executioner, forgotten that he never owned the right to *become* an executioner. The English professor shook his head in realizing he had played himself a far greater fool than DADT could ever have done.

Davenport assumed that he would be searched before boarding the airplane to the meeting, which presented the problem of how to carry his newly purchased Lady Smith. He did not want violence but must be prepared for it, and he planned to carry the Manifesto in his briefcase along with a few papers reasonably necessary for the conference. Lady Smith would be in a black felt bag at the bottom of the case where it might remain hidden during a hasty search. And if Gulf Stream found the gun, what of it? It was logical that Davenport should carry a weapon among his working papers. He was a member of DADT, a soldier who must always be ready for action. "We're not in the pastry business," he'd say.

The mild-mannered professor also practiced taping a switchblade knife along his spine just below the shoulder blades. The only pat-downs Davenport had ever seen came from movies and airport security, which suggested that the sides of the body and legs were target areas. Officers looked for a shoulder-holstered weapon or something hidden in a waistband, around the ankles, or along the inner thighs. They expected the bulk of pistol, so it might be possible to conceal a slim folded knife against his skin with surgical tape. Lady Smith was the weapon of choice, but if the gun were confiscated, a switchblade would be better than harsh language if push came to shove.

Davenport had one last ace up his sleeve—he could think on his feet and respond to the unexpected. Gulf Stream and DADT might rate him just poorly enough to lower their scrutiny to "chump-guard." If they did, and if Davenport and the Founder were alone, their impressions of the English professor might turn back to hurt them. The Founder could either politely answer reasonable questions, or the professor could impolitely draw blood. Davenport would, of course, maintain a genteel exterior image, but his previously genteel interior had been hardened by the subzero philosophies of Gulf Stream—the coldest man on Earth.

THIRTY-SIX

Tracking Gulf Stream

April 2008

Two days later, Emmanuel Cerrillo and Josie Waller huddled around a small video screen at the downtown Providence police station. Chief Margaret Ricketts was patched in with a video-chat system so they could review the hospital surveillance video from the night of Gulf Stream's visit.

"We have a shot of our delivery boy," said Ricketts. "He walked through the emergency room entrance, which is the only access between midnight and 6:00 a.m. The hospital locks everything else late at night, even for employees." Ricketts started the video. "The image is overexposed. Fluorescent lights play havoc with old-style VHS. Digital would have been better, but the hospital was trying to save money. Still, the picture is pretty good, and we're circulating digital copies to other agencies. Can you guys see this?"

"Yeah," said Waller.

Ricketts continued. "Gulf Stream must have been watching. He doesn't enter the building until the ER nurse steps away from the desk. Right there! See that. The man strolls in like a tourist. There are your flowers, Waller."

Cerrillo and Waller watched the playback with anger and frustration. The brazenness astounded them. One of the most wanted men in the country calmly enters a building, walks to a room with two police officers, and delivers a spring bouquet.

"That bastard has iron *cojones*," said Cerrillo.

"Not when I get through with him," said Waller.

Ricketts stopped the video as Gulf Stream walked beyond camera range. "That's all we have. He must have gone out another door," she said. "Won't help much. He's got a trench coat with an up-turned collar, gloves, a brimmed hat, and mock-turtle sweater. And he positioned the flowers to obscure his face—he knew the hospital would have cameras."

Cerrillo said, "The guy could be standing next to me and I wouldn't recognize him from the tape."

"Pretty sure he was wearing a wig," said Ricketts. "That mop top doesn't look quite real. Pumpkin-brown?"

"A nice shade of mule piss," said Cerrillo. "Maybe the guy gets his hair dyed at K-Mart."

"I doubt it," said Waller. "That coat looks tailor made. Or it might be high-end London Fog. He probably didn't buy it off the rack, so unless he stole his wardrobe, the man has money."

Cerrillo laughed. "I didn't know you were a fashion consultant, Josie."

"I'm not, but we bust rich guys right along with skid row. And in the City, if you care about staying dry, you care about raincoats. Umbrellas just drag you around in the wind."

"There isn't much to identify," said Ricketts, "but Gulf Stream is a big man. Over six feet, and I'm guessing two hundred pounds, a white male, late 30's to early 40's. Looks strong."

"With a disposition to hack off body parts and ship them to third parties," said Waller.

"So don't put him on the dinner invitation list," said Ricketts. "We'll try to come up with another video, but hospital surveillance was our best chance."

"Only four days until the attack," said Waller. "I hope Pearl turns out to be a lot of hot air because we can't stop it. We'll never find Gulf Stream in time... In fact, we can't be absolutely certain it's him on the tape. Might be one of his DADT flunkies."

"Then I'll arrest his ass, too. But I'm guessing that's our boy! Gulfy likes these kinds of games."

Rickets interrupted. "Just do your jobs. It's certain somebody delivered those flowers to Waller's room, and I want him. So keep moving. Turn over every loose board. Focus on anybody connected with Solomon. Gulf Stream is out there somewhere, and he was likely in Providence three days ago. He doesn't have superpowers. He's not invisible. And if we track him down, we might put the brakes on Pearl Harbor." Ricketts paused. "How's your hand, Josie?"

"Fine," said Waller. "I get the stitches out in three days."

"Glad to hear it," said Ricketts. "If you don't know already, SFPD has recommended you for a distinguished service medal."

"More like distinguished stupidity," said Waller. "Shot by a handcuffed suspect with another cop's gun. Brilliant."

"Nobody's asking you!" interrupted Cerrillo. "If the boss says you're recommended for a citation, you're recommended! Where I come from, it counts for something when a cop takes a bullet." Cerrillo had been one of the people to endorse the nomination. "And you'll take the damned medal and like it!"

Ricketts laughed. "Sounds like you two are still playing well together."

"Oh, I can tolerate him on a good day," said Waller. "And because I apparently have no choice but to accept a medal, be advised. I plan to shove it up one of Gulf Stream's bodily orifices."

THIRTY-SEVEN

The Founder

April 2008

It was April 14, the day before Pearl Harbor, but Professor Davenport didn't know that. He looked in the mirror and steadied himself. The knife was taped low between his shoulder blades; Lady Smith lay in the briefcase under the Manifesto and a batch of student papers. If needed, he might have a chance for one weapon or the other.

Tanish Padgett had registered at a Boston hotel under an assumed name, where she would wait until she heard from Davenport after his meeting with the Founder. If she received no information in twenty-four hours, Padgett should assume that Davenport was dead and escape to Mexico. If Davenport survived, the two of them might cross the border or continue to work with DADT, depending on what happened at the meeting. Either way, the English professor had resolved that if reasonable men could not be reasonable, he would fight.

At 1:55 p.m., a navy blue Ford Expedition with tinted rear windows pulled into Davenport's driveway. The suspension looked too high for a luxury SUV, the tires too rugged, and Davenport wondered if the vehicle had been modified to support armor and reinforced glass. It reminded him of the presidential limousine. To Davenport's surprise, both Gulf Stream and the driver emerged from the front seat. Someone else was in the passenger compartment.

Gulf Stream approached the front door threshold, where Davenport was standing, briefcase in hand, ready to go. "Good afternoon," said Gulf Stream.

"Afternoon," said Davenport.

"Mind if we come inside for a few minutes?" asked Gulf Stream.

"Not at all." Davenport gestured toward the vehicle. "What about your passenger?"

"Later," said Gulf Stream, without looking back. "Let's talk."

They entered Davenport's living room. Gulf Stream glanced around. The driver began a careful inspection, moving down the hallway and back again, peering into different rooms.

Davenport looked at Gulf Stream, walked into the living room, set his briefcase on the floor near the sofa, and took a seat. "We're not leaving, are we?"

"No."

Davenport nodded, his case within easy reach. "Do you plan to kill me in my own house?"

"Don't be ridiculous," said Gulf Stream, glancing around the room. "You have a meeting with the Founder. At this moment, you're one of the safest men on the planet."

The limo driver returned, nodded to Gulf Stream, and whispered into his jacket lapel. "All clear."

Outside, Davenport heard the vehicle door open and close, followed by soft, delicate footsteps. A small, oddly familiar man entered the living room. The driver lowered his head as the visitor walked past. Then he closed the front door.

"Hello, Professor," said the Founder. "I've been looking forward to meeting you."

Gulf Stream stepped back as the Founder approached Davenport, but he and the driver remained erect, watching. Davenport was certain that, despite Gulf Stream's reassurances, if he made any sudden motion, he would be shot.

"Good afternoon," said Davenport. "I'm surprised that you came *here*. It wasn't necessary."

The Founder smiled. "Perhaps, though because you now have doubts about our organization, Gulf Stream suggested that it might be prudent to keep my place of business, which is also my residence, secret. This seems excessive, but the government will soon be very interested in our band of merry men, so perhaps my security chief knows best."

"My guess is the Feds already have an interest," said Davenport. He wanted to begin his direct interrogation but decided to wait.

"Yes, that's true. Scrutiny is the price of overt action." The Founder, wearing an exquisitely tailored charcoal suit with a silk tie, had his hands behind his back and walked slowly toward the living room. "May I sit down?" he asked. "I am not as young as I once was, and I hope to chat at length about your concerns. I'd like us both to be comfortable."

"Please," said Davenport, gesturing toward the stuffed chair beside the sofa. "I would offer refreshments, but I didn't know you were coming. And I suspect that if I move beyond breathing, your associates will kill me."

"My dear professor, put that out of your mind, please. I did not travel all this way to have you murdered today." The gentle, almost feminine man then seemed to hard shift. His tone was glacial. "Besides, if I wanted you dead, you would be. If I wanted you to hang yourself in your classroom, that's where they would find your body." He resumed his softness, turned toward the stuffed chair, picked up Davenport's briefcase, and set it out of the way. "Oh, my," said the Founder as he sat. "From the weight of your attaché, one might guess that you planned to work during the flight. I hope the university is not overburdening you."

Lady Smith was no longer at hand, but Davenport held his courage. "On the contrary, most of my time has been devoted to a particular document I was asked to write. *Literature* is serious business to me, and I put a lot of time into it."

"Oh, yes. The Manifesto. You must beg my forgiveness. Oh, I meant to say I must beg your forgiveness, but I wanted to see what you would produce. It's unfortunate that Ms. Padgett stumbled on the preview copy of our dear departed Solomon-X."

Crap, thought Davenport. He hadn't known that Solomon was dead, which probably meant the cops were getting closer. Now, Davenport regretted not escaping with Padgett or perhaps even going to the police himself, but all he could do at this point was continue the dialogue and hope for the best. The fact that he and Padgett had been out of the loop regarding Solomon did not bode well for Davenport's future with DADT—or Padgett's. At least she's safe for the moment, he reassured himself, and I'm not dead yet.

"Why give the Manifesto to Solomon?" asked Davenport, trying to sound unruffled though he could feel his own heart beating.

"Isn't that what you call reader-response theory? I am not sure about the terminology, but I needed to be sure the least intelligent of my followers could understand most of the Manifesto. If Solomon understood it, the public would too. One thing we learned from Adlai Stevenson is that brilliance is wasted on the moronic majority. Solomon was merely a test, nothing more, and if the Manifesto passed the Solomon comprehension trial, it could be released on Pearl Harbor Day. We would have provided you with a copy in due course. Unfortunately, Padgett found the document and betrayed DADT by giving it to you. That's not how a tightly run organization should function. It cost us your allegiance."

Davenport leaned back, again hoping to appear relaxed. He felt the knife between his shoulders. "One thing? Who drafted the Manifesto? Some parts seem unnecessarily hostile, but it's very good."

The Founder nodded. "Thank you. I wrote it years ago with suggestions from my senior officers. I do think it comes off nicely. And as for the hostility, well, my dear professor, provocation is our method, but peace is our goal."

"Peace?"

"With the ultimate objective of disbanding the organization. We'll bury Don't Ask, Don't Tell when its members have *full* civil rights."

Davenport was sure that the Founder was lying though he didn't know why. "Turn swords into plowshares?"

"Precisely."

Davenport reasoned that the Founder was as dispassionately lethal as he was acutely intelligent, notwithstanding his professionally honed manners. He had managed to bring DADT together and inspire the kind of devotion now standing at attention in Davenport's living room; that required great skill. But Davenport, too, was an Ivy League intellect, and even with a knowledge deficit about DADT's inner-structure, Davenport thought he might spar with the man and win. To the Founder, on the other hand, the professor was in the somewhat pitiable position of a homeless kitten. The Founder could offer assistance or have him euthanized, depending on this meeting.

Davenport braced himself. "To get to my point in requesting this conference, why was I asked to work on a Manifesto that was already beautifully written?" The flattery was designed to put the Founder at ease.

After a discernible silence, the Founder said dryly, "I thought I answered that question. I wanted to see how your Manifesto would compare with my own, and the document would have revealed a lot about your frame of mind. It never occurred to me that I should need another reason. Rank has privileges, but perhaps I've surrounded myself with too many unquestioning associates."

Davenport wondered if Gulf Stream noticed the subtle insult, or whether he would even consider it an insult. "And suppose mine had been better?"

"I would have incorporated it into the final document, even supplanting the original if necessary. I'm not such a visionary fool as to discard the best available option. Surely you don't think that of me?"

Davenport remained cautious. "With all due respect, sir, I don't know you well enough, either way."

The Founder smiled. "How I wish, Professor, that you had not prematurely discovered the Manifesto. We have lost a wondrous potential."

"You seem to think I have turned on you," said Davenport, "which is not the case. I am, however, opposed to being played for a jester. I volunteered my services to DADT, and finding a second Manifesto would raise questions for anyone. Why trick me? Why the double booking?"

The Founder seemed to relax. "Because I wanted to know where your feet were planted. I wanted to add your name to the document and be sure it contained some of your, oh, distinct language. It was always meant to be collaborative. I apologize if you were led to believe otherwise. Surely you wondered why we recruited a tenured professor from a prestigious university, and it wasn't just because you had strong hands and were annoyed with homophobic colleagues. In our second phase, we want *thoughtful* terror, to throw a little fear at Middle America. Make 'em sweat."

"That might be over-reaching," said Davenport. "Prejudice has its own courage."

"Ever been in an earthquake?"

"Sure," said Davenport, "in California. I was camping in Big Bear when the 7.1 hit Twenty-Nine Palms. Rattles nerves, all right."

"When solid ground turns out to be fluff, there's a special emotional instability that goes with the realization." The Founder nodded with patriarchal certainty. "Similarly, we intend to rattle the middle-class social fabric as well as the intellectual and financial elite. With names like yours on the Manifesto or other DADT documents, and a few strategic burning buildings to accompany them, we expect to upset their pit-of-the-stomach security. The most self-righteous homophobes, from senators to janitors, will soon wonder whether one of our agents might be hovering nearby—a teacher, lawyer, doctor, anybody. That's Phase Two, Professor Davenport. A psychological earthquake that no one can predict until the ground moves and throats are slashed."

Davenport found himself growing annoyed with the Founder. Something about his speech said "sophomoric." And the mere hint of intellectual inferiority in an opponent empowered English professors in the same way alcohol empowered a drunk.

"But real names on the Manifesto would create real problems for the people on the list."

"We have a way around that," said the Founder.

Davenport was about to challenge this but decided against it. Instead, he asked, "Before going further, shall I remind you why I considered joining Don't Ask, Don't Tell in the first place?"

"By all means," said the Founder. "However, if you don't mind, I'd like my driver to set up afternoon tea and refreshments. I have a strict schedule, and I try to eat balanced meals as part of the routine. Please join me. Kind of a late lunch, more-than-a-snack affair." Without waiting for the professor's response, the Founder motioned to the driver, who exited the house. Gulf Stream remained steadfast.

"Fine," said Davenport, aware that he had been preempted.

"I took the liberty of having a few dishes prepared beforehand and placed in the vehicle's refrigerated compartment. My driver, who is also an excellent chef and valet, requires about twenty minutes, but you'll find the meal enjoyable. A lobster salad with imported mozzarella and a hearty cabernet sauvignon. For dessert, there's a semi-sweet port to die for. I trust you'll like it."

"Undoubtedly," said Davenport, sounding impatient. "In the meantime, shall I explain why I joined...?"

"I already know," said the Founder. "But tell me why you *think* you joined."

Now Davenport was really annoyed, which temporarily lessened his fear. "Because," said Davenport, "I desperately wanted to believe that first newspaper clipping, which I still keep in my wallet. You might have forgotten. It was a call to fight injustice, to become part of a unique and righteous organization. I had suffered humiliation because of the university's delayed tenure decision and the rumors as to why. I wanted ... *needed* to believe in something."

"I sympathize," said the little man. "By the way, I merely approved the language of that job listing. Gulf Stream wrote it with the help of our psychologists, and I'm sure he appreciates the compliment."

Gulf Stream did not move, and Davenport had not offered a compliment.

"He's very well trained," said Davenport, thumbing at Gulf Stream. "I've had some interaction with him, more with Little Boy, and I'm sure both have talents beyond what I know."

"They do."

Davenport leaned forward. "The battle against injustice! That's why we're supposed to be here. Yet from the Manifesto, and from what little I know about Pearl Harbor, I'd say that more than a few innocent people will be hurt." Davenport leaned back on the sofa, sure that moral authority had turned in his favor. "Tell me, sir. Why must the fight involve innocents? Perhaps we define justice differently. Or perhaps I'm confused."

The Founder smiled like a mad scientist in a clichéd movie. The professor tensed again.

"Doctor Davenport, before we leave this afternoon, you will know much more about Pearl Harbor and DADT. I promise. However, you are confused about the enemy."

"I don't think so," said Davenport. "I thought we were fighting bigoted, homophobic lunatics who torment gays and lesbians."

The Founder shook his head. "Extremists are not the whole issue, Professor."

"What?"

"No, the real enemy is a concept, a monster, very much like Mary Shelley's anthropomorphic creation."

Davenport sighed and said, "You've lost me. Shelley?" He expected an inadequate or evasive explanation.

"Let me tell a story." The Founder looked up at the driver who had returned from the vehicle rolling a service cart with lobster salad, cheese, red wine, polished sterling flatware, china, and crystal goblets. The cart stuck at the threshold, but with a brief assist from Gulf Stream, the driver wheeled it toward the living room.

"On second thought," said the Founder to the driver, "why not set up at the dining table. The professor and I can eat and talk more comfortably there. We'll return to the living room for the after-dinner port, which I am sure our guest will appreciate."

"To die for?" said Davenport.

The Founder smiled. "Yes. Is that all right with you, Professor?"

Davenport nodded, though the driver had already turned toward the oak dining set. "Everything will be ready in a few minutes, sir," said the driver, a man Davenport had not seen before.

"Thank you," said the Founder. He turned back to the professor. "And now, where were we?"

"You were about to deconstruct Shelley's monster," said Davenport, with a classroom tone of humored superiority.

"Quite right," said the Founder. "First, I am a preacher. Well, more than that, I am a rather successful church leader. I'm surprised that you didn't recognize me when I came in. I've done many televised ministries."

"To tell you the truth," Davenport said, "you looked familiar, but I assumed it was my imagination. I didn't believe *that man* could be the Founder of DADT. I hope you aren't offended."

"Not at all. Though surprisingly, it was my own congregation that revealed the nature of the monster to me, and I learned as Doctor Frankenstein learned, tragically. You see, I am heterosexual, raised with Baptist hellfire hovering at every corner and every infraction. Belief is very important to the faithful, and I earnestly wanted to be a preacher. So I spoke from my heart all the darkness that had been spoken to me about homosexuality. I embraced the spirit of those words, and I sowed and reaped a loyal congregation on the heels of burning, hateful rhetoric. Then, quite unexpectedly, and you must grasp that it was unexpected, God came to me. It was Easter. He spoke directly and only to me. Even for a man of faith, this was hard to fathom, but I fell to my knees and listened. The Lord praised my energy and devotion, said I was a good man, pure in spirit, and He was pleased about many things. There was, however, a problem with my actions." The Founder gestured toward the heavens. "I am sure my pulse stopped when I heard that."

"Luncheon is ready, sir," said the driver.

"Shall we move to the table, Professor?" The Founder extended his hand to the driver, who helped him from the chair. "This looks wonderful, Victor. Thank you. I could never travel without your help."

"It's an honor to be of service, sir."

"Bless you! I think we are both doing God's work."

Davenport and the Founder sat at the table. "We'll serve ourselves today, Victor," said the Founder. "Although, if you would be good enough to pour the wine."

Victor uncorked the cabernet sauvignon. "We should allow a few minutes before pouring, sir."

"To do it properly, we should. But with today's hectic schedule, let's proceed. This particular vintage should hold up even under such impropriety."

"Yes, sir."

The valet spoke with the quiet devotion of an automaton and poured an ounce of red-black liquid into a goblet. The Founder sniffed its bouquet, swirled the wine to coat the sides of the glass, held it to the light, and then drank. "I was right," he said, letting out a reverent breath. "Even haste cannot diminish this bounty from Heaven. Please serve, Victor."

The servant poured, set the bottle on the table, and retreated beside Gulf Stream.

The Founder lifted his glass toward Davenport. "Here's to Mary Shelley."

Davenport raised his in return. "I'll drink to that gal any day."

The Founder continued as from a script. "And God told me there was a problem with my views on homosexuality. He insisted that it should have been clear from the *Bible* that I was misguided, but greater people than I had been fooled by Satan, so He forgave me, and I was commanded to stop preaching against gays and lesbians, to stop immediately and completely. And more than that, God reached inside me. My heart started beating again. Every misgiving I had about homosexuals vanished, and I discovered as pure a love and understanding as I had ever known. God let me *enjoy* these feelings for several minutes before He spoke again."

Davenport listened. He drank his wine. He was frightened in a way that had nothing to do with his personal safety. An organization with great destructive power had been created by a madman.

"God said I was to spread a word of love, to challenge homophobia everywhere, but first and most especially in my own church."

"That must have alarmed you," said Davenport, surprised to hear his own voice.

The Founder chuckled. "No, I was too naïve to be alarmed, just as you are. After all, these were my people, in a church I had built from nothing. Surely if I spoke about revelations from God, about divine knowledge, my congregation would follow. They would share my joy." The Founder shook his head. His demeanor turned. "But like Doctor Frankenstein, I discovered that my creation was an uncontrollable brute, disobedient, ungrateful. And when the congregation turned against me, they turned against God. That was unforgivable. The insult to me personally would have meant nothing. But

to stand against the word of God? No! Like Frankenstein, I decided to undo my own handiwork."

The Founder leaned forward and clasped his hands
together. "I understood then why God had chosen me. I
was strong enough to challenge the self-same religious
body that I had stitched together from fragments of
moral consciousness; and I was smart enough to deci-
pher how God wanted this done, though He would not
tell me directly. Much like Noah had constructed his
Ark, I would painstakingly construct a new, specialized
organization to un-create the monster of prejudice,
starting first with my own congregation and branching
out from there." The Founder sighed and looked tired.
"Don't Ask, Don't Tell came together slowly, piece by
piece, secretly, over twenty years. I searched high and
low for the right men and women. It has been a heavy
burden, but no one who values his eternal soul may turn
his back on the Lord's command."

Davenport gulped the last of his wine. The Founder
looked pleased.

"And it is clear from our success that we have earned
His support."

Davenport held his empty glass half-way between his
lips and the surface of the table.

"I can see," said the Founder, "that you appreciate the
irony."

"What irony?" asked Davenport, barely realizing that
he spoke.

"I am a leader of an enormous religious congregation.
I have financial resources and devoted followers, devoted in the name of God. I use my office in the
prosecution of evil as others have used theirs in the per-
secution of homosexuality, and I am better at it because
I have God's support while they have only the pretense."

"I understand," said Davenport, rousing his consciousness. "But, sir, if you don't mind my saying, DADT
isn't exactly 'Jesus camp.' There are consequences for

violence. Just one betrayal from a follower, one person who knows you and becomes disillusioned, could put the brakes on the whole outfit, could endanger you." Davenport tried to sound concerned for the Founder, but he now hoped, earnestly, that he might be the person to stop DADT—if he could survive this meeting.

"We all live with risk, Professor, but to pursue a greater glory, who would not risk life and limb? I am the hand of God." The Founder set his wine glass on the table. "Besides, I expect to be betrayed sooner or later— same as Jesus—but I think it will be later, after the first-phase mission is finished. I have the best possible managerial talent, and they all have blood on their hands, which is the strongest of loyalty oaths. I am a pillar of the community. Pious beyond reproach. And because I once was the enemy, I must work doubly hard to make amends to the LBGT community. Think of it, Professor. I control the resources of a thriving, tax-free, nonprofit organization in a techno-industrial nation filled with semi-illiterates who want to be told what to believe and what to do. I preach to their pocketbooks, but I work directly under God. I have a volunteer army among the top percentiles of education and intelligence who are dedicated and invisible. And each one knows he's expendable." The Founder took a deep breath of satisfaction and chuckled. "The bigots haven't got a chance."

Davenport started to speak but was preempted again.

"Further," said the Founder, turning his palms toward heaven, "I answer only to Him in my direction of these resources. My supporters answer only to me."

"Some might say that kind of devotion is dangerous."

"God's wrath is dangerous...!" The Founder leaned back, took a deliberate sip of wine, and said, "I must apologize. It seems I've drifted into a sermon."

"I think I'm a little overwhelmed," said Davenport.

"Divinity is hard to grasp, especially for intellectuals. But regarding more earthly concerns, let's face it,

Professor. I am not the Founder of Don't Ask, Don't Tell. The real founder is hatred. I'm just the CEO that pulled things together." The Founder smiled. "And I'm probably the *only* chief executive who is willfully trying to put himself out of business. Unfortunately, there is an abundance of malice in the world, so I'll go on doing God's work." He gestured around the room. "I serve the Lord. Gulf Stream and Victor serve me. We shall take an eye for an eye, and unlike Gandhi, who thought this would leave the whole world blind, we understand it will ultimately endow them with new vision."

"And make the lion lie with the lamb?"

"No. We shall demonstrate what happens when the lamb, tired of sacrifice, becomes the lion."

Davenport grew dizzy, presumably from an unsavory mixture of platitudes and wine. "I still don't like the idea of collateral damage, hurting innocent people..." said Davenport.

The Founder smiled. "Nor do I, but with prayer, I have learned to accept it. After all, many died in the Great Flood, but that was necessary to cleanse the earth."

Robert Davenport realized that he was feeling more than revulsion. His vision blurred. He flexed his eyelids and said, "I don't see so good."

"I'm afraid you've been drugged," said the Founder.

"What do you mean?"

"The wine," said the Founder. "Victor used a hypodermic needle to inject a sedative through the cork into the bottle. I saw it done in a movie."

"And you?" asked Davenport.

"Oh, I took a counteracting agent before I arrived. Though I do feel a rather pleasant buzz."

"And what about me ... and Pearl Harbor?" asked Davenport, letting the glass slip from his fingers without realizing it.

"Don't worry," said the Founder. "You'll be an honored participant. We'll talk further tomorrow." The Founder paused and motioned to Gulf Stream, who braced the professor. "I am truly sorry, Doctor, but you must understand. God is our general. You are a regrettable casualty of war."

As Davenport was losing consciousness, one last thought occurred to him. "If you hurt her," he said, "it won't be God that comes looking for you."

"Do not trouble yourself about Miss Padgett," said the Founder. "We shall take care of her. We shall take care of everything."

THIRTY-EIGHT

Pearl Harbor

April 2008

April 15 began routinely. Police departments, the FBI, and Homeland Security were wary but had no specific leads regarding Pearl Harbor. Many officials hoped that Don't Ask, Don't Tell was mostly hype and hot air, but the Transportation Security Administration maintained heightened vigilance for potential hijackings. A few extra black-and-whites patrolled near public buildings and schools. Yet among the millions of civilians starting a normal workday across thousands of cities in America, there was little that law enforcement could do beyond preparations for a swift counterstrike should DADT materialize.

Chief Margaret Ricketts attended to civic business at the Pomona Police Station. In two hours, she would meet with the Mayor and City Attorney about the departmental budget, new recruits, and facilities' maintenance with a predictable negotiation ritual: The police would get less than they asked for; the city would concede more than it wanted; Ricketts would be bored to death. The closed-door resolutions would be followed in one week by public Council hearings that carried no real authority but allowed for community venting—an important democratic safeguard.

Agent James Ellington was in San Francisco, chasing leads about Don't Ask, Don't Tell. He had been to Smith's home three times, placed calls to Vegas and Washington, talked with Waller and Cerrillo, visited the zoo, searched Alex Craspen's former residence and business, and found nothing new. As far as Ellington could tell, DADT had evaporated as quietly as a disturbed dream.

Solomon-X was cremated in Providence, Rhode Island. The morning television and radio programs ran stories about tax return deadlines and extensions, deduction tips, and post offices that would remain open until midnight to ensure a timely postmark. And there were on-the-spot interviews with bedraggled taxpayers who habitually mailed their returns on April 15 but resolved to file early next year.

Tanish Padgett was alone in her hotel room. The lights were off and shades were drawn. She was crying. Robert Davenport had not called, but she decided to wait until April 16, tomorrow, before leaving. If Padgett hadn't heard from Davenport by then, she would assume he was dead and retreat to an obscure corner of Mexico. In the meantime, she would wait by the phone with a box of tissues.

Officer Josie Waller and Detective Emmanuel Cerrillo stopped at the Macaroni Grill for a late lunch in

Warwick, Rhode Island. They tried not to think about the date.

"How's your hand?" asked Cerrillo, sipping a glass of iced tea.

Waller flexed her fingers. "The doc did a good job, but I need to wean myself from pain pills. Starting to like them too much."

Cerrillo smiled and then grimaced. "I wonder what Gulf Stream's doing."

"Nothing, I hope," said Waller. "It's almost two o'clock. Maybe we got the date wrong. Maybe Solomon was blowing smoke, a ragamuffin with Ragnarok dreams."

"You believe that?"

"I'm trying to."

Cerrillo nodded. "I've run out of ideas about Gulf Stream. Not sure I could find him across the table. Some detective..."

"Let's eat. If he makes a move, about all we can do is chase him down afterwards."

"Probably, but I hate sitting on my thumbs." Cerrillo's cell phone chimed. "Hello," he said, swallowing a bite of rigatoni, listening, and jotting down an address. "Okay. Tell the boss we'll get on it as soon as we finish lunch. Anything else?" Cerrillo wrote a few more notes. "All right. Thanks."

"What's up?" asked Waller, pushing food around her plate like a child who doesn't want to eat her green beans.

"That was Henry," said Cerrillo, "the chief's assistant."

"Never met him."

"Wants us to check out some English professor in New Haven. Probably caught a student smoking in the hallway. I think they're grabbing at straws, but we'll drive down after lunch."

Waller shook her head. "Like Gulf Stream hires grammarians. What's the guy's name?"

Cerrillo glanced at his notepad. "Uh, Robert Davenport. Got his home address. If he's not there, we can drive to the university and ask around."

"I want Gulf Stream, not some Ivy League pencil pusher." Waller paused and asked, "How did Pomona get the tip?"

"Not sure. I think over the Internet."

Waller tilted her head. "Remember that radio transcript awhile back? Didn't it mention Daven something?" She stiffened. "Better call back. The only people who know we're working DADT are Judd, Ellington, the FBI, and..."

"Gulf Stream!" said Cerrillo, punching the cell phone and wishing the speed of light were a little faster. "Come on, Henry. Pick up the phone!"

Sergeant Brown answered. "Hello."

"Henry! It's Rob. How did that message arrive? Who sent it?"

"Came by fax," said Sergeant Brown. "From the home line of this Davenport character. We tried to call, but no answer. No signature either. Don't remember the exact wording, but it said, oh, wait a minute. Here it is: *Come to this house if you want to prevent a murder and discover the greater glory of God.* We figure it's a nut job, but the message said specifically to contact you and Waller. We weren't sure how the guy got your name. You've been working the area, so dispatch assumed you'd made contact."

"Does the chief know this?" asked Cerrillo.

"No. Didn't want to bother her; we get weird messages all the time. She's at City Hall and grouchy as hell. Maybe you better start to Connecticut." Cerrillo could hear a rustling of papers. "I can't find that damned memo that I just had in my hand. What's the city?"

"New Haven," said Cerrillo.

"About a two-hour drive by the speed limit."

"We'll beat that. Track down Ricketts and fill her in. I never heard of Davenport. If he knows anything about DADT, he knows more than us. Hope the guy's not nailed to a cross like that joker in Massachusetts. When did the memo come in?"

Brown hesitated. "Seven o'clock. Last night."

"And we're just getting it!"

"Sorry, buddy. Dispatch pegged this as routine crazy. Dropped it in my regular basket."

"Get the chief now! Waller just tried to call her, but the cell phone's turned off. Knock down the mayor's door if necessary."

"Right," said Brown.

"Alert New Haven PD to stand by," said Cerrillo. "Nobody moves unless we radio for backup. On second thought, keep this under wraps for now except for the chief. I don't want to risk tipping off somebody who might work with DADT."

"Got it, and watch your ass until we know status."

"Find Ricketts. We can take care of ourselves."

"The mayor won't like the interruption."

"Drag the chief out of there and give her the lowdown on Davenport. We're moving."

"Okay, but if 'His Honor' turns nasty, I'm going to tell him who gave the order."

"Ricketts can handle him."

"I'm on it," said Sergeant Brown. "Watch yourself."

Cerrillo motioned to his partner. "Let's roll."

Waller laid down a pair of twenty dollar bills, glancing around the restaurant. "I think our waitress is singing an aria."

Cerrillo gulped a hopeful bit of tea. "Now we talk with the English professor."

"Or pry him off the wall," said Waller.

***

Professor Davenport awoke to the high-pitched whine of a jet engine and the faint smell of kerosene. He recognized the interior of Gulf Stream's private aircraft. The cockpit door was open, the plane was in the air, and there was no one at the controls. Davenport tried to lift his arms but realized that he was wrapped inside a straitjacket and buckled into a rear passenger seat. The front row seats had been removed, and in their place were several black crates that bore no markings. They were also strapped down.

The cabin was pressurized and seemed to be at cruising speed. There must be somebody in the cockpit. Davenport called out. "Hello?"

No answer.

"Come on, Gulf Stream!" he said. "Are you up front? Who's flying the damned plane?"

A voice answered, and he recognized The Founder. "Good afternoon, Professor."

"Same to you, wherever you are."

"Oh, I'm at headquarters. The university-church complex. My schedule is very busy." The voice seemed to be coming from a radio at the rear of the plane.

Davenport turned his head and spoke loudly, guessing where the microphone might be. "Don't suppose you'd mind telling me what's going on. It doesn't take a Ph.D. to know that something's strange."

"Not at all, Doctor Davenport. I promised that you would participate. And here you are. Right in the middle of things. Right where we wanted you to be."

"That's nice," said Davenport, struggling to loosen the straitjacket to no advantage. "But by some odd mistake," said Davenport, "I seem to be wearing some of your clothes. A jacket left behind when you escaped from Bellevue."

The Founder laughed. "I like a sense of humor. But remember, many great men were deemed a little crazy."

He turned serious. "Really, Professor, I am sorry about our recent disconnect. DADT made great plans for you in the second phase. Miss Padgett forced our hand slightly, but we're on schedule after all."

"Leave her out of this. I warned you."

"You are in no position to warn anyone, sir. We shall find Miss Padgett, and perhaps after today's events, we can bring her back into the fold. If not, well, that's why we have men like Gulf Stream and Solomon, may he rest in peace."

Davenport was relieved. They didn't know Padgett's whereabouts. "What day is it?" he asked.

"April 15, an ascending historical moment. The visible fireworks begin in one hour. We also have some biological measures that were dispersed a week ago, incubation time and all, but those results should be felt soon enough."

"Who's flying the plane?" asked Davenport, suddenly remembering where he was.

"Gulf Stream," said the Founder.

"Good. If I die, so does he!"

"Actually, Gulf Stream is in Virginia, very near the orbit of your craft, flying by remote control. He's done a fine job with the technology. To taxi a loaded jet down a runway and get off the ground remotely. Very impressive. I'm not adept with electronics. *People* are my business, though I work with scientists and engineers from every field. And, of course, we have members of the literary arts. *Your* Manifesto will be delivered to the White House and several leading newspapers in about three hours. You're going to be famous in the morning, Professor, more than you could imagine."

"Oh, I don't know," said Davenport. "I can imagine a lot. You should see what's in my mind regarding your neck and my fingers."

The Founder laughed again. "Praise, Jesus. We could have been great friends. Such a shame. But you shall be held in reverence among the brethren. A man who died for his convictions, a great symbol in the fight for justice. My son, you are the sacrifice of Abraham without intercession. Of course, some will condemn you as a terrorist. Your Manifesto is so uncompromising and, what was the word you used, hostile."

"You mean *your* Manifesto."

The Founder was silent

Feeling sick, Davenport realized that Gulf Stream, Little Boy, and the Founder had long ago reserved this seat for him. He was the classic fall guy and would be portrayed as a gay Ivy League professor turned to violence because of an insane hatred of heterosexuals. The world prefers packaged scapegoat over self-examination, and the Founder meant to shovel responsibility for DADT's attack on a once mild-mannered professor. Davenport was certain he hadn't been the only intellectual considered for the role; they probably scoured the country for suitables; but he was the perfect choice. His biographical mixture of hurt, resentment, and professional standing fit their needs perfectly. Padgett said they had good psychologists, and Davenport had to admit they played him with Stradivarian precision. He just might be the stupidest smart man on Earth, and he was now locked on a suicide mission that would amount to a declaration of war against... Against what, exactly? Homophobia? Heterosexism? Violence? Davenport's academic mind screamed, "I need more time to figure this out!" But such time would never exist. He and many others were about to die. "At least," thought the professor, "I now know they're wrong."

Davenport asked the Founder, "What exactly is going to happen?"

"I can't explain all the details. Oh, how I wish you could read tomorrow's newspaper. A coordinated attack in sixteen states. DADT has worked very hard. Some of our members will die today, but many more of the enemy."

"And me?" asked Davenport. "How about that detail? I mean, we practically have a family relationship. I am wearing your straitjacket."

"Yes, indeed, Professor. You are important. The crates in front of you contain high explosives. Plastic, I think. I'm not into pyrotechnics, yet my comrades assure me that it will create a glorious bang. More importantly, at the center of that bang are ten pounds of plutonium. There wasn't enough time and know-how to go full out nuclear, but at least we're radioactive. That should inspire the tabloids for months."

"Pretty lame, your Imminence," said Davenport. "Radioactive cleanup is a studied art. A hazmat team will sweep up the mess, and the world will carry on. Your fifteen minutes of fame might stretch to an hour. Then you'll be hunted down and put out of business."

"You know what your problem is, Professor?"

"Aside from being strapped next to a bomb in a remote-controlled jet?"

"You don't understand the McMarten Effect."

"The what?"

"Three-mile Island and preschool hysteria. The 21st Century version of *Popular Delusions and the Madness of Crowds.* Kids or anything nuclear."

"You're preaching again," said Davenport.

"Nonsense. People are cattle waiting to stampede, and the hint of radioactive fallout is the contemporary equivalent of a voodoo zombies on a rampage. Our dirty bomb will push even pacifists over the edge. What disappoints me, Professor, is that you don't recognize the human spirit that's all around you. Men deliberately spit in your face for years, and you offer excuses about wind direction and gradual social change. I don't know which is worse, the cattle or the man who steps aside so they can trample someone else—or hides inside an ivory tower while others take a stand. Have you looked in the mirror lately?"

The Founder was at least partially right, and Davenport felt nauseated. Still, he tried to appeal to reason. "Look, sir," he said. "I know the world can be a bad place, not just to gays, but anybody. And perhaps I haven't ... resisted enough, but that does not justify mass murder."

"They murdered first. God keeps accounts, and I account to God."

"But innocent people will die. You are the Founder. You can stop Pearl Harbor, end the violence."

"We can stop the violence by winning the war. If ten people die so that a thousand may live happy lives in the future, isn't that worth the trade off?"

"I don't understand how Pearl Harbor will accomplish that, but the point is you're hurting folks who don't deserve it. Let the law handle criminal prejudice. Society is making progress. Democracy will eventually..." Davenport stopped.

"Don't make me laugh, Professor. The will of the people is the bloodiest dictator of all. Call it the October Revolution, zeitgeist, National Socialism, or better yet, *democrazy*; it's just an excuse to squash others at the polls and feel good about it. We prefer a more direct approach than begging for a bigot's compassion at the ballot box. The days of unopposed bashings are over. And more important, the days of quiet discrimination are over. We shall end them."

There was a sudden jolt of air turbulence. Davenport said, "Your violence will just create more of the same, and Pearl Harbor is wrong. You're trying to make the lion lie with the lamb by killing them both!"

"That won't be necessary in the long run," said the Founder. "Just temporary bloodletting for a better world."

"Nothing but words," said Davenport. "Talk, talk, talk."

"Until today!" said the Founder, who took an audible breath. "I thought you would understand, Professor. Our demonstration will be monumental. Sixteen states and the District of Columbia. I forgot to mention that we recruited a gay Secret Service agent and a high-ranking Pentagon officer. We expect noteworthy contributions at their venues."

"You're hurting innocents! You're as bad as they are."

"I grow weary, Professor. It's been a long time since I faced such thickheaded opposition. Were those men who murdered Matthew Shepard innocent? Or those, like you, who remained silent afterward? My supporters understand a lot about guilt and innocence. They are willing to die for justice."

"And if not, you help them along..." said Davenport.

He began to struggle furiously against his bonds. If he could work loose and get to the cockpit controls, he might have a chance. At the very least, he could turn the plane toward the Atlantic Ocean and spare innocent lives. Davenport would die, of course, but his own death no longer mattered. He *was* guilty. Guilty of malice toward a society that didn't really understand its sins against gays. Of envy for heterosexuals who seemed to have better lives without effort. And mostly, of a self-ingratiating belief that he deserved love and professional recognition that he had not earned. "Pride," he thought. "The sin that led me toward murder." Professor Davenport realized that his internal Mr. Hyde had temporarily overpowered his Dr. Jekyll, but he would make a final effort for redemption.

"Let me tell you what I understand," said Davenport to the Founder. "You're a holy rolling lunatic, and I'd rather be a persecuted faggot than saddle up with the likes of you. And somehow, I'm going to get out of this straitjacket and steer your damned bomb toward open ocean!"

The Founder sighed. "Professing themselves to be wise, they became fools. I must go, Doctor Davenport. Enjoy your flight. There is much to do, and whether you want to or not, you are already in the saddle. You will die for Don't Ask, Don't Tell and for the benefit of humanity. So in the name of God, I bless you, my son."

THIRTY-NINE

The Terrorist Professor

April 2008

Robert Davenport died in a plane crash at 3:49 p.m. on April 15. It would be several days before pieces of his charred body could be positively identified, and as near as could be determined, the presumably mild-mannered professor had flown a stolen mid-sized executive jet—loaded with fuel, high explosives, and radioactive waste—into a religious university at full throttle, traveling at four hundred miles per hour. The plane's black box data recorder had been disabled, and there were disturbing questions about how a teacher, who did not have a pilot's license, could plan and execute such an attack.

The aircraft's registered owner, a successful business executive, was interviewed after the identifying numbers were obtained from the wreckage. The man had no idea that his corporate Gulfstream liner was missing until the FBI contacted him; now, he was threatening to sue the airport where the plane had been maintained along with state and federal agencies for emotional distress because they had allowed his private property to be used as a weapon of mass destruction. The distraught executive was counseled, coincidentally, by a well-known church leader whose expansive Christian university had been the target of that attack. Yet, Robert Davenport's suicide mission had been only part of a coordinated strike against American institutions and citizens by a new domestic terrorist organization called Don't Ask, Don't Tell. As a result, most insurance companies were denying coverage under the Acts of War clauses in their policies.

Pomona Police Detective Emmanuel Cerrillo and San Francisco Patrol Officer Josie Waller, the two principal investigators of DADT, were propelled into the national spotlight after the day of devastation. They held a press conference on April 16 and confirmed the government's ongoing efforts to bring the terrorists to justice and apologized personally for their failure to prevent the attacks. This perceived humility only intensified their media celebrity. Waller and Cerrillo had reportedly first learned about the elusive Gulf Stream and his criminal conspiracy a year ago. Waller, herself, had been wounded in the line of duty and was even threatened in the hospital room where she recovered. Only Cerrillo's unwavering bedside vigilance had kept her safe, and despite increasing threats from DADT to their safety, the heroes had pressed on. A grateful nation claimed Waller and Cerrillo as its champions.

The twisted genius of Robert Davenport, cloaked by his tenured position at a prestigious university, had actually been the beating heart of a ruthless underworld. And Waller and Cerrillo's investigation ultimately led them to Davenport's home, where they found detailed plans of the attack, lengthy Manifesto drafts as well as a completed version, and a personal note:

Dear Friends: You were always one step behind me, and if it's any consolation, your pursuit has cost me my life. I could not risk endangering Don't Ask, Don't Tell should you catch me, so I sacrificed myself in a last act of defiance. I created DADT, and my death will protect it. Rest assured, however, that many dedicated associates shall carry on in my absence. Our declaration of war and terms for peace are offered in the attached Manifesto of Equality, *which is being distributed to several major newspapers around the world. It is time for America to do the right thing. Or else.*

Respectfully yours,

Professor Robert Davenport (aka Gulf Stream).

PS. When I get to Heaven, I shall apologize to Matthew Shepard and many others for society's pot-bellied bigotry.

Investigators also discovered in Davenport's home freezer body parts from one of Gulf Stream's known victims. The dead man's identity, a former FBI agent, was verified through DNA testing. This purportedly confirmed Davenport's dual secret identity as one of history's most notorious criminals; and while precise details of his murders were deemed too gruesome for public release, officials speculated that Davenport was a long-time serial killer with a disturbed childhood.

Preliminary interviews with Davenport's coworkers revealed telltale and problematic behaviors. A fellow professor, who wished to remain anonymous, said, "Davenport was moody, distant, and barely got tenure. Several people warned the department about his militant homosexual agenda. The man was a pyromaniacal Prometheus who threw fire at decent society." The University President hastily disavowed Davenport as a "praxis of evil," and the Academic Dean reported that he had watched Davenport closely for years and considered calling the authorities.

"I was suspicious," the dean told reporters, "but there was nothing anyone could put their finger on. The professor seemed polite and articulate, and he received excellent student evaluations. In hindsight, this was all a subterfuge so that we wouldn't look too closely at his dark side. Davenport could preach poetry with one hand and build bombs with the other. I wish we had taken to heart the mixed signals, but no one at the university can be blamed for one man's hatred of humanity."

The English Department secretary was not so sure. "I liked Robert," she said. "He was the nicest person on campus, even if he was gay. Very respectful, which is more than I can say about many of the holier-than-Moses prima donnas around here. If you ask me, there's some kind of frame up going on. Professor Davenport didn't know how to fly a plane, and he treated people better than they treated him. He was no terrorist." The secretary reported that she was already working on a book entitled *My Intimate Life with Robert Davenport*, which the publisher promised would be "raw and uncensored."

Mary Anne Shephard and Daniel Bradford refused to talk with reporters even as they were investigated by Homeland Security as possible Davenport accomplices. They issued a joint statement: "Robert Davenport would never hurt another human being, and he loved teaching and writing too much to ever give them up. The only logical answer is that our dear friend was assassinated by DADT and then framed for this murderous attack."

Davenport's parents were likewise hounded by the media. His mother was too heartbroken to speak publicly, but his father shook his head, solemnly, and said, "We haven't talked with our son in several years, but we always feared that his sexual perversion would deliver him to hell."

FORTY

Aftermath

April 2008

While the bomb flown straight into a religious university had been the splashiest part of the attack, Pearl Harbor also contained many other events. Newspaper psychologists claimed that Davenport had deliberately mixed the sophisticated ("Dirty Mary") with the primitive (mass shootings) to heighten social stress. Two gunmen opened fire with automatic weapons and grenades at a Mormon temple in Utah, desecrating artwork, architecture, and passersby. Another man blazed away at a City Council meeting in Idaho. Two men and a woman with M-16 Peacekeepers cut loose in a large shopping mall. And about twenty-five people were found murdered around hiking trails, golf courses, parking lots, bowling alleys, or in their homes. Each had a DADT business card on them. Some of the gunmen were caught or killed by law enforcement authorities; most were not; and soon the copycat shootings began. Violence inspired by violence.

And there was Washington, D.C., where a gun battle claimed three Secret Service agents and the Vice President. Details were sketchy, but a seventeen-year service veteran was apparently a member of Don't Ask, Don't Tell. On April 15, minutes after Davenport's plane crashed, the respected Secret Service agent drew his government-issued weapon and fired into the Vice President. Another agent emptied his pistol at the first. A third agent thought the second had gone crazy and returned fire. Thus, when the smoking guns stopped, agent three had killed number two, who had killed number one, who had killed the V.P. A surveillance video captured the action but would not be released to the media for reasons of national security.

The United States Capitol was effectively closed for three weeks. No one was above suspicion, backgrounds were checked and rechecked, yet authorities hesitated to directly offend gays or lesbians because the victim might not tolerate being victimized. If gay terrorists had gotten inside the Secret Service, they might be anywhere and everywhere.

There were also several releases of chlorine gas in public transportation corridors, which weren't particularly deadly—fourteen confirmed fatalities in three cities. But several hundred suffered ill effects, and the consequences included a chronically disrupted transit system. People were afraid to ride buses or trains, many refused to go to work until the government guaranteed their safety, and the economies of metropolitan areas were in shambles. Stock, bond, and consumer markets responded, and Professor Robert Davenport was blamed for every lost point in the Dow Jones Industrial Average.

The FBI claimed that they had opened a file on Davenport prior to Pearl Harbor but had no hard evidence of a threat to national security; therefore, the Bureau could not legally move against him before April 15. The Director was adamant: "We need greater investigatory power to scrutinize traitors. The Patriot Act doesn't go far enough. Law enforcement must have authority to detain and interrogate suspects for the greater general welfare. No one is above America's security, not even sanctimonious pseudo-intellectuals who preach the First Amendment while plotting to overthrow the government. To protect our freedoms, we shall propose to the Congress a new slate of "Liberty Laws" to squash terrorist loopholes in the Bill of Rights."

The National Education Association proposed a monetary reward system as part of a "Suspicious Neighbor Informant Program" (SNIP), suggesting that a nonprofit institute be created to solicit donations and distribute funds to citizens who turned in suspects. Payouts would be calculated on a sliding-scale of estimated lives and property saved, and special programs could be set up at elementary, middle, and high school campuses to enlist American youth in the fight against terrorism.

The rhetoric and fear intensified when people began to appear in New York emergency rooms with high fevers, trembling bodies, and long-forgotten skin lesions. A culture of smallpox had been released by DADT's biological warfare experts (the incubation period synchronized with the general attacks), and by April 17 the disease was spreading across Manhattan almost as fast as the panic across the nation.

Other reports indicated that people had apparently been murdered in dozens of health care facilities on April 15, and each victim was found with a plain white business card nailed to the forehead along with handwritten accounts of their homophobic crimes against humanity. And although no suspects had been arrested, officials speculated that Davenport had systematically developed an undercover medical network. Some of the subtle lethal agents used included insulin, cyanide, snake venom, morphine, asphyxiation, or toxins of the funnel-web spider; other less subtle methods offered cut throats or ice-picks in the brain.

Suddenly (as the Founder predicted), people were quick to point fingers regarding any death, explained or unexplained, in the aftermath of Pearl Harbor. It became difficult to die, even of old age, without relatives demanding an investigation; and medical providers became apprehensive when anyone passed away, whatever the reasons, because doctors or nurses might be accused of murder. And because people were increasingly afraid to go to a hospital, suspicious that DADT operatives might be waiting for them in white uniforms, their delayed treatments often transformed minor medical ailments into lethal conditions.

Business was brisk for newspapers, tabloids, talk shows, and evening television reports. Everyone wanted the latest about Don't Ask, Don't Tell. Who would be the next victim? What was being done? When would life become normal again? There were points and counterpoints about martial law and house-to-house searches in Davenport's hometown, fearing that he might have hidden weapons of mass destruction or corrupted former childhood classmates with propaganda. A Tarot card specialist revealed that she had predicted the attacks, but unknowingly reported the matter to an FBI agent who belonged to DADT. Astrologers claimed that Nostradamus foresaw the rise of gay terrorism and that the anti-Christ (Davenport) would be resurrected on the eve of global destruction. The Op-Ed ink was torrential.

Of course, not every Pearl Harbor event was successful. There were two biologists in Florida who had grown and stored Anthrax, which they released on April 15 in Palm Beach and waited for the deadly epidemic. Nothing happened. Nobody died. Nobody developed a runny nose. The culture turned out to be harmless white powder because the biologists turned out to be incompetent.

And there was the bomb in the backpack that was not delivered because the DADT member chickened out ten minutes before the appointed hour. She was young and afraid. She had mixed feelings. She wondered if she might be straight instead of gay and, therefore, the attack might be bad instead of good. Maybe killing people only seemed moral. The truth was that she didn't care about the cause as much as she did about herself, and the prospect of being blown to bits or caught by law enforcement gave her pause. Two days later that woman, along with her fully charged backpack, was tossed in front of a speeding Amtrak Acela by another DADT operative on the orders of Gulf Stream. A familiar white business card was left near the tracks in an envelope with a letter explaining her mission and that the organization did not tolerate cowardice among its members.

Veteran groups protested the name Pearl Harbor Day, insisting that it insulted the memory of December 7, 1941. And because of the gay agenda associated with "Davenport's Devils," a DADT nickname tagged by the Salvation Army, many conservative religious groups called for the registration of gays and lesbians as potential threats to national security. Some suggested that the federal government temporarily establish relocation camps for the LGBT community and their sympathizers until the crisis was resolved.

And, of course, there was retaliatory violence against gays and lesbians, including a mass shooting at an LBGT Florida nightclub, a lesbian lynching in Alabama, the firebombing of The Stonewall, a man choked with a Pride flag in Nebraska, and homes set ablaze in the night. Off in the darkness, DADT made notes regarding new homophobic incidents and plotted appropriate countermeasures. Each side vowed to defeat the other, but even so, it soon became clear that a too obvious homophobe might just encounter a card-carrying DADT agent. The odds were low, but the price for touching a wrong nerve could be like grabbing the wrong wire in a high-voltage circuit box.

Homosexuality might be a Biblical sin, but the Bible didn't kill. DADT did. And the corporeal here-and-now was much easier to interpret than disputed theoretical ancient verses. Magazines reported that while some people tried to politely avoid gays and lesbians, others seemed outwardly more courteous toward them. There were cautious blogs and tweets about April 15 and its effects on free speech, but when in doubt, silence remained the safest opinion. The carefree days of overt LGBT disdain moved underground in much the same way as racism had before it.

On April 16, a well-known evangelical minister, who had been known for homophobic remarks, delivered a nationally televised sermon, condemning Davenport and the brutality of the attacks. But he said, "Christian people must find Christian solutions to all forms of violence, hatred, suspicion, and retaliation, including the attitudes that led Professor Davenport to such extreme measures in the first place." The enraptured public had no way of knowing that this same minister was the real Founder of Don't Ask, Don't Tell.

Overall, Pearl Harbor proved a strategic success for DADT, and the Manifesto of Equality appeared in every newspaper or website to which it had been submitted. It would soon be available in hard and softbound editions. The gospel was spreading.

FORTY-ONE

Epilogue

After the events of Pearl Harbor, Gulf Stream resumed his business enterprises and simultaneously accelerated covert recruitment. The notoriety of Pearl Harbor brought more applicants than DADT could accept, and only the finest were considered for second-tier background checks and personal interviews. Some undisciplined radicals acted on their own, lashing out against injustice, and while Gulf Stream did not approve of extra-organizational resistance, he did not oppose it. And Little Boy, whose financial resources were themselves a miracle out of scripture, continued his work for Don't Ask, Don't Tell. The Founder commanded Little Boy's money with the precision of a gamma knife, cutting homophobic tumors from society as surgeons cut cancer from patients.

***

The U.S. State Department received a handwritten note one week after Pearl Harbor that read: *Be advised. Professor Robert Davenport is* not *Gulf Stream. I worked with them both, and Gulf Stream is alive and well. I don't know his real identity but he often operates out of New York and can lead you to the Founder of DADT. They framed and murdered Robert Davenport.*

The note was signed by a Tanish Padgett and post-marked from a small village in Mexico three days after the attack. Investigators found no fingerprints (other than the letter carriers') and believed the name was a pseudonym. Later, when Padgett saw Gulf Stream inter-viewed on a news program about his "stolen jet" used by the terrorists, she unexpectedly learned the identities of both Gulf Stream and the Founder. By then she had de-cided that personal revenge would be sweeter than mailing any more letters to authorities. Besides, she had no love for the government that had sanctioned the mur-der of her mother.

***

Many months later, Detective Emmanuel Cerrillo and Officer Josie Waller attended the secret funeral of Professor Davenport on the outside chance someone from DADT might have learned about it and been in at-tendance, but no such person was there. The services had ultimately been arranged by Mary Anne Shephard and Daniel Bradford after finally receiving permission from federal authorities and Davenport's parents, who were not present. The professor's few remains, sealed in an infant-sized casket, were to be cremated immediately after the memorial, and Mary Anne and Daniel planned to scatter his ashes at an undisclosed location along the Pacific Crest Trail on their next hike. Everyone, including Cerrillo and Waller, agreed that a marked gravesite would be regularly vandalized or worshipped by competing mindsets, and neither Daveport's friends nor parents wanted that kind of spectacle.

After the brief service, Detective Cerrillo pulled Mary Anne and Daniel aside and said privately, "I'm sure you'll be watched by the FBI for a while longer, but Waller and I know that your friend is not Gulf Stream. We heard that bastard's voice by radio, and it's not even close to the recorded lectures of Professor Davenport."

Waller added, "We're keeping this to ourselves for the time being, and we know you're not connected with DADT." She took a breath and said, "If it helps, I can promise you that my partner and I will bring the real mastermind to justice or kill him trying."

Mary Anne, a previously confirmed pacifist, answered as she stared at the urn containing Davenport's ashes, "I hope it's the latter."

***

Several years after the attacks, to help ease tensions among minorities who were becoming more vocal about their rights and among majorities who were less willing to oppose them, a legislative bill was introduced into the U.S. Senate to expand federal civil rights protection to include sexual orientation and to prohibit discrimination against members of same-sex marriages, which thanks to the Supreme Court had become legal throughout the country. Violence directed specifically against gays and lesbians would remain a hate crime, but penalties were stiffened. Further, the proposed bill declared, "Equal protection under the law shall not be denied or abridged on account of sex, sexual orientation, or gender." Thus, women who were disappointed that the first Equal Rights Amendment failed ratification in the 1970's were pleased to see its language mirrored in the new resolution, and feminist groups also understood that such legislation would simultaneously enhance rights and protections for women.

The new President of the United States threatened to veto this SB-101 if it were approved by the full Congress and submitted for signature. There were rumors of a secret memo from Don't Ask, Don't Tell that promised, "If the President does not sign, the Vice-President would soon have authority to do so." Some people laughed at the delusional hubris of DADT. Some at the delusional hubris of the President. Most did it silently because the memory of Davenport's invisible legions cushioned public dialogue.

***

As SB-101 moved quickly through the legislature, the President met with the delicate, soft-spoken religious leader whose university had been a primary target on Pearl Harbor Day. The two men had great respect for each other and often talked in private. The President called the preacher a wise and esteemed holy man. The preacher described the President as a fervent political leader thrust into a national spiritual crisis. They would pray together about the future.

"Do not worry, Mister President," said the Founder, alone with the President after an elegant dinner in the White House residence. "At decisive moments, great men always know in their hearts what to do. The Lord will guide you as He guides me. He shall carry your burden and point the way to an easy conscience."

"Thank you," said the President. "I appreciate your coming. You are an inspiration to the nation, especially after what happened to your own university. You are the embodiment of strength and forgiveness."

The Founder stood, moved to the center of the room, pressed his palms together, and intoned with robotic cadence. "God is good and powerful. He leads the worthy to salvation and casts demons to unending torment. You may rely on His wisdom and the infinite promise of His divine intervention."

The President, alone with the preacher, kneeled before him on the soft carpet.

The Founder placed his hand on the President's shoulder and said, "I, too, shall listen. Together we shall hear the word of God. And, soon, we shall become the word. Now, in this room, please ask for heavenly salvation."

The President lowered his head and closed his eyes. "Humbly, I ask for guidance."

The Founder bristled with reverence, chanting softly. "Without fear or reservation, you must submit before our Lord."

"I do submit."

"Blessed are the peacemakers, for they shall be called the children of God. Blessed are they who are persecuted for righteousness sake, for theirs is the kingdom of heaven."

"Blessed art thou, oh Lord," said the kneeling man.

The Founder held in his hands a large gold, jewel-encrusted ceremonial crucifix. "Ask for the power of knowledge and conviction and justice, Mister President."

"I so ask the Lord, who art my God."

"Blessed are the meek, for they shall inherit the earth. Blessed are the wise, for they heed the word of the Almighty."

"I heed the word."

"Trust in Heaven and not in the false idols of arrogance and pride."

"I trust in the Lord."

"You shall ask and God shall tell. Speak deeply and from the heart, Mister President. We are listening. We stand beside you. We shall hear." The Founder lifted the heavy crucifix high with both hands like a dagger.

"I ask God Almighty for help," said the President. "Please, Lord, speak to me in this hour of need and tell me what I must do."

The Founder poised motionless, gripped the crucifix with inspired strength, and stood ready and waiting for God's answer to guide him.

The man loved his work.

ABOUT THE AUTHOR

Claudine Griggs is a writer/teacher living in Fairfax, Virginia. She recently "retired" as the Writing Center Director at Rhode Island College and currently works as a writing specialist at the Daniel Morgan Graduate School of National Security in Washington, D.C. Her previous publications include nonfiction books *Journal of a Sex Change: Passage through Trinidad* and *S/he: Changing Sex and Changing Clothes*; fiction publications include "Raptures of the Deep," "The Cold Waters of Europa," "Growing Up Human," "Firestorm," "Maiden Voyage of the Fearless," and "Helping Hand," which has been adapted as an episode in the Netflix series *Love, Death & Robots*. She earned her BA and MA in English at California State Polytechnic University, Pomona. *Don't Ask, Don't Tell* is her first novel.

ACKOWLEDGEMENT

I am grateful to the following persons: Sydney Culpepper for her above-and-beyond efforts in helping me to turn the draft manuscript into a publishable book; my similarly dedicated Rhode Island writing coach, who wishes to remain anonymous; Benjamin Gorman, for believing in the book and moving it to publication; Carolyn Ekstrand, who read the initial draft manuscript and offered encouragement and good advice; and, especially, Karen Paley, my wife, my enduring love, and the first reader of just about everything I write.

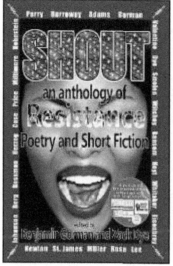